TRIUMPH OF THE WIZARD KING

THE WIZARD KING TRILOGY

TRIUMPH OF THE WIZARD KING

THE WIZARD KING TRILOGY

III

CHAD CORRIE

DARK HORSE BOOKS

Published by
Dark Horse Books
A division of Dark Horse Comics LLC
10956 SE Main Street
Milwaukie, OR 97222

DarkHorse.com

Maps illustrated by Robert Altbauer

Library of Congress Cataloging-in-Publication Data

Names: Corrie, Chad, author.
Title: Triumph of the wizard king / Chad Corrie.
Description: First edition. | Milwaukie, OR : Dark Horse Books, 2021. |
    Series: The Wizard King trilogy ; book three | Summary: "The first
    battle has been fought, but the war has just begun. As Cadrith savors
    his success, the mercenaries deal with the aftermath of their last
    confrontation. The thread that's bound them to this point is hard to
    break and is pulling them into yet another conflict where even the gods
    are bracing their gates. The battle lines have been drawn. The pieces
    are in place. The conflict to come will be waged on many fronts and
    through many faces, but victory is far from assured. Warring gods,
    secret plots, ancient feuds, and cosmic adventure fill this final volume
    of the Wizard King Trilogy, returning readers to a world rich in
    history, faith, and tales of adventure-of which this story is but one of
    many"-- Provided by publisher.
Identifiers: LCCN 2020024117 | ISBN 9781506716275 (paperback)
Subjects: GSAFD: Fantasy fiction.
Classification: LCC PS3603.O77235 T77 2021 | DDC 813/.6--dc23
LC record available at https://lccn.loc.gov/2020024117

First edition: August 2021
Ebook ISBN 978-1-50671-632-9
Trade Paperback ISBN 978-1-50671-627-5

1 3 5 7 9 10 8 6 4 2
Printed in the United States of America

THE WIZARD KING TRILOGY

Return of the Wizard King
Trial of the Wizard King
Triumph of the Wizard King

GREAT OCEAN

Napow

THE
WESTERN
LANDS

JASPER SEA

Rexatoius

SEA OF BITHAL

YOAN OCEAN

Breanna

IRON SEA

Irondale

Caradina

Black Isle

THE
PEARL ISLANDS

N

W E

S

0   500   1000   1500

MILES

THE BOILING SEA

2019

FROST OCEAN

THE
NORTHLANDS

Frigia

Troll Island

Baltan

ICE SEA

Valkoria

SEA OF GLASS

Arid
Land

THE
WIZARD KING
ISLANDS

THE
MIDLANDS

TRADITIC OCEAN

Colloni

TARNIAN SEA

CERULEAN SEA

GREEN SEA

Draladon

Talatheal

THE SEA OF ORTANIS

YOAN OCEAN

Belda-thal

THE DISCORDANT SEA

THE
SOUTHERN
LANDS

Antora

SEA OF SHADOWS

Menessa

GREAT OCEAN

N

W   E

S

0   500   1000   1500

MILES

RH
2019

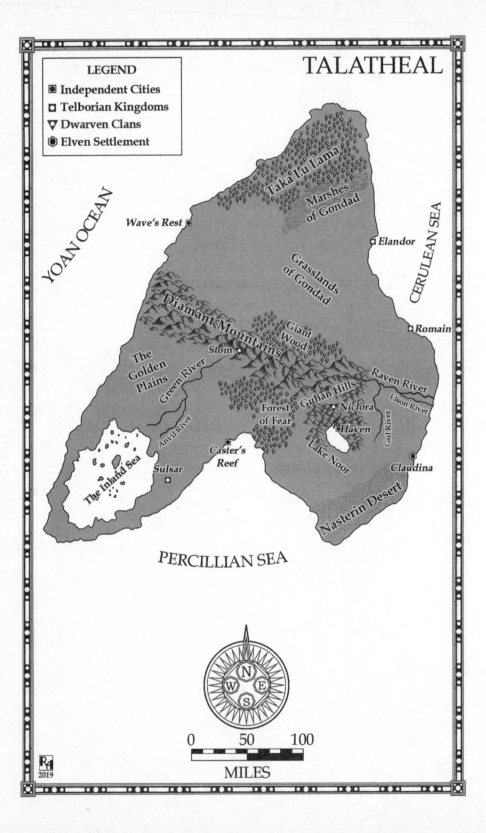

TALATHEAL

LEGEND
- ◉ Independent Cities
- ☐ Telborian Kingdoms
- ▽ Dwarven Clans
- ⬡ Elven Settlement

YOAN OCEAN

CERULEAN SEA

PERCILLIAN SEA

Taka Lu Lama

Marshes of Gondad

Wave's Rest

Elandor

Grasslands of Gondad

Diamant Mountains

Romain

The Golden Plains

Giant Wood

Stom

Green River

Raven River

Gulian Hills

Elson River

Niclora

Forest of Fear

Haven

Anvil River

Gul River

Caster's Reef

Lake Noor

Claudina

Sulsar

The Inland Sea

Nasterin Desert

N E W S

0   50   100

MILES

ARID LAND

LEGEND
- ◉ Tribal Capitals
- ▫ Unique Locations
- ▽ Nordic Settlement

YOAN OCEAN

Great Hawk Mountains

Hawk's Roost

Hawk Forest

Deer Forest

The Glade ◉

Boar's Lair ◉

Boar Forest

ARID SEA

Crystal River

Clear Lake

Conn's Home ◉

Moose Forest

Wolf's Seat ◉

Wolf Forest

Wolf Lake

Vanhyrm ▽

The Court of Beasts ▫

Gray Perch ◉

Owl Forest

Galba ▫

Arid Mountains

GREAT OCEAN

N E S W

0   50   100

MILES

R 2019

CHAPTER 1

B roken and alone, Dugan hung before one of the portals composing Galba's stone circle. He couldn't see the peaceful heather-covered hill behind him. He couldn't see anything as he floated between lucidness and unconsciousness. Each of his hands was affixed to a stone post by a twitching band of violet energy that bit into his flesh. He could feel most of his ribs had been broken. A few had even sliced into his internal organs, adding to his agony. His head sunk into his chest, chin digging into his sternum. He couldn't feel his legs or his arms past his elbows, but he kept a tight grip on life.

That tenacity had kept him alert enough to witness the final confrontation with the lich, following his own failed attack. He wasn't clear on what happened after that. It had all happened so fast, and it was getting harder for him to think. He recalled the violent force, the cracking of his back, and the searing set of claws assaulting him from within. He'd also been raised a good four feet above the ground. It looked like he was getting his crucifixion after all. No matter how far he thought he'd come, it had found him in the end. At least he'd have these last few moments of freedom.

It hurt to think, hurt to lift his head or look around. Before him was a battlefield. With its surrounding circle of stones, it could just as easily have been an arena. In the end, he couldn't escape that either. His body felt lighter—much lighter than it should. He began to wonder if he was still breathing. As he drew closer to Mortis, it felt as though he was on a *real* cross. Its splinters dug into his back as he struggled for life. In his mind's eye he could see the arena's roaring spectators shouting at the gladiator who'd suffered his whole life for their amusement.

As he hung on the cross, he saw his life play out before him. He saw himself as a fair-haired, scrawny youth from a village long since lost to Elyelmic violence. He watched his younger self play with a stick, swinging it like a sword as he fought off imaginary monsters and villains. There was an innocence about the boy that brought a deep sadness to Dugan. Another thing that had been taken from him. The images grew faint and his mind grew fuzzy before fading into darkness.

• ● •

Tebow wasn't sure if they'd won or lost. He'd barely survived the attack. The stench of burnt flesh and hair wafted through what he knew was his ruined nose, and there were constant agonizing echoes of the angry flames that had wrapped around his flesh.

Using his hammer as a cane, he rose on shaky legs before letting the object fall upon standing. He wouldn't need it anymore. He could see the bodies but couldn't see Cadrith anywhere. He knew they hadn't taken him down with their hammers, and Gilban didn't strike him with the scepter—the elf's dead body made that clear enough. So did the throne finish him off? That hardly seemed fair. Not after all they had gone through.

Too much to ponder and not enough time to do it. He could see Cracius was already at Sheol's gates, and knew he wasn't too far away himself. He might as well do some good while he could. He'd join him soon enough and then the next journey would begin. The Scrolls of Dust taught he'd get to serve Asorlok even in the afterlife, ushering souls to their final destination. The same thing they were called to do in this life for the living. And as long as he drew breath he might as well continue that mission. He could see Vinder, Cadrissa, Alara, and Rowan were wounded, but not as badly as Dugan—though Vinder was gaining ground on the Telborian. The dwarf would be Tebow's second stop if he survived his first.

He hobbled over to Dugan and placed his charred hand upon the Telborian's limp leg. Even though his hand, like much of his body, had suffered severe burns, the priest could feel the growing coldness in Dugan's veins. "Asorlok, Lord of Death, Master of the Afterlife, I humble myself before you. I beseech you for a peaceful transition for Dugan, a man who died in service of a great cause—one that you issued to your servants. Give him the assurance he needs to pass over without regret, without anger, and without fear. Grant him peace."

Dugan moaned and opened one bloodshot eye, staring through the loose strands of his blond mane.

"Rest, Dugan," Tebow said, looking him full in the face. "Be at peace." He knew his own face was far from the image of calm he wanted to project, but at such moments it was more important to convey the full weight of the words.

"I'm in the arena." His voice was weak and distant. "I-I see them . . ." Dugan drifted between this world and the next. "I have splinters in my back . . ."

"Be at peace. Don't fight it. Let go . . . Sleep." Dugan's eye closed again. His chest fell like tired bellows once more, and then Dugan was dead.

"Safe journey, brave warrior." Tebow allowed himself a rueful smile, ignoring the tearing of skin and fresh pain it created. He turned toward Vinder, who was also ready to cross into Mortis. On his way to the dying dwarf, he got a closer view of Gilban's body. His neck was broken, suggesting a quick death. Merciful, he supposed, and easier too, as he wouldn't have known how to offer comfort to the elf anyway. Gilban followed a different god. While Asorlok ushered all on to their final destination, Tebow didn't know what rituals were right and proper for a priest of Saredhel. It was better to let the body lie. His spirit was with his goddess anyway.

He didn't see Hadek anywhere, which raised questions the priest didn't have time to consider. Surveying the others, he wondered where Galba was. It would have been nice to learn what had happened with Cadrith. He supposed he'd find out soon enough, once he'd crossed over. He could wait.

Tebow shuffled to Vinder. The dwarf remained stoic as he fought to stay conscious, though savage pain was clearly gnashing its teeth over every inch of him. His gray skin and clothing were pitted with black circles of burnt flesh and cloth. His hair was singed and his salt-and-pepper beard was partially burned around his face, but his ice-blue eye still blazed with stubborn life.

Tebow studied the dwarf closely. Vinder stared back. Much of his brigandine armor still remained, but parts of it still emitted thin blue-gray, greasy plumes of smoke. His right hand held his rune-etched axe with a white-knuckled grip.

"You promised . . ." His lips bled with his words, black gel globbing in the corners of his mouth.

Tebow squatted beside the dwarf, biting back his own pain. "Vinder—"

"Don't . . . you . . . dare . . ." Vinder's eye blazed. "You promised . . . honor . . ." More blood flowed over his chin and down his singed beard and chest, where it spilled around and behind his head and neck.

"Once this was . . . done . . . you told me . . . I'd have . . . my honor. I did . . . my part . . ."

"Yes, you did." Tebow placed his hand on Vinder's battered chest and closed his eyes. No matter what had happened, they still had made a promise, and it needed to be kept.

"No tricks . . ." Vinder huffed.

"No tricks," Tebow repeated, then prayed. "Asorlok, grant this warrior the honor which he sought as he comes before your majestic throne for judgment. Honor the promise made to him by your priests so you are known as a fair and impartial god that looks favorably upon your priests and honors his word." With these words spoken, Vinder faded from sight. All that remained was a pool of blood on flattened grass, outlining where the dwarf's body had once lain. Tebow forced himself to stand. He needed to see to the others.

•●•

Vinder felt his spirit seeping away from his ruined body. He knew his time was short, and that made his plea all the more urgent. He wouldn't die without honor. He'd been promised this by the priests and would hold them to their agreement, even if they were dying with him. They owed him as much. He'd done his part. Now it was their turn.

He didn't know what followed Tebow's prayer. His mind was fuzzy. His vision grew more and more narrow. It was like he was looking through a tunnel. He didn't think he could hold on much longer, and that was fine with him.

He knew Tebow wasn't able to heal his wounds. The priest's beliefs and his god forbade such things. It would have been nice to go back to his family and clan . . . to live an honorable life for the rest of his days . . . but he understood his final return to the clan in death was just as important, if not *more* important, to him. If given a choice, he'd choose death with restored honor over more years with the ones he loved without it. He'd already made that choice when he'd stood at the mouth of Cael's lair. He knew he'd probably die, but he also knew it would bring him the redemption he desired.

Now as he lay dying, Vinder had an epiphany. The most important things in life *were* faith, honor, and family. Duty was only the byproduct of these ideals. Only in death did it all make sense. What would he leave behind? What mark would his existence make on the world? And how would he be remembered? Life was not so much about being alive, but how one lived, and what one left behind. That was the basis of the dwarven philosophy. Without death, life would have no meaning. Here was the purpose and meaning of it all. Here, on the precipice of death, he learned what he should have been living for all along.

Vinder didn't even realize the scenery had changed. The green grass had given way to cool, rocky earth. The blue sky had darkened to a foggy twilight, and the stone circle had transformed into a womb of rock. There was something familiar about the place. He struggled to sit, his fading vision weakly scanning the area around him. A smile found its way across his pale and worn features, even as he coughed up blood. He was back in Cael's lair. He noticed the Troll's bones beside him, skin and muscle melted away by the death priests' earlier attack. He fixed his narrowing gaze upon the skeleton. It was nothing but a hollow, meaningless thing now. It would be the last thing he saw when Drued called him to his ancestors.

As he contorted his body to better view the Troll's remains, he understood this wasn't enough. This wasn't going to win him his lost honor. He may have been willing to die in battle with Cael, but now his foe was dead. Failing to fall in battle wouldn't win him anything if he died alone here on the cold stone floor. Though those who would find his corpse later would assume he'd died in battle with the Troll, he and Drued would know the truth. His family might have comfort in his perceived restored honor, but he'd be unable to rest in his afterlife knowing the truth.

Worse, if it wasn't believed that Vinder died in battle, his death would serve no purpose. His family would have lost not only a son, but honor within the clan as well. No, something had to be done. Reaching under his clothing, he retrieved the small figurine of Drued he'd worn around his neck since heading out with Alara and the others into the marshes.

He gave the quartz pendant a kiss. Suddenly his head lolled backward and his body grew cold and slack as it slammed into the rocky ground. A bloody groan escaped his mouth, jarring his mind toward action. He had one last thing he could try.

Slowly, fighting against the cold numbing of his flesh, he turned his head toward Cael's skull. He forced back the growing blackness long enough to fix his gaze upon the skull's empty sockets. For what seemed like a great span of time he eyed the jaws that would have split his bones and torn muscle and skin. Now they were dull and silent.

With one last burst of will, he called upon the deepest reserves of life that yet remained. He'd have to face Drued on the merits of his own life—as all dwarves did—and live with the verdict his god decreed, but he could at least leave behind some comfort for his family.

Vinder forced his numb right hand to tightly grab his axe. Laboriously, he focused his mind, his will, and his faith on the task. He watched Cael's skull fade into darkness before it disappeared altogether, and then his heartbeat ceased.

The dwarf took a deep, rattling breath. It was slow, painful, and labored but gave him his last bit of strength. He let out a powerful yell that fueled the weapon's arc, severing the skeleton's neck with a single hit. The head rattled away and struck the nearby wall like a child's spinning top. And with his final strike, the last of Vinder's life fled from him.

•●•

Alara managed to sit up, ignoring the throbbing in her gut and temples. She tried to make sense of the scene coming into focus. Her stomach was bruised, she knew, and there was going to be a welt on the side of her head, but she'd live. She spied Gilban not too far from her. His body lay on its side, neck broken and face staring blankly into space. Near him was the silver scepter, half-hidden from view. He didn't deserve this— none of them did.

She didn't see Cadrith anywhere. She wanted to believe that was a good thing—perhaps the throne took him—but in her heart she knew that wasn't true. And then Tebow came into view. The priest was a horrid sight. His body was as black as his singed sable cloak, most of his dark brown hair was gone, and the remaining skin on his face barely covered the bones beneath it. A thick black ichor oozed from his ruined flesh.

"Are you able to stand?" His voice was rough, crackly.

She didn't answer.

Tebow drew closer with careful steps. She was surprised he was able to stand at all. He was probably in a great deal of pain—*much* more than she—and yet he seemed unconcerned.

"Take care of the others," he said, placing his cinder of a hand upon her shoulder. "You're all they have left to hold on to. You have to be strong for them in the time to come. You still—"

His speech was cut short as he fell to the ground. He landed on his side, his eyes locked on hers in a gaze holding the last of their fading light. A heartbeat later, the priest's body and even his charred clothes crumbled into dust, leaving only a pale gray blanket of ash. She thought of Cracius and dared a look, only to find another swath of gray dust a few yards away. Even their silver hammers were gone.

First Gilban and now Tebow had appealed to her leadership, urging her to guide the others. With Gilban she had accepted it, in part knowing she'd be able to let it go once the mission was over. Now everything had changed. Part of her didn't want to do anything but run to Rexatoius as fast as she could. But she knew that wouldn't change anything. Then there was Rowan, and her promise to him.

Sliding on her right side, she dragged herself close to Gilban and the scepter. With her left hand, she pulled it free. She used it to prop herself up and rose with agonizing effort.

She didn't want to lead anymore. She didn't want to fight. She felt beaten and tired, alone and afraid. This wasn't what she'd pictured on the fields where she'd been a child, watching her father's herds and practicing with her imaginary sword. She didn't see the suffering behind such actions and quests, only their completion. She never would have imagined what it might be like to truly suffer defeat.

Alara forced her feet forward. She made it to Rowan, lying unconscious across the dais' white marble steps. Thankfully, he didn't seem too much the worse for wear. He'd have a headache, but the measured rising and falling of his chest showed he still lived. She couldn't find Vinder and assumed the lightning had totally consumed him. A grisly fate, for sure, but at least it was quick. She also saw no sign of Hadek. She hoped the goblin met his end as painlessly as possible. If anything, he was an innocent in all this. He'd had the potential to live a decent life in Rexatoius, she supposed, but now she could only hope he'd found some peace somewhere.

To her amazement, Cadrissa was awake and sitting upright. From how Rowan had reacted, Alara had thought she'd been killed, yet here she was looking better than any of them. When last they'd been together Cadrissa had been wearing travel-soiled golden robes. Now she was dressed in a clean white gown and hooded gold cloak with matching sash. As with many things she'd been encountering, Alara wasn't sure what to make of this new attire.

"What happened?" Cadrissa's movements were weak and labored. Her face was lined with fear and exhaustion.

"That's what I'd like to know," said Alara. "I thought you were dead."

"So did I." Cadrissa's mind started to clear. "How did you get here? The warding was almost too strong for—" She broke off suddenly. "Where is he?"

"The lich?"

"Yes." A note of fear crept into her voice.

"I don't know." Alara figured that was the best answer for the time being. She didn't want to explain everything, not until Rowan was awake. And at the moment she was more interested in what Cadrissa could share about her time with Cadrith than anything else.

"Then did he become—"

"I don't know."

Cadrissa nodded, lost once more in her thoughts, until she caught sight of the crucified Telborian. "Dugan!" She bolted for the dead man, her feet betraying her a few times in her rapid flight. Alara followed, wincing.

Tears filled Cadrissa's green eyes. "You're going to be okay." The image in the portal behind Dugan had changed to a snowy wasteland—a flat arctic tundra of white winds. "We just have to get you down. We—"

"He's dead, Cadrissa." She tried to be as gentle as possible, but there was no way around the truth. "Leave him be."

"He's just wounded," Cadrissa said, tenderly stroking Dugan's knee. "He'll be okay."

"He's gone, Cadrissa. There's nothing we can do." Alara's eyes misted at the finality of the words, feeling the weight of all she'd seen since she herself woke to this nightmare.

Cadrissa sobbed violently, burying her face in Dugan's lifeless legs. Alara tried to administer some comfort, but she knew the wounds of the heart were painful to endure. While helping Cadrissa, she pondered how she'd deal with the same grief. Even if she and Rowan lived to a ripe old age, she'd still outlive him. Worse still, anything could happen to them in the meantime. Events even worse than what they'd just survived. Silently, she thanked the gods Rowan hadn't left her yet—there was *one* positive note in this dark ballad.

She'd become so absorbed in her own thoughts that she failed to notice the portal's image behind Dugan change once more. The frozen wasteland was warping into a desert realm with tall volcanic mountains, meandering streams of lava, and roving flames resembling fiery serpents.

Cadrissa jumped from Dugan's body as if bitten by a snake. "It's like he's on fire." No sooner had she spoken than a geyser of flame erupted from Dugan's chest, spreading over his whole body with such speed that his entire frame was devoured by the famished fire before either of them knew what was happening. It consumed him entirely, melting his flesh and blackening his bones into a fine dust. Neither could do anything but stare open mouthed at the empty stone posts. Nothing of the former gladiator remained.

CHAPTER 2

AT THE CENTER OF THE COSMOS WAS THE WORLD OF THANGARIA.
—The Kosma

"I trust this was all part of what you've already seen," said Asorlok. He entered through an intricately designed wooden door. Sooth, Saredhel's realm, was far removed from Mortis, but Asorlok thought it wise to come in his true form anyway. Though the pantheon were using guises to meet in their council, the gods could engage in other matters as their true selves. This also allowed for momentary distraction, which would serve the god of death's purposes well.

Saredhel was undisturbed by Asorlok's sudden arrival. She kept her back to the door and her mind focused on meditation. It wasn't customary for a god to burst into another's realm unannounced, but Asorlok wasn't in the mood to move through the normal channels. Such things could take extra time, something he didn't have a great deal of.

The bald goddess' eyes remained closed as she hovered near the edge of a reflecting pool. The white skirt about her waist, slit on both sides to her light brown thighs, dangled between her crossed legs and bare feet, almost touching the smooth water.

"What brings you to Sooth?" Saredhel asked, keeping her pose. The pool was six feet deep and at least twice that in width—its smooth lavender-colored stone lining like glass shimmering beneath the calm water. The pool's surface reflected the brilliant torches lining the top of the chamber, whose pure-white radiance was akin to the brightest of days.

Besides the torches and the scrying pool in the center, the chamber was rich in design, opulent frescoes painted on its domed ceiling and bright mosaics encircling the walls. The images and scenes were of events that had taken place in the realm from its beginning all the way up to the coming of Saredhel and her rule over it.

"I think you know very well what brings me here." Asorlok curled his lip. His blue eyes, hawkish nose, and clean-shaven head only accentuated his air of royal discontent. The god of death stood fifteen feet, just like his floating sister, but was more somberly attired. A deep claret cape flowed down his back, stopping at tall black sandals. His black samite robe was encircled by a red satin sash.

"One of two options," said the goddess, "neither of which need concern you."

"We went through all that effort getting them to the circle. And for what? They're dead."

"Not all of them." Saredhel spun in midair. "You should know that." Rays of light struck the various jewels and gems she wore—most noticeably the silver chain connecting her left nostril and earlobe. Twin silver serpents, which made up a portion of her metal brassiere, glistened in the light.

"But they just as well *will* be if he's left to enact Nuhl's will."

"And what *is* that will?" Saredhel's solid white eyes stared deep into the god of death.

"I don't have time for your games."

"Then why are you here?" She floated to the middle of the pool, returning her gaze to its liquid confines. The opaline shawl she wore over her head hid part of her face in shadow.

"I want the truth for once. You told Endarien and me that we needed to join you to stop Cadrith, and we did. But I couldn't help but notice that new revelation you shared with the council. So which is it? Or are they *both* false?"

"What I've seen, I've seen." Saredhel fixated on some rainbows sliding across the pool's surface.

"And what's *that* supposed to mean?" Asorlok's frustration grew.

"And why does this trouble you so?" Saredhel raised her head. "Why is the god of death so concerned over the possible destruction of Tralodren and its gods?"

Asorlok took a deep breath and slowly let it out before saying, "I just want some answers. You can't have this both ways. What we did at the circle was supposed to be the end of this. Now we have Endarien looking to go and fight this lich with what's left of Vkar."

"A choice he made," she explained. "As did you when you joined him in gathering the others at the circle."

"Which you also led us to undertake."

"That isn't how *I* recall it."

"Then what *did* take place? Can you tell me *that*? In fact, what's going on right *now*? Because I don't think any of us really have a clue."

"All things serve their purpose." Saredhel's voice was calm and clear. "The artist who must give an explanation of his work to the viewer is indeed a poor craftsman. It is in the interpretation that the piece comes into its own."

"This is pointless." Asorlok slashed his hand through the air like an angry blade, as if the action could clear away the verbal clutter. "You could at least give me *something* of an answer."

"You haven't asked the right question—not the one that matters most."

"Which is?" Asorlok crossed his arms, causing his silver bracers to shimmer in the light of the room.

"You already know it but have yet to ask it of yourself. When you do, I will be here to help you find your answer," she said, turning away from him to resume her meditation. "I have other matters to attend to. I'm sure you do too."

Asorlok glared at Saredhel until it was clear nothing further was going to be said. He released a snarling huff as he stormed from the room, slamming the door behind him. With the loud clap still vibrating off the walls, Saredhel closed her eyes and focused on the pool.

"I'll see the final piece is put in place, but what is chosen shall be counted as final." With these words the pool swirled into a solid white, as if the water was liquid marble. This whiteness shimmered with a brilliance like sunlit snow, covering the goddess in a living radiance and making all the colors onto which it fell a few shades paler. "And no choice will be made under compulsion."

A voice arose from the pool. It was both feminine and masculine at the same time. "What is chosen shall be respected."

"Yes, it shall," said Saredhel. "For good or for ill."

• ● •

Asora joined the rest of the pantheon, save Endarien, in their adopted guises deep beneath the Hall of Vkar. She and the others had finally made their way through the maze of disused tunnels and corridors beneath the ancient palace. Like much of the hall above, the area felt like an old shrine, a relic of days long since past. Days that would never—could never—be again. No gods nor titans roamed the tunnels anymore; none had any reason. The cosmos had changed with the deaths of Vkar and Xora, a sudden and irreversible change that had forged the current pantheon. A new order for a new age, which now faced a similar fate as its predecessor.

Ganatar had led the council though ironclad doors, twisting tunnels, and a seemingly endless number of stairs. Lit by the radiance of the god of light's presence alone, the corridors they traveled eventually slithered to a cold dead end. It was here, amid the rock walls, that a small, plain silver chest sat nestled in a tight niche about waist level to a titan.

A nod from Ganatar told Asora to gently pull the chest free. The container was no larger than a human head, the goddess' large frame dwarfing the object as her delicate fingers enveloped it. It was amazing to think that something so powerful could be contained in such a small vessel. Vkar had been the first to rise to godhood and had ruled a far-flung empire for years. And now here was all that remained of the Eternal Emperor.

The other gods were silent as Asora brought the small box to her chest. She rested it just above the swell of her stomach, where still more life waited to be birthed. As she brought it to the others, they formed a circle in the open area of the tunnel. She was loath to do what they were about to do, but she understood the greater benefit. Any loss of life sat poorly with her. But if it would keep death's grip from claiming many more, it was worth the sacrifice. It was with this resolution she'd convinced herself to hold true to the task. She entered the middle of the circle; the others closed ranks around her. Taking the center of the circle for her mark, she stared at Ganatar.

"Let it begin." His voice was even, measured.

Asora opened the chest. As she did, an aggressively bright light manifested, overpowering Ganatar's luminous presence with a blinding white glow. Together, the gods concentrated, digging deep into the chest's contents, using their wills to draw forth that which had been held inside for millennia.

They had to subdue it, to make it obey their command. Though Vkar had been the strongest of the gods—and still was, even in death—what remained of him wasn't able to stand against the collective will of his progeny—or the Race Gods—even in their guises. A moment later, the pantheon had hold of Vkar's essence and were wrenching it free from the silver box. As it was removed, it took the shape of a globe of bright white light, a foot in diameter, and began to hover above them.

"We must send it to Endarien," said Ganatar.

Once more, the gods concentrated their wills. The globe became hot, flaring with a life all its own so that the room became like the center of a sun. Just as quickly as the heat and light had come, the globe disappeared. Though she feared what they were doing was dangerous and potentially wasteful, Asora tried to reassure herself it would work out well in the end. She couldn't help reflecting on how Vkar's essence had been able to resurrect and restore those wounded or killed in the last attack against the pantheon. And it had served so well since then in various other matters the pantheon had faced, including raising Panthora, Aero, and Drued into the pantheon.

It had always been there as the last resort, a secret defense or weapon they could call upon if all else seemed lost. To give it up now felt like arriving naked to a battle. But they had nothing left. This was their best option, and now it was enacted. Still . . . this was a sacrifice, and that was what Saredhel said was needed. They had done all they could. It was in Endarien's hands now.

• ● •

Endarien hovered over the peaceful deep blue orb of Tralodren, waiting for the others to send him what remained of his grandfather. Scattered with dark green and brown islands and continents, it seemed *too* idyllic, *too* perfect to be home to mere mortals. But that had been the intention. The pantheon had wanted a world to reflect their glory in the cosmos, a sign of their own splendor mirroring and even rising above what had been when Vkar had ruled Thangaria.

Even though everything hadn't gone as they'd planned, it was still a world worth saving. Tralodren was part of a collection of planets making up its solar system. Unlike the other planets and moons, this one had a mystical barrier powerful enough to prevent a god from entering. Visible only to divinities, the barrier was meant to protect the world from their incursions.

When Tralodren had been created, it was amid memories of terrible conflicts that had split the cosmos into wars and factions. None of the pantheon wanted their creation to endure such woe. It was decided those on Tralodren would be given free will, the ability to live their lives without direct intervention. They'd only receive guidance from the pantheon, which they could either accept or decline. The gods would be able to act chiefly through their followers, and only in matters related to their areas of dominance and influence.

More direct interaction would require a special guise of mortal flesh that housed a spark of their true divine self. Through these forms they managed to circumvent the barrier, but they were still limited in their influence. While they couldn't be fully present on the world, in their weakened mortal guises they could walk the planet as they wished. With such guises they'd been able to accomplish a great many things and, in some cases, hinder the causes of others along the way.

When the Race Gods were raised to godhood during the aftermath of the Imperial Wars, the council wisely waited until their spirits had departed Tralodren before bestowing godhood upon them. Doing so allowed the three their apotheosis without trapping them on Tralodren, behind the barrier, where they'd have been able to do incredible harm if they so wished without any direct intervention from the council.

Cadrith had done just the opposite. He had attained godhood inside the barrier and was thus blocked from leaving Tralodren. He was also protected from the pantheon's direct retaliation. This was the main reason the former lich had to be stopped before he gained a stronghold over the planet. Only with the last remaining essence of Vkar could Endarien hope to circumvent the barrier in his true form. If they tried to destroy it outright, they wouldn't be able to raise the barrier again without Vkar's throne to aid them, thus introducing Tralodren to dark days similar to the ones the pantheon had endured before the rise of the council.

In his true form, Endarien was fourteen feet tall, his massive body covered in sinewy, tanned skin. He wore a silver cuirass emblazoned with a golden eagle on his chest and back, its outstretched wings covering much of the armor. The cuirass covered a white toga that draped over much of the god's upper body. On his feet were black leather sandals with silver greaves shaped as upward-arching wings, which matched his silver bracers. He sported two majestic cordovan wings, similar to a hawk's, but with gold speckles that sparkled like stars. His head was crowned with a silver helmet shaped like the head of a screeching hawk.

His radiant yellow eyes scanned the globe below him with eager anticipation. He'd brought his best weapons for the battle. His right hand grasped an imposing twelve-foot spear of solid light, which possessed the searing intensity of lightning itself. Its cruel head sparked with charged snaps and bursts. His left arm held a large, circular silver shield with a detailed relief of a hawk in flight. It radiated a gentle silvery-white aura of its own.

Knowing that every moment he waited, Cadrith's threat grew, Endarien became restless. He began to sense something swimming around him. It was subtle at first, slowly growing in intensity. He fixed his keen vision on a distant star. He squinted, then smiled. The time had come. As the globe of light approached it came into clearer focus. The foot-wide ball rushed toward him at incredible speed before striking him full in the chest. He doubled over from the impact.

White lightning sparked and arched about his frame, creating a spiderweb of living light. It was like liquid fire flaming over his body, mind, and spirit. But instead of consuming him, *Endarien* consumed *it*. The last remnant of Vkar soaked through his mind, overshadowing his being and molding it into a new and grander image of the deity. With this essence, knowledge and insight flooded his thoughts. Endarien worked to fight the onslaught of confusion that came from the bombardment. He had to focus. He needed to find the answer to break down the barrier, or all was lost and this last bit of Vkar would be wasted.

The Storm Lord struggled to focus his mind. Vkar's essence had entered his spirit now and was reinforcing it with its own presence, strengthening him for the task to come. Body awash with snaking tendrils of flashing white energy, he could feel his eyes flare into twin gouts of silver fire. By their aid, he could see the way past the barrier. Stretching out his left hand, he fluttered forward and touched the protective surface. As his fingers caressed the barrier, a ripple spread upon its now-cloudy surface.

He smiled.

With one swift action, he thrust his spear into the barrier. Thunder boomed from the impact, echoing into the cosmos beyond. In its wake a hole appeared. At first no larger than his fist, the opening continued to grow until it was large enough to allow him passage. He retreated a few yards and positioned himself to fly headfirst through the opening.

Closing his eyes, he began to glow white hot as he called upon his own might and that of Vkar, his mind focusing on where he knew Cadrith to be. He sped for Tralodren as a bolt of vengeful lightning. As a great quake of thunder rolled over the world and into the outer reaches of the cosmos, the opening in the barrier closed in on itself like a rapidly healing wound. Not even a thin scar remained where Endarien had pierced it.

• ● •

After sending the remains of Vkar to Endarien, the gods had returned to Xora's chamber and the reflecting pool. Once more everyone took in the large circular room's fresco- and mosaic-covered stone walls rising some one hundred feet into a painted dome. And while there was a massive battle displayed across it, Vkar and Xora's images dominated the scene. Indeed, the first god and goddess almost seemed focused on what their children and grandchildren were doing below.

The dome's large crystal oculus funneled pure light that fell into the center of the room, where a clean, calm pool rested in a brass basin deeper than a human was tall and four times as wide. The pool's granite lip peeled up around it, silver rails worked into a display of delicate twisting vines.

They'd all need to watch together in case a sudden vote might be needed. Their presence was crucial to ensure a quick resolution. All would watch Endarien battle Cadrith, hoping for a swift and relatively easy victory. Some of the gods believed Endarien could best the upstart. Others were not so sure, and a handful thought he'd bitten off more than he could chew and would perhaps lose his very existence for the sake of his pride.

"Are we prepared for the worst?" Olthon solemnly asked the others.

Their faces grew grim at the remark. Though they didn't want to speak of it aloud, they'd seen the havoc that had followed the last encounter with Cadrith's dark patron and knew what would follow should Endarien fail.

"Win or fail, the vote has been made, and this council has ruled," said Ganatar. "The time for debate has ended." With a wave of his hand, he caused the pool's surface to swirl with a rainbow of hues that morphed into a single scene. The gods watched as the blotches of color merged and cleared to reveal Endarien and Cadrith coming to blows.

"Well, I just want to see this battle first." Khuthon clung to the silver railing with a death grip. His smile held a sinister mirth.

"But are you really ready to take up arms should Endarien fail?" Olthon repeated her concern, searching the gathered gods with her golden gaze. "Are we sure that there's no other way?" Only Asora's soft green eyes seemed to share her concern.

"We're all pledged to follow through on the council's vote."

"Even you?" Olthon was surprised at Asora's resignation. She quickly took in the pool, avoiding her sister's hurt expression.

"So far it seems just fine," Khuthon assured Olthon, his face brimming with excitement. "Endarien looks like he's holding his own."

"But what if he becomes trapped on Tralodren once he succeeds?" Asora kept her question tempered, just like her viewing of the pool. It was rare of her to view most fights. They oftentimes had a way of getting to her more than others in the pantheon. "He could become locked behind the barrier regardless of this battle's outcome. What should we do if that happens?"

Rheminas' lips curled at the thought; his yellow eyes flickered with some hint of glee. "I don't think we need worry about that. Endarien isn't that foolish, and it won't happen to him anyway. Not with the infusion of Vkar inside him now. It will take some time for the last of it to work its way through him."

"Still," Asora continued, softly, "should that fail, Endarien could be trapped on Tralodren forever."

"Our cousin knew the risks when he took on this task." Perlosa's hard stare never left the pool.

"But would that be such a bad thing, though?" Drued rubbed his beard in thought. "To have all of Tralodren to yourself . . ."

"But you'd be trapped there," Olthon reasoned, "cut off from your own realms and domains, as well as your followers. You might even lose your vote in council."

"But you would rule Tralodren," Khuthon countered, clearly internally weighing the pros and cons. "Not the most intelligent of ideas, but you—"

He interrupted himself by jabbing a fist skyward. "That's right, Endarien! Make him suffer!"

"Enough!" Ganatar's stern rebuke killed all further discussion. "We have a battle to watch." The pantheon resumed their viewing. Only Gurthghol dared a final look away, his gaze fixed on an image of an enthroned Vkar on the wall across from him.

CHAPTER 3

WRATH AND AMBITION ARE QUITE SIMILAR;
BOTH TEND TO BLIND THE EYES TO TRUTH.

—Douglass Fuller, gnomish philosopher
(1400 BV–1147 BV)

Cadrith materialized near his tower in a burst of azure light. The black stone structure rested on one of the Wizard King Islands, far from any source of civilization. He needed time to prepare, and there was no better spot for the time being. He thought of his last trip here, after escaping the Abyss. When he'd left the tower for Galba, he was a lich. Now he was a god. The first to have survived the quest for Vkar's throne.

He'd toyed with the idea of using his tower and the island as his divine seat, but had decided against it. It was better to start out someplace more populated. He wanted to build his base and power as fast as possible, and that would require access to people who could see his glory firsthand. The gods would try to stop him, of course, but he wasn't concerned about that. He was in his full strength on Tralodren, and they were only able to oppose him in a lesser state.

Cadrith knew, as did just about every resident of the planet, that the gods had sealed off Tralodren long ago, keeping it free from meddling divinities and safe from harm. But this didn't stop the gods from mingling with their creations from time to time, nor other divinities from doing the same. While the barrier kept Cadrith free from the full force of direct reprisal, it also prevented him from leaving Tralodren in his true form. He'd only have access to a lesser manifestation in the realms beyond. The very place where his more powerful enemies dwelled.

This meant he now was living in an existence exactly the opposite of how the gods lived, and in a way, Tralodren was both a realm and a prison. But he was confident he could find a way out of this situation if given enough time to understand his new power and reality. He'd done the same when he'd first escaped to the Abyss centuries before and was sure he'd be able to find another way soon enough.

He stood on the grass, looking at his hands. He tried to bring a spell to mind but found he was unable. Angered, he tried again, to no avail. Was Galba hindering him? No. She'd told him she wouldn't hold him back from his plans, and he didn't feel like it was the other gods either . . . not yet. As he struggled with what had once been so normal—second nature to him—a deep well broke inside him, filling him with immense energy like a flood of searing might surging out of his fingertips into the sky. He laughed at his success.

He'd been thinking like a *human* wizard, trying to cast his spells from formulas, corrupted ancient phrases, and esoteric training. This wasn't the way of a god. Deities were beings of will and spirit. All he had to do was think of a desired result and the deed was done. Even his own words could bring things into existence. No longer did he have to tap into a well of magical might. Now he *was* a well unto himself.

Putting this new understanding to the test, he thought of hovering above the ground and found himself floating over the grassy hill, his feet no more than a foot above the grass. It was so fast acting. So potent. So limitless in scope. Only his will and the strength of his spirit hindered him. He'd soon be a master of these abilities. He just needed a little time.

Cadrith had always assumed once he'd become a god it would be easy to enact his plans to gather followers, incite worship, and have temples built in his honor, but now as his mind drifted into the concept of eternity, he felt a tug at his core telling him to let go of his former life. The longer he existed in his divine state, the more his former plans seemed like the desires of someone else. He was seeing things more clearly than ever before, latching onto a deeper understanding of what was possible. In the face of such revelation his former desires began to melt away like wax before fire.

Even as he marveled at his new powers, Cadrith felt like needles were riddling his body. In that moment he knew what the sensation meant: there was a more powerful being nearing his location. The thought was troubling. Who could be his equal on Tralodren, if all the other gods were hindered by the barrier? Holding out his right hand, he conjured a staff of polished oak, capped with an azure globe the size of an apple and held in place by silver clasps. An old comfort, but it still felt right to have it in hand. It was getting easier to control his power. It flowed about him, running over his frame like raging rivers. The process was beyond gratifying.

The sky grew dark, and thunder rolled across the heavens. Dark gray and black clouds spread like a growing cancer as far as the eye could see. Then came the birds. They burst from the dark mass of clouds like rain, scattering everywhere. They descended upon the grassy field and the trees around the open glade with such a massive flutter it sounded like an army on the march, covering every green blade and leafy branch with a rainbow of feathers. Their beady eyes glared at Cadrith. Songbirds and parrots, ducks, geese, quail, and birds of prey surrounded him. All that was allowed him was the circle of grass where he stood.

A great screech rose over the rumble of thunder. This was followed by the sound of massive wings raising a gale around the former lich, scattering stray debris and a whirlwind of feathers his way. Looking up, Cadrith saw the tower's crown had become a roc's roost. The rest of the tower was dominated by still more birds: ravens and kites, doves and hawks perching on whatever footholds they could find alongside eagles and vultures, condors and falcons, and a host of smaller, brightly hued birds.

Cadrith could see still more birds circling about the isle. Their heckles and cries added to the unsettling medley of those who'd managed to find a roost. Behind him—all about him—they covered the earth, forming a feathery canopy.

Unable to move without stepping on a bird—which he would do without the least amount of concern—he stayed still. He knew who'd come to face him just as he knew this was only the prelude. The wind picked up, becoming a screaming zephyr. He was battered by the gale, yet it left all the birds untouched. How or why Endarien had come to Tralodren, Cadrith didn't know. He only knew it was an act of desperation. Endarien risked being trapped here, regardless of the battle's outcome. A foolish and impulsive choice, but that was the Lord of the Winds.

Swifter than an intake of breath, a colossal bolt of lightning shot from heaven like a javelin, parting the slate clouds as it exploded into the ground before Cadrith. Birds scattered in all directions. The impact rattled the earth in unison with the accompanying burst of thunder that would have shattered a mortal head, though it left the birds unscathed. In its wake the bolt left a good-sized crater. Cadrith had to right himself with his staff to keep from falling into it. An azure globe of energy protected him from the flying chunks of rock, dirt, and sod.

From out of the ten-foot pit, Endarien's silver helmet emerged. His head, the tops of his wings, and his shoulders rose above the maw of shattered earth as he stood defiant. Even with much of his body sheltered by the crater, Endarien was an overwhelming sight. His spear crackled with ravenous hunger. His skin spit and snapped with white serpentine bolts leaping like attacking cobras, before they fizzled away with a spark-filled snap.

Cadrith met the gaze of the god's large yellow eyes with calm. He stood defiant before the towering deity nearly three times his size. Around the island, thunder rolled and the birds continued their cacophony. Winds went wild, dancing drunkenly. They came from the east, then west, then north—crashing together like a flurry of fists.

"You're breaking your own laws," Cadrith shouted over the screaming gales and squawking birds.

"The pantheon's granted me the joy of killing you myself." Endarien's voice echoed into the heavens.

A sardonic smirk crossed Cadrith's lips. "I'm a god now. We're on equal footing."

"Hardly equal," Endarien replied, releasing an aura of silvery white, which rapidly grew brighter than a solar flare. Cadrith felt it dig into him, tearing at him, dissolving his own essence like vinegar mixed with baking soda. The experience was almost unbearably intense. He fell to his knees, clinging to his staff lest he fall over completely.

"You can't even stand my mere *presence*." Endarien lessened his aura's radiance, reducing it to a soft ambient light, and climbed from the crater. His strong hands lifted his gigantic frame in one smooth motion.

As soon as Endarien's aura diminished, Cadrith willed himself to fly up and out of the god's range. But twin silvery-white bolts burst from Endarien's eyes, striking Cadrith as he started to take off. They hit him so fast and with such force the dark god was flung through the air for miles before the Tarnian Sea embraced him. Throughout his flight the energy set upon him like a mass of vipers gnawing his bones—picking away at who he was and what he would become.

Once aware of what was happening, Cadrith willed himself to stand again before the rival god. Instantly, he appeared before Endarien, dry and free from any injuries. Time and space were malleable in the divine understanding of reality. Cadrith had come to realize it wasn't so much the strength of the body or great insight that gave divinity its power, but the muscle of imagination.

Endarien responded with a swift jab of his spear, violently piercing the island's crust where Cadrith stood. Rapid reflexes spared him from the strike. "You learn quickly," Endarien said, eyes shimmering with a silvery glow. "But it won't save you."

"We'll see." Twin azure jets of flame blazed out of Cadrith's eyes. Like coiling serpents they entwined Endarien, searing his exposed skin. Endarien remained stoic. A shrug of his shoulders and wings dislodged the clinging flames.

"Is that the best you can do?" Endarien said as he drew back his empty spear arm. A glint in his eye was all that proceeded the volley that shook the earth as a bolt of fierce lightning exploded through Cadrith. The ground shook like an earthquake. Birds scattered and spun, forming a funnel below the turbulent clouds. Cadrith was shoved into the earth, a small smoking crater forming beneath him. Over the thunderclap he could hear Endarien's laughter.

"*That's* how gods fight!" he said, peering into the depression where Cadrith lay.

Cadrith didn't move. Not yet. He needed the right moment for action. It seemed this fight would be more challenging than he'd thought. He smoldered inside the pit, which stank of ozone and charred flesh. Such an attack would have incinerated a mortal, yet he felt as if he'd only suffered some bruises.

The hole was just five feet deep, not deep enough to swallow him whole. He could get out of it easily when he had to. With will and spirit he would be able to heal any damage, re-forming his frame. It was when the will gave out and the strength of spirit dimmed that gods began to die. He was far from that.

"Come on, Cadrith," Endarien said, drawing closer to the pit. "Get up." He uprooted the spear and directed its sparking tip at Cadrith's center.

A silence fell. The thick clouds stopped their motion. The lightning and thunder ceased. The birds halted their cries. Even the air stilled. Cadrith thrust his hands forward and rose to his feet outside the crater's lip. The action pulled up the earth all around him, transforming it into a worm-like form. Its rocky mouth swallowed Endarien in one gulp and then covered him with stone and sward as it pulled him deep into the island. The birds scattered from the grassy glade in a flutter of feathers, then settled on the tower and trees or took to the slate-colored heavens, circling above for any sign of their creator.

Arrogant thunder and lightning paraded across the heavens, but Cadrith remained silent. It was too soon to declare victory. He knew it would take far more to defeat Endarien. Still, it had been a great joy to try it. Soon enough his new abilities would be second nature. He jabbed his staff into the earth and worked his hands as if kneading dough until he formed a ball of cold azure energy that crackled with its own malevolent life. Before he could do anything further, a column of silver burst from the ground beneath him. In an instant the unquenchable flame had reduced him to charred bones.

Cadrith's will was unable to stand against such an attack. He couldn't even begin to, for it was the will of Vkar, the first god, he faced. He knew all this in his spirit as he did many things he was beginning to more fully comprehend. His strength faded like sweat from his pores. He knew he was dying; he knew he'd lose the battle of wills and spirit, and would fade from existence like a puff of smoke.

"The Abyss is ready for your return," said Endarien. Cadrith couldn't see him anymore, but sensed him floating somewhere in the gloomy, bird-riddled clouds.

• ● •

After a moment, Endarien slowly fluttered down, his great wings parting the charcoal vapors and mist before him. His jubilant expression melted when he gained a better view of the battlefield. Cadrith's tattered remains were being remade.

"I destroyed you by the power of *Vkar,*" he said, confused, as he hovered above. Fresh skin was unfolding over Cadrith's pinkish sinew. "Unless . . ." The words were a whisper on the wind. And then he saw it. Nuhl's tendrils twisted around Cadrith's body. It had shielded him from the brunt of the attack and allowed him time to recover and heal. The arrogant fool had no idea. But Endarien had the power of his grandfather coursing through him. Vkar had defied Nuhl before, and through Endarien he'd do so again.

"It seems not even Vkar can stand before me." Cadrith's voice faded in and out of existence. "Imagine what will happen when I gain a *full* understanding of my abilities."

"You'll *die* and *stay* dead!" Endarien dove with his spear lowered, hungering to skewer the impudent godling. But the spear's sparking point got no closer than an inch from Cadrith's chest before the former lich faded into nothingness. Endarien, unnerved, continued his charge. His spear bit into the earth with a jerk, sending him somersaulting so his face landed in the crater where Cadrith had once been.

A violent curse blew out of the god's lips as Endarien struggled to stand. "You won't be able to hide from me forever." He stood under the black canopy of clouds, gnashing his teeth and gripping his spear with alabaster knuckles. Anger, thicker than molasses, coursed through his veins, and he craved to release its full force. "You can't leave Tralodren. You're trapped here, and there's nowhere on this world where you'll be safe from me. Nowhere!"

Turning with a gust of brooding air, Endarien spied Cadrith's tower. Letting loose a scream, the god flung his spear at the demon-shaped doors at the tower's base. The spear transformed into lightning and struck the doors with a rumble that shook the entire island and shattered the ancient wood into fiery splinters. The birds who were using the tower for a roost scattered with caws and cries, fluttering to the trees and the sky for safety. Even the large roc on the tower's ramparts departed for the stormy sky.

"Come out and face me!" Endarien screamed as he approached the charred opening. Small puddles of flame bubbled through the grass where bits of debris and sparks had conjured the fires. The closer he drew to the door, the smaller Endarien became, until by the time he reached the doorway, he resembled a human in height. He stopped and retrieved his weapon. Once in hand it shrunk into something better suited to his new size.

Stepping inside, he beheld a wonder of richly decorated art and fine tapestries. In truth it seemed more a museum than the home of a fiendish lich. Rich rugs sat under exquisite furniture made only for the use of kings. He stopped in the middle of the foyer. Here he spotted many odd, horrifying, and beautiful objects from all ages and places on Tralodren. Sculptures of elven maids bathing, powerful dragons, great griffins cast in bronze, unspeakably obscene creatures ripping young human females apart, and other pieces of artistic merit filled the space.

Endarien was far from impressed and passed on without a second glance. He knew Cadrith wasn't here. But with his patron still latched onto him, helping cloak him from detection, he didn't know if he could find Cadrith before what remained of Vkar's essence was spent. This was obviously part of its plan: getting the threat Endarien posed reduced and ultimately eliminated.

"At least you won't have your tower to return to," he continued, strolling to the first black marble step of the ascending stairs. Closing his eyes, his body began spitting off a series of silvery white whips of energy. These were joined by rings of silvery white energy rising and falling from his body, mimicking the snaps and pops from his spear. He held these rings for a few moments before releasing them in a cascading explosion of forked lightning.

Hounded by strong winds, the ravenous bolts charged up the stairs, laying waste to everything in their path. Metals melted, precious stones were pulverized into powder, and tapestries caught flame and quickly transmuted into ash. Fanned by the wind, these fires cruelly ravished their victims, devouring all they could with supernaturally accelerated hunger. The destruction continued all the way up the stairs, which cracked and exploded from the lightning's heat, spreading the Storm Lord's wrath. The bullying winds fast on the lightning's heels tore down wall coverings, blew in doors, and scattered the tower's treasures and mysteries. When they could, the aggressive gusts burst into closed chambers housing books and scrolls, toppling the antique shelves, throwing the volumes to the floor, and scattering ancient scrolls to tattered dust.

When he was finally content, Endarien left the tower, taking on his full height as he moved into the open. With a beat of his wings he was back in the air and glaring down upon the tower with a cold eye. Leveling his spear, he released the most deadly barrage.

Fat silver shafts of light slammed into the top of the tower repeatedly. Black bricks exploded and fell like rain from gaping holes in the stone cylinder. Again and again the bolts punched into the sturdy dark stone, until the tower started to teeter. Finally, it crashed in upon itself with a cloud of smoke and ash. And the birds who had remained scattered.

Flames sprouted like weeds amid the broken stone. Soon they'd grow into a strong bonfire and consume all that remained. Satisfied, Endarien rose high into the slate clouds and then beyond them.

"Find Cadrith," he commanded the great company of birds circling him. The new god might have been cloaked from divine eyes, but Endarien wasn't sure that held true for others. The birds, heeding his command, scattered across the sky.

Endarien flapped his wings and headed east.

• ● •

Cadrith didn't know where he was. His eyes swam across the endless gloom surrounding him. He was *unable* to know where he was. He was blind and confused, a wraith hovering in unfathomable darkness. Events rushed by him as a blur. Nothing seemed to make sense.

"This won't help you, Endarien," he shouted into the black emptiness.

"That was very foolish." A new voice, soft as silk, slithered around his body. It wasn't Endarien speaking. It was clearly unique, a kind of blend of a male and a female voice. "You could have been destroyed before you completed your task."

Cadrith peered about the landscape, discovering nothing.

"Were it not for the part you play, I would have let Endarien kill you." The voice took on a hateful tone. "You wasted enough time on these reckless actions."

Cadrith didn't know what the voice was talking about but wasn't about to be spoken to in such a manner. He was ready to unleash his newfound might but found himself powerless. All he could do was hover in place—helpless. The voice didn't speak for some time, as if it could read his thoughts and wanted him to truly understand his position.

For the first time in his unnaturally long life he felt fear slide down his spine. He wasn't in control. A glimmer of insight dawned, allowing him to see it was something even greater than a god who had taken hold of him. He didn't know *how* he knew this, but he understood it was something existing on a level he could never ascend to. The proposition rattled him to the core.

"What do you want with me?" he said, his voice falling flat, as if the force of his words dissipated as soon as they left his mouth.

"You will serve my purpose," the voice said ominously. Cadrith still couldn't find where it was coming from. "I wouldn't have been so direct, but since my opponent has made a rather direct intervention—"

"I serve no one!" He turned to where he thought the voice might be originating. "I'm a *god*!"

"You're my pawn and part of my plan."

"Show yourself!"

Mocking laughter rebuffed the demand. It encircled him, swimming about his head, echoing out of time, making a chorus of ridicule. The blackness around him diminished. Cadrith was in a cavernous chamber built of ancient marble. He couldn't see the ceiling nor the end of the room. Both were cloaked in swimming night, but from where he stood he thought he was in some kind of temple.

"You're as arrogant as you are naive." The voice was the same but the one who spoke it wasn't. From out of the swimming darkness came Raston, his former master. He appeared the same as he had over seven hundred fifty years ago—impossible, given the lich had died before Cadrith ground what remained of him into dust. He didn't have the staff that Cadrith took from him, but otherwise it was a totally convincing replica, down to the torn flesh on his face that revealed the naked bone beneath and the black gloves he wore to keep his fleshless fingers hidden.

"Did you really think you could have earned the right to godhood?" the semblance of Raston continued. "Did you really think you were skilled enough, that you were worthy of such power? Many have searched for that privilege since the beginning of time. Even the so-called gods stole what they now have—but even with their theft, they're still of higher worth than you."

"Still too afraid to show your true face?" Cadrith asked Raston, who stopped a few paces from him. "If you're trying to intimidate me, you're doing a poor job. I succeeded where Raston failed."

"Only because I helped you," said Raston. "I was going to use your master, but you showed yourself a more viable option."

"I did *everything* on my own." Cadrith sneered at the thought of being as weak as his former master. "I had to take all I could—do all I could—to succeed. What I did was by my own hand."

Raston laughed, and his form started to shift, morphing into that of Kendra. She appeared as Cadrith would always remember her: blond and willowy. The pregnancy of her final days was gone. The voice changed to match hers, so perfectly that it was a bit unnerving. He supposed that was the idea.

"I had been grooming Raston," said Kendra, "but when you proved the better choice, I took hold of you. You wouldn't have gotten any further than him if it wasn't for me. I guided you. I helped you, until now. If not for me, the portal would never have let you leave Tralodren. I brought you out, and I brought you back in when the time was right. Not to mention how I made sure you were kept safe in the Abyss—even extending your spell to have you awaken at a more *opportune* time. And then there was my help with the circle . . . and the throne . . ."

"Lies," Cadrith spat in disgust. This had to be a pathetic attempt to slow him, to hinder him or trap him while Endarien got whatever he needed in place to take him out for good. "So who are you *really*? Gurthghol? Asorlok? One of you must have come with Endarien to Tralodren."

"You really think the gods are the highest beings in the cosmos?" Kendra mocked.

"Galba!" Cadrith's face contorted with wrath. "You swore you wouldn't stand against me."

"Idiot!" Kendra snarled. For a moment the sight reminded him of their final confrontation, and it jarred his thoughts with a fist to his heart. "Galba's *nothing*—a form that's taken on, much like the gods use when they wish to walk Tralodren. The force behind Galba's true form is something else entirely.

"You studied us, Cadrith. I made sure of that. You had to have some knowledge of us to get this far. The scrolls and tomes you stole from your former master, among other things. You were never given the true picture of things, but enough to begin to understand and prepare you for the work I'd have you do. You couldn't have done what you did without knowledge of us. That was what led you to Galba in the first place."

A thought began germinating in his mind. It shot up and took root in a flash. But he couldn't believe it . . . it seemed too impossible. If it was correct, then he was the biggest fool ever, and in great danger.

"The Cosmic Entities? You're saying Galba was one of the Cosmic Entities?"

"Now you begin to understand," the voice said, rich with sardonic mirth as black tendrils began seeping out of Kendra's body.

"But if that's true, then you're—"

"Your master." The voice that first greeted him returned as Kendra's form mutated into an amorphous glob of darkness with scores of twisting tendrils. Each ended in a white-fanged mouth.

"Wh-what do you want?" He knew he had no control over his life or death anymore, that his movements had been carefully calculated. He'd been a pawn from the start. These revelations revealed the great emptiness of his future, the barren potential in attempting to achieve his plans and dreams. He withstood these thoughts. He had to if he had any hope of using this to his advantage.

"To serve your final purpose," said the voice. "So listen carefully."

Gurthghol's brisk pace made it hard for the much shorter Kardu to keep up, but somehow Erdis managed. The oval-headed chaotic incarnate had been summoned to the god's side a short time earlier and tasked with listening to a set of orders relayed at a rapid pace.

"And you will make no mention of this to anyone until after the battle is over, is that clear?" Gurthghol turned his head to make sure Erdis was understanding everything he was saying.

"As you command," Erdis said with practiced skill, though his mind was racing with what his lord was putting into place. Gurthghol had turned to him some years back to take on the role of chamberlain when the previous one finally decided it was time to move on. Death wasn't really an end in the realms and planes—all were immortal, after all—but not every position need be forever. And when you have a chaotic incarnate serving a god of chaos, longevity in a position isn't assured; change is inevitable. But for as long as he'd have him, Erdis would continue to serve Gurthghol to the best of his abilities.

The position of chamberlain was a vaunted one that at times outranked the twin viceroys of Altearin, and as such it hadn't been held by any Lords of Chaos or Darkness so as to keep the balance of power among the factions. For all the talk of Gurthghol being a wild-eyed madman, he was very astute in the way of politics and the managing of his affairs and realm.

"What about Mergis and Shador?" Gurthghol asked as they neared a corner in the heart of his palace. They were moving through the secure and private areas where Gurthghol kept his more precious and personal items for safekeeping.

"They have been informed, as you instructed."

"And the men?" They turned the corner, coming face to face with a large black walnut door at the end of the hallway. Reinforced with wrought iron, it was clearly strong enough to withstand a fair amount of abuse. Beside it stood a Chimera. Like Erdis, Chimera were chaotic incarnates, but they were quite different than the Kardu. While humanoid in shape, they stood with the hind legs of a goat and the torso and head of a tawny-furred lion. This one had a black mane with matching curling ram's horns. He wore a suit of plate armor that allowed his black bat wings and serpent-like tail to pass through without impediment. His golden eyes carefully watched their approach while a clawed hand gripped his two-headed axe.

"The last I heard, they had them at the ready," said Erdis, watching Gurthghol retrieve a black key from a pouch on his belt. Upon reaching the Chimera, he gave a nod and stepped clear of the door and lock he'd been guarding.

"Tell them to meet me at Galba, on Tralodren." Gurthghol inserted the key into the lock and turned it in one smooth motion. There arose the sound of metal gears moving followed by the clear click of the lock releasing.

"Galba?" Erdis knew he shouldn't have asked as soon as the word left his mouth.

"Is there a problem?" Gurthghol eyed the Kardu with a shrewd glance.

"I was just remembering the pact," Erdis confessed, careful to not get too far into paths he need not tread. There was wisdom in knowing when to step into a matter and when to let it be.

Gurthghol returned his attention to the door, giving the wrought iron loop handle a strong tug. The door opened without protest. A burst of low light revealed a room a few feet taller than Gurthghol and about double that in length and width. But while it might have been small and rather utilitarian when compared with the rest of the palace, it served a very important function.

Erdis watched Gurthghol step inside, noting the sparkling rows of assorted arms and armor that lined the walls of the god's personal armory. "We won't have to worry about the pact for much longer." He peered back over his shoulder. "Just get those warriors there. I'll be leaving shortly."

"Yes, my lord." Erdis turned on his heel, resuming his hurried steps to carry out his lord's wishes. A final look over his own shoulder caught Gurthghol examining a cruel-looking flail with great interest.

• ● •

Cadrith was speechless after hearing the plan. He might still have been hovering in darkness, but he'd been enlightened about something he didn't even know was possible. It dwarfed all his previous schemes. The scope and implication were beyond anything he'd known or thought possible—even with his new insight. But as staggering as it all was, there was one central truth he couldn't shake loose: his present destiny was never of his own making. All his boasting and scheming—all the tireless work and sacrifice . . . In the end he'd been nothing more than a tool—a pawn advancing another's agenda all along.

"Now you understand your place," said the voice.

"It seems I have little choice." Cadrith stifled the rage that wanted to leap out of his throat and strangle his would-be master. All this time he'd been thinking it was his own efforts that had gotten him this far. But the curtain had been pulled back, showing him what a joke it all had been. Any other would have been crushed under the weight of such a revelation, falling headlong into despair, but not Cadrith. He was a god now. That had to count for something.

"You always have a choice." There was just a hint of sarcasm in the voice.

"And what do *I* get out of all this?" It was time to push around the edges of the cage in which his supposed master sought to contain him. "I'm not content to just be your pawn."

"I'll let you exist when this is all over . . . should you survive."

"That's not enough." He put on the best act of confidence he could muster.

"You presume much."

"If I do what you want, I not only want my freedom but—"

"Power." The voice echoed from the darkness. "So be it. I'll grant you greater insights into the power you seek. You'll learn things that few of the gods know or dare to seek out . . . should you survive. I trust that's enough incentive?" It seemed the cage door wasn't fully shut. There was a crack he could exploit . . . if allowed enough time.

"Yes." Cadrith resumed the dutiful servant act he'd mastered so long ago. As he did, he couldn't help but think how, with just a simple repurposing of his previous plan, he could position himself to cut the strings of his puppet master while empowering himself on a whole new scale. This could actually work even better than his original plan.

"Good," said the voice. "Now be about your task. The longer you wait, the more your opposition grows." The darkness melted away, revealing more of his surroundings.

He had a general sense of where he was, having been in similar surroundings, but needed to be sure. With but a thought, the globe on his staff burst into brilliant azure light, illuminating all around him. He found himself in a structure that had been built for people much taller than himself. Others might have guessed giants, but Cadrith knew better.

Even if his new master hadn't told him, the ancient text scrolled across the tops of the walls made it quite clear this was a titanic structure. A titanic temple.

It was large and empty, save for an iron-reinforced wooden door across from him. This was flanked by two titanic statues: one male, one female. Their flowing robes hid much of their bodies, but their eyes were sure and focused. It was easy to imagine them staring at the observer, bearing down with a penetrating gaze.

He'd learned in his studies that most of the titans originally didn't worship the pantheon. Instead, they honored the Cosmic Entities said to be the true power behind all things. To many a modern-day priest this would seem a strange religion, focused on abstract forces rather than personal deities. Some might even have called it blasphemous or cult-like, which was ironic in that it was from this ancient religion that all others flowed.

Cadrith kept alert as he walked to the door. While he'd been told what he needed to do, he hadn't been told where he would be doing it. Having this all take place in a temple added another level of irony. As to where this temple was, he had no idea, though it had to be somewhere on Tralodren.

He shoved the door aside and moved beyond it into a narrow hallway ending with a plain iron door. He stopped before the door, looking it over with a bit more care than its common exterior would warrant. It had no keyhole, latch, nor even—apparently—hinges, on this side anyway. But he knew it was where he was supposed to go.

Placing a hand upon the door, he closed his eyes and willed it to open. There was a flash of azure light, followed by the door melting away. It wasn't exactly his intent, but it accomplished the same end. He thrust his staff forward, letting the azure light illuminate the square room. It was fairly plain when compared to the rest of the temple. The only thing standing out was a titanic corpse. Long dead, its leathery flesh held together the bones of what appeared to be a fifteen-foot frame slouched in a heap on the empty floor.

"Sidra." Cadrith stepped closer, holding the glowing globe of his staff forward to better reveal the body's shrunken and dehydrated breasts and swan-like neck. He couldn't miss the ebony pieces of armor. Parts of it were damaged, and others still showed splashes of old blood that looked more like cankerous rust, but the ancient metal still clung to the shriveled body. He'd heard the stories as a child, like many others had, about the legendary battle among Sidra, the pantheon, and even Vkar and Xora themselves, but never dreamed he'd see part of it in the flesh.

"Still here after all these years." When he had first heard this part of the plan, he didn't believe it. She'd been destroyed by Gurthghol, or so the legends said. And yet here her body lay.

"Waiting for you." A shudder of darkness rippled across the gloom around him, slithering around the mummified woman and Cadrith. He noticed it didn't venture too far into the circle of light created by his staff. He wondered if he was being watched more closely than he thought. Best to assume he was until everything was in place.

"Lay hold of what remains of my mantle upon her and come into your full potential." The familiar voice returned, more tangible than before. "Up until now I've only been resting *upon* you, but now I will be *within* as well. And none shall be able to stand before you."

As he'd already been briefed to do, Cadrith willed the tatters of the former power that had once resided so greatly in her bones into his own body. It was a simple matter once he put his mind to it—easier than he thought it should have been, but then again, he was just getting used to his new abilities. His actions produced a dark aura about him. Along with the aura, Cadrith gained some height, growing in size to match Sidra's corpse. As the last of what had been kept in Sidra flowed into him, he became accustomed to his larger, more augmented nature. He also enjoyed the increase of power that came with it. If he was amazed by what he'd already experienced, he was even more so at the potential even a taste of Nuhl's power granted.

And his size wasn't the only thing that had been changed by the infusion of Nuhl's power. His skin had paled to a very light porcelain, and he now wore pure-black robes and a long charcoal-gray cape. He also knew his eyes were outlined with a soft azure light and his short hair was a shimmering black. A fitting reflection of the merger, he supposed, that could be altered or changed as he wished once he was free of Nuhl's chains.

Cadrith watched a slick tar-like substance slide up the bottom of his staff all the way to its top, encasing it in liquid night. Instead of the azure globe, a black pearl polished to a mirror-like sheen rested at the top. Even so, this new darkness didn't hinder the azure light from continuing to shine.

"Now finish them off," ordered Nuhl. "Every. Single. One."

"I know just where to start," he said, grinning darkly.

CHAPTER 4

EVEN THE THICKEST OF ROPES CAN SNAP
WHENEVER ITS CORDS START TO FRAY.

—Old Tralodroen proverb

Rowan's head felt like a blacksmith had mistaken it for an anvil.

"How you feeling?" Alara pushed some stray hairs from his forehead. She was seated beside him on the hard steps of the dais that were digging into his back.

"I've been better." He made an effort to sit up. As he did, with Alara's help, the blood rushed to his head, increasing the throbbing between his temples exponentially. Shaking as much of the sensation away as he could, he tried to put everything together. From the looks of things it had been a fierce fight. Almost on reflex, he turned to see the throne. It was empty.

"What happened? Did he—"

"I don't know," said Alara. "We took some heavy losses, though. Tebow and Cracius are dead. Dugan and Vinder, too. I can only assume the same of Hadek."

"And Gilban?" He already knew the answer, judging from the troubled look on Alara's face.

"Dead."

"What about Cadrissa?" He stood, albeit shakily. There was something about waking up lying down after a fight that didn't sit well with him. Especially when he learned he was the last to awaken.

"She wasn't even hurt."

"But I saw her—"

"See for yourself." Alara pointed out the wizardess seated in front of a portal to his right. She seemed very much alive. Her back was to him and so he couldn't tell entirely how she fared, but from what he could see she seemed well enough.

"It's a miracle," he said. "I thought she'd been killed."

"I know." Alara's comment reminded him of how he'd dashed off into the fray, heedless of anything else after concluding Cadrissa had been slain. His actions had been foolhardy and were probably to blame for what had followed.

"I'm sorry," he said, noticing Alara's tired sapphire eyes and the bruise on the side of her head. He could have prevented that too if he'd just been more level headed. "I should have stuck to the plan. All of this is my fault."

"We fought our own fight," she assured him. "Whatever happened is on our own heads."

Rowan wanted to say more, but knew Alara didn't want to discuss it. "So what do we do now?"

"I don't know. I suppose keep heading to Valkoria. You helped free Cadrissa, so that's all that *is* left."

"I didn't really free her," said Rowan. "But now that she *is* free, I guess that's all that's left to do . . . like you say . . ." Only that wasn't what he felt. There was something else gnawing on his gut, growing more frenzied with every heartbeat. Panthora had sent him here—well, given him the choice of coming here—saying that he'd also find the answers he'd been seeking. But he knew no more than he did before. If anything, he had even *more* questions to ponder.

Had he made the right choice? Was this nothing more than a diversion from his main objective? Was getting back to the knighthood the goal all along? But Panthora had said he was free to make his choice—that he had to decide. And he did decide, and had been feeling good about it . . . until he woke up and saw the aftermath.

"How is she?" Rowan carefully inquired while looking Cadrissa over. He figured it best to get through one thing at a time.

"She's upset about Dugan's death," said Alara. "She was pretty fond of him."

"As I am of you." He gently stroked Alara's cheek, amazed at how easily the gesture came to him. Only a few hours before, he was torn about just how to respond to Alara—or even if he should. And now here he was embracing his deepening affection. "Did you give as good as you got? That bruise looks pretty deep."

Her expression didn't change. "I think we all tried our best, but in the end it wasn't enough."

"You don't know that for sure. He might have gotten past us but died on the throne. And we still have the scepter." He pointed at the object clasped in her hand. A minor victory, if anything.

"Which we don't know how to use anyway." She sighed.

"Have you seen Galba?" he asked, eager to find some bright lining in one of these gray clouds. "She'd be able to tell us what happened."

"No, it's just been us."

"Then we'd better see to Cadrissa," he continued, stooping to retrieve and sheathe his sword before making his way to the wizardess. He left his shield where it lay. "She might be our only way back to Vanhyrm—unless we want to spend weeks trying to get through these woods."

Alara followed him. "So you've decided to head back to Valkoria for sure?"

The gnawing in his gut increased. "It's all I have for now . . . Cadrissa," he called to the mage. She didn't answer, engrossed in the portal before her. It displayed a peaceful oasis in the middle of a desert.

"How did he die?" he asked Alara.

"He was crucified."

"Where? I don't see his body."

"Between those two posts." Alara's voice grew softer as they got closer to Cadrissa. "Once he was dead, his entire body was consumed by flames."

Rowan stopped. "Consumed by flames?" Alara nodded. That certainly wasn't natural. But what of any of this *had* been natural since he started? The dreams. The visions on the boat ride here. And for what? Resuming his stride, he walked around to Cadrissa's side, where she could see him.

"Cadrissa?" This time she responded to his voice. She'd been crying for some time; her eyes were moist and cheeks slick.

"Are you okay?" he asked.

"I'll survive."

"I'm—I'm sorry about Dugan, but happy that you're safe. Alara and I were actually looking to find you . . . to free you. We never guessed we'd cross paths like *this*."

Cadrissa wiped what wetness remained on her cheeks. "*None* of us had this in mind when we signed up. If I had, I'd probably still be in Haven right now, enjoying a nice cup of tea and some good books." She made an effort to stand, but Rowan took her hand and helped lift her up.

"That gown new?" he asked. While they were much better than the soiled golden robes she'd been wearing when he last saw her, he wasn't sure if the change was a good thing.

"*He* gave it to me." Cadrissa's features were flat. He didn't need to ask who "he" was. She'd already been through enough with Dugan as it was. No need to stir up other memories for the time being.

"Rowan and I are thinking of heading back to Vanhyrm," said Alara. "It's a fortified settlement a long way from here. We thought, if you were up to it, you might be able to help us get there faster than we could on foot. You'd be able to rest there yourself until you decide—"

"He survived the throne." Cadrissa's flat voice drained the blood from their faces.

"How do you know that?" Alara asked. "You weren't even awake for the fight. And none of us saw anything after that."

"I-I just know." For a short moment Rowan thought Cadrissa's green eyes had flashed pale blue. It was faint and sudden and could have been a trick of his tired mind. Even so, he couldn't help recalling the similar occurrence back in that lizardman village. "He survived . . . and now he's a god."

The awkward silence was broken by Alara. "You've obviously been through a lot," she began cautiously, "and I can't *begin* to imagine how—"

"He survived the throne, I'm sure of it." There was a fire in Cadrissa's face that shocked even Rowan. It was the conviction of the most ardent believers—only this wasn't a matter of faith or religion but of a lich rising to godhood.

"Is that even possible?" he asked Alara.

"We were supposed to be the last line of defense," she said, raising the scepter for added emphasis. "If we failed, there was always a chance he could have survived the throne."

"I thought Galba wasn't going to let that happen," said Rowan.

"The throne is always the final judge." The new voice belonged to Galba. She stood a few paces from them, as calm as ever.

"So did he survive?" asked Rowan.

"He did."

"And you didn't stop him?" He was beside himself. To go through all this—to even have Panthora help guide him here—and then to have the lich *survive*? It was beyond all comprehension.

"He faced his trials—as do all. He just made it further than most."

"So now there's a new god in the pantheon?" Alara was amazed at the thought.

"Not in the pantheon, just on Tralodren," said Galba. "But that too can change—and in very short order."

"What do you mean?" Rowan didn't like Galba's tone.

"She wants us to stop him." Cadrissa laughed a humorless laugh. "He was more powerful than any wizard I've ever known or read about *before* his apotheosis. Assuming we even were insane enough to *try*, how can you think we'd stand a chance *now*?"

Galba's gaze rested on the silver scepter clasped in Alara's hand.

"What's that?" Cadrissa asked, suddenly drawn to the object.

"Something Gilban thought could stop the lich," Alara explained. "He said he got it from Gorallis and that it would allow the person who used it to sap even the strength of a god."

Cadrissa's eyes widened. "The Scepter of Night."

"You've heard of it?" Rowan didn't know if he liked her sudden enthusiasm. Especially after that flash of blue in her eyes earlier.

"Any mage worth their craft has," Cadrissa answered eagerly. "It's one of the greatest artifacts left from the ages of the wizard kings."

Alara fixed her gaze on Galba. "Is that what you want? For us to face a god?"

"It's not what *I* want," Galba returned, "but what you *choose*. Cadrith may be a god, but he cannot leave Tralodren. Once he comes to understand his full strength and nature, he'll look to make Tralodren his realm, subjecting all to his rule . . . until this world is destroyed."

"He won't destroy Tralodren," Cadrissa countered. "He's been after godhood for years. He wants to *rule*—to have *power*—not *destroy* the planet."

"*He* might not," Galba continued, "but his *patron* has other ideas."

"Patron?" Alara went from Cadrissa to Rowan.

"The black tentacles . . ." Cadrissa shivered.

"Black tentacles?" Rowan was just as lost as Alara.

"The *real* power behind Cadrith's boasts," Galba explained. "And it has an agenda all its own. One that calls for the destruction of Tralodren and even the pantheon."

"*What?*" He couldn't believe what he was hearing. "He's going to take on the *pantheon*? That's madness."

"Not for a god," Galba countered gently.

"A god who can't leave Tralodren, you just said," Alara responded.

"A god backed by the same power that challenged them before and nearly succeeded, while also taking the lives of Vkar and Xora in the process."

"What did you mean when you said *black tentacles*?" Alara asked Cadrissa.

The mage took a breath, then said, "I was taken to his tower after we left the ruins. When I tried to escape, I-I encountered some black tentacles covered with mouths. At first, I thought it was part of the tower's defenses, but when I saw it again outside Galba's circle I knew it was something much greater. In the tower it told me I had to help Cadrith succeed. The implication was fairly clear of what would happen if I didn't. But when I saw it again outside the circle . . ."

Alara turned to face Galba. "Is it still outside?"

"No." Galba's answer brought some visible relief. "It had to detach itself from Cadrith so he could enter the circle. But it reclaimed him upon his departure. It's now plotting its next move, which gives you very little time to make up your minds about what you'll do next. Decide quickly," Galba said sternly as she began fading from sight. "I'll return when you've made your decision."

"Why do I have the feeling we don't have much of a choice in any of this?" Alara mused.

Rowan was tempted to agree with her but wasn't ready to relinquish his hope for answers just yet.

"I'll need some time to think," he said, withdrawing himself.

• ● •

Cadrissa watched Rowan retrieve his shield and then take a seat at another part of the circle. "So you really were going to come after me?"

"That was the plan," Alara confessed.

"Even though you had no idea where I was?"

"I didn't say it was a good one."

"Well, we might as well know what we have to work with." Cadrissa extended her hand. "Can I see the scepter?" Alara handed it over.

Since her final encounter with Cadrith, she'd been feeling strange. A wreath of whispers swirled about her head. They weren't saying anything she could understand, just constantly mumbling amid her thoughts. She was growing rather annoyed with it all and would welcome an opportunity to focus on something else.

There was a greater sense of magical might inside her too. She felt the necklace she'd placed in the hidden pocket of her robe burning with an intense heat—even hotter than before.

But despite its heat, it didn't harm her, allowing her to quickly put it out of mind and focus her full attention on the scepter.

"Did Gilban tell you the incantation to activate it?"

"No," said Alara. "He even got pretty stubborn when I asked him about that. I don't think he thought he'd fail."

"Guess he didn't see that coming," Cadrissa added, then wished she hadn't. Worse, there was a faint echo of laughter in her head at the comment—a cold levity dancing in and out amid the whispers.

Alara bit her lip in sullen silence.

"Sorry," she said, her face softening. "It just slipped out. Gilban was a good man."

"Yes, he was," Alara returned, then added, "so was Dugan."

Cadrissa returned her focus to the scepter as she turned it in both hands, looking over the minute details of its simple design, searching for anything that might crack its mystery. Her training didn't aid her, but that same added energy she'd felt since her capture continued beating through her veins, greatly augmenting her abilities of discernment. She was growing to like it.

"After all the stories I've heard, I never thought it would be so plain looking."

"Maybe that helped to keep it hidden," Alara offered.

"Maybe." It was a decent theory and one she was willing to accept for the time being. "It seems to be of marvelous craftsmanship and resonates with an energy I can't pinpoint. It's almost like it has power built up inside it, waiting to be released." Raising her head, she asked, "Was Gilban able to use it?"

"I don't think so."

"I'm still amazed he convinced you to let him make the attack in the first place." Suddenly she envisioned a comical image of the blind seer repeatedly swinging into the air while Cadrith laughed mockingly mere inches from the elf. She knew it probably hadn't happened that way, but the scene was hard to ignore, seeming to have a life all its own. And once more she felt a pang of regret at having even entertained it to begin with.

"He knew he had the leverage as long as he kept the incantation to himself," said Alara. "At least that's what I think he was thinking."

"Which doesn't do us much good now." Cadrissa sighed.

"We can't change what's passed."

"Well, if it's still active, then you might be right about it not being used properly. I couldn't tell you more without having time to study it better."

"Do you think if we found Cadrith, we'd still be able to use it against him?" Alara's question was a surprise. She hadn't expected her to be so willing to rejoin the fight.

"I don't know the first thing about it." Cadrissa struggled with the whispers. They were more like flies buzzing louder and louder around her head. It was starting to disrupt her concentration. "There's a lot of energy in it, but until I have that incantation I don't really know."

"But if it *is* the Scepter of Night, like you say, could it really stop Cadrith?"

She pushed back the whispers and stared Alara straight in the face. "You really want to face him again?"

"If it means saving the world, yes." And there it was, the clear-cut answer she'd seen poking out here and there for the last few moments. Madness. And yet, if what Galba said was true, it might be the only option *to* take. For right now no one had anything else to level the field, which was what the scepter could do—if they knew the incantation. They might not have wizard kings to challenge Cadrith, but if enough of an opposing force could be roused to stand against a greatly weakened newly risen god . . .

"Well, without the incantation there's little good it's going to do anyone."

"I see." She watched Alara's countenance fall.

Expelling the last of her lingering reservations with another sigh, Cadrissa said, "But I do know a place where we might be able to find it."

• ● •

Rowan sat apart from the others, facing a portal showing a woodland scene not unlike the terrain of Arid Land. He'd dropped his shield beside him and was watching the opening between the stone posts shimmer. He wasn't sure how long the sight had held his attention, but eventually he returned to the present and pulled out the panther paw necklace from under his armor and tunic.

Grasping it in his left hand, he prayed to Panthora for wisdom and strength and felt peace wash over him, stilling his heart and mind. He continued to desire an understanding of the necklace's purpose. But that, like so many other answers, eluded him. He didn't really know what to do or where to go. Cadrissa was free from the lich, so that obligation was fulfilled, but now there was Cadrith.

He couldn't help but feel that he was duty bound to stop this new threat, since he was, in a way, responsible for its creation. Though he was obligated to report back on the success of his first mission, he kept finding himself in new situations calling for action. If he continued this way, following all the threads through as they were woven into the next, he'd never get back to Valkoria.

He knew it was time for a choice, but what should he choose? For it wasn't just duty that called him. What would he do about Alara? Should he stay? Should he go? The questions were tearing him up. Whereas before he had a focus to his purpose in life, everything now was blurred by his growing attachment to—perhaps even dependency on—her presence.

Coupled with this were Panthora's words telling him he had a great calling in his life, greater than he realized. He even had been told the knighthood might not be that important to her; at least it was seeming that way the more he considered the visions he'd had back in Vanhyrm and outside Elandor. Still, Cadrith was a threat to the whole world and therefore *all* of humanity . . . and there was the possibility of staying to help put an end to that too.

So if he was honest, it really all came down to what *he* wanted, what *he* felt was right in *his* mind, *his* spirit, and nothing else. Alara had helped him separate his true self from the dogma he'd learned in his training. Now he had to search out what his true self wanted, and his true self alone. The knighthood was important, but wasn't saving the lives of millions of humans more important than heading back to report on his mission? Weren't the words and implications of Panthora more worthy of consideration than the edicts of a superior knight?

Once more he stared at the old, shriveled panther's paw. "Please, Panthora," he begged, "show me a sign. What do I need to do next?"

You decide . . . came the faintest of whispers. So faint that Rowan wondered if he'd really heard anything.

"Panthora?"

"Rowan?" Alara's voice came softly from behind him. Rowan shook himself awake as if from a dream. Standing, he saw Alara. "I didn't want to bother you. If you don't want to be disturbed—"

"No. You're not bothering me at all." Even in the midst of his chaotic thoughts the sight of her brought a sense of calm to his heart.

"How's your head?"

"Probably better than yours looks." Rowan noticed the bruise had darkened. It would be a while till it healed, as it looked to be all the way down to the bone.

"What's that?" Alara pointed to Rowan's necklace, and he realized he hadn't placed it back under his tunic and armor, as was his habit.

"Something very dear to me." He was about to tuck it away but stopped. What reason was there to hide it now? Alara had already seen it, and there wasn't any harm in it remaining exposed for the time being.

"I've never seen you wearing it before." She stooped to get a closer look. "Is it a dried-out panther's paw?"

"Panthora gave it to me in the ruins of Gondad. I was led to it after I ran inside the ruins."

"And you hid it all this time?" She sounded a little confused and surprised.

"I didn't want to draw any attention to it," he explained. "There were enough distractions as it was."

Letting the matter drop, Alara progressed to the real matter at hand. "Cadrissa thinks she knows a place where we might be able to find the incantation for the scepter."

"Where?"

"The Great Library."

"Where's that?"

"In Clesethius. It's the capital of Rexatoius. There's a library that's been filled with all sorts of knowledge and texts from all across Tralodren since the foundation of the republic."

"Is that where Gilban took the knowledge from Taka Lu Lama?"

Alara hesitated. "Yes. That's where it'll probably wind up in the end."

"And so if you find the incantation, what then?"

"We use it against Cadrith."

"Sounds like a pretty far-fetched plan."

"As far fetched as going to find some wizard you only knew about from legend to help save a human mage?"

"No." He frowned. "Even *more* far fetched."

"Well, it's the only option we have." He could see she was starting to get upset. He wasn't sure why.

"Is it?"

"Did you hear what Galba said?" she pressed. "The fate of the world rests with *us*."

"That's not what I heard her say."

"Oh, really," said Alara, arms akimbo. "And what part of destroying the pantheon and Tralodren escaped your hearing?"

Rowan saw Cadrissa working her way toward them out of the corner of his eye. She was holding the scepter Alara had given her. She was also watching their exchange with obvious interest. *Too* much interest for Rowan's liking.

"And why do you think it's all up to us?" he asked.

"Because we have the scepter and know what to do."

"No, we don't," Rowan half shouted, half laughed. "None of us have a clue what to do next, and you're just hoping your idea will work."

"And you have something *better* in mind?" Alara clamped her lips tight when she saw Cadrissa draw up beside them.

"Did I miss something while I was abducted?" The mage looked from Alara to Rowan, seeking a reply. None was given.

"You're right." Alara sighed. "This doesn't have to be your fight."

"But somehow it's *yours*?"

"The scepter's the only way we can hope to stop him. And if Tralodren goes, we're going to die anyway. So why not die doing something to stop it?"

"Now you sound like a Nordican." Rowan felt his lips curl up at the edges.

"You must be a corrupting influence." Alara shared in the guarded smirk, the tension melting between them.

"I could say the same thing about you," he added.

"Yeah." Cadrissa reinserted herself into the conversation. "It must have been something pretty big."

Rowan looked Cadrissa square in the face. "You really think you can find that incantation in the library?"

"This scepter's too old for us to find anything of worth in my academy or any other I can think of. The Great Library is the only place where I'd have a chance of ever figuring it out with any degree of certainty."

"And you're with Alara on this?"

"We share the same logic. If Tralodren really *is* at stake, and we have something in our power to try to stop it, we should do what we can."

"You still don't have to join us." Alara's face softened with her voice. "You've already rescued Cadrissa, and Rexatoius is a long way from here. You'd probably be better off just heading back to Valkoria."

You decide . . . The two words haunted his thoughts. It would be so much easier if Panthora made the choice for him. At least then he could be confident it was the right choice. But to have such a matter left to his own choosing—if he made the wrong decision . . . But the longer he mulled it over, one path stood out, along with a rising peace he felt with it.

"I'm coming." Rowan's voice was as serious as his face. "There won't be much need for a knighthood if there's no Tralodren—or Panthora to serve." Turning to Cadrissa, after collecting and slinging his shield over his back, he asked, "So how do we get there?"

"I could try to cast a spell, but I haven't been there before, so I won't be able to anchor us that strongly, and I don't know how it will work in this circle or if we can even get out of it to begin with."

"You have a spell that strong?" He was rather impressed. "You're planning on going almost to the other side of the world. Aren't you tired by now, after all you've been through?"

"I should be able to get us to the library if I have a strong-enough connection." Cadrissa studied Alara carefully. "Have you been to the library before?"

"Yes," said Alara, "many times."

"Recently?"

"Just before I left with Gilban, why?" Before Cadrissa could answer, Alara guessed. "You want me to be your anchor."

"Yes."

"Do you think it would be dangerous to try this in the circle?" Concerned, Alara scanned the stones around them.

"I'm not sure." Cadrissa joined her in surveying the scene. "It could just do nothing, or it could do something really bad."

"Like what?" Rowan was hesitant to ask but still curious.

"Like scattering our bodies over the entire planet."

"Oh."

"Then perhaps now's a good time to tell Galba we're ready," Alara suggested.

"Very well." A familiar voice brought everyone back around to the front of the dais. Galba stood before it, sparkling as if she'd been sprinkled with diamond dust—her rich green eyes ensnaring them in a comforting and inviting gaze. "It seems you've made your decision."

"We have," said Alara.

"And I will not hinder any one of you from leaving." Galba's voice was like a peaceful breeze.

"So then I can take us out of here with a spell?" asked Cadrissa.

"I will not hinder you." Galba motioned to a nearby stone portal. "Cast your spell on that portal and you will find success.

"However . . ." She moved closer to Gilban's body. "The dead shall stay. Only the living may leave this place."

"But Gilban—" Alara started.

"Will be taken care of with the others." Alara attempted to speak, but was halted by Galba's upturned hand. "Let life be for the living. What is dead has now passed on to a new journey. You'll have your own soon enough. For now, if you wish to be free of the circle and able to enact your plans, then your way is clear." Galba's alabaster hand again pointed out the portal.

"Can I at least say goodbye?" Alara's eyes had become wet, her lips thin and tight.

"Certainly."

•●•

Alara slowly approached Gilban's body, pondering his fate with each measured step.

She prayed it was a good one. He'd been her mentor, her friend, and in many ways . . . her inspiration. The journey seemed to take years, though he was just a few feet away. His body seemed nothing like it had in life: empty . . . and so frail. So still. She didn't want to remember him how he looked now. She wanted to recall him as the kind and wise man who had been so much to her, who had served his nation and his goddess admirably in this life and, she was certain, would in the life to come.

She bent down and smoothed out his mussed robes as tears started to flow. She knew he was gone, and she had to go on. There wasn't any time to grieve his loss. She had to lead now. The plan was still forming and was weak at best, but she had to do something to try to stop this thing she'd helped unleash . . . even if unknowingly. The mantle of leadership was heavier than she thought she could bear, but as she viewed the fallen seer, she drew strength from his example and life. It was time to place the pain and emptiness behind a wall so she could do what needed to be done. The moment called for action, not the mourning of things that were fading away.

"Safe journey," she whispered. She remained there until she heard soft footfalls approach from behind.

Alara turned to see the peaceful face of Galba peering down at her. "You'll make sure his body is taken back to the temple?"

"Yes." Galba had adopted the face of a loving mother.

"Thank you." Her smile was brief and bittersweet.

"Now go. Your place is not here among the dead, but with the living."

• ● •

"You know the spell," Galba told Cadrissa as Alara rejoined them. "Speak it and be gone from here." Cadrissa watched the nearest portal become black and empty. "I will see to the rest."

"Rowan, grab my hand." Cadrissa extended hers toward the knight. "Now, take Alara's."

"You sure this is going to work?" He shot a nervous glance the mage's way.

"The worst thing that could happen is we miss the library and end up in a more familiar area that might be stronger in her mind." Cadrissa focused her attention on Alara. "So you need to keep the image of the library your main thought at all times. Focus on that, and we should get there."

"What do *I* do?" asked Rowan.

"Just close your eyes, and clear your mind of any thoughts other than going to the library, then follow me through the portal."

"But I don't know what it looks like," he said.

"It doesn't matter." Cadrissa bit back her rising frustration. This spell was already a stretch for her. The longer the strain, the greater the discomfort—and she'd like to be rid of it as soon as possible. "The thought alone has weight and will carry you there on the strength of Alara's will. Just concentrate on my voice, but don't open your eyes until I say so, or the spell will be ruined."

Both Alara and Rowan closed their eyes and tightened their grip on the other's hand. Taking a breath, Cadrissa tried to clear her head, but found it still cluttered. On a strange urge she couldn't explain, she reached out to the necklace, focusing as much as she could upon it. Even with the fragile line she was able to muster, she wasn't prepared for the surge of energy that shot into her.

The faint whispers completely ceased. In their place rose a steady—almost addictive—hum of magical power. Infused with this energy, she heard herself speak the words to the spell as if she herself was far away, listening to someone else saying them. It was as if the words came to her mind and then bubbled to her lips of their own volition. Her whole frame shook as the magical surge increased even more. Her mind raced in fearful awe as the hidden necklace blazed in its secret pocket like the fires of Helii itself. It was too late to wonder if this was the right thing to do, for she was compelled by it now more than anything else.

"Kanree loth ra. Ambi lo-deen. Uth vos angri." The spell released itself from her grip. Birthed of a nature that both frightened and excited her, the spell worked at such a level of power it astonished her. Before her, the portal began to spin and twirl like a kaleidoscope. Colors and patterns bloomed and faded into one another until a new scene materialized between the posts and lintel: a tranquil park-like setting with freshwater lakes and leafy trees.

Cadrissa quietly watched as the image became clearer. "I'm going to start moving," she informed the others as she took the first tottering steps toward the portal. It was hard to move, almost as if she was drunk. The energy released and sustained throughout her body was just short of euphoric. But with each careful step, she managed. The others followed slowly behind her, eyes clenched tight in concentration.

She stepped up to the flat image between the posts, then into and through it with a continuous stride. It would have looked to any who saw it as if she'd stepped into a puddle. Her entrance into the image sent out ripples that bounced into and back from the posts framing the portal. With another step her body vanished from view completely with only her hand sticking out, pulling Rowan fast behind her—and Alara behind him. Following their exit from the circle, the image in the portal faded, as did the images of all the other portals. Each became a soft gray haze.

Silence again descended over the circle. Only Galba, and Gilban's body resting at her feet, remained. Galba peered down at the elf with a face devoid of emotion. A nimbus of light radiated from her, spreading outward to cover the entire circle and the glade beyond. Anyone who might have seen it could have imagined the area being home to a star rather than an ancient monument. However, as fast as it appeared, the light faded. When it did, Galba and any signs of their confrontation had vanished. Only the dais, statues, and throne remained.

CHAPTER 5

THERE IS DEATH AND THEN THERE IS NOTHING.
I AM CONVINCED OF IT BEYOND ALL REASONABLE DOUBT.
ALL WHO SAY OTHERWISE ARE CHARLATANS AND FOOLS.

—**Cyrin, dranoric philosopher**

The last thing Dugan remembered was the agony weighing down his body like a shirt of mail. He recalled hanging between the posts and even taking his final breath. How he was now standing in this strange terrain was beyond him. Thankfully, he was no longer in pain. The wounds he'd suffered had departed, leaving him with a strange sense of numbness. It was an odd sensation but a welcome one after his torturous death. His eyes looked up at the gray, lifeless sky. No cloud sailed the dismal domain. Only the persistent glow of either twilight or predawn ruled. The overwhelming silence was both dreadful and peaceful.

The silence gave him another revelation: he wasn't breathing. Placing his hand upon his chest, he noticed another two things: first, his heart no longer beat; second, he now wore new clothes. Closer inspection revealed a long-sleeved copper-colored robe with amber and orange embroidery around the hem and cuffs. The garment fell to his ankles, where he was glad to see he was still wearing his boots. A small bit of comfort in this otherwise surreal scene. Everything else he'd last had on—including his weapons—was gone.

He surveyed the broken gray landscape stretching on for an endless expanse all around him. For miles upon miles in all directions, it displayed shattered columns like petrified trees in a strange and unsettling forest. Mixed among them were toppled statuary, open scrolls and books scattered about the stones like dry hides—flaking and crumbling into minute debris. Here and there were a few open areas where the clutter of ruins gave way to small puddles—even lakes—of powdery dust. This same dust covered all in a thick, undisturbed layer, like a gray cloth smothering out all life beneath its folds. There was no sign of life, no wind, not even the sensation of air itself. It all smelled of dust and was so dry that Dugan's throat and eyes itched.

If he was dead, then where was Helii, Rheminas' realm? He didn't see any fire. Could he have been sent somewhere else by the lich? Perhaps *before* his death? He didn't think so. He remembered Tebow praying for his safe passage. No, this was someplace else . . . But where?

Dugan stooped and picked up a fragment of a shattered statue. The chunk of granite bore the visage of a comely woman with flecks of red still on her lips and green chips around her eyes. He studied it a bit longer and then dropped it as his interest waned. The sound of the stone hitting the ground was muffled to the point of nonexistence—as if the noise was swallowed whole upon impact.

With nothing to direct his way—for all was the same or seemingly the same in all directions—Dugan chose a path at random and started treading ahead. He noticed that his feet left no trace of his movements. He walked on for what felt like miles. The ruins changed here and there— cultural differences, he thought—but nothing living came into his field of vision. He didn't stop to look at much of any of it—didn't want to. There was no reason. He wasn't going to get any answers digging through these endless rubbish heaps, of that much he was sure.

After what he was sure had been hours, he stopped. Again scanning the sky, he saw it remained the same, neither dimming to a deeper twilight nor brightening to a shimmering dawn. Odder still was the impression he hadn't traveled for any great distance at all. Had it not been for the scenery changing he wouldn't have known that he'd moved anywhere.

With no heartbeat or breath, it seemed his body would be able to go on indefinitely. He realized it didn't matter how long he traveled—he could walk from now until the end of the cosmos and still not grow tired, nor see the sky above him change. If this was what it was like to be dead, then he wasn't looking forward to his afterlife.

He spotted a tall statue to his left. It was more intact than the others he'd seen so far. There also was some writing on it, which he could barely make out. Thinking it might be a marker he could use for direction, he made his way through the rocky, dusty soil to what he came to see was a carving of a female warrior sitting on a throne. The statue had to be about double his height and was carved of cold gray rock. It was smooth to the touch, almost pristine. He took in what appeared to be a single word, carved in a large, strange script at the throne's base. He couldn't decipher it. The writing was like nothing he'd seen before, though in truth that didn't mean much since he hadn't seen much of *any* writing outside of Elonum and Telboros.

Giving up on the word, he studied the woman instead. She was young and stern. Even he could see the battle-hardened features on her face. He was unable to discern her race, though he was sure it was some type of human; probably Telborian from the looks of it. Dressed in plate armor as she was, it was hard to make out the rest of her features, and in short order he gave up. If this was a signpost, he couldn't make heads or tails of what it meant.

"Ah, there you are . . ." The familiar voice spun Dugan around. "It seems you wandered off by yourself."

"Tebow?" Dugan almost didn't recognize the man who stood before him. It *was* Tebow, but a much younger and fully healed version. The gray hair and lined face were full of new life and a renewed health. It was like Dugan had somehow stepped back in time and now saw the priest at his prime.

"What are you doing here?"

"The same as you," said Cracius, who stood beside Tebow. Of the two, he was the least changed in appearance, only slightly younger and healthier than Dugan remembered. Both were dressed as they'd been in the circle, but they no longer carried their silver hammers.

"And what's that?" asked Dugan.

"Making our way to our fate," answered Tebow.

"Why are you so young?"

"The spirit is eternal and never ages," Cracius replied.

"It's not a wise idea to go wandering in Mortis," Tebow continued.

"Mortis?" Dugan scanned the scene behind the priests once more. "*This* is *Mortis*?"

"That's right," said Cracius.

"So I'm dead."

"Yes." Tebow nodded.

"And you're dead too?"

"Yes," Tebow repeated.

"But how can I be alive if I'm *dead*?" Dugan held out his hands to contemplate as he spoke. "It feels like I'm still alive. But I'm not breathing and don't have a heartbeat."

"You're seeing your spirit," Tebow explained, "your *true* self."

"I don't look or feel any different." Dugan studied his hands more closely, carefully closing and opening them.

"Most don't if they strive to live an authentic life," said Cracius.

"So *everyone* has *two* bodies?" Dugan was still trying to get a foothold in this logic. It was almost beyond his reach, but if he strained just enough he could latch onto a small ledge and try to pull himself onto it.

"*Three*, actually," Tebow corrected. "Your physical body, your soul, and your spirit." He counted each off with a finger of his left hand.

"Soul?" Dugan studied Tebow carefully. "Isn't that the same as your spirit?"

Cracius held up the same three fingers before the former gladiator. "Spiritual body." He moved his index finger forward. "Mental body, which is called the soul," he said, wiggling his middle finger. "And the physical body," he added while moving his third finger forward. "All three"—he combined the fingers into one mass of digits—"form the existence we call life. Such was the way of our creation. When one body goes away, like when the physical body dies"—the priest moved his third finger away from the other two, which he left combined—"then the other two go on without it. The spirit and the soul are eternal. In fact, they're *so* tightly intertwined that in some cases people can say *soul* and mean *spirit* and vice versa."

Dugan's mind raced at this new understanding. "So if someone were to sell their soul, then it wouldn't be their *spirit*, but their *mind* they were selling?"

"You can't sell your soul or your spirit." Tebow's words hit Dugan at his core. "They can only be given to another by the yielding of their owner to another, such as yielding them in devotion to a god."

"So I can't sell my soul?" He wanted to make sure he understood correctly.

"No," repeated Tebow, "but you can give it to another, as I've said. I suppose the terminology could be changed a bit to offer something for the yielding of a soul, and in that sense you could say a soul was 'purchased,' but it wouldn't really be true."

"Besides," added Cracius, "you couldn't really yield your soul without also yielding your spirit. The two go hand in hand."

"I thought you said they were separate?" Dugan was getting lost in these theological waters.

"They are," Cracius continued but was stopped by Tebow's upheld hand.

"Why all this sudden interest?"

"I have my reasons."

"Which involve Rheminas, no doubt." Dugan hid his surprise at Tebow's deduction, though not well enough to escape the priest's notice. "I thought as much. You wouldn't be the first he's made offers to."

"He only wanted my soul," said Dugan, "not my spirit. So if you said this"—he pounded his fist against his chest—"is my spirit, then I could still be missing my soul. And if only my soul's going to Helii, then my spirit—"

"Is also going to Helii." Cracius pointed at Dugan's robe. "There's no mistake. That's your fate."

"He has your body, soul, and spirit." Tebow landed another verbal blow. "I could see it when we were on Tralodren, and it's even plainer now."

"I only sold him my *soul*," Dugan growled.

"And he's laid claim to all three parts of your being." Tebow's voice was more subdued than before.

"But how?" Dugan embraced the swelling rage inside him. He knew he'd been used before, of course, but the old feelings of hatred and anger rose to the surface anew.

Cracius glanced at Tebow, his face full of uncertainty. Tebow gave a nod to Cracius, who returned to Dugan, saying, "It's been said the soul is the gateway to the spirit. Control the mind, the emotions, and the will of a person and you can influence their spirit enough to eventually take control of it. You gave Rheminas your soul, and he rushed in to take your spirit as well. Your body simply followed where your spirit and soul told it to go."

"The pain in my heart . . ." Dugan recalled that moment the fiery serpent had slid down his throat and into his chest back in his cell in Colloni. It felt as if his heart was on fire and that he'd lost something in the process. Now he knew he had: his spirit.

"He's not always known for his trustworthiness." Tebow's words were meant as a form of comfort, but offered little. "He took what he wanted."

"And I let him . . ." Dugan hung his head.

You have already been burnt, Dugan. You can't be wounded any more than you are now. Rheminas' words came back to him, along with a terrible understanding. Looking back, he saw how he gave himself to Rheminas with his oath—swearing his allegiance to him before he'd even come to him in his weakest moment to take advantage of his desperation. And he could see how Rheminas had waited to make sure that oath had sunk in and was weighed down with more hatred and despair, all connected through fear. It was the chain binding the anchor to him.

But what could he do now? Like he'd been branded in Colloni, he'd been branded by Rheminas and was just as much his property as he'd been the elves'. Only with the elves there was a chance for escape—a fleeting hope of a better life to flee to. But with Rheminas . . . this was the end. He was dead and in Mortis. There was nowhere else to go.

Nothing else to do. It was over, and the sooner he grasped hold of that with both hands, the better.

Dugan raised his head. "So why am I here, then, and not with Rheminas?"

"Every creature in the cosmos—except animals—has a spirit, soul, and body," Tebow explained. "Animals have only a physical body inhabited by a soul. When our body is destroyed, it sets the spirit free for its final destination and a new body to claim—an *immortal* body everyone will possess throughout their afterlife. You, along with us, are on such a journey. Soon enough we'll have our new bodies to live out our new lives, but only *after* our judgments."

"What *sort* of bodies?" Dugan was half dreading what might await him in Helii.

"Our new bodies," said Tebow, "will be suited to the realm chosen for us."

"So, if this is Mortis, then this is where you'll spend *your* afterlives?"

"We've been sent to take you to your destination," Cracius continued.

"You wandered away before we could come and collect you," said Tebow. "You don't want to do that here. Mortis is no friend to those who wander from the path."

"I didn't see any path." Dugan searched again for anything that might remotely be considered a trail. Nothing. Not even his own tracks or those of the two priests. "I just started walking."

"And you would have wandered forever." A solemn spirit settled over Tebow as he spoke. "If you veer off the path, you'll never arrive at your destination."

"So where is this path, then?" Dugan still wasn't seeing anything that could qualify as a path.

"You'll see soon enough," replied Tebow.

"Wait," he said, pointing at the statue behind him. "Who's that?"

"What does it matter now?" Cracius didn't even turn around, desiring, as did Tebow, for them to return to the path.

"I just—she seemed important and I was curious."

Silently, the priests exchanged a long glance.

"That's Sidra," said Cracius.

"Who's that?" Dugan continued staring at the statue, trying to make sense of it.

"She was the first real threat to the pantheon, long before Tralodren was formed," Cracius continued, albeit hesitantly.

"So she's dead?" Dugan returned to the priests. He'd learned something about the gods in searching for freedom from Rheminas, but had never heard anything about anyone named Sidra.

"Indeed." Cracius made an effort to dust off his robes, which didn't really do much since they weren't dusty to begin with.

"So what did she try to do?" Dugan returned to studying the statue.

"Kill the gods." Tebow was curt.

"Then she failed."

"She came close enough." It was Cracius' turn for curtness.

"We really have to get moving, Dugan." Tebow's patience was slipping.

"*Both* of you need to escort me?" He allowed a small smirk at the thought. "Is he afraid I'd try to escape?"

"We're not here to escort you anywhere but Sheol," said Tebow. "From there you'll be sent to your final destination."

"Sheol?" Dugan looked from priest to priest. "Never heard of it."

"It's where Asorlok and the fourteen gates reside." Tebow spoke as if that should be common knowledge. "Everyone who dies goes to Sheol, and then their afterlife once they're judged."

"So where are the others?"

"If you're referring to the others from Galba's circle, not all have died yet, and those few who have, besides us, have already passed on to their destination." Tebow turned around, walking away from the gathering. "*They* stuck to the path."

Cracius joined Tebow. "If you're referring to the other beings who've died and still *are* dying with each passing moment, when we get closer to Sheol you'll see the large throng around it."

Dugan started to sigh, swallowed it, and then joined the two priests. What he did now didn't matter. He had a fate, and now that he was dead, he was bound to it. He didn't see the point or even the possibility of trying to squirm out of it.

"So how did she die?"

"Sidra?" Tebow raised an eyebrow. "Her father killed her."

"And who was her father?" He glanced over his shoulder and was surprised at how far away the statue was after such a short amount of time.

"Gurthghol," said Cracius, who kept his eyes forward.

Now that was a name Dugan knew. It was hard to go through life not knowing the god of darkness and chaos. "And how do you two know all this?"

"It's in the Theogona and Kosma," stated Cracius.

"I've heard of those. They're supposed to be some collections of myths, right?"

"Not myths, but stories of what took place before recorded time." Cracius continued on, keeping to a path only he and Tebow could see.

Seeing the current conversation had become the proverbial dead horse, he changed his focus, instead trying to figure out where they were heading. He still saw nothing but unending ruins and dust.

"So how far is it till we get to Sheol?"

"You wandered far from the path, but we'll be there soon enough." Tebow kept an even pace with Cracius. "Once you start to move along the path you'll find it pulls you forward and compresses even the most drawn out of journeys into a rather short trek."

This was far from the fiery greeting he'd been expecting to encounter upon his death. This endless expanse where time, purpose, and reason were nonexistent was more than a little unsettling. It was also growing more than a little frustrating. He would have preferred things were more rapid in their resolution. Dragging everything out just made what was to come even worse.

"How long till we get there?" he asked again in the oppressive silence.

Cracius kept his eyes on their invisible path. "We'll be there before you know it."

"I thought Mortis was filled with ghosts and ghouls, not ruins and dust," he said, tending to the conversational kindling.

"More misconceptions about our god," said Tebow. "What most people don't understand is that all things have a lifespan. Even things without a soul or spirit pass away. Though they may not share the same process as living, breathing creatures, all things have an allotted span of existence. Once that time has expired, they fade from the cosmos—'die,' if you will—and end up here."

Dugan noticed a broken bust to his left whose shoulders were the only things remaining intact. The head above them had long since shattered. "So even *art* comes here to 'die'?"

"Yes," answered Tebow. "Artwork, bricks, houses, palaces, planets, stars, even whole empires, when they've met their demise, end up here. The world may see them as falling to flame, rust, moth, war, or some other such thing, but even as their remains are scattered over Tralodren and the cosmos, their very nature—their concept of design and purpose—comes here. And this isn't just for tangible things either. Ideas end up here too when they've been forgotten or abandoned or suppressed, even philosophies and understandings dying the slow death of dark ages. All come to Mortis in the end."

Dugan found himself wondering just how many ages sat here in the dust. How many layers of time had come to rest, not only from Tralodren, but from other spots all over the cosmos? How many stars contributed to the dry dust on which he was walking?

"So Mortis is one massive graveyard?"

"Yes," said Tebow.

"So if Rheminas hadn't already claimed me, where would I go?"

After a long silence, Tebow responded with a question. "Why worry about it now? You can't change anything that happened once you've come to Mortis."

"It's something to pass the time."

"Your afterlife is determined entirely by what you believed while you lived in your physical body," answered Cracius. "If you held to a certain god or goddess, then to them you would go; if you held to more than one—as is the case in some areas of the world—then you have a potential set of options for your afterlife. But those who held to no god . . . well, they're sent to the Abyss."

"*The Abyss?*" He was surprised at the rage that rose in him so quickly, though the priests appeared unaffected by his outburst. "What kind of reward is *that?*"

"A true one," Tebow stated flatly.

Dugan couldn't believe it. "So a man who lived a good life but didn't really care about the gods would still end up in the Abyss?"

Tebow glanced over his shoulder. "All who have made their way into the Abyss have done so for one of two reasons . . . and sometimes *both* reasons. They've either warred against the gods or they've denied them their due as powers greater than themselves."

"So I would've gone to the Abyss?" Dugan spoke more to himself than anyone else.

"Don't trouble yourself about it." Cracius made an attempt at encouragement. "It's been decreed since the dawn of creation. There's nothing any can do to change it. Just be thankful you're going to Helii. Though it's a harsh realm, the Abyss is far, far worse."

"Yes." Tebow nodded. "A small hope, but at least you won't have to know the despair and horrors of the Pit. Even the gods shun it."

"Sounds like the gods want us all to be slaves," Dugan continued. "And if you don't serve them in life, you're made to suffer for all eternity."

"The gods created Tralodren and all things in it, Dugan," Tebow returned with a steely confidence. "I think it fair that they make the rules of their own creation."

"What about those that hold to more than one god?" Dugan continued. "Where do *they* go?"

"Well . . ." Cracius slowed a bit, letting Dugan come up beside him. "That's for the Lords of Death to decide. They judge all who pass their way, determining where they should go based upon what they believed and how they lived out that belief. So most go to one of the gods they worshiped, whichever deity matched their strongest beliefs. You can tell such people right away because they don't have a robe. Nor do those destined for the Abyss."

"So that's it?" He searched Cracius' face for anything more the priest might be keeping from him. Though why he would do so now, he didn't know.

"Yes." Cracius returned the gaze. "Were you thinking this matter more complicated?"

"I guess so."

"Well," Cracius continued, "there *is* the matter of Paradise."

"What about it?" Just as the Abyss was known far and wide by just about everyone on Tralodren, so too was Paradise—the exact opposite of the Abyss. But everyone had their own idea of what it was like, as they did the Abyss.

"Just as the Abyss is unclaimed by any god, Paradise is also unclaimed by any of the pantheon," Cracius explained. "It's here that pure goodness is manifested, and those who have done incredibly noble and righteous deeds have been known to qualify for the plane from time to time."

"Even if they didn't believe in the gods?" asked Dugan.

"No, they have to believe in the gods or a god," Cracius answered. "If they hold to a god, though, and do a noble and good deed which brings about their death, then they have been known to enter into Paradise, but the judge who grants passage through that gate is a hard one to get past."

"Who's he?"

"Asorlok," Tebow curtly replied as he slowed to a stop.

"How fair is he?" Dugan also came to a stop beside the priests.

"He's impartial and doesn't judge by his own authority," Tebow continued, "but by the authority given him by one greater than himself."

"What are you talking about?" Dugan grumbled. "I'm dead. You don't need to keep going with these mysteries."

"We've told you all that you need to know." Tebow sounded irritated, as if he'd grown tired of the former gladiator's company. His tone wasn't cold, but it was certainly formal and meant to put an end to any further inquiries. "It's a matter that doesn't concern you, nor will it affect you where you're going.

"And besides, we've reached our destination." Tebow pointed ahead of them. Dugan followed the priest's finger. In the distance he could see a huge gray mountain ascending into the dim sky. At its peak stood the bone-colored walls and silver-capped towers of Sheol, the city of Asorlok, Lord of Mortis. Millions of people pooled around the mountain's base, streaming in from beyond like living rivers and snaking up its rocky trails.

They came in all shapes and sizes, from all races that covered the world. Rich and poor, great and small—all had been made the same in death. Each had to wait for their audience with those who judged their fate. Many of the throng were bedecked in robes of various colors, forming a breathtaking spectrum that washed the drab mount in vibrant brilliance.

Dugan couldn't believe there were so many people in all the world. He had never even heard of—let alone seen—so many of the creatures who now waited in line for an audience. More amazing was the fact that still more seemed to emerge out of the landscape as Dugan and the two priests had just done, adding to the back of the congested mass. It was an eternal progression of bodies beyond comprehension. The process itself had to be a miracle, for he didn't have the words to explain what he felt or thought.

"Come," Tebow said, resuming his previous pace. "We should be there shortly."

CHAPTER 6

The bright sun reflected off the Great Library's high bronze dome. The grandest and oldest building in Clesethius, capital of the Republic of Rexatoius, it was a sight to behold, even for the City of Wonders. Said to have been built before the palace outline was drawn across the dirt, it safeguarded all the knowledge and history the Patrious had collected over their many generations.

The Great Library was under the control of the Dradinites, priests of Dradin, god of learning, literacy, and magic. His nearby temple, called the Temple of the Eternal Book, was the largest to the god in all the world. And the priests of the temple, more numerous than bees, busied themselves with various tasks: copying old manuscripts, maintaining the library, and recording new knowledge in the form of historical accounts, day-to-day events, and other documents.

The Dradinites were a cautious bunch when it came to protecting the library. Such a precaution was one of many meant to safeguard the books from fire or structural failure. Planting a grand botanical garden around the library was another such precaution.

A marvel in its own right, the lush grounds were home to a collection of tall shade trees, bubbling fountains, of both the geometrical and the humanoid type, and soft green grass. Visitors were free to wander the cobblestone pathways through the rainbow-hued flower beds and shrub mazes. Several small artificial lakes also dotted the landscape. These ponds were arranged at strategic points to serve as natural firebreaks should the worst come the library's way. Many of these ponds had small footbridges, others were left more natural, but all were the destinations of the waterfowl that had come to make this park their home over the centuries.

All this, of course, was mere dressing, a necklace around the neck of the *real* beauty: the library itself. Even amid the tallest trees, it stood out still higher, its gigantic bronze dome rising above them all to shimmer in the sun. A series of smaller domes rose up all around its base like mushrooms: two in the front, two to each side, and two in the back. Each of these was topped with bronze—gray granite composed the exterior of these buildings and the Great Library itself. Upon first observance most eyes fell from the central dome to the eight red marble caryatids. They supported the pediment of stone and roof tile fifty feet above the white marble steps leading to two massive, gold-plated doors some thirty feet back.

The pediment above had been carved with the image of a cloaked man holding an open book. Both were painted, and the figure seemed almost lifelike in his green attire. The six caryatids were spread out along the entranceway. They were attractive Patrician maidens wrapped in himatia, with an ampyx crowning their heads. All stood an arm's length apart, looking out at those nearing the library while holding the roof aloft with their delicate hands. Their sandaled feet rested on a platform of smooth red marble some five feet off the ground.

Another two caryatids followed these six, each standing near the doors. These were turned slightly inward, identical in every way: a himation-, sandal-, and ampyx-clad elven maid holding the weight of the roof with her head. Both faced approaching patrons with a congenial expression, a subtle smile, and a rolled scroll in each hand crossing over their breasts to form an X.

At the base of the library steps three people started to appear, coming into greater clarity like solidifying smoke. Surprisingly, their arrival wasn't noticed by many of the Patrious milling about the stone roads. These were too preoccupied with the beauty around them or their own daily routines to take any notice. They did little more than walk past them, looking at them with distant eyes which only told them someone needed to be stepped around to avoid a collision, but nothing else. A few, though, took notice of two of these newcomers with a small degree of wonder as they caught sight of a Nordican and a Telborian in a predominately Patrician world.

•●•

Upon opening his eyes Rowan noticed two Patrician maids walking up behind the newly arrived trio. Both of them turned a curious eye toward the knight as they passed. They looked no more than sixteen winters. He felt himself flush with their curious stares and girlish giggles.

Alara was mildly amused. "Most Nordicans don't come this far west."

"I don't want to cause a distraction." He looked around for any more who might have been drawn to his sudden appearance. Apparently the girls had been the exception. "We have enough to worry about without me drawing attention and slowing things down."

"We're here to do research. I don't think your being a stranger here will interfere with that," she said. "Besides, with that tan you look more Telborian than Nordican, and we see our fair share of Telborians in this part of the world . . . What?" Alara was obviously confused by Rowan's sudden interest in her face.

"Your bruise," he said in amazement. "It's gone."

She gingerly touched the area where it had once bloomed across her pale gray flesh. "Not even sore to the touch." Another hand went to her stomach. "Nothing. There's no pain anywhere. How about you?" She studied Rowan carefully. "Your head took a pretty good pounding."

"Nothing." Rowan smiled. "I feel better than before we met up with Brandon. But how?"

"Galba," Cadrissa answered. "She must have done something when I cast the spell."

"But I thought only Asora and Panthora could heal." Rowan tried to wrap his head around this development.

"*Panthora* can heal?" Cadrissa was intrigued by the idea.

"Oh yes," Rowan confidently returned. "It's one of many ways she favors humanity."

"But just humans," Cadrissa continued, "no one else?"

"She *is* the goddess of humanity."

Cadrissa didn't appear entirely convinced by Rowan's statement.

"How about you?" Alara gave the mage a quick visual inspection. "Are you all right?"

"I'm fine."

The bright sky took hold of Rowan's gaze. He could have sworn it looked like only late morning, yet he knew they'd left Galba's circle in what he'd thought was the afternoon. "Did your spell take us through time too?"

"No. Just across distance. Time is something much more difficult."

"But it looks like late morning."

"If you travel far enough east or west that will happen," Cadrissa assured Rowan. "The world is really a globe orbiting another globe—the sun in this case. And when the two pass each other—" She must have seen the confusion filtering into his face and stopped in midsentence. "The further west you go, the more time you gain," she summarized. "The further east, the more time you lose."

Rowan's countenance brightened. "So then we have more time to search."

"Not really." Cadrissa squelched any further optimism. "Time still continues all over the world, it's just measured differently in different locations. Time is really a relative thing when it comes to the individual. We're still living the same hours, just in different ways . . . *and* you really didn't want a lesson on time differences right now, did you?"

He declined gently. "Maybe later."

"Sorry. I guess I'm just a little excited about having someone *living* to talk to again."

"There's nothing to be ashamed of," said Alara. "I'm sure it was a terrible ordeal, and you'll need some time to recover. Actually, you're doing much better than I would have thought, given the situation."

"Well, it's not all over with yet. We still need to find that incantation."

Turning from the mage, Rowan renewed his focus on the library, trying to take it all in as best he could.

"Beautiful, isn't it?" Cadrissa's gaze was as admiring as Rowan's. "I've only heard stories, but seeing it in person . . . It's breathtaking."

"So this is where Gilban brought the knowledge from the ruins?"

"I thought we'd moved beyond that." There was a hint of concern in Alara's voice, even some possible dismay in hearing him broach the topic. While it was tempting to try and find where the lost knowledge had ended up, he wouldn't know where to begin—even if it *was* in the library. And Alara was right: there were more important matters before him.

"So what do you do with all this knowledge?" Cadrissa asked.

"What do you mean?" Alara seemed a bit lost by the question.

"You have all this knowledge—this amazing wisdom and insight—so what do you do with it?"

"The idea behind the library was to store all the knowledge and keep it safe."

"Safe from what?" asked Rowan.

"From falling into the wrong hands." Alara acted as if the answer was self-evident.

"But *whose* hands are the wrong hands?" Cadrissa inquired. Rowan had to admit, it was a good question. One he'd thought about himself back outside the ruins when they'd been debating about what to do next. Neither Gilban nor Alara had given a good answer.

"We really don't have time for this," Alara said, moving briskly on her way. And, in truth, Rowan knew she was right. Right now there were more important matters that needed his immediate focus and effort.

"It's so huge." Cadrissa followed Alara. "It's even bigger than some of the temples in Haven."

"I've heard you can spend years in just one section and still not read everything there." Alara continued to spark the mage's excitement.

Rowan shook his head at such a thought. "Do you have any idea where to start?"

"Inside is always good." Cadrissa followed Alara up the marble steps. "They should have a directory of what materials are stored where, correct? All the same information about a certain topic in one area?"

"Yes, but the directory's pretty large too, and a lot of it can only be found with the help of the curators."

"Then we'd better get started." Rowan took up the rear. Before them were the great gold-covered doors that were double a person's size in both height and width. But as impressive a sight as they might have been, he was drawn to the caryatids. Their beauty reminded him of Alara. But he quickly dropped the thought, focusing on what lay ahead.

Through the open doors, Patrician men and women, scholars and priests—even a few wizards—filtered in a steady stream. The trio passed by without incident, and neither were they hindered by the two guards clad in silver scale mail standing on either side of the doorway. Each wore a green silk cape attached at his shoulders and fastened to his mail shirt. In one hand each held a long spear. The other hand gripped a medium oblong shield, painted with the image of an open book.

Near the guard on Rowan's right was a fat chest with a slot at the top. He noticed those who entered dropping some coins into it. "You have to *pay* to get in?" He had never seen anyone forced to pay money to enter a building. It seemed almost insulting.

"Don't worry," Alara said in equally hushed tones. "There's no set fee; it's just an offering—a token of thanks for getting to use the library and its resources. We have enough to get inside." She pulled out a few coins from her belt pouch and dropped them into the chest. As they passed, the guards eyed Rowan with slight interest. They didn't even take notice of the scepter at Cadrissa's side. He supposed he might have expected more from them, given he was essentially an armed and armored stranger, but was happy with their lack of interest. Perhaps he really was more Telborian than Nordican in appearance, like Alara said.

As soon as he entered the library, Rowan felt like he'd passed into the realms beyond, and was in some god's chamber. Candelabras hung from shimmering chains high above in the domed ceilings. But these candelabras didn't hold candles, but slender, crystal rods of light instead. Daylight poured in from stained glass windows, spreading across the walls of the upper and middle levels, where galleries snaked around the entire building. These windows created a rainbow of hues that mixed with the light from the rods in the candelabras in a most breathtaking way.

Added to this light was the illumination falling from even higher arched windows that encircled the great dome at the library's apex. Numbering forty-seven in all, the windows were crafted to hold golden-tinted glass, which served to enrich the already splendid light dancing about the library's interior. This rich illumination accented the lustrous mosaics covering the ceiling, forming portraits of people who Rowan could only surmise had contributed to the library in some way.

The strong aroma of cedar and strange perfumes hung heavy in the air, wafting from specially crafted incense burners dangling from the ceiling. It was an almost overpowering mix that mingled with the odors of the dry leather and time-aged pages of the countless tomes, scrolls, and sheets that filled every opening of the towering shelves. As Rowan walked into the great entrance chamber, he felt his tongue and mouth dry up and eyes grow sore and itchy.

"All these books and scrolls suck the moisture from the air." Alara explained Rowan's sudden need to rub his eyes. "Your eyes will get used to it shortly."

"What's that smell?" His nose had wrinkled up as they passed into the antechamber.

"Cedar shelves help keep insects away, and the incense is a special mixture the Dradinites make to keep any other destructive pests from coming inside," Cadrissa answered. "Ingenious, isn't it?"

"I guess." Rowan was reminded of the strong perfume worn by the harlot who'd harassed him when he first came to Elandor. Perhaps not the best comparison, but a strong resemblance nonetheless.

"You'll get used to the smell, too," said Alara as Cadrissa passed them both to approach a tall wooden cabinet, lined with perhaps a hundred small wooden drawers. The cabinet was as tall as she was and at least twice that in width. It stood at the base of a six-foot-tall dais, upon which stood a life-sized statue of a middle-aged Patrician male dressed in archaic armor.

Some twenty feet away from the stone figure began the rows of ten-foot-tall cedar shelves, stretching as far back as the eye could see, dotted with the odd statue or crumbled sculpture placed in alcoves like relics on display. There were also long oak tables and chairs, along with smaller, more intimate options scattered here and there, at which were seated a smattering of scribes and common folk alike. He noticed he didn't see them as he would have before—as just elves—but rather as people. He took that as a sign of progress since leaving Vanhyrm.

"All these people come here just to read?" he asked Alara, amazed.

"Hundreds a day, at least," she replied.

Cadrissa pulled out one of the directory's square drawers at chest level like a child opening a box full of candy. Inside was a row of parchment sheets cut so they neatly stood upright within the drawer. The mage's digits dug into them, quickly moving down the line like dominoes. As he waited, Rowan lifted his head and studied the level above him. Through arched openings in the wall, he spied yet more of the same trappings that made up the lower level. It was a world of books and scrolls and strange-smelling incense. A world in which he felt very much an outsider. He'd had his education from the knighthood and wasn't a stranger to tomes and scrolls, but this . . . this was something else entirely.

"We're going to have to locate the section on the wizard kings and narrow it down from there," Cadrissa stated while still perusing the parchment sheets with her fingers. "I'm going to focus on the third and fourth ages, as those would be the key times when such an item might have been crafted. Maybe even the Wars of Magic too . . ." She stopped and pulled out a card. "Alara, is everything here in Pacolees?"

"Everything but the source documents." She joined Cadrissa at the directory.

"That could be a problem." Cadrissa faced Alara, adding, "It's one of the few languages I can't read that well." Cadrissa's shoulders sunk with a sigh. "But I can read a few others."

"And I can read all the human languages," Rowan offered, though he didn't know how much that would help, given they were in a land of elves.

"Well, that's better than nothing." Cadrissa returned to her search.

Rowan raised a finger to the statue before them. "Who's that?"

"Cleseth," said Alara. "He founded the Republic of Rexatoius after leaving Colloni." Rowan took a few steps around the statue, studying the man from a different angle as Cadrissa and Alara conversed between themselves. The statue didn't really look that much like a Patrious elf, nor entirely Elyellium either. He actually appeared more a mixture of both, if that was possible. Intrigued, Rowan continued his study, inspecting the various details and angles, until finally his concentration was shattered by Cadrissa's frustrated voice.

"Well, I can't make any sense of this directory. You'll have to find what we're looking for, Alara: some books on the Fourth Age of the Wizard Kings." She relinquished her position, letting Alara take a turn with the drawers.

"Give me a moment and I should be able to find something."

Knowing he wouldn't be much help at the moment, Rowan made his way across the mosaic floor behind the statue of Cleseth, stopping below the great dome. Gazing down, he took in the image portrayed in the tiles: a wizened, green-garbed Patrician man bent over a table and writing in a book. Quill in hand and an inkwell at his side, the figure was a mystery.

"Who's this?" he asked Cadrissa as she approached.

"Dradin."

"I didn't know he was an elf."

"They've taken some artistic license, but the iconography is clear enough. This whole library is owned and kept by the Dradinites as a service to their god, whom they see as the Great Chronicler."

"So this is a *temple*?" Rowan lifted his head, taking in the high domed ceiling once more. He noticed the dark images of more green-clad figures in some kind of collective pose amid other geometric and figurative mosaics spread across the ceiling.

"To a follower of Dradin, *all* places of knowledge are holy sites." Cadrissa joined Rowan in his upturned gaze.

"So then Dradin's *your* god?" Rowan's question jarred Cadrissa from her thoughts.

She appeared as if she was about to answer when something else caught her attention. Curious, Rowan followed her gaze toward what appeared to be a sort of sundial. Only it was much larger and flatter than a normal sundial—about a common tavern table in diameter—and hung on a wall close to where they'd entered. It also appeared to be made of a solid piece of polished brass. It was such a curiosity he was surprised they didn't notice it earlier.

"I haven't seen another annualis since leaving the academy," she replied, clearly taken with the sight.

"What's an annualis?" Rowan was still lost on the device. Unlike what he knew of sundials, this one had three movable brass strips that formed what he assumed was the dial part of the object. Each strip pointed to its own concentric circle, with a fourth and final circle of metal resting at the annualis' center, where the metal strips were attached to a larger brass knob.

"It helps measure time," Cadrissa answered.

"I've never seen one before." He followed Cadrissa, seeking a closer look.

"The shortest hand keeps track of the hours in each day." Cadrissa pointed out the innermost circle, which besides having the shortest metal strip was also divided into twenty-four segments. Rowan noticed the hand was pointing into the ninth segment of the circle. So presumably it was the ninth hour of the day.

"The next longest hand keeps track of the days, and the longest hand keeps record of the months," the mage continued. "It's a pretty ingenious system, but expensive to make and maintain."

Rowan continued his study, noting the second-largest circle was divided into thirty segments, which would make sense since there were thirty days in each month. The largest circle had twelve segments, which also coincided with the number of months in the year. Because of the greater amount of space between these segments there was some room for writing. Though he couldn't decipher the script used, Rowan assumed they were the months' names.

"Wait. That can't be right," said Cadrissa.

"What's not right?"

"The date"—she motioned to the two larger circles on the annualis—"it's not right."

Rowan took a second look, noting that according to where the hands pointed it was the thirtieth day of the fourth month—Sharealia.

"According to this we're one day in the past."

"Maybe it's broken."

"No." Cadrissa shook her head. "The Dradinites would never let it fall behind—especially when it's being used in the Great Library."

"And you're sure nothing else happened with your spell?"

"Positive. It must have been Galba."

"But why?"

"Found it." The two turned around and saw Alara closing the drawer with a look of triumph. Noticing they were gone, she quickly looked around and then made her way straight for them. "I think the section we want is on the second floor toward the back of the library." As Alara approached, Rowan saw her expression change. "What's wrong?"

"I think we may have traveled back in time." Rowan was amazed at how calmly Cadrissa relayed such news. Though she did so with a lowered voice, making sure no one else might overhear their conversation.

Alara momentarily froze. "Can you *do* that—go back in time?" She looked from Cadrissa to Rowan.

"How do you read this?" Cadrissa turned round and pointed to the annualis.

Alara studied it carefully. "It says it's *yesterday*." Looking at Cadrissa, she asked, "How is that possible?"

"Galba," said the mage. "It has to be. I don't have that kind of spell at my disposal."

"But why send us back a day?"

"Wait a moment." A new option came to Rowan. "If we're really in the past, then maybe we can go back and fix what went wrong at the circle. We might even be able to beat the lich!"

"I don't think Galba would let us return." Cadrissa's words dampened his rising optimism. "She wanted us here for a reason—to find answers on that scepter."

"And so she gave us some extra time to do it." Alara nodded, putting everything together.

"But what if we went back and rescued you earlier?" Rowan wasn't ready to relent. "It might stop him from getting to the circle at all."

"No." There was certainty in Cadrissa's voice and face. "Cadrith would have continued without me, and even a day before we arrived in the circle, it wouldn't be any easier. What he did in the circle he'd just do again—if not worse—outside it."

Rowan sighed, his momentary hopes rapidly dashed by Cadrissa's firm tone. "All right."

"Trust me." Cadrissa finally put the matter to bed.

"So then where do we start looking for that scepter information?" He shifted gears, eager to resume where they'd left off.

"Follow me." Alara strode quickly to a set of wide marble stairs lined with golden railings and nestled beside a corridor alongside the library's outer wall. It had an identical twin across from it on the far right of the library. Rowan and Cadrissa followed, matching her pace.

"Can you tell me anything more about what Gilban shared with you regarding the scepter?" Cadrissa inquired.

"Not much more than I have already," said Alara. "He said it could be used to stop a god. Then, of course, he told all of us it can only be used once in a lifetime."

"Yes, that once-in-a-lifetime clause again . . ." Out of the corner of his eye, Rowan noticed Cadrissa trace her finger along the scepter's plain head with her free hand.

"I don't think Gilban meant it could only be used once in a genera- tion. The wizard kings wouldn't have put so heavy a restriction on such an artifact—of that I'm sure. So I think it best to assume it can be used only once in the lifetime of the *wielder*."

"And how do you know that for sure?" Rowan was staring at the scepter now. Cadrissa either didn't notice or didn't mind. Either way, he didn't see anything new.

"I just have a hunch." Cadrissa returned the scepter to her side.

"So what do we do?" Rowan asked as they reached the foot of the grand staircase populated with ascending and descending Patrious.

"I guess just start looking through the books and scrolls to see what we can figure out." Cadrissa took the first step.

"Then let's get started," said Alara, following.

CHAPTER 7

COME NOW TO THE CITY OLD,
WHERE ALL MUST PASS THROUGH ANCIENT GATES.
COME NOW AND SEE WHAT MUST UNFOLD,
AS EACH WILL LEARN WHAT FATE AWAITS.

—Old dranoric song

Dugan, Cracius, and Tebow had made their way to the back of the massive sea of creatures around the base of Sheol. From his slightly higher vantage point atop a broken mound of columns, Dugan could see masses of goblins, giants, humans, elves, and all manner of creatures that called Tralodren home.

Every one of them stood still and silent, waiting for their chance to ascend the mountain and enter the city. It didn't matter if the person would be going to a favorable end or not; all were silent in the massive press. Dugan took another look behind him. Others had already filled in behind them, the sea of bodies extending to still further banks. He didn't see any marks that could tell him if it was a sword or a sickness that had taken them into death. Moreover, none of them were old. All were the exact picture of youth, strength, and health. It was very odd and somewhat unnerving.

When he'd finished looking about, he stepped down from the crumbling mound, rejoining the two priests. As he did, he felt like he'd moved forward but knew he'd taken only one step, just one down from the column. He'd been standing in line this whole time, and no one in front of him or behind him had moved forward. Though Dugan knew this to be true, the scenery around them seemed to suggest they were closer to Sheol than before.

"Did we just move?"

"Though it looks long, the line is rather swift." Tebow cocked his head to one side, adding, "Asorlok and his lords are very efficient."

Dugan let the silence settle in again, letting his mind wander while waiting. Though from what Tebow had said, it might not be as long a wait as he'd thought. Even so, new thoughts came. His mind was as barren as the rest of Mortis. What could he do but wait? He was boxed in by the group on every side . . . with more and more coming from who knew where and how. It was a seemingly endless procession of the dead, which Dugan knew would go on long after he'd passed this way, continuing for all eternity.

"If the dead keep coming, won't the realms they're sent to fill up eventually?"

"No," Cracius answered. "The realms of the gods are very large, and while they could be filled in time, albeit a very *long* time, it will never get to that point."

"Why not?"

"The realms continue to grow with the rest of the cosmos," explained Cracius rather matter-of-factly. "So unless everyone and everything dies at once—before there's a chance for the realms to expand—things might get crowded but only then for a short while. The cosmos is always expanding."

Dugan noticed the scenery had changed once more, and all three of them had moved to the base of the mountain on the long, flat path ascending the gray rock. He'd be happy to be done with all of this, and soon. All this strangeness and delay was too much for a man who just wanted to die and get on with his afterlife. And so he resigned himself to waiting, experiencing the strange sensation of forward progress without any movement under his own power.

In short order, before him and thousands of others, appeared the open silver doors of Sheol, the great city of Asorlok. They stretched to a tremendous height, no doubt allowing access to beings of all sizes. He studied the walls as he neared them. They were built in a large circle around the city and were composed of fat blocks at least as tall as Dugan and twice that in width, all worn smooth. Now that he saw them up close, he noticed their resemblance to bleached bone. In contrast to the gray mountain, the weathered tone helped the structure stand out even more, like some cairn of bones.

All passed beyond the walls in silence. The whole gateway was filled with it, hovering over everything like a funerary shroud. This was a sacred place, and all knew it. On each of the doors was a relief of a leering skull flanked on either side by a sickle. For a moment Dugan's eyes locked on the ring of keys under each of the skull's jaws. He counted fourteen keys on each ring.

Dugan passed the doors and moved into the interior of the city. He thought it was rather drab when compared to other cities he'd seen in his short life of freedom. It was parchment colored inside with only a few glimpses of red cloth here and there. Asorlins in bone-colored robes broke up the rest of the scenery. It was a far cry from the glorious displays he thought should have been present in a god's city.

It was well maintained and looked newly constructed—though he knew it wasn't—but it was also very plain, with no carvings, no statues, no artwork of any kind. All was as lifeless and utilitarian as a common tool. He noticed some Asorlins looking down at the ever-present throng from a high set of balconies. These stuck out overhead from the tall build-ings along the very wide cobblestone road funneling the masses forward.

These priests, at least the ones Dugan could see, were observant, like a farmer inspecting his livestock as they passed before his eye. They kept their gaze fixed upon the creatures passing before them, under them, or above them. Giants, gnomes, and even a few dragons—that towered over these balconies but not the walls of the city—made their entrance silently beside, before, and behind Dugan.

The cobblestone roadway he'd been traveling came to an end in what appeared to be a central hub like that of a wheel. The road he'd just arrived on was one of sixteen spokes that radiated from a large tower in the center. From what he could see, each of these paths was a different color.

Dugan noticed red-robed beings going down a roadway decorated with rubies and red silk, green-robed beings going down a brilliant green thoroughfare—all the paths followed this system that tied the robes and paths together. All save the one upon which he'd entered and the two to his left and right that stood out due to those traveling them lacking robes. Everyone on them apparently wore the same clothing they'd died in. From what he'd learned from Cracius and Tebow, he knew these two paths led to the Abyss and Paradise.

The paths themselves were richly paved. One was made of pure gold, the other pure silver. From the handful of creatures who traveled the two paths, he'd say it was a safe bet to name the golden path as the one leading to Paradise and the silver one as that leading to the Abyss.

The tall tower in the center of the hub had a base of the same bone-hued rock as the city and its surrounding wall. The tower was carved to look like a pile of skulls from a variety of creatures. These changed into a series of keys as they ascended the tower to its silver-capped top. All along this tower were dark, narrow windows where beige-robed Asorlins watched the throng below move off to their assigned destinations. This assigning was conducted at the tower's base by a handful of priests, some of whom now approached Dugan.

Dugan found himself standing before a muscular Celetor dressed in the parchment robes of an Asorlin with a red sash at his waist and the Silver Cross around his neck. Behind his tall, dark-skinned frame were two more similarly dressed Asorlins, one an Elyellium, the other a Telborian. Each was young but radiated a great wisdom and maturity from their eyes.

The Celetor looked over Dugan for a moment with a practiced, assessing gaze. His clean-shaven face remained stoic as he spoke. "You have an audience with Helii and its god."

Tebow placed a hand on Dugan's shoulder. "Here is where we part. May you find peace at the end of your journey." Dugan said nothing as

Tebow left to talk with the Elyelmic priest. "Safe journey, Dugan," Cracius said as he headed for the Telborian priest.

"Go your way," said the Celetor, pointing a finger to a roadway where others who wore the same robe as Dugan had been gathered. "Helii awaits."

All at once, Dugan felt himself move. He hadn't taken a step or even changed position, but rather everything around him had, realigning itself in relation to him so that he now stood at the start of this new path. It was constructed of copper-colored stones interlaced with pieces of basalt and small chips of topaz and rubies, composing a simple design. Besides a few giants and a handful of lizardmen, the path wasn't populated with too many humans. Those he did see were Celetors. He squinted, trying to see what was at the end of this seemingly unending path. As he did, he was brought further into a coppery light that grew brighter and brighter until it was finally all around him.

When his eyes had grown accustomed to the light, he found himself standing inside a large chamber. It rose to a staggering, indiscernible height, covered from the floor to its copper dome with precious rubies, onyx, topaz, and a strange orange-colored stone he couldn't identify. Though it was large, the chamber was packed with Celetors and Telborians; a few Nordicans, Elyellium, Patrious, dwarves, gnomes and halflings; and many, many monstrous races, including giants and other kinds of creatures Dugan had never seen before. All of them had on the same robe he wore and were standing before a disk of light. The disk, which he took for a portal similar to the one he'd seen in the ruins of Taka Lu Lama, was built into the basalt-lined, gem-studded wall and was large enough to allow a dragon to pass through.

This was the gate to Helii, one of fourteen gates watched over by the Lords of Death. Dugan knew this the moment he saw it. As he looked at it, he realized the lip of the massive opening was lined in gemstones that mimicked the look of flame. The light spilling out of the opening was the same hue, but more organic than the glittering gems encircling it. And it was into this opening the people and creatures moved silently at a moderate pace.

There was something else, though, something just outside his vision and inside the light from the gate: a shifting form he couldn't clearly see. His unease grew as he drew closer to the gate.

As he neared, the indiscernible form took shape. What he saw filled him with dread. The figure he beheld was at least twice his height and covered in a long, flowing robe and cloak, the hood of which obscured its features. The figure was so emaciated that the black cloth covering it seemed to hover under its own power rather than being supported by anything of substantial weight. The few aspects of the figure's body he could see gave him even less comfort.

Bony, long-nailed fingers crept out from behind velvet cuffs, directing the petitioning person before it into the portal. But that wasn't what made Dugan's stomach clench. Rather it was the unnatural nature of the skin covering those hands: a strange incandescence whose cold sheen was reflected by white, icicle-like fingernails. Furthermore, the skin was translucent, allowing the viewer to actually see the bones beneath, which were a dark charcoal-gray color.

"What's *that*?" Dugan's words came out in a hushed murmur.

"Charbis," a Celetor beside him answered with equal reverence. His whisper was nearly swallowed whole by the heavy silence smothering the chamber. Dugan barely heard the answer, as he couldn't take his eyes off of the divinity.

An eyeblink later, Dugan found himself just outside the tangible aura of this dark-clothed judge. Only one Elyellium stood between him and Charbis: a woman Dugan assumed to have been a warrior. He now noticed how the light of the gate was really caused by flame flickering all about and through the opening, though he couldn't feel any of its heat . . . not yet.

Daring another look, he could see the Lord of Death did indeed have a face under his hood. Like his hands, it was a strange and awful sight. Charbis' dark gray skull was clearly revealed under a transparent, shimmering face. Inside his sockets rested two eyes; the parts that should have been white were instead a medium shade of gray, his irises and pupils glowing a pure white. While Dugan could see Charbis' face, the Lord of Death didn't seem to acknowledge him.

When the Elyellium before Dugan had finished her business, she bowed her head, moved through the gate, and disappeared from Dugan's sight. When she was gone, Charbis drew his hooded head down toward Dugan's small frame as he took the elf's place. From his new location, he could see farther back into Charbis' hood. Under it, stringy, flat, and lifeless strands of pure-white, phosphorescent hair fell from a rough onyx circlet crackling with a charcoal-gray energy like a smoky serpent twisting around his brow.

Dugan felt himself pierced through by a thousand spears under the Lord of Death's gaze. It was as if Charbis was looking all the way through him—past even his soul and spirit—and he wanted to cover his utter nakedness, but nothing could hide him from the Lord of Death's sight.

"I have been expecting you." The Lord of Death's withered whisper filled the entire room. Dugan shuddered.

"You"—Charbis pointed at Dugan with his skeletal digit—"have been claimed by the god of Helii. To him you must go."

It felt as if a blast furnace behind the gate to Helii had been opened. If Dugan still had a physical body, sweat would have poured from his brow in rivers and his chest would have constricted from the harsh, metallic vapors.

Once again, he was pulled forward, feet and legs moving into the flaming gate under their own accord. He helplessly felt his body make the passage up to the gate and then through it. There was a brilliant flash and then a searing heat overwhelmed him as he passed onward. But just as quickly as it started, it ended.

The light. The heat. Everything.

CHAPTER 8

To fight with the gods is madness,

but most do so every day, more than they realize.

—Bolin Miders, Telborian philosopher

(5340 BV–5231 BV)

Cadrith materialized in the ruins of a temple of Endarien. That was his part of the plan, which Nuhl allowed. However, the time in which he appeared was under Nuhl's control. There was a timeline to all this that Cadrith had yet to fully understand. Between getting the instructions and appearing in the temple, it had already been hours since he last faced Endarien at the tower. Just how many hours, he wasn't exactly sure. Time differences across Tralodren muddied the waters, but he believed it was still the same day.

Nuhl had told him it wanted to use up more of Vkar's energy inside Endarien. And the longer Endarien wasted his time searching for Cadrith, the less of Nuhl's old enemy remained. The further benefit, of course, was that Endarien would be allowed more time to grow enraged, and so might be easier to unbalance when they next faced each other.

He could almost see Endarien hurrying this way and that, desperately trying to find him. He and his pathetic birds squawking and screeching across the planet, not able to locate even a single sign of where he might have gone. It was almost comedic. But a fitting fate for the first of the gods who tried to stand against him.

Cadrith surveyed the ruins he'd helped create nearly eight hundred years ago. From how the place appeared, Endarien didn't want to do anything about changing them. He wondered why. The matter was obviously on the god's mind, given the frequency of their clashes since Cadrith's return to Tralodren, but Endarien's motives and thinking could be clouded at times.

He strode through the wreckage, noticing the bones of the fallen had never been buried. Instead they'd been left to lie where the elements and animals who picked them clean had scattered them. Things really hadn't changed since he'd last been here with Kendra for their final encounter with Raston, nor their earlier visit with the rest of Raston's pupils who'd been sent to secure the remaining pieces of their master's plan.

As he walked the ruins he relived the memory of that initial visit. Together, he, Kendra, and the rest of Raston's pupils had managed to slay all the priests before picking much of the temple clean. He stopped at the place where he recalled the old high priest kneeling before him, begging for his life. Cadrith hadn't given it to him. His action revealed the weakness in Kendra, who'd rebuked him.

He should have seen it then, but it'd taken him longer to realize her weakness was more deeply rooted and had a greater grip on her than he knew. She wouldn't have been able to survive the Abyss, let alone the trial that was needed to take the throne and their divinity. And she certainly wouldn't have had the guts to do what Cadrith had done with Cadrissa—whom he'd never have been able to use if Kendra hadn't deserted him centuries before. Yes, in many ways she did him a great favor by fleeing when she had. Like Raston said, the path of power is better followed by yourself.

His thoughts were interrupted when he noticed a seagull landing atop a shattered column to his left. Once settled, it started rebuking him with high-pitched cries. It didn't take long for the noise to grate on Cadrith's nerves. He released a small, crackling bolt of azure lightning, incinerating the bird midsquawk. The bird was a clear sign Endarien would be here soon. All the better, as the god was nothing more than an annoyance now anyway.

He felt the change in temperature before the wind picked up. What were small puffs at first quickly transformed into great gusts, harrying all in their path. Looking up, he spied thickening clouds, and grasped his staff tightly. From out of the cumulus canopy descended Endarien. Cadrith was amazed at his speed. Regardless, it would still end the same.

"Cadrith!" The very wind howled with Endarien's rage. If he noticed Cadrith's change in size, he didn't show it. And he was confident Endarien hadn't a clue about what else had changed since their last confrontation.

He readied his staff, standing defiantly. Endarien wasn't one to wait, though, chucking his spear with all his might. With a smooth sidestep, Cadrith watched the spear bite into the hard stone a foot to his left. It was getting easier to control his new abilities . . . much to his enjoyment.

As he landed on running feet, Endarien barreled forward with fists intent on pummeling Cadrith's face. He ducked the first swing while shoving his staff into Endarien's chest. The strike stilled the god's advance but not his fury.

"I couldn't have chosen a better tomb for you." Endarien swung again. Cadrith parried it with his staff.

"My thoughts exactly," he said, lowering his staff and sending an azure blast of energy into Endarien's face. The god stumbled back with a curse, hands going to his eyes, which he rubbed furiously.

Using the opening he'd created, Cadrith unleashed a series of azure beams into his opponent's frame. Endarien wrapped his wings about him, shielding himself from the assault. Cadrith's blasts burned through feathers, flesh, and bone without care. With a shout, Endarien flung open his wings and knocked Cadrith onto his back. In a mere heartbeat, Endarien was above him, spear again in hand, shield at the ready, totally restored from the previous attack.

"Back where you belong," Endarien sneered as he brought his white-tipped spear down upon Cadrith. The crackling tip slammed into and through Cadrith's chest and heart, digging into the stone beneath. He could feel the fire of the weapon inside him, singeing his heart and flesh even as his blood splashed out of him.

"You've failed." Endarien gave the spear a hard twist, causing Cadrith to grit his teeth in rage. "Accept it."

Closing his eyes, Cadrith focused on the power flowing in him. The power that even the once mighty Vkar, first god of the cosmos, was unable to withstand. As he reached out to it, he felt the bleeding stop and his flesh start to mend. But that wasn't all he felt. There was power rising within him—greater than what he'd tasted since his ascension.

He sprang to his feet with a fluid motion, knocking Endarien back with a violent impact. Even as the other god rose, Cadrith grabbed hold of the spear poking through his back. He yanked it free and tossed it aside like waste metal. Endarien spread his fingers and unleashed a spray of white-hot lightning Cadrith's way. But the lightning did only minor damage.

Cadrith had tapped into the full might of Nuhl's boons. With them he knew nothing had a chance before him—at least when it came to the gods or their allies. No, he'd finally done it: risen to the highest rank of power he'd ever thought possible. But better yet, there was still a place he could climb . . . and he'd be able to get there soon.

Following his attack, Endarien took flight and then rammed Cadrith in the gut. The collision was jarring and effective. Endarien slid Cadrith across the ground, slamming him into a nearby building. The brutal collision caused the wall to crumble and the entire structure to topple in upon him. From under the debris, Cadrith could hear Endarien summoning a storm.

As much as he would have enjoyed letting the matter play out, and really getting a chance to humiliate his old foe, he knew he had to end this to keep the rest of the pantheon from digging in their heels more deeply. Still, it would be wise and rewarding to send them a clear message about his true capabilities by means of Endarien's defeat.

Cadrith shot up from his makeshift cairn with an explosion of broken stones to hover a few feet off the ground. Endarien deflected any rocks that came close with his shield and wings while keeping his gaze solidly on Cadrith. The god of the air had regained his spear and was restored to his former strength. A quick glance heavenward also revealed the pitch-black sky and the twisting finger of a funnel cloud drawing near.

"It's over, Cadrith."

A coiling black serpent sprang forth from the inky pearl on top of Cadrith's staff and flung itself around Endarien. It sunk its teeth into his neck even as it looped about his throat. Endarien grimaced as he wrenched the serpent free. It left behind a bloody and burned wreath about his throat. He threw the serpent to the ground, where it shattered into sparks and dust.

"Pathetic." Endarien drew up his shield as the funnel cloud touched down between the gods with a hungry roar. Cadrith willed himself to remain unmoved, even as the rest of the ruins were pounded and shattered. An azure globe he'd summoned for protection kept him safe from the flying rocks and other material as they pounded the transparent construct, seeking entry.

"You're serving a lost cause," Endarien shouted over the noise. Cadrith couldn't see where he was through the muddled, swirling winds but didn't have to. All he had to do was close his eyes and concentrate. A black fire erupted across his right hand as he did. A fire that didn't burn but merely outlined the hand as he raised it and then brought it down with a strong chop. Though he didn't strike anything but empty air, the funnel cloud was cut in half from top to bottom. A moment later it unraveled, dumping all that it once held onto the two gods below. Endarien joined Cadrith in creating his own protective globe—his a silvery white—to keep from being pummeled by the raining rubble.

"I know why you're afraid," said Cadrith. "But you can't stop me— none of you can."

"Then you realize what you're being used to do?"

"Yes." Cadrith lowered himself to the ground, letting the globe around him fade as he made his way to Endarien.

"Then you know it's not just us it wants but Tralodren too." The globe around Endarien began crackling with silvery-white threads of energy.

"A small matter." Cadrith stopped just outside Endarien's globe. The stench of ozone was thick at such close range. "I'll just find another world to rule over."

"And you really think you'll be allowed to live when you've finished?"

"It's not a matter of what I think"—Cadrith punched into Endarien's globe—"but only of holding up my part." The globe melted away like snow in fire.

Faster than lightning, Endarien propelled the full force of Vkar's essence from his frame into Cadrith's. It was unlike anything he'd ever felt before. Fire, lightning, acid, and pure hatred incarnate gnawed away at his being and spirit on every side as the white light surrounding him passed through him. Even as Cadrith forced himself to remain standing, he found himself facing the disturbing sensation of being unwound like a spool of thread. It took all he had to hold back the onslaught. Reaching deep inside, he pulled up the full power resident inside him, tapping into it as he once had done with his well when he'd been a human wizard.

Using that strength, Cadrith twisted his staff around and shoved the base of it into and through Endarien's body. Instantly, the onslaught stopped. Endarien's face was filled with a mixture of wonder and worry. Cadrith had plunged the staff from Endarien's left shoulder all the way down and through his body so that it emerged out of his right side. The hesitation on Endarien's part was only momentary. He struck Cadrith with the back of his hand, turning him aside and back before kicking him in his gut and sending him flying into one of the few solid pieces of wall that still remained. But Cadrith simply sat up and stretched forth his hand. The staff inside Endarien twisted and leapt out of his innards with all the grace of a butcher's hook yanked out of a side of meat. A gulp of breath helped Endarien repair his injuries.

Cadrith had played with this long enough. Endarien had given his best effort, and still Cadrith stood. Endarien couldn't defeat him and wouldn't. His message had been sent to the pantheon, who he was sure were watching. It seemed Endarien wasn't accepting that same message. He let loose a roar while flying straight at Cadrith. Spear set to charge, and shield covering his right flank, the god continued screaming his rage. Cadrith waited.

Cadrith once again covered his hand with black flame as he focused his own rage and the power of his patron into it. When he was ready, he released the full brunt of it through an uppercut that sent Endarien reeling up and back into the sky. He watched the god soar heavenward like a shooting star in reverse. Endarien sailed past the atmosphere and into the star-speckled mantle of space, where he struck the Grand Barrier around Tralodren, broke through it, and continued his flight without slowing his ascent. He'd been rendered unconscious by Cadrith's blow and was unable to stop the hurtling path taking him straight for the sun.

Each passing heartbeat saw the helpless god soaring through the stars, shining brighter and brighter as sweat, birthed by the heat of the approaching sun, glistened over his body. He would have been flung into the burning star and quite possibly destroyed had an invisible force not stilled his progress. In short order, Endarien was brought to a complete stop, hovering in space. The sun was still close but not enough to put him in any real danger.

Back in the temple complex, Cadrith smiled at his accomplishment. He didn't see Endarien's fate—he'd lost track of him when he broke through the Grand Barrier—but figured this would keep him away long enough to work the rest of the plan.

You should have killed him. Nuhl's disapproving voice filled Cadrith's head.

"Soon enough," he said to the being he imagined turning and twisting all around him yet invisible to even his divine eyes. "I just need to better prepare," he lied.

Treachery will get you killed, the voice reminded him with the deepest of hate. *You have all the power and knowledge you need to get to Thangaria and finish them off.*

"I'll need something more."

You already have my patronage—what more do you need?

"One last precaution against a certain desperate defense they might employ."

You mean the scepter? It won't come to anything.

Cadrith hid his surprise at the mention of the ancient artifact. He realized how foolish he'd been in assuming he was the only one who knew about it or what role it might play in the time to come. "I don't want to take any chances. Galba kept me from it before, and I wouldn't put it past her to try to use it against me—or your plans." He made sure the last part was spoken with the proper submissive tone. "I know you might not see it as a threat, but if they should find a way to use it, and I lost access to what you've given me so far . . . it could make things more challenging."

An uncomfortable silence followed, during which Cadrith envisioned the invisible darkness pacing around him, searching every part of his being for any hint of deception or flawed logic. In that moment he also had another revelation. For all Nuhl's threats, it still needed him. If not, it would have been done with him already. No, there were some rules in play, and Nuhl couldn't violate them. Now he knew what Cadrissa felt when she'd found out the same thing about his own bluffs and purposes. But unlike her, he'd keep what he'd learned to himself, continuing the act of the humble servant.

"It won't take long," Cadrith carefully added. "I know exactly where it is."

You'll be brief. The others are already digging in their heels.

Cadrith smiled. The puppet had taken hold of a few of its strings. It was a promising development. Now he just had to set the rest of his plan in motion . . .

CHAPTER 9

ONLY AFTER ALL OPTIONS HAVE BEEN EXHAUSTED
SHALL YOU CONSIDER WAR. BUT DO SO GRAVELY AND WISELY,
KNOWING THE COST OF EACH LIFE THAT SHALL BE REQUIRED.

—The Book of Peace, one half of the Holy Dyad

"Is he dead?" Asora peered over the silver railing into the large scrying pool. All of the gods were standing silently around it, observing the aftermath of the battle between Cadrith and Endarien with a more subdued air than they had when the fight first commenced.

"No." Rheminas' reply brought some small relief. "I still sensed his life when I stopped him from hitting the sun."

Once more the gods fell silent, letting the heaviness of the situation weigh down their words as well as thoughts. Finally, Drued lifted his face from the pool.

"So now what?" he asked no one in particular.

"We prepare for war." Khuthon stepped away from the pool and faced the others.

"War?" Panthora wasn't the only one jarred by the statement. "Isn't there some other way?"

"Not now." Olthon solemnly joined the conversation. "We have to raise a defense or be laid waste as were Vkar and Xora."

"What about what Saredhel said?" Panthora persisted. "That's got to be the answer to victory. Maybe there's another meaning we've missed."

"Well, it didn't seem to help us in stopping Cadrith, now did it?" Gurthghol grumbled. "And we have little time to debate the meaning of riddles either."

"We've weathered this threat before and won." Khuthon sounded like a general inspiring his troops. "We just need to raise an army and—"

"It isn't going to be like it was before." Dradin cut Khuthon's speech short. "We can't be cavalier about what we're facing."

"Yes," Ganatar gravely agreed. "We need to be wise about this."

"And while we talk, the threat only grows." Khuthon grew more restless. "What we need is action, and fast."

Rheminas nodded. "Agreed."

"And what then do you propose?" asked Ganatar.

"We gather our forces and make a stand." Rheminas nodded in Khuthon's direction.

"But how do we know where he'll attack?" Aero's uncertainty was shared by the other Race Gods.

"He'll come to us," said Gurthghol. "Wherever we are, he will follow. He's been consumed by Nuhl, and has no choice but to carry out its desires."

"How big an army are we talking about?" Drued rubbed his chin in thought.

"A select few," said Khuthon. "The best and most loyal. There's no need to bring whole armies."

"Agreed." Asora quickly spoke up. "I don't want to have more lives risked and lost."

Khuthon viewed his wife with a puzzled expression. "You already think we'll lose?"

"I just don't want to risk more lives than we have to," she explained.

"It's not like they're really going to die." Rheminas chuckled at his mother's comment. "Their bodies perhaps, but their spirits—"

"Are you certain of that?" Asora's stare strangled the levity in her son's throat while chilling the rest of the air in the room. "Nuhl wants the end of *all* life: spirit, soul, and body—divinities and nondivinities alike."

Khuthon clasped Asora's hand. "Which is why we're going to fight and win."

"Then we should go to Endarien," Shiril reasoned. "If there's anything left of Vkar's essence—"

"It'd be spent before you arrived," said Gurthghol. "Between the battle and everything else, I doubt enough would be left to make any difference anyway."

"I wouldn't be too sure of that," Rheminas countered.

"You saw how well Endarien was able to stand before Cadrith," Gurthghol retorted. "You think any of us could do any better?"

"Yes." Rheminas was more than confident.

"Why are we not surprised?" Perlosa's disdain only heated her brother's resolve.

"At least I'm *going* to fight." Rheminas' wrath flared out at his sister. "You picked out the cave you're going to hide in yet?"

"Enough!" Ganatar commanded. "Your petty bickering is only helping to serve Nuhl and its plans. We need to stay focused on our own."

"So then where's our battlefield?" asked Aero.

"What about here?" The rest of the gods fell silent at Shiril's suggestion.

"We have laws and oaths forbidding it," said Ganatar.

"Perhaps it's time to break those rules, to stand and fight for a greater purpose than the old customs and habits, which will keep us in an unfavorable position when the attack comes."

Ganatar and the pantheon quietly contemplated Shiril's words. None had seen this side of her before: the active, engaged goddess who seemed more deeply committed than anyone would have guessed. To many, it showed just how dire the situation was.

"Thangaria *is* an easily defendable area," Khuthon told Ganatar. "And conveniently free from our own realms too. It could allow us the space and opportunity to really let loose, without concern for anything else."

"It'd also be great to exact our vengeance in the same setting as the first attack," Rheminas added with wicked glee. "Irony is always a wonderful addition to such things."

"And the loss of life would be lessened if we kept it here too." Asora took a brighter view of the matter.

"Then it seems we've found our battlefield," Dradin concluded.

"If this is what you all wish, then so be it," said Ganatar. "Who then agrees to this offer? Shall we assemble an army on Thangaria to fight off our ancient foe and his new pawn?"

The gods all raised their hands in a unanimous vote. "So be it," said the god of light.

"But what about Endarien?" asked Panthora.

"I'll send someone for him," said Rheminas. "I'm sure he'll be eager for another encounter. And if any of Vkar's essence *should* remain, then so much the better."

"Go and gather what forces you can and begin to place them outside the hall. We'll make our stand there." Ganatar dismissed the council.

•●•

As the gods dispersed—some vanishing, others making their way for the door—Panthora jogged up beside Saredhel before she'd left the pool.

"Can I keep you for a moment more?"

"That depends," said Saredhel, stopping to face Panthora.

"On what?" Panthora peered into Saredhel's white eyes in reverence. No matter how long it had been since she'd become a goddess, she still felt like a simple human among them. She supposed she always would. Saredhel and her family had created her along with all of Tralodren. Panthora wouldn't have anything to boast about if it wasn't for their good graces.

"On how long your moment is."

Panthora gave the room a rapid inspection. All the others were distracted or departed. "I just have a few questions." She lowered her voice, adding, "About your dealings with Asorlok and Endarien."

Saredhel was silent. Panthora didn't know if that was a good or a bad thing but ventured onward anyway. "You told them to assemble that group at Galba."

"Yes, I did." There was no sign of deception or rising wrath in her answer. A good start.

"I wouldn't even ask you about this if it wasn't—"

"For Endarien asking for your help." Saredhel finished Panthora's thought for her.

"So he told you of our meeting."

Saredhel made no reply.

Panthora paused, pondering how to put her next comment in the best light possible. "I don't pretend to know everything, but it looks to me as if what you said failed."

"Does it?"

She carefully chose her reply. "You saw the fight in Galba's circle. Everyone gathered has been either defeated or killed, and Cadrith survived the throne."

"Why did you send your knight there?" The question startled Panthora.

"I didn't. I gave him a choice."

"But you didn't have to do that," she continued. "You could have left him alone, and he'd be blissfully ignorant of all of this."

Panthora didn't like being on the defensive. She'd come for some answers, not to be interrogated herself. "From what Endarien said, it sounded like the right thing to do. And since he got his information from you, I thought to go right to the source."

"So you think Endarien lied to you?" Again, Panthora was shaken by the bluntness of Saredhel's words.

"I-I just want to be sure I understand what's going on. Neither you nor Asorlok brought this up in council, and now we have this new plan you seem to endorse, even though you had the previous one that was supposed to work instead."

"And again, who said it hasn't worked?" Saredhel calmly inquired.

"We all saw it." She was growing flustered by Saredhel's evasive manner. "Cadrith defeated them and survived the throne. And now Endarien has failed to stop him too. I think that's pretty obvious."

"You still haven't answered my question," Saredhel continued. "Why did you tell that young Nordican about Galba?"

Panthora stopped. It was obvious she wasn't going to get any further if she didn't at least humor Saredhel's query. "It just felt like the right thing to do."

"Because you're fond of him?"

Panthora's eyes went wide at the suggestion. "He has a good heart," she replied. "I did what I did because I knew he'd make the right choice."

"Which was to join the others in Galba," Saredhel continued, "which you thought was the right thing to do."

"Yes . . ." Panthora drew the answer out, not sure if she liked what Saredhel was getting at. She was impossible to read: her blank eyes cloaked any hint of what she might be thinking.

"So what's changed?"

"I already told you." She bit back the frustration growling in her throat. "We just watched—"

"What one sees isn't always what is true," came Saredhel's cryptic reply. "And it's often the unexpected that takes place when no one is watching."

"So what does *that* mean?"

"Each of us has called another to fight in this battle, and they've done so in part, but some have yet to complete their full purpose. But once all is in position, the final battle can be had."

"So this was all just a lead-up to what you put forth to the council?" This didn't make much sense. Innocent lives had been lost, and for what? "If you knew they were going to fail from the start, why—"

"Again," Saredhel interrupted, "who said they failed?"

Panthora sighed. This was pointless. She'd been hoping for an inkling of insight but was just going in circles.

"The time grows short." Saredhel's face took on a soft, maternal quality. "You'd best make ready."

Trying one more time for at least one clear answer, she asked, "Are we going to win?"

Saredhel simply smiled. "What do you believe?"

"That we will."

"Then let your belief lead you." She was as unreadable as always.

"But—"

"Let your belief lead you," she repeated and turned away, ending their conversation.

Panthora could do nothing but watch her go. She had plans to make and forces to rally, and only a belief in victory to tie them to . . . It would have to be enough. The time of questions was over.

•●•

Gurthghol emerged out of the darkness of the greater cosmos, his plum-colored skin helping him blend into the infinite blackness even as the brilliance of the nearby sun outlined his figure. He'd come in his true form. He'd need his full strength and ability for what lay ahead. He'd also come dressed for war.

He wore a sleeveless suit of black scale mail, falling from his neck to just above his ankles. It was slit up both sides to his waist, where a black leather belt held it fast. The coat of scales seemed more organic than metallic and could well have been the hide of some beast. His shoulders were capped with wrought iron pauldrons carved to resemble the upper portion of a dragon's head. This allowed for the illusion of the dragons devouring the arms underneath. Similar motifs covered his wrought iron greaves and gauntlets, except these were of linnormic rather than draconic origins.

On his right side a flail ending in a spiked metal ball hung on his belt. On the opposite side rested a silver khopesh. Only his head and feet remained naked.

With the other gods focused on preparations for war, he didn't want to miss the opening presented him. As an extra precaution, he made sure to cloak himself from scrying or any other attempts at location. He'd learned how to do so while sitting on Vkar's throne centuries ago. It was one of the few positive things he took away from the experience.

There was a great deal he could have tapped into and learned if he'd stayed on the throne longer, but he wasn't as much of a glutton for punishment as his father had been. Any such power and insight the throne could give was at the cost of his freedom. What he'd learned had served him well in the ensuing millennia and would help him now with the matter at hand.

Turning, he viewed Endarien's unconscious frame. He'd lied to the others about Vkar's essence being lost. He had to if what he wanted to do next would stand a chance of success. But the longer he waited, the less of it remained. Gurthghol would need everything possible. Wasting no further time, he willed himself to move through the empty space between them. Once near the body, he rested both hands upon Endarien's shoulders and proceeded to drain what remained of Vkar's essence into himself.

It felt like someone was pouring molten metal into his veins, but the discomfort didn't stop him from laying hold of all he could. All the while, Endarien slumbered. It was a restorative sleep, which Gurthghol could also tell was using some of Vkar's essence to heal. It seemed Cadrith, like Nuhl's pawn before him, was a rather formidable opponent. All the more reason to be quick about his work. The more he dallied, the greater the cost for his family and their allies.

When he sensed he'd taken all that remained, he released Endarien and turned himself back around, facing Tralodren. He hadn't seen it from this position for quite some time. After he and the rest of the gods had created it, they had gotten wrapped up in their own affairs.

The blue globe in the distance brought a smile to his lips. His only regret was that his parents weren't there to see it with him—to bask in the glory of their achievement. For while Vkar and Xora had been great and done great things, they had never created a new planetary system or populated it with a people made entirely from their will. The pantheon had crossed over into a higher level—a greater reality—when they'd crafted their creation. In some ways it was the pantheon's version of their own personal cosmos. And all of it under their control.

So long as the planet and its people remained, it was a sign of victory over their former rank. There was nothing they couldn't do—but only if they pushed aside the one thing holding them back. And finally, after so long a time, he was ready to clear that obstruction. It wouldn't be easy, he knew, but a sacrifice had to be made. And when it had been, he and the rest of the pantheon could finally rise to their full potential.

Closing his eyes, he brought the raw power of Vkar's essence fully into his control. In some ways it reminded him of tapping into the throne. Once done, he made sure to cloak himself from anyone who might be seeking him out. He also made sure when he entered Tralodren no one would notice his arrival—including Cadrith and his patron. What he did next needed his full attention and no additional interference. He'd have plenty of that later as it was.

His thoughts focused, a burst of plum-colored energy emanated from his body. A moment later thin streams of dust started flowing his way. From every direction they appeared, finding their way to the god, where the line of fine particles joined with others in rapid succession. Soon enough these thin strands wove a rough, rocky cocoon. Inside, Gurthghol kept the effect going, thickening the black stone barrier. It would need to be strong enough for what was coming. As he continued thickening the rock, Gurthghol also sent a small amount of Vkar's essence into it, making sure it would be able to handle the barrier when it encountered it.

Finally, after enough cosmic dust had been compacted around him, Gurthghol adjusted his direction, focusing on a certain spot on Tralodren before willing himself for it. The black rock shot forward with a sudden burst of speed.

•●•

Far from Thangaria, Rheminas, in his true form, stood on a balcony overlooking the strange beauty that was Helii. Rugged black peaks and jagged brown crests and valleys of hardened lava rimmed the horizon. All was lit in the constant reddish-orange haze of the rivers and lakes of magma flowing down a circle of volcanoes. He had been so taken with the site, he'd built his basalt-walled and ruby-studded fortress palace, named Crucible, in its center.

In many ways, his true form didn't differ from the guise he'd adopted in the council. The god of fire and magma was dressed in a copper-colored tunic with brown pants and boots. A sword was strapped to his side. A dagger was sheathed on his right hip. His wild orange hair and beard fluttered in the breeze, giving one who might have seen him from afar the impression he was crowned with a pool of flame. His clawed hands were crossed under his elbows as he stared out over the vastness of his realm.

Behind him, near the doorway back into his palace, stood two Lords of Fire. Their reddish-brown skin helped highlight their deep blue eyes, full blond beards, and hair. Both wore dark brown pants and a tunic: one red, the other dark yellow. Each was armored in a cast-iron cuirass and bracers. A cast-iron circlet—studded with spessartite garnet, citrine, and yellow topaz—crowned each as a titan lord. These men were special guards, a fact made evident by the spears each gripped in his right hand, whose white-hot iron tips constantly danced with flame.

From the opening between them emerged a Lady of Fire. While she resembled the two titan lords in most respects, her long hair was of an orangish cast, and her black cuirass rested over a black-hemmed red-and-yellow dress. The clicking of her heels as she walked caught the attention of Rheminas, who cast a look over his shoulder.

"And where is he now?"

"As far as I can gather, still in Mortis," said the Lady of Fire.

Rheminas returned to his view. "Let's hope he didn't get lost along the way."

"I don't see how he can, given how you've already claimed him."

"Oh, he might still try to find a way," said Rheminas, "but in the end he'll learn to embrace his fate just like the rest. But who knew how useful he'd actually become? *That's* what amazes *me*," he said, twirling on his heel. "Prepare two furies with the necessary equipment. I want them ready the moment he arrives on Helii. We don't have much time as it is."

"Yes, my lord." The Lady of Fire gave a shallow bow.

"Once he's been transformed, the furies will need to give him his first mission. I trust I don't have to repeat it?"

"No. You made it quite clear the first time."

Rheminas smirked. "Good. Have him bring the scepter to me. If he's on time, I'll be with the pantheon in the hall. If he takes longer, I'll be with the rest of the troops outside it.

"Now go," he said, gesturing for her departure. "And tell the others to make ready. We'll be leaving for Thangaria shortly."

The Lady of Fire gave another shallow bow, then departed. Rheminas watched her leave before walking to the end of the balcony and hunching over the railing.

"Finally, we'll have our revenge."

CHAPTER 10

From high above the heavens it had burst forth, scattering clouds on its fiery descent while wide-eyed creatures and people alike stared dumbfounded at its passing. The fire enveloping the charcoal stone gnawed away at its edges, incinerating any small pebbles it managed to chip away. Behind it a trail of oily smoke slithered into the atmosphere and would soon be gone altogether.

Its arc of descent took it over Talatheal, Colloni, and the deep Yoan Ocean before it sunk low enough to scrape the mountaintops of Arid Land, scattering ancient pines and mountain-perched boulders and cremating anything within reach. Finally, it crashed in an earthshaking explosion just outside Galba's stone circle, spitting debris, dust, and flame all around. Only the circle itself was unaffected in the ensuing quake.

The silence that followed was deafening. The settling dust fell like snow. The thirty-foot crater was only yards away from the timeless stones. The ageless trees that had feared to approach the glade had been swallowed by the crater. The lip of its rough outline crumbled in the dwindling quiet. More trees had been toppled near the edge of the crater and now sprawled out like warriors laid low—defeated and harmless. But with all that had just happened, the sanctity of the glade still held.

Outside the ring of stones, the crater's center smoldered and spat, crackled and sputtered. Amid that churning fire, something moved. A shadow at first; insubstantial and fleeting, it danced amid the flames, growing more solid and rigid as it rose up and above the crater's blackened, rough walls. The shade gained the semblance of a man who grew more massive and spectacular the closer he drew to the crater's lip. He took hold of the edge with his plum-colored hands and pulled himself up and into the light. Once risen from the crater, he took in all around him with a calculating gaze, stroking his long black mustache. The god moved forward with his bare black-nailed feet.

Gurthghol stopped a few yards from the circle. "You know why I'm here." His voice was strong and clear.

"Very well," he continued. "If that's how you'd have it, then you leave me no choice." He raised his hand, and four beings emerged from the shadows of the trees and stones around him. They were similar in appearance to humans but the same size as Gurthghol. Their dusty, grayish-purple skin seemed to grow grayer in the light and more purple in the shadows as they moved to stand beside Gurthghol.

Each of the four Lords of Darkness wore a somber robe. The color was like liquid twilight that darkened and lightened as they moved, making it impossible to determine its actual hue. On top of these robes they wore charcoal-gray cloaks. Each of their hoods was drawn forward, masking their faces in shadow. They approached in silence, long robes hiding their feet and giving the impression they hovered rather than walked.

"Be ready," Gurthghol told the Lords of Darkness. He had a hunch he wanted to explore. Well, more of a burning conviction than a hunch. In order to make it work, though, he'd need to have some help. He hoped it wouldn't come to that but figured it would, as Galba wasn't going to be the least bit friendly to his demands. And if she was, he'd have some serious doubts about the validity of Saredhel's prophecy.

Another small gesture brought forth four more beings, similar in size and shape to the previous four but different in appearance and nature.

Each of these men wore a long-sleeved tunic, pants, and boots—the colors of each varied between the four. A silver cuirass with matching bracers was the extent of their armor. A half cape took the place of a cloak, leaving their heads and olive-skinned faces free of any covering. Their hair was short. Two of their number had monkey-tail beards. The other two were clean shaven.

Their amethyst eyes scanned the area. These were the same color as the amethyst diadems crowning the four as Lords of Chaos. All four kept their hands close to the silver scimitars holstered to their waists.

Gurthghol said nothing as they took their places beside him and the four Lords of Darkness. Lifting his hands before his chest, he summoned a wrought iron helmet with nose and cheek guards. At its crest a ridge of sharp spikes, much like a wicked-looking spine, followed the curve of the helmet. These spikes started small at the nose but grew in size as they climbed to the top of the helmet. From there they again became smaller as they journeyed to the end of the helm.

"You know what to do," said Gurthghol, solemnly donning his helmet.

The eight nodded. Together they made for the stone circle. Behind and between its posts the image of a soft, tranquil glade appeared as it had to all who had come before it, but Gurthghol knew the truth. He knew what it really was and why he was now seeking it. He and Galba had made a pact, and he doubted Galba would go back on it now after so many millennia had passed. In truth, he wasn't really relishing breaking the pact, but then where would be the sacrifice?

He stepped forward and drew his flail. The chain chimed as it fell from the wooden handle, letting the spiked metal ball half the size of a human's head dangle freely near his knees.

The Lords of Chaos rapidly approached the stones, drawing their scimitars and delighting at the conflict to come. Their grins bordered on maniacal as they sprinted ahead. Each abruptly collided with the invisible barrier around the circle. Disconcerted, they peered back at Gurthghol. He simply nodded. They raised their weapons, and the Lords of Darkness called forth some of their power to help. Velvet darkness flew from their outstretched fingers and onto the barrier. It clung and spread over the structure like syrup. In moments the entire barrier, once invisible, appeared as a half globe, shading everything beneath.

When the liquid night had covered its prey, the Lords of Chaos struck. They screamed as their blades rang true, striking against the black barrier with a thick thud, as if they were chopping wood. Though their attack had no effect, they continued raising their weapons in a wild frenzy, hacking away at the dark dome. For a few moments the bedlam continued until Gurthghol came to join them. Upon seeing him draw near, the titan lords halted their attack.

Gurthghol began swinging his flail overhead, gripping the handle with both hands. His face darkened and eyes squinted. His brow furrowed with the effort it took to build up the force he needed. Soon he'd created a vortex of darkness above his head. With a grunt he unleashed the full force of his strength with the weapon. It struck first into the barrier and then the force behind it. The attack was massive. The black dome rippled with the vibration of the impact. The dome's destruction mimicked the shattering of glass, but magnified to an unearthly pitch.

"Your fight's in vain," Gurthghol bellowed. "Why battle me now when you know what's at stake?" He lowered his weapon and stepped into the circle. The firstborn of Vkar and Xora, he was the best suited to the task, since he had once used the power which Galba watched over. None of the other gods would have known what they were getting into. After all, he'd dealt with the first pawn sent against them, sacrificing much for their victory. And he'd also sat in the throne before. He wouldn't need as much time to get accustomed to it as they would.

"Can you really afford to waste such time with everything that's at stake?" he asked as he entered the circle's center, striding to the throne atop the white marble dais. He wasn't sure what to make of the statues of his parents on either side of the throne—which were obviously recent additions—but wouldn't let them distract him. He needed to keep his mind and eyes on the throne. The same throne he'd once been shackled to for too many years before finding his way to freedom. A sacrifice had to be made.

"The life of this planet is insignificant when compared to the whole of the cosmos," Galba's disembodied voice admonished him. Undaunted, he continued his march to the dais.

"I'd remind you of our pact to make it safe from interference—"

"No." Galba suddenly appeared before the god. She'd grown in size to match his own, her green eyes deep pools of stern rebuke. Her left hand rested upon his armored chest, holding him at bay. The delicate appendage was stronger than it appeared.

"You may be gods, but you're not—nor ever will be—our *equal*." Galba's voice was as firm as her blocking hand. "If it weren't for your father's throne, you and your kin would have gone the way of all created things millennia ago. Now that reprieve has ended, and things must work their course."

"And if not, you use those you can to bring about your wishes," Gurthghol said, curling his lip in disgusted anger.

"Fighting me won't reverse Sidra's choice. She made it freely."

Gurthghol flinched at the mention of his daughter. After all these centuries a part of him still missed her, and perhaps a sliver of guilt still pierced his heart for what he'd done to put an end to her threat . . . A sacrifice had to be made.

"Don't make this more difficult than it has to be," said Gurthghol as he tightened his grip on his flail. "Move aside."

"You're strong, Gurthghol, as all firstborns are, but you're not your father, and even *he* was limited by the throne as much as he was its pris-oner." Galba didn't move her hand or change her stance. "Claiming the throne again will just make matters worse, increase your own pain, and bring greater doom upon the pantheon."

Gurthghol said nothing but merely gave a mental command calling for the eight titan lords to spring into action.

The Lords of Chaos rallied against Galba first. Their blades struck her soft alabaster flesh, but didn't drink from her blood or even shred her gray gown. The Lords of Darkness met with similar results as they lobbed black daggers at the divinity. But amid all these assaults Galba remained like a statue. Only her green eyes moved, seeking out Gurthghol, who'd found a clear path for the throne. She continued to watch him from the corner of her eye as he drew up to the white marble dais.

With but a thought, Galba vanished from the ensnaring circle of attackers, appearing before Gurthghol once again. She materialized right in his path, only one step above him—a porcelain-skinned, gray-gowned pillar with flaming red hair. With her absence from their midst, her attackers ran into one another, tumbling into a pile. The Lords of Darkness hurried to their feet and focused their gaze on Gurthghol, ready for his next command.

"It's not yours to claim," said Galba.

"Nor yours to bar."

"Remember the pact." Galba's face remained as stern as it was lovely. Gurthghol searched for some pathway around her, but knew he could only gain the throne by going through her. It would be a waste of time, but he'd have to do it—have to suffer through the process to claim his prize. Galba followed his wandering eyes, ready to counter whatever action he might take next. "Even *you* break your own rule in your rush to shatter our pact. No god nor divinity can be here—not even in another guise."

"It's in my nature to challenge rules."

"But it's not in your nature to defy the will of what must be—to defy change."

"Your change is nothing but the destruction of everything. I never agreed to that, nor did the others. I'd thought we were through with your meddling after Sidra—especially after the pact. None of us expected you to mark us as prey again."

"Change is something I thought you'd favor," said Galba. "After all, here is the time and place to see all things refashioned, to witness a new age being born, a shaking up and off of the old to give birth to the new—be it a new age or a whole world."

"*Your* game"—Gurthghol placed a foot upon the stone step, putting his face mere inches from Galba's—"will have no winners if allowed to continue. I won't allow something I helped create suffer destruction before I wish it to."

"Are you referring to Sidra or Tralodren?" Galba questioned gently.

Gurthghol's countenance darkened. He'd had enough of the mockery and threats she was trying to pass off as appeasement and appeals to some better part of his nature. It was time to be done with this.

"So I see." Galba was crestfallen. "You favor change only if *you* originate it—if it comes from within *your* understanding . . . *your* control." Galba sighed. "Someday you'll learn—all of you—that as great as your family may be, there is something much greater still."

While the glare he returned was anything but inquisitive, Galba's eyes pulled him deeper and still deeper into the truth of her words. He could see the veil being pulled from them so they became windows to things beyond the gods and their titanic forefathers. He knew then the fathomless reaches of nothingness and everything being combined into one location. One reality . . .

He felt himself being pulled away with this feeling. At once he was swallowed by the vision of endless darkness and light, churning and tossing about for thousands of miles in all directions. There was nothing but these two things—these two entities. They were all and all, eternal and unending in scope and power. Who was he—*what* was he—to think he could contend with a force that had given life to all the cosmos? Compared to it he was nothing. He was . . . His thoughts stopped when he caught the faint outline of an outstretched hand amid that churning mix of light and darkness. It was the hand of his father, Vkar, reaching for the very things that gave him existence—the very things from which he stole and crafted his own divinity and passed it on as a legacy for his offspring. The very hand of the first to dream and reach for something far outside his station.

Gurthghol snapped out of the ensnaring disillusionment swimming across his mind and senses. When he did he could see an endless cycle returning to Tralodren and other worlds. Even if Tralodren was spared and the pantheon victorious, they'd have to stand up against the threat once again. At some point the end would come, an end that was not of their own choosing. His father had been right. Vkar had sought knowledge and power from the throne by dominating those ancient entities.

But domination wasn't the answer. Vkar had begun the right course, but Gurthghol could now see it through to its completion.

"Out of my way." Gurthghol introduced Galba's smooth cheek to the back of his hand. There was a peal of thunder from the strike as Galba fell to the ground. She didn't remain down for long, returning to her feet like a flash of lightning and appearing beside Gurthghol in the twinkling of an eye.

"There are greater things afoot than this foolish action." She matched him step for step until she weaved her way before him, blocking his path once more.

Gurthghol knew what she was referring to but also knew she was trying to distract him—lead him away with whatever options she had left outside of violence. "Your coming war on Thangaria is a distraction. As is this."

"A distraction to whom?" Gurthghol swung his flail at Galba. It passed right through her, viciously biting into the marble steps instead.

Galba rose a few feet above the shattered steps. Gurthghol knew his lords had recovered and stood ready as they continued intently watching the battle, eager to obey however he directed. Another mental command called them into action. The Lords of Darkness called upon more darkness, while the Lords of Chaos made their reckless charge, happy to be free to slaughter once more.

Galba paid them no mind. She kept her attention firmly on Gurthghol. "If you want to fight, then we shall fight."

"To the winner goes the throne," Gurthghol said, clenching his teeth in a snarl.

"If that's what you wish . . ." Galba waved her hand and the eight lords vanished from sight. "But only you and I shall fight; your minions have no place in this battle. If I'm being forced to kill, then I wish it to be only *one* instead of *nine*."

"Agreed." Gurthghol never removed his gaze from Galba. He knew the lords had returned to where they'd been called from. He'd expected nothing less from Galba, though it was a token gesture. Both of them knew that unlike Gurthghol, who'd arrived in his true form, the lords relied on guises and as such couldn't be killed in the true sense of the word. But he supposed Galba had to make her point, and it was probably better this way, since the lords could be used for troops at Thangaria, where they were needed now more than they were here.

"I'll try to make this as quick as possible." Gurthghol finished mentally lining up his attack, making sure every move and counteraction was in place. He couldn't afford any mistakes.

Galba struck him with such force his helmet flung off his reeling head. Recovering himself quickly, he whipped a trail of blood from a split lip with the back of his hand.

"Not bad." His smile smeared more blood over his teeth. He threw his weight behind his next attack. Galba simply sidestepped the swing with startling speed.

"Your father couldn't take me. How could you?" Galba remained calm, her body fluid but straight.

Gurthghol swung again. Once more Galba moved from his strike faster than the eye could see. The god of chaos gave out a shout of rage, which accompanied his flail as it flew into, and then through, a nearby stone. The damaged object collapsed around the hole in its center, tumbling to the ground. The lintel it had supported slid and came to rest at a diagonal angle.

"You really would kill me?" There was clear disappointment in Galba's voice as she moved in front of Gurthghol.

"If you stand in my way, yes."

"What you're seeking to do I cannot let you do."

"So you'll let us *die* as you did before?" Gurthghol drew his khopesh.

"There are rules, Gurthghol—ones that we *all* agreed to. Would you threaten everything you created with your fellow gods by seeking the throne once again?"

He lunged with his khopesh. It only nipped Galba's gown and tore off a piece of fabric. She countered with a fist to his nose. It struck hard and fast. Warm crimson blood spurted from the wound, trailing down his lip and coating his mustache. His nose had been broken, the building pressure and pain making it hard to breathe. He needed to finish this.

Gurthghol's eyes glowed a deep plum and the god was joined by five duplicates of himself, each surrounding Galba with a deadly khopesh in hand. Galba merely stood amid the bodies, waiting for them to attack. When they did, it was a flurry of swords and screams. Each of the six blades found a sheath in her flesh, but there was neither blood nor cry of pain. Instead, she remained still, digging deep into Gurthghol's unique eyes with her own unwavering gaze.

Seeing that she didn't move, Gurthghol willed himself from where he had been at the lowest steps of the dais to the opposite side. Without hesitation he resumed his ascent before hearing Galba shout her defiance. A heartbeat later Galba leapt away from her attackers and flipped in the air to land back in front of Gurthghol. His five duplicates were amazed by the action, staring dumbfounded at Galba before fading away into the nothingness from which they were spawned.

"Recall what happened to you before," said Galba. "You wanted nothing more than to shed the throne when we first met. Do you really want to claim it again?"

He knew little time remained. This battle was a pointless exercise and had to be finished soon, for everyone's sake. And there was only so much of Vkar's energy he could keep using. And he wanted to have some still flowing through him when he reclaimed the throne. "I won't be played by either of you like last time. This isn't a game. We're fighting against one of your own creations—"

"It wasn't I who—"

"You're just as guilty."

"Yet you still won."

"Only by a great sacrifice." Gurthghol's voice seethed with barely subdued wrath. "We have nothing left now. No net to catch us should we fall . . . and we will."

Galba's face softened. "Then leave Tralodren. The stakes are only one world—you could go and find or create another."

Abandon the very jewel of his creation? Would he allow himself to be tempted by such a thought? Would he really be willing to run away like some battered dog who hoped to live another day? Could he?

No.

In his heart he knew there was nowhere to run. He would be tracked down and called to fight this threat, but perhaps without the same face presently staring back at him. He supposed Ganatar would find his mind-set rather noble, but Gurthghol knew the truth. In his heart, he knew it wouldn't really end with Tralodren. It would only grow and spread over time, and eventually the whole cosmos would be in jeopardy. To be true to himself and what he believed—to what Saredhel had seen—he needed to take the throne and put an end to this threat once and for all.

Galba continued her refrain. "There are other worlds, Gurthghol."

"But there's only *one* Tralodren."

"What's a world filled with lesser life—weaker beings who would go on for generations without coming close to you and the other gods in rank—compared to your existence?" It was a good question, but he'd hear none of it. He had decided on his action. It was time to see it through.

He swung his weapon, but Galba weaved around it, pounding his chest with a hard shove and sending him sprawling to the sward. He rose and charged Galba head on, shoving his shoulder into her collarbone. The collision jarred Galba enough to cause her to lose her balance for a moment. And it was in that moment that Gurthghol took his advantage and seized Galba's neck with his hands. He began to squeeze.

Galba tried to claw the plum hands away from her throat, but Gurthghol held her fast. He tapped into what remained of Vkar's essence still coursing through him. By its aid, he started draining away the substance and power of Galba and absorbing it into himself.

Galba's eyes went wide as she struggled to speak. "What are you doing?"

"What my father should have done when he had the chance," he said, tightening his grip.

Galba dropped to her knees. He could feel the power ebbing from her body into his hands and then up his arms and into the rest of his body. He'd learned some secrets from his time on the throne and was pleased to finally be able to put them into practice.

"If you . . . break your word . . ." Galba's raspy voice assailed Gurthghol through his strangling grip . . . "Then I'm not bound . . . to our agreement."

The form of Galba melted away and folded into an expanse of white light, blinding Gurthghol. The blindness lasted only for a moment, but the stranglehold he'd had was now useless. The living energy flowed through his fingers like mist. He might as well have tried strangling a cloud. When his vision cleared, he found a huge ball of white light blocking the throne, a milky aura that spilled to Gurthghol's bare feet.

"There's still time to repent of your intended action." The voice was like Galba's but also different—more expansive and regal, less feminine— but not yet totally devoid of the softer undercurrents of her voice.

"I have no intention of turning back," Gurthghol snarled at the luminescence.

"You were warned." The light shimmered all about him in a blinding shower of dagger-like rays. It covered everything, filling up the whole interior of the circle and spilling outside the stone posts into the empty glade beyond. Gurthghol shaded his eyes with his arms and took a step closer to the throne.

The light was intensely corrosive to his flesh and garb. He could feel it digging into him, eating him away, defeating his will and spirit. Even gaining just one step closer made him feel the full force of just the fragment of the being it represented. If he had dared to face that entity in its true form, he'd be gone in an instant. But here, in its partial manifestation, Gurthghol stood a chance. Yet even with that chance he wouldn't be able to hold out much longer against such an onslaught.

However, he could still feel a tingle of the remaining presence of his father within him. Amazingly, Endarien's foolishness and the attempt to drain Galba hadn't used it up. Better still, the trace amounts of what he had managed to siphon off of Galba were also still present. He had to use what was left of them to make it to his goal, or die in the process.

"Father, grant me victory." Gurthghol raised his voice as he tapped into the last bit of Vkar's essence and mingled it with the pilfered pieces of Galba in his veins. He began glowing hot white. His whole body and even his armor cast a flickering light like fire. It was under this glow that he took another heavy step forward. Then another. Each time he was fighting against what felt like a wall. But the more steps he took, the more spongy it became. Better still, the burning had stopped. It was just the weakening barrier and him willing himself through it.

His eyes narrowed and brow perspired under the focused pressure. When he pressed his way into the center of the white globe—into the very heart of his opposition—he let out a roaring shout of defiance as he pushed forward with every aspect of his being. And then the globe of light swallowed him whole.

For a long, hushed moment, there was nothing but that brilliant globe of light. But then a plum-colored hand shot out from the back of the globe, reaching out for the throne behind it. This was followed by another hand and then a head fixed upon the object of its maddening devotion with a painful grimace. He was almost there. Though his body had the look of suffering some sort of grievous beating, he continued pushing forward.

He brought a foot through the globe, planting it with a mighty effort. He used it as an anchor, pulling the rest of his body behind him out of the mire-like illumination, which threatened to pull him back into the glowing globe. He slammed his other foot down and pushed forward. He was almost free of the luminous tendrils. He could feel the last of the extra power of his father's essence fading away with the lessening intensity of the glowing aura encasing him.

Even as he freed the last of his person from the globe's hold, the light shook and quaked like a bowl of jelly. He spied the wondrous gems of the throne beckoning him. He saw the familiar stone seat on which he'd sat for countless years, shackled to it like the drunkard to his bottle. If there was any other way, he would have done it; if Saredhel's words were true, then he had to follow through with his plan.

He took one last step, turned, and then seated himself in his father's throne. The entire circle shook. He could feel the familiar sensations of being connected with the whole of the cosmos.

"You've made a great mistake." The light had become a pillar of snowy flame, the voice more saddened and stern.

"Let's hope not," he replied. Sitting in the throne again was like putting on a pair of well-worn shoes. The fit was comfortable and familiar, more than easy enough for him to make full use of its powers instantly—even after his long absence.

"You've now set yourself against us," the white pillar chastised Gurthghol. He merely smiled, opened his mouth, and sucked in the flaming light. Yes, it was definitely easier with the throne. He could feel the power enter him even as he focused on using it to fuel him and the next part of his plan. And there was some added delight at watching what remained of Galba fading away more and more with every heartbeat.

When he had finished absorbing Galba's essence into his person, Gurthghol surveyed the circle. There was nothing left to oppose him. He had the throne and had gotten rid of Galba. And the warm tingling flowing over his body told him he was being healed from his recent injuries. There was only one final task to complete, and then it was all over.

No sooner had he closed his eyes than metal bands appeared on the armrests of the throne and slapped over his wrists. Another band appeared and snapped his legs against the lower part of the throne. He struggled for release but was held fast.

"Galba!" he screamed. "I won't be—"

He was stopped in midsentence by the sensation of his body stretching across a wide expanse. It was similar to how he felt whenever he traversed great distances, which he wasn't trying to do. There then arose a blinding flash of white light, and Gurthghol vanished from the circle.

CHAPTER 11

BE MINDFUL THAT YOUR STUDIES DO NOT CONSUME YOU.
FOR WHAT GOOD COULD COME FROM GAINING GREAT
KNOWLEDGE AT THE COST OF YOUR LIFE?

—The Great Book

"How about this one?" Rowan held up a dark purple tome for Alara's inspection. The binding was made of some type of scaled hide he couldn't identify. Alara stood in front of a small reading table on the upper gallery of the Great Library. Tucked away from the other patrons, the three had taken to a collection of books they'd assembled from the shelves.

While Rowan couldn't read any of these texts, as they were composed chiefly in Pacolees, along with a few other nonhuman languages, he could play gofer to Cadrissa and Alara. Both were hurriedly scanning through the pages and scrolls looking for something worthwhile. Cadrissa sat beside Alara, piling a small hill of scrolls before her tired eyes. The scepter rested on the table before her. Alara was really the one doing most of the work, skimming the texts for anything mentioning wizard kings in the third or fourth ages, and then asking Cadrissa if what she had found was relevant or not. It was tedious and tiresome, but needed to be done.

"Let me see." Alara stopped her reading and took up the weighty volume. Turning it over, she saw it was devoid of a title. Undaunted, she carefully lifted the cover. The book opened with a dry crackle.

"I'd like to think we're getting somewhere, but with all these books—"

"We're closer now than we were before." Alara interrupted Rowan without even raising her gaze from the vellum pages.

"I thought you'd say that." He returned to a nearby bookcase with a worn but steadfast frame, like a champion athlete who's run a great distance and continues his stride as he enters the final lap.

Alara peered up from the tome. "If you want to take a break—"

"No, you're right," said Rowan. "There's no time to rest when we didn't have that much to begin with."

Cadrissa made her way through more scrolls. The small puffs of dust birthed by the action caused her eyes to water and nose to twitch. "Well, I can make some of these out, as they're source documents, but nothing of interest is coming up."

"There's nothing here either." Alara sighed. "Just more biographies of the Patrious who opposed the wizard kings." She set the book Rowan had given her among the others on the table.

"What if the answer *isn't* in the library?" Alara asked Cadrissa. "Are there any other places we can look?"

"*Not* in the library?" Cadrissa was shocked by the statement. "If it isn't here, then we aren't going to find it anywhere else, I assure you."

Rowan didn't listen to the rest of their conversation. He had made his way back to the library shelves cluttered with the strange, spidery written language of the Patrious. He realized just how hopeless and frustrating this all was. Even with the extra time at their disposal, it was worse than trying to find a needle in a haystack. At least then he would know what he was looking for, but here . . . here he couldn't even make sense of the scribbles in front of him.

Thankfully, he'd long ago shed his shield; it was resting against the table. It wasn't a great weight, but he would have certainly felt it by now if it were still slung over his shoulders. And then there was the added benefit of standing out less without it—though since he still wore his armor and sword, it wasn't like he was easily blending among the library's other patrons.

Sighing, he tried to locate a book he felt might be closer to what they needed. He'd been instructed on what symbols—or Patrician words—to look for and in what basic area he should be looking. He might just as well close his eyes and pick one at random. It would be just as effective.

Rowan.

He jerked himself free from his melancholy thoughts, spinning around the gallery. He didn't see anyone nearby.

Rowan.

This time the voice, which was in his head, attached itself to a gray panther that had appeared a few feet from him. It was the same gray panther he'd last seen in the ruins of Gondad.

Follow was all the feminine voice said before the panther made its way down the aisle of bookcases. Rowan did as bidden, stepping closely behind the great cat. He was led through the gallery's wide assortment of texts and towering shelves, a virtual forest of knowledge. He had no idea where he was going, only that he needed to stay close.

As he walked, he passed beside a wall of stained glass windows depicting Patrious from a time long before Rowan could even imagine. It was like they were posing amid their daily tasks: farming, building cities, assembling to fight some kind of giant, and getting married, as well as recording history and of course reading scrolls and books. While he might have been tempted to stop for a closer inspection the panther kept moving—and so did he.

He passed through the midst of some silent Patrician scholars. They kept to their own work, never acknowledging Rowan or his guide. Could they see the panther? Judging from their lack of response, he thought not. He'd become comfortable enough with visions and portents from Panthora to know when something could be seen by him alone. He was sure of that much, at least. What he wasn't sure of was why he was being led all around the library to the gallery opposite the one he'd been in. He supposed he'd get an answer soon enough.

And so they continued, the panther leading Rowan, until he came to a stop before a single bookshelf stacked tight against a wall rising far into the ceiling above. The area around it was empty of people and seemed almost like a deserted part of the building—neglected for some reason. His guide, though, had curled itself at the bookcase's base like a common cat beside the warmth of a fire, waiting for Rowan to approach.

"What now?" he softly inquired.

The panther did nothing except yawn. Seeing no help there, he focused on the books and scrolls. When he caught sight of the text, he smiled. The familiar runic shapes of his native tongue cheered him to no end. Not only because he felt like he could be useful again but also because of what one of the books was titled: *The History of the Valkorian Knights.*

Read and begin to understand.

Rowan turned, hoping to see what he thought would be Panthora. He was sure she was standing right behind him—had to be. Instead, there was no one. Turning back to the bookcase, he saw the panther was gone as well. No matter. The creature had done its job.

He made his way to the shelf, withdrew the fat leather-covered volume, and began reading. Though it was of an older time period—the text containing a few anachronisms—Rowan read it quite easily, thanks to his training. Thumbing through a few pages, he stopped when something caught his eye:

The location and environment of the Northlands have long been both aid and hindrance to the Nordican. Aid in the sense that they have helped foster the independence each Nordican craves and thrives in while also stopping the softness of civilization common to the southern lands and races from taking root. They are also a hindrance, because this isolation has prevented any strong form of unity from being established among the Nordic people.

We have been little more than packs of wolves striving for our own causes, pitting ourselves against the other for countless generations. Only with the coming of the knighthood could we start to make a better future for ourselves. For here is an institution which unites common Nordicans rather than splintering them. It gathers men from all sides of the continent, and then even beyond Valkoria's shores, to bind them in one brotherhood. And in this unity I see a great and glorious future for my race.

And to think we owe this new beginning to the elf, who gave the builders of the knighthood the energy to follow through on their commitment far more than the belief in Panthora ever did. For it has been told to me by some elderly knights, who have also come to see themselves as scholars, that following the Imperial Wars, a group of Telborian refugees fleeing the devastation of Gondad made their way to Valkoria.

Here it was that they made up a small camp, and with the aid of a nearby tribe who took pity on them, survived through the winter. They were mostly men, the women and children having succumbed to the hardships of refugee life before making it to Valkoria's shores. The men who survived were convinced that they were in danger of elven aggression and started to build a walled village to protect themselves.

They also took up arms and the art of warfare to further defend themselves, and taught it to the children who had come from mixed Nordic and Telborian unions. They were even able to convince some of their neighbors of the threat of this coming elven invasion, and these neighbors joined them in their walled town, which soon became home to a tribe in itself. More years passed and the elves didn't come, but the Knighthood of Valkoria had been born. They saw the time they had as an opportunity to reach other Nordicans, recruiting them for their growing army to stand against the elven aggressors who were soon to come upon Nordic shores, hungry for imperial expansion.

That invasion never came, but each generation was ingrained with the fear of it and the elves who caused the destruction of great Gondad—the origin city of humanity, as the Telborians saw it. While their fortunes waxed and waned over the centuries, they were strictly a martial order run by Nordicans holding to Telborian ideals who came to believe they had founded the knighthood themselves. The main purpose, though, remained protection from elven invasion.

That is, until it was challenged by another migration from the south.

Once again a group of Telborians came up from the Midlands to visit Valkoria. These, though, were of another stripe—missionaries for the new goddess Panthora, said to be a goddess for all of humanity. The faith took root around the knighthood, making converts as the martial dedication of the knights merged with the spiritual devotion of the Panians, as they were called. The faith took root so quickly that in one generation the knighthood had dedicated itself to Panthora and the protection and unification of all the Northlands, and to a lesser extent, the whole of humanity.

Once more the Telborian blood ran thin and Nordic dominance over the knighthood returned. But the new mission and purpose stayed. And in time, as had happened with its founding, those who lived in the Northlands soon forgot its foreign origins, taking it as a wholly native construction. If not for the few elders to whom I spoke, and the scraps of ancient history I've been able to discover and save here and there, I would share the same belief. It is my hope that by writing this book I will keep this knowledge alive for those who still wish to learn the true history of the Knights of Valkoria.

Rowan stopped reading.

He couldn't go on, not while his mind was frozen by what he'd just read. Here was the whole history of his knighthood in a nutshell, and it was nothing like he'd been told. Whereas before he might have doubted what he'd just read, now it only served to confirm what Panthora had told him. There were no brave souls of the far north who had seen a vision of Panthora and moved to the south of Valkoria to build her a place of worship and a knighthood to honor her. It was all lies.

He had given himself in service to a lie. No, that wasn't quite true. He had given himself in service to Panthora, to serve *her*. The knighthood had just been a means by which he could honor his pledge. Panthora's words now made much more sense. She *hadn't* built the knighthood, but *allowed* the people there to follow her because she could use them to spread her influence. She might have sent the priests, but certainly not the band of refugees who founded the knighthood in the first place.

So then where did this put him and the calling Panthora had placed upon him? She said he had a great purpose in life, but what did it have to do with this knowledge of the knighthood's foundation? Should he go back to them, knowing what he knew now? Sadly, he knew he didn't have time to dwell upon these matters, and so he opted to read just a bit more to glean what he could now, for he didn't believe he'd ever have a chance to access this information again. He planned to make use of the rare gift, yet another of the blessings Panthora had granted him, while he could.

• ● •

Cadrissa's head lifted from the scrolls she'd been reading. She'd become absorbed in her studies. Of course, that didn't take much, given the rich trove of knowledge within her reach. Removing herself from her work helped bring her back into reality. That and realizing it was just her and Alara at the table.

"How long has Rowan been gone?"

"I don't know." Alara glanced up from her own reading. "How long has it been since you last saw him?"

"Maybe half an hour."

"You think he might have found something?"

"More likely he got lost," said Cadrissa. "He would've brought something back to us to check if he'd found anything."

"Or maybe he sat down for a moment and fell asleep." Alara stood up to stretch her back and arms, grimacing. "We *have* had an eventful day."

"Yes, we have." Cadrissa was amazed it was still the same day. Just a few hours ago she'd been the captive of a lich who'd now risen to godhood, and now they were in the Great Library. What an amazing contrast . . . and a very surreal few hours.

"So *did* I miss something?" Cadrissa asked. "With you and Rowan, I mean."

Alara paused. "What do you mean?"

"Things just seem a little . . . *different* between you. The last I knew, you didn't really have too much in common, and now—well, things seem a bit *different*." She went up to the edge of what she thought was wise to inquire about.

"Since you were taken by Cadrith"—Alara was choosing her words more carefully than normal—"we've had some adventures of our own, which have helped us come to an understanding."

"You could have done worse." Cadrissa's comment clearly caught Alara off guard. "I take it you're older than him, right?"

"Now really isn't the time to be talking about this." Alara became businesslike again, shifting her attention back to the tomes on the table. "We need to stay focused on finding that incantation. Which means we'll need as many eyeballs as possible." Looking back at her, Alara asked, "Do you think you could go look for Rowan?"

"Sure." Cadrissa rose. "I'm not much help right now anyway."

"Of course you are." Alara waved her hand over the collection of scrolls and books they'd amassed since entering the library. "I certainly couldn't have gotten this far without you."

"I'd believe that more if we'd actually *found* something."

"We will."

Cadrissa wasn't sure if she believed Alara, but found her optimistic outlook sturdy enough to latch some hope to for the time being.

"I'll be back as soon as I can." She took a few paces before shooting Alara a sly smile over her shoulder. "You do make a nice couple, though."

Alara said nothing, shooing her away, clearly not looking to get any-where near the topic. Cadrissa left the scepter with Alara, not seeing the need to carry it around the library. Alara would do a good job of keeping it safe until she returned. And with two free hands, she was ready for anything that might suddenly appear as she wandered the aisles of books.

Rowan shouldn't be too hard to find. He *was* the only Nordican here, after all. In the meantime she had an excuse to enjoy more of the library. It really was a lovely sight, and she never would grow tired of looking at it. For someone who loved knowledge, where else could she go? It was her shrine. How would she dare leave it? If not for the matter with

Cadrith, she probably wouldn't. In fact she'd be content living out her days in Rexatoius within walking distance of—

The necklace flared into life with a near-searing heat so overwhelming she almost screamed. This was followed by whispering voices and a new pressure around her head as if a metal band was tightening around the top of her skull. Slowing her stride, she clenched her jaw, gnashing her teeth against the pain. It wasn't working. The pain only increased. She stopped near the end of a bookcase and leaned against it. She felt like she was going to faint.

It was clear the necklace and the whispers were linked in some way. She focused all her mental strength on remaining calm while enduring all those faint echoes climbing around her head like spiders weaving a web around her consciousness. Soon she could no longer concentrate on where she was and what was going on. Terrified, she focused all her effort on holding back the fire in her brain that matched the blaze she felt from the hidden pocket where the necklace rested.

It took all her strength to flatten her back against the hard wood of the shelf. She was breathing hard, like she'd been in a long, torturous run. Forcing her hand to function, she sent it in search of the necklace. Once inside the hidden pocket, her fingers cramped up after taking hold of the object. With another strenuous effort, she willed the hand back out.

The pain around her head increased. Through pinched eyes she took in the golden disk-shaped pendant and matching thin chain. Both glistened with a pure bronze light. The strange carvings and symbols covering the medallion were alight with a white glow. She wished now she'd taken some time to try to decipher them. But the events that followed the necklace's discovery hadn't allowed the opportunity.

When she pulled it out of its hidden pocket, she'd felt it calling to her somehow, speaking to her with scores of voices. She felt compelled just like a moth to flame and couldn't stop herself, even if she wanted to. And part of her didn't want to either. And that made her even more concerned.

Her fears grew when she observed her empty hand move to meet the other, and together they placed the necklace over her neck. Instantly it felt like someone had wrapped their hands tight about her throat and were trying to choke the life out of her. But as quickly as it began, the sensation left. The pain fled her brow and the whispers stilled. As they faded, her mental clarity returned.

Remaining still for a moment, Cadrissa waited to be sure it was all over. When a few more moments passed without incident, she dared a breath. A study of the space around her revealed no one else had seen what just took place. Or if they did, they chose to ignore it, or they didn't care. In any case, she hadn't drawn unwanted attention, which was good. She'd have to sort this all out later. While the library might have been a good place to search for information about the necklace, the scepter was more important. And if the whispers and heat didn't return, she could wait until a more opportune time for digging into what just occurred.

For now, she was in full control of her mind and body, and there was still a lost Nordic knight to find. Releasing a soft sigh, Cadrissa stood to her full height, got her bearings, and resumed her search.

•●•

Rowan was so engrossed in his reading he didn't hear Cadrissa speak his name the first time, nor the second. He only returned to reality after her hand lightly shook his shoulder.

"I've been looking all over for you," she informed him with mild frustration.

"Sorry." He used his finger as a bookmark as he closed the book he'd been reading and faced Cadrissa. "I must have wandered further off than I realized."

"I'd say. It took me over a quarter of an hour to find you."

"Only a quarter hour?" he asked with some degree of relief. "I thought I'd been reading longer than that."

"You have," she said. "It's probably been an hour altogether since you left."

"An hour?" A knot grew in Rowan's stomach upon hearing the news. Here he was indulging in something unrelated to why they'd come, and he'd made them waste an hour looking for him.

"I'm sorry."

"For what?"

Rowan was about to answer when Cadrissa spied the book he was holding. "What's that?"

"I just found it in that bookcase," he said, pointing with the book to the case behind him. "They're all in Nordican. I guess I must have gotten into what I was reading and lost track of time." It was a feeble apology, since he knew he wasn't being that helpful with the search in the first place.

"Anything good?" Cadrissa's eyes lit up as she strolled closer to the bookcase for a peek.

Rowan stepped aside, letting the mage pass. "I've just been reading this one so far, but I did notice that there are books on various areas of the Northlands and tribes—"

"And a few that might be of some interest to *us*," Cadrissa interrupted, pulling a slender green hide-covered book from a lower shelf. She hurriedly opened the volume, thumbing through the vellum pages with some speed—though not so rapidly as to risk damaging them in her haste. Her smile widened.

"What is it?" She ignored him, continuing to flip through the volume as delicately and speedily as she could. "You can read Nordican?" he continued, surprised.

"Better than I can Pacolees." She kept her nose in the book, fingers turning pages. "And it comes in handy more than you might think. There *were* some Nordic wizards, you know. Not many, mind you, but enough to leave some records about things . . ." Cadrissa stopped to scan a new page she'd just turned to before suddenly stopping, head bolting up into Rowan's face. "I think this is it." She began to head briskly back the way she'd come. "We need to tell Alara."

"Tell her what?" Rowan called after her as she sped through the aisles and around a few patrons who paid her only mild interest. Cadrissa didn't reply, only continued on her way.

Rowan sighed, removed his makeshift bookmark, and returned the book to its proper place. He supposed he'd read enough to get a truer understanding of what Panthora had been saying. But he couldn't concentrate on that now. He had to finish what he'd come to do in the first place. One mission at a time. That was all he could do.

He hurried after Cadrissa, who was now a fair distance ahead of him. He was curious to hear what she'd found. Even more curious to know why Panthora had shown him to the bookcase which contained not only what he needed to know about the knighthood, but possibly something relating to their search too. Truly, she was watching over him, and that only increased his faith in a favorable outcome.

For a moment, he wondered if this would have all been possible had he returned to Valkoria from Arid Land. Not likely, he surmised. So him choosing to go after Cadrissa on Arid Land instead of returning immediately to Valkoria must have been the right choice. It clearly benefited him with insight into the knighthood and confirmation of Panthora's words. Not to mention providing them with aid in stopping Cadrith as well. He still didn't know what to make of it all yet, but was confident Panthora, and a little more time, would help sort everything out.

CHAPTER 12

IF THERE IS NO ENEMY WITHIN, THEN THE ENEMY OUTSIDE CAN DO NO HARM.

—Old Celetoric proverb

"So *this* is what we're looking for?" Alara asked Cadrissa, who felt giddier than she had been upon first finding the book. She had sped back to Alara, Rowan not far behind. Alara was glad to see them—she'd begun to think Cadrissa had gotten lost or sidetracked as well. But when she presented the book to Alara, any worries or concerns evaporated. The book told about a wizard king in the wilds of Frigia, where the author would have the reader believe the Scepter of Night had been crafted in the Third Age of the Wizard Kings.

"I'm certain of it." She watched Alara turn the book over in her hand. It was an amazing find, given all that had led them to it, but Cadrissa didn't want to dig too deeply into the matter of how fortunate it was. She had enough to contend with as it was without rousing any more flames by stoking more fires.

"Frigia?" Alara looked at Rowan, who'd taken a seat beside her.

"That's what it says," he replied. They really did make a nice-looking couple.

"Frigia," Cadrissa responded, with so much excitement she could barely contain herself.

"The exact same place you wanted to go to meet your wizard to help us find Cadrissa." Alara slowly shook her head. "What are the odds?"

"You were going there before?" she asked.

"It was an idea for a *very* short while," said Alara, sharing a look with Rowan. She figured it was an inside joke.

"It's still a long way from here," said Rowan. "And it's even less hospitable than Valkoria."

"And you're sure about this Lann Mirson?" Alara asked Cadrissa for the second time since she'd presented the cursory summary of her findings.

"Yes. And from what I've read so far, he's named as a powerful wizard king."

"You're sure?" Alara pressed.

"As sure as I can be without reading any more," she said as she took her former seat.

"Well, you're the one who's going to have to make sense of this." Alara relinquished the book into the wizardess' eager hands. "How long do you think you'll need?"

Cadrissa gripped the book like a child receiving an extra-large piece of pie. "It shouldn't take me too long. I'll just skim the high points," she said, placing her hand over the top of the scepter. Without thinking, she pulled it closer. When she did, the necklace flared up with an intense heat—even hotter than before—and she felt a painful spike invade her head. Fear gnawed on her gut while she envisioned passing out on the table or something worse. Thankfully, the episode was brief. Even better, neither Rowan nor Alara had noticed anything amiss. Well, almost. She looked down and saw her fingers tenderly stroking the necklace's pendant. The action wasn't missed on Rowan.

"It was part of my reward from the ruins," she hurriedly explained. "I figured I'd wear it rather than keep it in my pocket. I might as well get some use out of it—especially if we're looking at the end of Tralodren and all." She figured that sounded decent enough.

"You think that's wise?" Alara asked. "I've heard stories about objects being enchanted and the user donning them to their own hurt."

Cadrissa looked for a way to end the discussion. It wouldn't do having her focus divided. She'd need all her mental energies to hurry through the old book. She found her solution hanging around Rowan's neck. "No less wise than Rowan using that shield he found or wearing that necklace of his." She pointed to the shriveled panther paw he'd taken to wearing since Galba's circle.

"Mine was given to me by Panthora," Rowan corrected, "in the very ruins of Gondad."

Cadrissa shrugged her shoulders. "Let's just forget about it," she said, burying her face in the book. "I'll just need a few moments," she told herself just as much as the others. She hoped she sounded natural. To her relief they let the matter pass.

•●•

Content to let Cadrissa read, Alara stood. Rowan followed her a few feet away from the table.

"You okay?" she asked.

He turned his back to the table and Cadrissa to get some privacy. "I'm fine." Rowan had said nothing as he listened to Cadrissa give her explanation of the book. He'd told her about coming across the books and bookcase but nothing else. Nothing about Panthora or the panther that had led him.

There was too much going on as it was to add his recent encounter to the pile. He didn't see how it was any of Alara's business anyway. That was only part of it, though. He also didn't want to taint her opinion of the knighthood until he'd had some more time to come to his own conclusions. The other truth was he didn't want to think right now either. There were just too many things to deal with. Life kept getting harder and harder for him the more he strayed from his home. Or was it the longer he stayed with Alara . . . or the more he learned about the truth of his calling from Panthora . . .

"What?" Rowan asked after noticing Alara was staring at him.

"What's bothering you?" she asked.

"What makes you think something's bothering me?"

Alara crossed her arms.

He knew she wasn't going to stop digging, so he decided to relent. "It just seems like I'm in the middle of this stormy sea, and these waves keep crashing over me. It's all I can do to keep my head above water."

"I know," said Alara. "And I have a feeling it's only going to get worse before it gets any better."

"Now you sound like a Nordican," he teased.

"You just keep rubbing off on me, I guess."

"I've also been thinking about how you're back home now," he cautiously continued. He didn't really know how Alara would react, though he was sure the matter hadn't escaped her notice.

"And?" Her face and body became unreadable.

"And . . . I just wanted you to know if you *did* decide to stay, I wouldn't blame you."

"If you'd suddenly made it back to your keep, do you think you'd be able to endure the burden of knowing you had the chance to do something to save so many others but instead did nothing?"

"No," said Rowan. "I don't think I could, but I'm a Knight of Valkoria, and it's my duty to protect others. You're just—"

Alara finished his thought. "Someone you still don't know that well."

"Maybe not," Rowan confessed, "but I'd like to."

"Then we need to do all we can, while we can. Even if that means trying to find a hidden and possibly even forgotten incantation for some relic of the wizard kings."

"You don't really think this is going to work, do you?"

Alara was surprised by the question. "Why would I be here looking for answers if I didn't?"

"You're not one who likes to sit around and do nothing. I know *that* much about you." Rowan saw the hint of a smile on her lips.

"Seems I've been rubbing off on you some too."

"You still haven't answered my question."

Alara became serious again. "What if I don't want to answer it?"

"If you're afraid of swaying me, you won't," said Rowan. "I've already made my choice."

"I'm more afraid of what I'd hear myself say." Her eyes left him for a moment to contemplate the floor, but her focus returned to him in the next breath. "It's just better to stay focused on one thing at a time for right now."

"Faith and patience." Rowan nodded, repeating the same phrase Alara had been known to repeat herself over these last few days. He found himself latching hold of it more and more with everything he encountered.

"So how far away is Frigia from your keep?"

"Some distance to the north, but a lot closer than Arid Land."

"So we're making progress on more than one front," she said.

"Did you really mean what you said about Cadrissa's necklace?" A new thought redirected his thinking.

"About things being enchanted?" Alara asked. "It's just a wise precaution. Especially if she found it in some dranoric ruins." Upon seeing concern rising on Rowan's face, she quickly added, "But I trust her judgment. She is a mage, after all, and helped us find everything in the first place. I'm sure she's able to tell what's potentially dangerous from what isn't. And *you* did fine with your shield."

Rowan nodded. "It's saved my life more than once now."

"And *I* think that's a good thing, don't you?"

"I got it." Cadrissa's voice interrupted their conversation.

"You sure?" Alara asked while making her way back to the table. "That couldn't have been more than—"

"I told you," she said, "I just stuck to the high points."

"Must not have been too many," Rowan said, coming up alongside Alara.

"Enough for our purposes."

"So what did you find?" asked Alara.

"I think I know where we go next."

"The wizard king's tower," Rowan said. "We already know that."

"Yes, but I know now where it's located and what we'll need to get inside and past its defenses. And thankfully, his tower still stands because of some powerful protective spells he put in place."

"But those were cast hundreds of years ago," he continued. "Are you sure they could last that long?"

"I've seen the sort of thing firsthand." Rowan didn't need to ask what Cadrissa meant. If she'd been captured by another wizard king, it stood to reason they would have some things in common.

"So where's this tower?" Alara asked.

Cadrissa pointed to her head. "I've memorized the map. I just need to cast a simple spell, like the one that took us all here, and we can be there instantly."

"Simple spell?" Rowan's brow wrinkled. "You're talking about finding a wizard king's tower that none of us have been to, and this time we don't have Galba's help to get there."

"He's right," Alara added with a touch of concern. "You sure you don't need more time to study or rest a little?"

"No," Cadrissa said, absent-mindedly stroking her necklace. "I have enough strength to get us there. And I'm sure I know the way."

Rowan glanced at Alara and saw, like himself, she wasn't entirely convinced of Cadrissa's plan.

"Are you sure this is the only way?" she asked.

"Yes." Cadrissa stood, grabbing the scepter. "And the sooner we get there, the sooner we can get this scepter working again."

"And then what?" Rowan said what all of them had been pushing aside until now. Finding a way to activate the scepter was one thing, but what to do with it once they'd done so was something entirely different.

"We don't have any other options." Cadrissa voiced the other truth they'd been holding on to since arriving.

Alara sighed. "Then we'll need to get some warm cloaks and gear."

"No need," Cadrissa countered. "I can get us right inside the tower. We won't need anything other than what we already have. We can be in and out and off to wherever we need to go next with ease."

"What about those defenses you were talking about?" asked Rowan.

"I told you." Cadrissa's lips parted ever so slightly. "I've got it all locked in place. We can be there instantly, retrieve the information, and then move on." Rowan wasn't sure he liked the way she was now constantly rubbing the pendant of her necklace with her free hand.

"If you're sure you can handle the spell," Alara continued, "then what do we need to do to get there?"

"Just what we did before we came here, except I'll use Rowan and myself as an anchor and we won't have a portal to walk through. And it probably will be better to cast this spell outside the library to avoid any counterspells that might be in place."

"All right," Alara said, making her way toward the stairs. "Then let's get moving."

Rowan reclaimed his shield and followed.

• ● •

Soon enough Rowan, Alara, and Cadrissa found themselves outside the Great Library, in a secluded cluster of trees. "This should be far enough," said Cadrissa. Now that they were back outside she felt better. She hoped it would last. "Now we need to hold hands and focus as best we can on the Northlands. You'll help with being our anchor there, Rowan.

"Just keep your focus and it'll be fine." Cadrissa slid the scepter under her belt, freeing her hands so she could take hold of Rowan's and Alara's. Rowan hurriedly tossed his shield back over his shoulder, freeing both hands. As she began the spell, a familiar sharp pain jabbed into her temple. She felt colder as a chill penetrated her spine and legs, traveling down her arms and up her neck and head. Bone-cracking frost licked the inside of her skin, giving her goose bumps.

Rowan and Alara didn't notice she was struggling. They had their eyes closed and focused on the upcoming spell. Cadrissa tried to push the grip out of her mind, and she could for a moment, but it returned, desperate to gain control. Fear was threatening to swallow her whole and end the spell as well. What was happening?

"Grastal yorn-leem. Rasbin olin ion olin contris." She forced the words from her mouth, drawing in a hard breath to uncap the reservoir of magical might she somehow still possessed. In fact, she thought there was more power inside her now than before she'd donned the necklace.

It wasn't natural and she knew it, but she was starting to like it too . . . the sensation of unlimited magical strength for whatever she wanted. To have such power at her fingertips was tempting. She was certain it was one of the factors that allowed her to hold out against the cold clutches threatening to overtake her before the spell had ended.

"Resbin olin tress." She forced out the rest of the words, and then the world was swallowed in darkness. She saw the night sky wrap about her and realized she was looking out over the vast expanse above Tralodren as she had seen it from the roc's clutches not that long ago. She, Alara, and Rowan were floating in it, holding hands and concentrating on where they were going. And because Cadrissa's eyes remained open, she was the only one who could see the growing specter racing toward them.

It was Cadrith. Not in the flesh, but as she'd first encountered him in his skeletal form—the one that had most frightened her when she'd been his prisoner. His fleshless hands reached out for her as his ghostly frame towered over everything else like some decayed giant. Cadrissa could do nothing, say nothing. All her energy and focus were tied to keeping the spell set on reaching its destination. She couldn't react without jeopardizing their lives.

She tried to speed up the spell—forcing it to end in Frigia—but something wasn't right. She could only watch as Cadrith's hand ensnared her. Vise-like, yet ethereal, its arctic grip shook her to her core. She could feel her mind getting tugged from her like a child being yanked from a mother's grasp. She could feel Cadrith entering her body, mind, and spirit, possessing her with his own chilled, dark presence.

Suddenly, she remembered her nightmare in Arid Land, the one where Cadrith had tossed her aside to that horrid tentacled mass in the darkness. The sensation was the same, but now the dark entity had been replaced with Cadrith. She'd been able to push those violent memories and fears down, but at that moment they came bursting back to the forefront, fears and memories spilling out.

Yet even in the midst of such turmoil Cadrissa felt something else. The necklace was heating up, driving Cadrith's frosty presence away from her. In fact, the heat quickly began to radiate over her whole body, around her head and out of her hands, filling both Alara and Rowan with the same warmth. A moment later, a sudden force unnervingly similar to the punching sensation she'd felt when Cadrith had used her to cast his spells in Arid Land exploded in her gut.

The blow set off a chain reaction all around the trio. Cadrith and the night sky faded from sight in a shower of rainbow-colored sparks. She was falling. The attack had caused them to separate their hands. They were all now plummeting like meteorites toward the planet. Cadrissa could see the continents swimming under them as they fell closer and closer to the Northlands. The sight reminded her of the roc crashing into all those pine trees back on Arid Land.

Shoving the bile-producing fear aside, she focused on what was at hand. There was still the spell. It was still in effect. She could sense its presence all around them. It was their best hope—their *only* hope—of getting out of this in one piece. She clamped her eyes shut, holding tightly to the image in her mind of the place she still hoped they'd all reach: Lann Mirson's tower.

CHAPTER 13

A WISE WIZARD KNOWS TO KEEP A CLOSE EYE ON HIS STUDENTS.
FOR NO MATTER THEIR INTENTIONS, THEY WILL ALL BETRAY YOU IN THE END.

—**Raston Tolle, Telborian wizard king**
Reigned 34 BV–6 BV

Cadrith stopped what he was doing. He knew something wasn't right. Something that involved a certain contingency plan he'd put into place with Cadrissa. Thanks to the Mirdic Tome he'd been able to find a way to secure his victories as well as overcome any losses. But it wasn't as complete as it should have been—there was something blocking him somehow . . .

You're wasting time. Nuhl's voice hissed in his head. *And my patience.*

"I thought I saw something," he said, resuming his search of the rubble that remained of his tower. He had to be careful. Nuhl already knew about the scepter, and with part of the entity already flowing in him, he wasn't sure how much of his own plans could be discerned. He did his best to conceal both his plans and additional actions, hoping such efforts wouldn't jeopardize anything else in which he was engaged. That said, should Nuhl suspect something was off, all such efforts would be wasted.

He was able to get a short glimpse of a spell being cast by Cadrissa. They had been going somewhere, but something wasn't entirely right. He got the sense he was looking into both the past and the present at the same time. He didn't know how to really describe it, only that he knew he'd done it. Could all gods really see into the past? He thought such things were only in the realm of Saredhel. Perhaps as he mastered his new nature, he'd uncover still more hidden truths long kept secret from mortals.

Cadrissa had been trying to go somewhere—somewhere crosswise to his purposes—and he had tried to stop them . . . and then . . . Then something blocked him. But what? Cadrissa should be fairly weak by now, making his efforts all the easier. He was reminded of how strong she'd been in Arid Land—even after all he'd done to her right up to Galba's circle. How she could still be as strong even now wasn't clear.

What was clear was that she had the scepter. He saw that much in the brief glimpse afforded him. Which meant Galba had, no doubt, given it to her and whoever had survived his first assault to use against him. Then it was a good thing he was here making his final preparations. And a good thing that what he'd earlier enacted with Cadrissa was autonomous, sparing him the time and mental effort required for his present task.

The mess that had been his tower was obviously the work of Endarien. He'd probably destroyed it in a fit of wrath at being denied Cadrith's death. He could rebuild later if he wished, but knowing now that he was going to be able to flee Tralodren for the cosmos beyond had started filling his thoughts with all the better possibilities now within his reach. Why settle for just one world when he could have dozens or more? And who knew what other insights to still greater power were just waiting for him to find them?

So far he'd managed to sort through a good portion of the burnt stones and damaged debris. There wouldn't be much of anything left anyway, he knew, but the tome . . . That would have survived. He was sure of it. He had been stalling for some time, looking to make his plans with Cadrissa a reality so he could bring everything into alignment before he departed for Thangaria. Now that things had taken a turn, he knew he wasn't going to be getting much more leeway. Already he felt Nuhl's irritated pressure growing inside and upon him.

Never had he felt so much energy coursing through his veins. When he'd reached godhood he thought he'd found the pinnacle of his being, but now he knew there was something beyond him. Something he both feared and craved. He was determined to master it and make it his own rather than be at its whim. But all was still going to plan.

He'd bought himself the time needed to finish weaving the last few threads of his new plot into place. All he had to do was wait until the right time to make his final move. Until then he needed to keep pretending to obey as best he could. For the present, Nuhl's desires and his own overlapped.

Another motion of his hand scattered rock from a small pile on his right. But this time he stopped for a closer inspection. A familiar book cover poked through the rubble. The binding was torn and the cover itself had been gouged in a couple of places, but it appeared solid enough. He beckoned the object to him. It rose up and then floated to the dark god as if toted by some invisible servant. As it came, a few pages fluttered free from the spine. Cadrith didn't mind. He could see they weren't important. What he wanted was still inside the volume's guts.

I've indulged you long enough. Nuhl's voice was hot in Cadrith's ears. "I'm almost ready."

Almost? Cadrith thought he could feel a snapping mouth nearly take off his right ear. *You've done nothing but give them more time to prepare.*

"No matter what they try, they'll fail. You know that as well as I," he said, taking hold of the book. When he did, he was reminded of his now greater size. It might have been a slightly hefty book to the common man, but in his new frame it was more akin to a small journal. He flipped to the middle of the book, ignoring the pages drunkenly spilling out as they came undone from their stitching. It had served his former master Raston well and would do so for Cadrith one last time. He stopped when he saw what he'd been searching for. There were a few diagrams drawn on the vellum amid fanciful script. These were images of a scepter with some notes and information about what Raston thought was the incantation to activate it. Yes, this would do nicely for his last fail-safe.

He tore the page free and let the book drop to his feet like so much refuse. That was all it was now that he had the full power and soon the greater knowledge of the gods. Whatever Raston had thought he'd mastered had been eclipsed by what Cadrith had already achieved. He was above the best of the wizard kings and soon would be above the rest of the gods . . . and then *their* masters.

"Now I'm ready," he said, folding the page before stuffing it into one of the pockets of his black robes.

Then take hold of what I've given you and put an end to the pantheon. Get to Thangaria and destroy them all.

Cadrith was only too happy to comply. A burst of azure flame went out from his hand. It consumed the rest of what remained of his tower and books. He was done here. Done with Tralodren. Done with the gods. The cosmos was open wide before him, and he would take his fill of it. Already dreaming of the possibilities, he faded from sight. Behind him the last pieces of his mortal life quickly crumbled into ash.

Frigia had long been divided between the Nordicans and the Jotun. Of all the Northlands, Frigia was the most dominated by these giants, who'd made their claim to the land in ancient times. Ever since, an uneasy tension had existed between the two major races, each testing the other with expeditions along their borders in the hopes of gaining more plunder and terrain to govern. A common place for such contention was in the Spears of Shiril. This mountainous region was constantly troubled by invasions, counterinvasions, and wandering bands of monstrous races who'd managed to scrape out an existence among the dragons, linnorms, and Trolls that called the region home.

Like much of Frigia, the area could tell many a bloody saga to those who'd listen, but it also held some secrets—one of which was about to be discovered by the three figures who'd just appeared at the base of a mountain. There was no grace to their landing. None of them was expecting to be tossed face first into the hard earth with as much care as someone dumping garbage into a pit. One moment they'd been holding hands with their eyes closed and the next they were tumbling over the ground in the hope of doing as little damage to themselves as possible.

Alara made a side roll after striking the rocky surface, spinning out of the way just in time for Rowan to come to a stop after a short, clumsy somersault. Only Cadrissa managed to avoid a rough landing. A quick spell caught and held her a hand's breadth above the earth. If she hadn't stopped, her face would have slammed straight into a particularly nasty-looking stone about twice the size of her head. Letting out a slow sigh, she forced the spell to stand her upright and set her gently down. All the while she kept a firm grip on the scepter.

"Everyone all right?" Alara asked after sitting up, inspecting herself as well as the others.

"Yeah," Rowan said as he slowly rose to his feet. Once righted, he took in Cadrissa with a curious gaze. "You trying to get us killed?"

"There must have been some counterspells affecting things," she explained, conveniently leaving out the part about her struggle with Cadrith.

"I don't see the tower," said Alara while accepting Rowan's assistance in standing. "Are you sure we're in Frigia?"

"We're further east than we were," she replied, observing that the time had changed again.

"Everything okay?" Alara noticed her growing wonder and unease.

"Yeah. It's just—I think we moved back into the present somehow."

"Was that part of the spell?"

She paused, pushing away thoughts of Cadrith again. "No." Shaking her head helped shift the memory completely from her mind.

"So it must have been Galba again," offered Rowan as he came up alongside Alara.

"I guess." It was sighed more than spoken.

"Then how much time have we lost?" Rowan tried gauging the heavens for himself. "It looks close to when we first left Galba."

"So then we have some time," said Alara, "but not much. But are we absolutely sure we're where we need to be?"

"We're in the Northlands," Rowan confirmed.

"But in Frigia?"

"I'm sure of it," Cadrissa replied, confident that much of the spell had worked. "We just got . . . detoured from our original destination."

"*How* detoured?" Alara's raised eyebrow momentarily made Cadrissa's shoulders tighten. The sooner they could get some answers and start moving, the better—for everyone.

The mage craned her head, taking in the surrounding peaks. Desperate for answers, Cadrissa frantically scanned the distance, rubbing the necklace with her free hand. Her anxiety soon parted, however, with a knowing grin. "There," she said, pointing with the scepter to a large structure on a mountain peak.

"And how are we supposed to get up there?" Rowan asked. It was hard to see any details from where they stood, but it was obviously large and a good distance from them, with no discernible way to reach it.

Alara and Rowan both turned to Cadrissa, who appeared lost in her thoughts, absently fingering her necklace. They exchanged an uncertain glance. "Cadrissa?" Alara softly inquired while taking a step forward. If she heard Alara, there wasn't any indication. "Cadrissa?" Alara repeated. The wizardess suddenly shook herself from her stupor, staring Alara clearly in the face.

"I think I have just the spell to get us there."

"Another spell?" Rowan cautiously stepped up beside Alara. "Isn't that dangerous? You said the counterspells—"

"Can be broken through." A fresh confidence surged through the mage.

"How?" Alara asked.

"The necklace." Cadrissa smiled.

Another uneasy glance passed between Rowan and Alara. If Cadrissa noticed, she didn't care. She'd fixed her gaze upon Lann's keep.

"I don't like this," Rowan whispered to Alara.

"Me either, but the best thing for her and us is to get to this keep, find what we need, and leave."

"We should get her some help," Rowan gently countered.

"And where would we find it around here?"

"She could cast another spell and take us to—"

"And leave behind the only chance we have of saving Tralodren?" Alara's voice raised with her question. "If we turn back now, it won't matter if she gets help or not. Tralodren will be lost."

Rowan nodded grudgingly.

"We just need to keep a close eye on her. If she gets too bad you can take her back with you while I—"

"We leave together," said Rowan. "I'm not going to leave you here alone."

"And I'm not going to give up," Alara added. "I thought you knew that about me."

"And what would you do if you found it?" Rowan crossed his arms. "You're not even a wizard—what good would it do you then?"

Alara sighed. "One thing at a time. Let's just worry about getting inside first."

Rowan gave a small nod of agreement.

Alara tried getting the mage's attention. "Cadrissa?" She didn't respond, her eyes locked on the keep high above them.

"Cadrissa?" Rowan half shouted. Startled, she came back into the present.

"I think I have just the spell to get us there."

"Yes," Alara said as she stepped up before the mage, "you told us that before."

"I did?" Confusion swept over Cadrissa's face.

"You said you think that necklace is trying to help us," Alara continued. "Why do you say that?"

"Because it's been talking to me, and telling me how we need to get to the tower, and what we need to do once we get there." Cadrissa didn't change her pose, but her voice grew more distant, like she was slipping back into a stupor. "I didn't understand it at first, but now it's talking to me clearer and clearer. It wants to help us. And wants to share its power with me." Her face was washed with delight. "So much power . . ."

"Cadrissa?" Alara dared a hand on her shoulder. The action pulled her back from her trance. "You all right?"

"Fine," she said. When Alara's stare didn't relent, Cadrissa laughed nervously. "I'm fine, Alara. Really. If you're ready, I can cast that spell and take us right up to the front gates." The smile that followed was more a veneer than anything else. "You ready?"

"I guess," said Rowan. "You want us to hold hands again?"

"No. I have something much easier in mind." She whispered some indiscernible words and then all three of them were hovering a short distance above the ground in a violet-tinted bubble. "This should get us there without risking any more of those counterspells."

No one said anything as they rose into the sky. The bubble was transparent, allowing an unobstructed view in all directions. This proved helpful in looking over the hard rock of the mountain into which Lann's keep was built. The faint outline of a stairway traced its way down the peak like a faded scar. The stairs themselves had long since crumbled away, making the bubble the only way the trio could have reached the ledge jutting out before the keep's main level, serving as a type of outer courtyard.

The gates were made of iron-reinforced wood and still stood strong after many centuries. The walls were windowless at the base but gained a few at higher levels as the two towers jutted out of the mountain. Both had conical shingled roofs which had also withstood weather and time without damage.

"It looks more like a fortress than a wizard's tower," Rowan observed as they rose up to the ledge.

"You were expecting some sort of palatial estate?"

"No, it just looks like a keep more than a palace."

"Probably with good reason." Cadrissa guided the bubble to the ledge. "Wizard kings often had a good many enemies, and I suspect his fellow Nordicans weren't too favorably inclined toward him either."

"So how do we get inside?" Alara carefully studied the keep, searching its various angles.

Cadrissa peered over her shoulder. "From what I've read, Lann was a bit of a recluse who protected his residence from anything, whether a common wandering animal or a giant. He did these spells in layers. So it will be just a matter of pulling them back, layer by layer, until the way is clear."

"Are you sure you're up to that?" Alara inquired cautiously. "You've been through a lot recently."

"I have it covered," she said with another dreamy smile before returning her attention to the keep.

Rowan and Alara exchanged another uncertain glance.

•●•

Facing the gate, Cadrissa started reciting the words to the perfect spell for this situation under her breath while her free hand clasped the necklace. She was aware of the habit she'd adopted but wasn't able to do much about it. It took all her energy to keep the whispers out of her head and remain fully in control of her thoughts. Her focus came and went in waves, and it was taxing when she was engaged in casting spells, where she had to be precise.

For a moment she thought she'd run into more of Cadrith's attempts to hinder her efforts. She was thankful when none manifested. She didn't think she had the mental mettle to stand against him anymore—though it wasn't her that had stood against him before, but the necklace. As before, the circular pendant grew warm in her hand as she cast the last of the spell. The ancient gates started to shimmer with an amber aura, letting her know all was progressing as it should. Now she just had to finish the last part.

"Open," she whispered amid the murmurs in her head.

Nothing happened.

"Open." Cadrissa spoke the word again, this time with greater volume. *Focus. You have to focus*, she thought. *Feel the words as they are spoken.* She recalled the words of one of her instructors.

Closing her eyes, she gave herself to the spell, focusing all her strength upon it. As she did, the necklace took hold of her. She felt as though she were on fire—consumed by an incredible heat from inside to outside. So much heat, in fact, that she broke out in a sweat. There was a tidal wave of power swelling inside her. So much power birthed from such force she couldn't have kept it back even if she wanted to. The revelation was as alarming as it was intoxicating.

She could understand why Cadrith and many of those who had followed the path of power were so consumed with it. To wield such power in her veins made her feel like she could do anything. With but a whim and a word she could manifest her will all around her, raising her station in the cosmos to the very heels of the gods themselves . . . Shaking her head, she caught herself midthought. These weren't her thoughts—not the ones she wanted to concentrate on. She would always follow the path of knowledge. She could never be tempted by the path of power . . . Never.

"Open," Cadrissa repeated, almost shouting. The tidal wave inside her surged forward and crashed upon the keep. When it did, there was an outpouring of such magnitude she couldn't believe it had all been stored inside her . . . But it wasn't, was it? No, the power had been—and still was—stored in the necklace. She wasn't doing *any* of this. It was the necklace using her, as Cadrith had done before. She understood this with crystal clarity before collapsing into darkness.

The bubble holding them burst as a nimbus of energy, shimmering like liquid amber, raced for the keep, ramming into the protective barriers surrounding it. A ferocious display of rainbow-colored light and energy was unleashed as various protective spells fell like dominoes. Thankfully, Cadrissa hadn't left them very far off the ground. Rowan was able to land on his feet, as was Alara. He wasn't fast enough to catch Cadrissa, though. She dropped to the ledge without much harm. Rowan stood still, watching the last of the colors fade before turning to Alara.

"She okay?" she asked.

"Nothing from the drop," said Rowan as he looked Cadrissa over from where he stood. "But who knows about what happened before then."

"She just might have overtaxed herself. It was a pretty powerful spell."

Rowan gave a thoughtful nod, then asked, "What now?"

"I suppose we try the doors," she said as she started walking toward them.

Rowan bent down and slung Cadrissa over his shoulder. At the higher altitude the wind had picked up and now whistled about his head and body.

"No. No . . ." Cadrissa's voice was faint and weak. "Put me down, Dugan."

Rowan ignored her, taking it as a sign of her being well enough to face whatever was before them. "You're *really* just going to open the doors?" he asked Alara.

"You have any better ideas?" She'd nearly reached them.

"Not yet," Rowan said, nearing Alara's side.

She pushed against one of the doors with her shoulder. It didn't open upon her first effort but with the second, a grinding creak accompanied the door's inward movement. Alara continued pushing until enough space was created for them to enter. Once inside, Rowan gently set Cadrissa against the plain white marble wall of the dimly illuminated room.

"*This* is a wizard king's keep?"

"Disappointed?" Alara said from Rowan's side.

"I just thought it wouldn't be so . . . *empty*." Save for a few sconces giving off faint light among other lifeless ones lining the wall, the room swam in puddles of darkness. Though large, it wasn't endless, and Rowan could see a set of double doors—white pine by the look of them—just on the edge of the darkness. The ceiling was another matter. He surmised it had to be at least twenty feet or more in height, most of it hidden beyond the light of the flickering sconces. They seemed more like stars in the night sky as he stared heavenward.

"It's been deserted for some time. I'm surprised it's even stood this long—*especially* after Cadrissa's performance."

He noted Cadrissa was still struggling for consciousness. "Do you think it was all from the necklace?"

"My guess is yes."

"It looks like things are getting worse," said Rowan. "If that necklace can destroy a wizard king's spells and it's already gotten ahold of her—"

"There's still nothing we can do, only try to find what we're looking for faster than before."

"But where do we start? This place is huge."

"We'll have to just start combing each room, hoping we'll find something to help us." There was a slight weariness in her voice. He didn't blame her. He wasn't too excited about turning over every rock either. "Hopefully, Cadrissa can help us stay on the right path."

"That's a pretty big gamble."

"It's also about all we have." Alara tried to keep herself optimistic, but she wasn't doing such a great job.

"She's right." Both turned to see Cadrissa struggling to stand up against the wall.

Alara instinctively went to her aid. "You should rest. That last spell took a lot out of you."

"Out of *all* of us," Rowan muttered under his breath.

"I'll be fine." Cadrissa shooed away Alara's hand as she managed to stand upright once again. "The longer we stay, the greater the chance of more dangers finding us."

"*Dangers?*" Rowan's hand moved to his sword hilt.

"I've broken the counterspells. And that will allow us to move about freely without magical impairment, but it also means all spells that were at work in this tower have been removed."

"So what does *that* mean?" Rowan was growing unsettled by his surroundings.

"It means that any spell that was used to, say, hold up a load-bearing wall or contain a creature that had been held prisoner for research or some such thing has now been removed."

"Great," he muttered into the empty hallway.

"There's not much we can do about it now," said Alara. "So let's just get moving. You sure you're up to this?" she asked Cadrissa. "If you like we can wait—"

"I'll make it."

"Did you want me to hold the scepter?"

"No." Cadrissa brought the object closer to her side. "I've got it."

"Then let's go." Rowan pulled out his sword, and Alara mirrored his example.

Cadrissa gave a wave of her hand, sending new life into all the sconces lining the walls with a sudden burst of cold but helpful white flame. "Might help to have some light." Alara shot Rowan a questioning look, which he shared before following the wizardess as silently as possible.

CHAPTER 14

HELII IS ONLY FOR THOSE WHOSE EXISTENCE HAS BEEN TRIED
BY THE CRUCIBLE OF THIS LIFE AND FOUND WORTHY.

—The Solarium

The darkness fled as Dugan opened his eyes. He found himself in the midst of an incredible landscape. One he knew he couldn't have survived if he were still alive on Tralodren. He stood amid fire and lava, smoking volcanoes, and a sun's intense heat radiating from every direction. Oddly there wasn't any of that sun's light, which apparently was unable to penetrate the charcoal-gray clouds overhead. Molten rock in organ-red shades splashed and splattered in rivers and pools amid byzantine igneous formations. These glowed in a dirty yellow cast from the lava's glow and the periodic jets of fire spurting through tiny fissures in the rough terrain.

Why anyone would want to spend eternity here was beyond Dugan. If he had his old lungs, they would have been burning from the thick atmosphere. However, he now found he had a new pair suited to breathing the harsh air. Placing a hand over his chest, he registered a familiar rhythm. It was a small comfort.

As best he understood, he had a body again, or he at least *felt* alive again, as opposed to how he'd felt in Mortis. Other than his skin having a more bronzed appearance—like one who has spent their whole life under the sun—he didn't really feel or believe he appeared different than he always had.

He was surprised by this rapid transition in what was to him just a few breaths, but he put further thoughts of it from his mind. He needed to figure out just what was going on and how he would deal with it. As far as he could see there was nothing alive in this brimstone-caked expanse. Worse still, the emptiness just repeated itself for miles, only broken up here and there in the distance by craggy reddish-brown mountains. If this was Helii, it didn't seem he'd have much company during his stay. But, as with many things he was discovering, not everything was as it first seemed.

Two strong hands grabbed his arms. "Welcome to Helii, Dugan," a low, measured voice said in his left ear. Turning toward it, Dugan was greeted with a fantastic sight: a bluish-gray human torso covered with a bronze cuirass, sitting atop the lower half of a serpent. On its shoulders was the head of a bull with a bristly black beard covering its lower jaw. A pair of pure-black eyes reflected Dugan's amazement.

Ebony bovine horns glistened in the constant firelight as the bull's head nodded a greeting. "We've been expecting you." Its mouth spoke as plainly as any man's, though it was more surreal than anything he could have dreamed. The sharp teeth inside only added to the figure's unsettling nature.

"Who are you and how do you know my name?" Dugan's hands instinctively went to his waist, but he quickly found he was defenseless. Nothing but his copper robe graced his frame.

This wasn't the case with the creature, whose wide belt held a great sword in its scabbard. Dugan paid special attention to the weapon and the blood-red whip coiled opposite it. The figure's bronze bracers displayed a painful motif: sharp, jagged edges which seemed to mimic tongues of flame. The sword was mostly hidden in the ruby-studded scabbard, but the tiger-eye pommel was quite impressive.

"We've been sent to collect you upon your arrival," another voice answered. This one was from Dugan's right. It was much more animalistic and rushed than the bull-headed being's, peppered with snarls and even a growl.

Dugan jerked toward the new voice and saw a creature who resembled a humanoid wolf: bipedal with wolf-like legs but a human torso and hands ending in sharp claws. Unsettling wild yellow eyes gleamed as the creature smiled a predatory grin, revealing its deadly teeth. A wispy goatee trailed from its muzzle. Dugan noticed the sword on this one as well and the bronze chain mail shirt. Two well-armed potential foes in a forsaken place . . . not the best situation to find himself in. Then everything hit him all at once.

"You're furies!" He half spoke, half whispered. "I thought you were just a legend."

"We are very real," the wolfish fury returned. Both he and the other were a full foot taller than Dugan, and he caught sight of its curled ram's horns on either side of its head as it stared down at him. "And we take our assignments *very* seriously." Except for the chain mail shirt, the creature was naked. His gunmetal-gray fur covered him from head to clawed toe. He appeared as strong and well versed in physical combat as his bull-headed companion—a paragon of physical aggression.

Dugan called to mind the old tales he'd heard swapped in the arena about furies. He didn't know much about them, but he'd heard it said they had some sway over matters of revenge. As to whether they were free agents or enforcers of Rheminas' will, the tales never seemed too clear. Gladiators often invoked them for aid in staying alive long enough to take their revenge on their chosen enemy in the arena. Some even petitioned for retribution against their masters, Dugan among them.

"You're a Furor?" Dugan asked the wolf-headed fury. He returned a small nod. "And you're a Keraff?"

"Kezef," the bull-headed fury corrected.

"You think I'm going to run off?" Dugan struggled against their grip. "I'm here now. I couldn't escape Rheminas even if I tried."

"You're not going to see Rheminas," said the Furor.

This didn't make any sense. He'd been sold to Rheminas and was now here as his property. Why didn't he want his possession delivered to him? What further bump in the path to his final destiny would he have to endure? A beating? Another change of clothes?

"And we have a deadline to maintain," said the Kezef as he slithered into the lead, tugging Dugan forward.

"Come on," the Furor growled.

He could do little but comply. Their grips were uncompromising. He couldn't push past them, no matter how hard he struggled for release. He tried to see more of the terrain he was hurried through, but it all was so alien to him and their march through it so fast he didn't really have much of a chance. After some time of walking, which brought back memories of his trek through Mortis, he spied a tall cylindrical structure rising among low hills in the distance.

"We were told to ask you about a certain scepter," said the Kezef. "There was one you had with you back on Tralodren, was there not?"

"Yes." Dugan watched the cylindrical structure draw nearer. "But I didn't get to use it. Gilban was supposed to." He noted the structure had no roof. The more he contemplated it, the more it reminded him of a chimney.

"What was it supposed to do?" asked the Furor.

"I guess it was meant to weaken Cadrith. Gilban said it could make gods and divinities or maybe even destroy them. Little good it did us, though." He could now make out two large brass doors at the base of the cylinder. Each was decorated with the image of a winged humanoid in bas-relief. If he hadn't known better, Dugan would have sworn they looked something like what he heard angels were supposed to look like. And angels weren't something he was expecting to find in Helii.

"What was the scepter called?" the Furor asked.

"The Scepter of Night, I think. I didn't really pay too much attention to that part."

"Good enough," said the Kezef as together he and the Furor brought Dugan before the two doors. They opened into a large circular room, into which Dugan was escorted. Immediately, he noted the bronze hexagonal tiles lining the walls. Each had to be as big as his head, and they climbed up the walls into the hazy sky far above. The floor was polished black marble and shimmered with the reflection of the column of yellow flame flickering in the center of the room.

This blazing column had to be at least twenty feet tall; the curved walls of the room climbed for another twenty feet beyond that. He could smell the sulfur from the flame as well as feel its intense heat. It was the hottest flame he'd yet felt in this world of fire. And then he started putting things together. It was now clear what fate awaited him. A fitting one, he supposed, given how Rheminas had burned him in life. Now the god would do so in Dugan's afterlife.

"Where are we?" he asked the Kezef, who seemed the calmer of the two and thus a better one to pester with questions. The furies had stopped some yards from the dancing fire, releasing their hold upon him. Another clear sign there really was no escape. This truly was it—the end of his old life and the start of his afterlife . . . his final fate.

"The place where you're going to get your reward. Now step into the flame." The Kezef pointed at the burning column. Dugan tried to see into it—past it even—but could see nothing save the flame's impenetrable core. The all-consuming flame.

"Get moving," said the Furor while giving Dugan a rude shove.

He lurched a few steps, stopped to take some short breaths, and then continued with a measured march. Dugan strode with purpose, taking one last bit of fatalistic joy that these were the last steps he was making as a free man. Once he was inside the flames, that last taste of liberty would be gone for good. He would be Rheminas' forever. What that eternity would be like he had no clue. He'd always imagined himself being chained once more as he had been in the arena, tortured or locked away, or something worse. In truth, he didn't know what might befall him, but it was too late to worry about that now.

Even as he neared the towering flame, he remembered the truth he'd learned from Galba. Acting on fear had brought him here as surely as the baited hook snares the fish and reels it in. Hindsight was always the clearest and cruelest form of vision. There were obvious snares that could have been avoided, lies that could have been seen through, if he'd been in his right mind to think and see clearly. Instead he'd let hatred, fear, and his lust for revenge blind him to anything else. He saw what he wanted to see, believed whatever he wanted to be true.

As his robe began to spark and flame away from his body, Dugan could see how he'd chosen to be a slave even after he'd attained physical freedom. A slave to fear. At first, fear had served as a comforting lie, but it had slithered back into the shadows of his mind and forged his chains. And he knew now that how he'd tended his thoughts had been the key. That was the gateway—as he'd learned from Cracius and Tebow—to his spirit. It was too late to change his fate, but not too late—at least for a moment—to reflect upon what might have happened if he'd never given bitterness a foothold, hoping it would somehow change the future.

He reached out to the fire. It didn't feel like anything. It was like touching empty air. He latched on to this clear and truly free vision as he stepped into the column of towering flame. Keeping the thought tethered to his heart, he closed his eyes and waited for what was to come. It was his last thought before all fell into darkness . . . the flames consuming all . . .

• ● •

And then he was aware once more.

"Arise."

Dugan didn't know who had said it or when, only that the word had been spoken and he felt compelled to obey. He opened his eyes and saw that he was still inside the flames. He could also see outside them, as the flames had become strangely transparent. Beyond them were the furies. Both were watching him but now from farther below. He wondered if he was perhaps hovering above the ground. No. He could feel his feet securely resting on the floor.

"Come forth," commanded the Kezef.

Dugan watched a large bronze-skinned leg step out of the flames. It was long and thick with muscle. Stranger still, it was his own! Eager for answers, Dugan studied his hands, taking in their massive size. He was a giant! A giant with bronze skin.

"Put these on," the Furor said, lifting a pile of garments above his head. It was then Dugan understood he was naked. He dared a closer look at himself—as best he could manage—and was overcome with emotion. His flesh was a brilliant bronze hue. There was no hair on any of his body. Not even his now-bald head, which he affirmed by passing a hand over his smooth skull. But he was more surprised at two new developments: he no longer had any genitalia and now possessed a set of peacock wings.

"You're now a fellow servant of Rheminas," said the Kezef. "You're one of the Galgallim."

"Galgallim?" Dugan was shocked at how his voice sounded. It was still his voice, but at the same time it wasn't. Something new was there—a resonance birthed from a sense of command he'd never known in life. "Aren't those—"

"Avenging angels," the Furor interrupted while Dugan donned a simple white sleeveless tunic. Crafted with skill, it fell to his knees and felt a suitable garment to wear. Next he put on the tall black leather sandals he discovered standing beside him. "You're one of their rank." This wasn't what he'd been expecting at all. To go from thinking he'd take the place of some log in an eternal bonfire to this . . .

"And you have an important mission to undertake," added the Kezef, "so be quick about your dressing."

The final piece of his garb rested beside the sandals. It was a gold, diamond-encrusted breastplate with glowing silver runes carved on the outer edges. He had no idea what the runes stood for, though he recognized the script from the statue of Sidra he'd seen earlier in Mortis. He sensed they were important, and he should be proud of wearing them boldly on his chest. He donned this piece of armor, thick leather straps fixing it between his new wings, which remained free of his tunic via a set of clever slits in the cloth.

"Your sword is a tool of judgment," said the Kezef while lifting the massive blade, which took some effort to get over his head and into Dugan's reach. It was a wonderful weapon to behold: a broad sword with a ruby-encrusted handle. It rested in a finely crafted cordovan leather scabbard etched with more runes he couldn't decipher but somehow knew were important.

"Use it well." The Kezef's dark eyes beamed with what Dugan supposed could be pride.

Dugan took the weapon, studied it for a moment, then tied it about his waist. He felt more complete somehow, like he was finding more of himself with each new piece of armor and dress given him. The Furor tossed two large bracers up to him. Dugan caught them with one hand and inspected them in wonder. These were of gold and studded with onyx, emerald, and lapis lazuli. Amid the oval-cut gems were spirals of shimmering gold arranged in a truly mesmerizing fashion. He couldn't wait to put them on and feel them against his naked new skin. Somehow these were also very important—an important part of his new identity.

"You're here because Rheminas favors you," the Kezef informed Dugan. "This is your place now and forever."

"This is what I sold my soul for?"

"No." The Furor snorted sarcastically, bursting the bubble of euphoria that had been swelling around Dugan. "You were raised to this position when you carried out Rheminas' wishes regarding that cult in Haven. You were acting as a Galgalli then, and your success impressed Rheminas enough to bring you into his service once you'd arrived on Helii."

Dugan tried to make sense of what he was hearing. "So by getting my revenge against the cultists—"

"You were proving your worth for this position," said the Kezef. Regardless of how he came to the position, he found great delight in his new form. Somehow it just seemed to fit him . . . to *be* him.

"Here." The Furor drew Dugan's attention to a black silken object in his outstretched hand. Even folded, it appeared oversized in the Furor's uplifted palm. "Your final garment and the authority to complete your task."

Dugan bent down and retrieved the item. Unfolding it revealed a unique combination of mask and cowl. In some ways it reminded him of the masks the followers of Shador had worn—as it cloaked most of the upper half of his face. In reality, he supposed it was closer to an executioner's hood with its opening for his mouth and chin. Besides the unique design it also had fine writing on the fabric that covered the forehead. It was tiny and so artistically rendered Dugan wondered if the marks were even words at all. But he was sure they followed the same style of script as the rest of the writing he'd already seen. And though he couldn't read it, he knew it was important.

"This mask is what declares your authority to judge and the one who must receive your judgment," the Kezef continued.

"Put it on," the Furor insisted. "There's not much time. The judgment has been decreed and now has to be enforced." Dugan obeyed, pulling the cowl over his head.

"Now listen to what has been decreed and what you are to do," said the Kezef. "No Galgalli has ever failed in their mission. However, should *you* fail, it will be the doom of all, for none will be able to stand against what's coming. All of the pantheon are gathering in Thangaria. They plan to fight a war against one whom they've marked for judgment. That judgment has been placed on your mask." The Kezef stared right into Dugan's eyes. "Cadrith Elanis must die."

Dugan's eyes narrowed. Somehow he could feel the words on his mask burning into his head. When the Kezef spoke the order, it told him all he needed to know to find him and how to deal with him as the gods had decreed. It was at once both odd and familiar, like taking up an old skill you've half forgotten.

"I understand," said Dugan.

"But before you confront him," the Kezef continued, "Rheminas has one other task for you to complete."

CHAPTER 15

THIS IS FRIGIA, THE GRAVEYARD OF MEN.

—**Kestor Morrison, chieftain of the Hawk Tribe**
Reigned 799 BV–659 BV

"What are we looking for exactly?" Rowan asked Cadrissa. She was in front of him, leading them down a dark marble hallway with only the flickering sconces to light their way.

No decoration of any kind adorned the walls; not even relief carvings sprung up to greet them along the way. It was cold, silent, and empty. Like some bleak tomb. A shudder shook his frame at the thought. It was quickly followed by concern for Alara, who kept pace beside Cadrissa as a precaution against future surprises. Rowan insisted on following behind to better secure everyone from the rear.

"Probably a book or a scroll," said the mage.

"Could those have survived after all this time?" Rowan gave the hallway around him one last study, making sure he didn't miss anything. It seemed to stretch on forever, but he knew that to be an illusion. It had to be. Even in their brief exploration he'd seen just how deep Lann had carved into the mountain to build his keep. It was impressive, but couldn't continue indefinitely. At least, that was what Rowan told himself.

"Given the state of the tower and the counterspells still around it," Cadrissa continued, "I'd say it's a *very* safe assumption."

"It seems kind of foolish to keep the instructions for such a weapon, doesn't it?" asked Rowan.

"Not really," Cadrissa returned. "Most wizards record their work in order to study it and see if they can improve upon it."

"And how could you improve such a weapon?" Alara wondered aloud.

"Well"—Cadrissa lifted the scepter as she spoke—"making it *lethal* to gods would be a start, I suppose." Rowan didn't like the tone of Cadrissa's voice, but then he caught himself. Was he reading too much into her actions? Worrying too much about nothing? She was looking and acting better than she had been earlier. Maybe the necklace only had a temporary hold over her . . . Maybe . . .

"So where do you think we should go?" Alara asked.

"Probably upstairs. From what I've read and know about other wizard kings, the lower levels were for their warriors and servants. They didn't do much of anything in them and kept them practical and simple. If we want to find anything, it will be upstairs."

Rowan couldn't help but wonder if one of those "other wizard kings" was really the one who'd abducted her. He also wondered just how much of that encounter still lingered. And recently he'd begun toying with the thought of whether that had anything to do with the necklace. Not the most pleasant thought, but as they continued their silent walk, it was what filled his head.

An occasional small sound broke the stillness. A creak here, a ping there, mixed with random sounds so faint he found himself debating whether they were real. Rowan peered over his shoulder more than once when he thought he heard the sound of a muffled footfall behind him. The swaying darkness beyond didn't allow him to guess what, if anything, it could be. After turning his head for a fourth time only to find nothing, he assumed it was just the wind.

A short while later they found a flight of solid stone stairs. He'd lost all sense of where he was in the structure, not sure if they'd moved closer to one of the towers he'd first seen outside or were somewhere completely different. All he knew was he hoped these steps led to better pickings.

They followed Cadrissa up the steps to yet another hallway, similar to the one they'd just left. This one too was illuminated by the occasional gleam of sconces still eerily burning after all this time—even after Cadrissa's spell had allowed them entrance.

Eventually, they stopped behind Cadrissa in front of a tall, iron-clad wooden door. The door itself was simple and plain, almost rustic. She opened it with minimal effort, leading them into the room. As soon as she had done so, more sconces lining the walls sprung to life. Or rather, they tried to spring to life. Though there were a fair number of sconces in the room, only two—one on the wall opposite the doorway and another on an adjacent wall—flickered with cold white flame upon their entry.

The room itself, like the door, was practical and simple, a place evidently set up for conversation. A fireplace was built into the wall opposite the door. A collection of simple wooden chairs rested around a circular table sitting on a carpet made to look like a mosaic of a battle scene between two human nations Rowan didn't recognize. The two walls to either side held red floor-length tapestries, each emblazoned with a golden dragon. Other than that, a small bookcase sat beside the door with a few old scrolls and dusty tomes resting on its shelves.

Rowan found himself drawn to a bronze statue of some kind of fiendish creature sitting on the top of the bookcase. Probably no more than a foot tall, it was crafted with enough detail to give him a twinge of unease in the pit of his stomach.

"This could be something worthwhile." Cadrissa made a beeline for the bookcase. Alara and Rowan were more cautious in their assessment. They examined with steady eyes what was, in truth, a very dark room. When they felt all was well, their attention returned to Cadrissa and her feverish digging through the rolled parchment and tomes.

"Anything?" Rowan kept his distance.

"Oh, there's a lot of material here." Cadrissa was more than a little excited at the prospect of getting into such knowledge. "But nothing that can help us with the scepter. This was an understudy's collection."

"And how do you know that?" Alara asked with curiosity.

"It's too plain," said Cadrissa. "A wizard king's main library was much larger—it had to be for them to amass the insight they had."

"Do you know how many apprentices Lann had?" asked Alara. "We don't want to be looking into empty rooms and wasting more time."

"I'm not sure of an exact count," Cadrissa responded amid her wild rummaging, "but I'd guess he'd have had at least a dozen."

"A *dozen?*" Rowan was shocked by such a high count—and of amateur mages at that. "We'd be lucky to find that many in all the Northlands."

"Magic was more common then." Cadrissa moved past Alara and Rowan on her way out of the room. "And it was a sort of status symbol too. Most wizard kings didn't teach too much to their apprentices. It kept them from outshining their masters and possibly even coveting their station.

"Having a bunch of apprentices, though, showed that the wizard king wasn't too worried about those he trained rising to his skill level and also demonstrated how powerful he was because of the desire of so many to be instructed by him." Rowan watched Cadrissa closely as she passed. She was acting more like her normal self, which was good.

"So then how much higher do you think we have to climb?" Alara followed Rowan out of the room.

"I'm not sure." Cadrissa's face became contemplative. "Maybe all the way to the top. These corridors and stairs are more like a maze within a maze." She rested her hand on the necklace, fingering the pendant absently while she thought.

Rowan's heart sank upon seeing the action. "It's definitely bigger than it appeared. He carved his way all over this mountain. It would take us days to—"

A noise from somewhere within the darkness of the hallway snapped everyone's jaw shut. Rowan almost had his shield off his shoulders and on his left forearm by the time he ventured a look beyond the doorway. He didn't see anything, which only made things worse when the second noise came. This one was muffled but louder than the first. However, it was clear it originated from where they'd just come, allowing them the chance to escape down the other part of the hall.

He ducked back inside the room long enough to motion for Cadrissa and Alara to remain silent and start making their way down the hallway. He let them pass while standing guard by the doorway—listening. After giving them enough of a lead, he followed. He was just closing the gap between them when Cadrissa pointed out a familiar sight.

"More stairs," she whispered.

"Good," added Alara. "The sooner we can leave this—"

Another noise froze everyone's step. It was much closer and louder than the previous ones had been.

"Get up those stairs!" Rowan whispered.

Neither Cadrissa nor Alara moved.

A hearty roar filled the hallway. Their stalker was now visible. It was a Troll—and a fairly angry one at that. His ten-foot frame dominated the hallway. With only a breechcloth to cover him, the giant gave Rowan a clear view of his strong but lean reddish-brown flesh and hairy chest and arms. The clawed hands and feet didn't improve his appeal.

Another bellow brought his sharp teeth into clear view; all the while his cruel yellow eyes never took their focus from Rowan. And then there were the curled ram's horns. Rowan had heard old stories of just how deadly they could be in an attack. There were the other tales, too, of how Trolls often enjoyed eating their victims raw—sometimes while even still alive.

"Go!" he shouted, waving them on with his sword. The Troll raised his meaty claw and swiped at him. Rowan blocked it with his shield. The force behind the blow was so strong it caused him to retreat a few steps.

Rowan chanced a glance back and saw it was Cadrissa who led Alara to the stairs. Alara happened to look back at the same time, catching Rowan's eye. Even in the midst of peril, she put on a confident face. The short moment they shared strengthened his resolve.

He saw the Troll's abdomen as the best place to attack. Though his blade only nicked the giant's flesh, drawing out the tiniest river of dark red blood, it was a good sign the Troll could be wounded. He had to use a great deal of muscle to hold back the Troll's counterstrike and slid back a few paces from the blow. He knew he couldn't keep this up for long. Either his shield would break or he'd be shoved onto his back. First blood or not, it was foolish to think he could defeat a Troll. Not even the best Nordic warrior would take up this fight without a great deal of consideration.

He could smell the giant's rancid breath and felt the hot gusts upon his neck and face. An angry claw followed another snarl. Rowan raised his shield in time and blocked it, but was unable to hold his ground, sliding back another foot.

The Troll laughed. The giant was toying with him—playing with his rag doll before he sank his teeth around the neck for the kill. It was clear the Troll knew he had the advantage and was enjoying it.

Rowan knew when he was beaten and began looking for a way out. If he could get to a more defendable position, where he could have some better options, even put his back to the wall—he'd stand a chance of defending Cadrissa and Alara. If he died here, he'd be of no use to them. So he opted to run, Nordic logic aiding the choice.

Swinging and jabbing hard into the towering creature, Rowan felt himself land a few good strikes, though the giant didn't make any sign he'd been wounded. In the fraction of time it took for the Troll to return in kind, Rowan made his move.

He ran backward as fast as he could, keeping his shield and sword leveled until he felt he'd gained enough of a lead. Once he had it, he ran full force for the stairs. But any lead he thought he'd secured quickly evaporated when the Troll gave chase. Pushing himself as fast as he could, Rowan vaulted up the steps.

His joints ached and his body was wet with perspiration. His breath pulsed in rhythm with his frantic heart, pounding faster than the Troll's footfalls behind him.

A bright flash of bronze light rushed over his shoulder so quickly he nearly lost his footing. All he could see were incandescent spots before his eyes. It barely missed him but hit the Troll hard. The giant was struck straight in the chest and rolled backward with the momentum of the blast, tumbling down the steps.

Rowan could hardly move. He dropped to his hands and knees to support his hunched frame. Panting, heart thumping in his ears, and eyes still dancing with tiny green globes of light, he didn't notice Alara and Cadrissa descending the steps to meet him. Only when Alara's hand touched his shoulder did he register anything other than his physical condition.

"You all right?" She gave him a rapid once-over as Cadrissa wandered a few steps down. She was lost in her own thoughts and fingering the necklace.

"Just let me . . . catch my breath." The panting had lessened but he was still winded.

"Is it dead?" Alara asked Cadrissa, who hadn't moved from her place— eyes searching out the oily darkness below with a trance-like stare.

"Yes," Cadrissa said, returning to her full senses, hand dropping from the pendant as she rejoined Rowan and Alara.

"You sure?" Rowan huffed out between gulps of breath. "Trolls can be pretty hard to—"

"I'm sure. The spell was quite lethal."

Rowan stared down at the Troll's body near the base of the stairs. He didn't see any signs of life, but the light and distance made it hard to get a clear view. The one obvious thing he could see, though, was a hole the size of a fist that went clear through his chest and heart. There was no blood, only the circular wound.

Impressed by the sight, Rowan turned to the others. "So why didn't you do that earlier?"

"I didn't know I could until just then." Cadrissa's faint smile was unsettling, chiefly because of the odd disconnect between it and her face—as if she were wearing a mask.

"Do you think there are any more?" He tried to stand. Alara helped him up.

"Probably." Again, there was a strange distance in her voice and face.

"Then we can't afford to stand around wasting time." Rowan drew himself together, wiped his slick brow with his arm, and arched his back in a stretch. He was confident his vision would clear momentarily.

"Where to now?" Alara asked Cadrissa.

"Up." Cadrissa resumed her ascent. She still wasn't fully herself but seemed aware of her surroundings. He took that for a good sign.

Rowan grabbed Alara's wrist, halting her own advance. After he was sure Cadrissa was out of earshot, he asked, "What happened?"

"We were running up the steps, and then she just started casting that spell."

Rowan released his hold. "Nothing else?"

"Not that I could see. But she isn't as bad as before. If we can make better progress, I think—"

"And what if we can't?"

Alara said nothing more, instead taking a few steps past Rowan, leaving him once again guarding the rear.

CHAPTER 16

COINCIDENCE IS REALLY NOTHING MORE THAN PROVIDENCE AT WORK.

—**Baxter Natter, half-elven philosopher**
(1 BV–119 PV)

Thangaria had been readied for war. The rocky debris of the shattered world was filled with the forces assembled in the courtyard around Vkar's palace. With ancient laws and customs suspended, the place of meeting that had always been a neutral ground of peace was now littered with the forces of war, and the pantheon itself willfully supported it. Arriving with a small company of warriors, each of the gods also came in their true form. To face down the same power that had killed their progenitors, they'd need to be present at their full strength. Their enemy would spare nothing, and neither would they.

Shiril's silver eyes watched the growing throngs from atop the outer wall. The gate was closed and a motley collection of watchmen posted. The divinities, gods, and assembled warriors prepared themselves in this tense atmosphere. Whereas before each might have been the others' enemy for now they were united across philosophical divides and various allegiances, forming as solid a resistance as possible.

She'd been one of the first to arrive at the hall, bringing with her some Lords of Earth. She had gathered the smallest force, even compared to Asora's allies, who rallied behind her, but Shiril was still as passionate about this fight as any other.

With the semblance of an athletic fourteen-foot-tall woman, the goddess easily stood out among the growing throng. Her skin was a soft brown, her cascading hair the color of freshly turned earth. Around her neck was a string of rough-hewn gems—emeralds, rubies, topazes, and diamonds. Though unrefined, they still caught the light of the strange illumination of Thangaria's sunless sky, their fire adding to her splendor. A rose-tinted marble circlet with a princess-cut sapphire the size of a plum crowned her as the goddess of earth. A form-fitting, finely scroll-worked steel cuirass encompassed her upper body, resting firmly above her steel-studded black leather belt.

"My lady, more have arrived," a Lord of Earth's low, gravelly voice said from beside her. He was a stern figure, a solidly built male with the look of a titan, standing a foot taller than Shiril with black eyes, short-cropped black hair, and reddish-umber skin. His garb was utilitarian: leather breeches, wide brown belt, and dusty chestnut tunic with small plates of various metals attached to his garments and the toes of his boots. Most of this was covered by his field plate armor.

The chain mail and plates were polished and in good condition. All of them would be using their best—presenting their best—in what would no doubt be a battle remembered throughout the ages. The only finery he wore was on his head. Like all titan lords at important occasions, he wore his diadem. And like those of all the Lords and Ladies of Earth, it was crafted of polished brown chalcedony and studded with brown diamonds and tiger-eye gemstones.

"Who now?" She observed the great gate being opened.

"Rheminas has come with his troops," said the titan lord.

"I see," she said as she watched the ragtag group of furies, Lords of Fire, Lords of Magma, and even a few others she didn't readily identify march through the gates. She knew Rheminas would be eager to join the others in plotting their strategy. He had a love of such things.

In times past there had been an ancient portal on Thangaria that the gods and titans used in traveling to other locations, but it had been ripped away during Nuhl's first assault on the pantheon. Miraculously, it had remained intact, floating on a small piece of planetary debris. It was through this portal all traffic typically arrived. The distance wasn't great enough to hinder movement between the portal and the palace. Though never had so many been brought to the former planet as there were today.

"He's so much like his father," she said, shifting her weight from one foot to the other. The action showcased the segmented plate armor flowing from her trim waist to her ankles, where the steel-capped black shoes took over. Her arms were covered with sleeves of the same armor that flowed and flexed from shoulders to wrists.

"How are you and your kin holding up?" She returned her attention to the Lord of Earth.

"Well enough," he replied. There was no hint of resentment at his present placement or fear for his fate in the upcoming battle.

"I suppose I should see what aid I can offer to my family before it becomes too crowded. I assume Khuthon has already been elected to lead the troops."

"Yes."

"Then the plan's been laid. They just need me to vote on it." Shiril continued watching the scene below her, observing Rheminas' troops making their way inside the courtyard and forming their own unit of warriors among those already gathered. It was becoming quite a motley host indeed.

"See to the comfort and care of your own." Her normally stoic visage took on some slight compassion. "I'll be unable to help you in the battle. My place will be beside the pantheon and my own defense."

"I understand," said the Lord of Earth with a nod.

Shiril faded from sight, appearing outside the entrance to the chamber of the Great Eye. It was now guarded by two Tularins. She made her way past them with a soft, self-assured grace. Though about half her size, the paradisal incarnates were well known for their attention to duty and strength in combat. The pair watched her with their bright blue eyes; a soft white aura shimmered off their golden cuirasses, bracers, open-faced helmets, greaves, and long swords as their swan-like wings rustled softly.

The chamber beyond the guarded doors was the same one where earlier they'd watched the battle between Endarien and Cadrith. Only now a gargantuan rectangular wooden table, standing taller than most mortal men, dominated the room's open space. Around this table several of the gods had gathered in discussion. They pored over a collection of parchments illustrated with various strategies and a running tally of forces standing at the ready.

"Shiril." Rheminas greeted her arrival. In his true form, he was the same height with pointed ears and a reddish-copper cast to his skin. His bright orange hair stood up in wild display. His yellow eyes beamed with pleasure at the prospect of the upcoming battle.

"It's so nice to see you in person again." His grin widened. She didn't quite know what to make of his lingering gaze, but it appeared he'd dressed up for the occasion. Copper-studded red leather armor sleeves and pants jutted out of a thigh-length coat of copper ring mail. For added flair, he'd donned an orange half cape emblazoned with his own symbol: the sun with the silhouette of a dagger that had been stabbed into it all the way up to its hilt. Tall boots, which also doubled as bronze greaves, matched the fire motif found on his bronze bracers.

"Rheminas." Shiril's tone was dry yet cordial. While the two were never really at odds, they weren't quite allies either. Nor was she with the rest of her family, preferring to leave them alone and expecting the same from them in return. So far this had worked quite well.

"You were right," said Khuthon, noting Shiril's arrival. "This place *is* well suited for a battle. We already have a *great* advantage in the terrain." Khuthon motioned to some of the parchments on the table approvingly. His suit of full plate armor sported spikes at the elbows and knees. An open-faced helmet rested on the table close by, complete with nose and cheek guards. At his waist a long sword was strapped to a thick black belt whose buckle was the Steel Cross—his personal crest consisting of two crossed falchions.

Shiril wouldn't be surprised if he had a few more weapons hidden on his person. Once he got going, Khuthon was known to enjoy a good fight and appreciated having the right weapon for the job.

"And we'll need all the advantages we can get." Causilla spoke in a low, melodious voice beside Khuthon. How such beauty could be conceived of, let alone represented in a living being, was a wonder even for the divine mind. Causilla's soft olive skin shimmered with youth and health even in the chamber's mixed lighting. Her bright hazel eyes shone with an innocence that added to her appeal, and her long red-tinted chestnut hair curled into a bow around her face. Though, like her cousins, she was equal to Shiril in height, Causilla seemed more like a standard of womanly grace and splendor than a great hulking figure.

Though she had dressed for war, the nature of her armor seemed more decorative than protective. A form-fitting silver cuirass covered her chest. This too wasn't without its charm. The breastplate was carved with thorns wrapping around the metal with two full rose blooms etched over the convexity of her breasts. Attached to this piece of armor was a clinging, gossamer-like material. It flowed from her shoulders and hands and looped around her fingers, making a sort of attached fingerless glove and skirt that ended at her knees. The material resembled a miniature form of scale mail and shimmered like liquid mercury.

Thigh-high brown leather boots climbed her shapely calves as a slit on the right side of her skirt rose to her waist opposite the slender sword sheathed at her left hip. Like her armor, the weapon seemed more ornamental than practical. It was covered in jewels and twisting thorny vines. The handle and hilt were a mixture of thorn and leaf, ending in a pommel shaped like a blooming rose.

"It sounds like you've chosen the best spot for a battle," Shiril said as she approached the great table. The others gathered there made room for her.

"I've chosen several fronts." Khuthon reminded her of a wolf stalking his prey. "We'll attack on at least three sides and then close ranks on a fourth to surround and *destroy* him."

"Do you think we can count on the others showing up to make this defense?" Shiril asked Ganatar.

"The others will show up in time," he confidently replied. His face was fatherly and wise, with gentle blue eyes and straight white hair that ended in a square-cut mane about his neck. White stubble made a neat oval under his nose and around his mouth and chin. "They have yet to rally their troops and get all things in order." A soft white illumination emanated from his pores, bathing the god in a faint aura.

Ganatar wore his regalia with a royal bearing that none of the others possessed. Though at first glance he resembled a fifteen-foot-tall Telborian knight, the subtle touches of his dress added to his refinement. These were the shining golden plate armor, the silken black cape attached at each shoulder by means of golden gavel clasps, and the black-plumed golden helm resting beside him near the map of Thangaria on the table.

"What about Gurthghol?" Shiril knew her uncle sometimes kept to his own timetable, even in the most inopportune times.

"Gurthghol will be here, as will all the rest" was all Ganatar would say.

"I don't think we need fear Gurthghol retreating from *this* fight," said Olthon. She resembled her husband in height and racial appearance, except for her white dove-like wings. Dangling blond locks covered her neck in thick curls. Her soft flesh was pink with health, adding all the more life to her bright green eyes beaming with a great inner peace. She had no helmet, instead wearing a golden laurel crown. Like Ganatar, she was dressed in solid plate armor—a form-fitting silver—under which a white tunic, tied with a silken green sash at the waist, made up the rest of her attire.

"Still," added Khuthon, "it *would* be nice to have his—"

The door to the chamber opened, allowing Asora inside. "It seems you didn't waste much time." Of similar height and build to Olthon, Asora was great with child, which she handled rather well despite her hurried gait. Her bright green eyes complemented the fiery red hair curling about her neck and face.

"There's little *to* waste," Khuthon returned. "I can't think of the last time you even picked up a weapon." He referenced the wooden club at Asora's side. In comparison to the goddess' natural beauty and presence, it was a roughly hewn and almost ugly thing. "You sure you know how to use one of those?"

"I'm not interested in killing another creature, but I'm not above self-preservation." Asora wore only a form-fitting white gown that stopped at midcalf, allowing brown leather boots to take over from there.

"Are you sure you want to fight?" The concern in Olthon's question was obvious. "You're not just risking your own life."

Asora placed a hand upon the swell of her stomach, letting Olthon know she was well aware of what she was doing. "When you consider how many *more* will suffer if I don't act, the choice becomes quite clear. I'm doing this for the protection of the pantheon and *all* living things on Tralodren."

"So how many warriors did you bring?" Khuthon inquired.

"Enough to help, mostly Lords of Life but a few Lords of Animals and Plants as well. A total of some twenty-five persons in all."

"Twenty-five?" A half-cocked smile spread across his face. "I'm impressed."

"Don't be." Asora was curt. "This isn't about bloodshed and slaughter."

"Believe what you will," he said, resuming his study of the maps and parchment on the table. "As more troops arrive, we'll start building up our other fronts."

"Who'll lead the main assault?" Asora found her place around the table beside her husband. Khuthon shot his wife a knowing glance.

"I thought as much," she muttered.

Olthon turned to Shiril, asking, "Where's Saredhel?"

"She should be here shortly, I would think." Just as she didn't keep up with the rest of her family, Shiril didn't keep too close a watch on her parents, nor they her. They were more inclined to encourage her independence, which allowed them more of the same for their own endeavors. While some might have thought such attitudes foster coldness in a family, Shiril didn't share that opinion. She enjoyed a relationship with both her parents that was probably better and deeper than others in the pantheon had with their own immediate family members.

"She'd better." Khuthon cast a wary glance up from the table.

"Do you have any contingencies?" Causilla inquired.

"My plans don't fail." Khuthon's countenance darkened.

"But still, with what we're facing, don't you think it would be wise to—"

Khuthon glared back at Causilla. "We are *going* to win." His face grew darker and sterner, the very cauldron of slaughter and warfare staring back at Causilla in full fury.

"But—"

"We are going to *win*!" Khuthon's jaw locked as he slammed his fist onto the table.

CHAPTER 17

THE QUIET BEFORE THE STORM IS SOMETIMES THE LOUDEST TIME OF ALL.

—Old Tralodroen proverb

It took Hadek a moment to realize he was airborne. He only understood he was sailing through the air shortly after the lich had slammed his staff into the earth. He had felt the powerful explosion of force and rose a good ten feet or so above the ground, flying to and then over the dais. He made it through the space between the female statue and the throne smoothly and safely. He was happy about that. He could easily imagine how painful it would have been to collide with either of them.

The only problem was he wasn't stopping, and just a short distance from the dais were the edge of the circle and what he knew to be hard stone posts and the impregnable openings between them. Shifting his head around, Hadek was able to see what was fast approaching from behind. He was going to hit the circle before the ground. The scene inside the posts, which had a habit of changing from time to time, had shifted into some sort of underground room or chamber. He couldn't make out much more than a stone floor and maybe a wall before he spun his head around and closed his eyes, bracing himself for the impact.

Instead, to his utter amazement, he flew into the scene between the posts, sliding and rolling to a rough stop on the stone floor he'd seen just moments before. He ended up on his stomach, a bit winded and with a few scrapes and cuts, but alive. He lay there, letting everything that had just happened sink in. When it had, he pushed himself to his feet.

He realized he was in a circular room—a *large* circular room. Looking behind him, he saw the portal he'd passed through was gone. There was only the room, nothing else. It was tall and encircled with a few torches, giving off a strangely brilliant white light. Unease bubbled within his gut. In the center of the room was a pool. And hovering above it was a giantess. She floated with her light brown legs crossed. Dressed in silver and white, she had her back to him. This vision alone was enough to send his head reeling with a swarm of questions.

Instinct, birthed from fear, told him to arm himself, but he couldn't see anything to do so with, and the dagger Dugan had given him was gone. Perhaps he'd died in the fight, and this was the afterlife, maybe even one of Asorlok's agents to judge him.

"Welcome, Hadek," said the giantess, whose back was still turned. Hadek said nothing, nor did he move. He was petrified by a mixture of awe and fear.

"Be at peace," she continued. "You're not dead, nor are you anywhere you should be afraid of." She kept her gaze on the pool beneath her. From what he could see of the pool's reflection, the large woman had solid white eyes. "This is Sooth, and you are my guest."

"And who are you?"

"Saredhel."

Hadek dropped to his knees. "I thought—"

He'd barely lifted his eyes and started to speak when he grew frightened at how small and hollow his voice sounded. He was stunned for a heartbeat more, but then he found the courage to continue. "Why have you brought me here?"

"You have to fulfill your destiny." Saredhel's words pounded anew the old drum he'd been hearing so often of late. He'd thought—hoped, really—all that would be over once he'd finished his encounter with Cadrith. Apparently not.

"My destiny?" Hadek felt a cold sweat wash over him. Could you still sweat if you were dead? He wasn't sure. Assuming he *was* dead, of course. While Saredhel had said he wasn't dead, how else would you be able to see a god if you weren't?

"Yes." Saredhel lifted her head but still kept her back to him.

Hadek's heart kicked into a gallop. "I thought that was all over. I helped fight. *That* was something *great*, right?" He didn't know what to say or why he'd been called to Gilban's goddess, and he didn't think he wanted to know either. Why he had such fear interlaced with the revelation he wasn't sure, but it couldn't be good. Why couldn't he just be dead? It would all be so much simpler.

Saredhel slowly turned around, hovering in the air like a serene cloud. "Rise." Her voice was soft but powerful. He did as bidden. He kept his eyes low, though, to avoid looking into her face.

"There is much you don't understand and much more you still need to do." The goddess descended silently before the goblin, bare feet touching the floor like silk on satin. "Time is not an ally for you, but neither is it an enemy." She stooped to one knee, lifting Hadek's tiny green head with her finger so that he could peer directly into her hooded face. "All are born with great potential. Some find it; others never do. Still more have it forced out of them through challenges and circumstance."

Hadek's eyes found themselves in Saredhel's. In that moment he saw his reflection. But it wasn't just his reflection he beheld. No, this was something far more compelling. In her eyes he saw not only himself as he presently was, but also from the days of his youth and as he would be, he supposed, in later years—if he lived to see them.

All three images he beheld at once, superimposed one atop the other in an otherworldly image reflected in the goddess' smooth eyes. He couldn't explain it, but even though they overlapped he didn't see a blurred image of himself; each image was at once distinct from and simultaneous with the other.

"You were born with a great potential that has to be realized, else we'll all suffer a great defeat . . . perhaps even an eternal one."

"Why *me*, though?" Hadek sounded so small—so distant—like his reflection resting in Saredhel's eyes.

"It's *your* destiny," came the goddess' strong reply. The words stiffened Hadek's spine, pulling him straight and tall.

"What if I don't want it?" His voice was stronger now, but still far away. He was lost in Saredhel's milky pools and couldn't free himself even if he tried.

"You've been given a great honor—the greatest ever bestowed upon a goblin. But the choice to receive it is always yours to make." Saredhel released Hadek from her gaze, rising to her full height once more. Hadek, for his part, shook his head to clear it from the past few unnerving moments before gazing at his shoes.

"Come here," she said, motioning for him to stand beside the pool.

He hesitated.

"There's nothing here that would harm you, save yourself."

"Now you sound like Gilban." Hadek sheepishly made his way forward. He saw no advantage in disobeying Saredhel's command. It was foolishness to resist a god—everyone knew that . . . at least they should if they wanted to keep breathing.

Saredhel motioned for him to stand at the lip of the pool. "Look deep into the waters, and you'll understand."

Hadek drew in a slow breath, let it out, and then did as instructed. At first he saw nothing but his reflection staring back at him from the clear waters above the bottom of the pool, where bluish-gray marble tiles encased the bowl of water. But that didn't last long. The surface of the pool began swimming with an oily mix of colors. This rainbow soup spun and blended in wild dervishes of silent passion as he did nothing but stare into it helplessly. And then a strange scene appeared before his eyes . . .

Hadek wasn't in Saredhel's chamber anymore. He was standing in the middle of an even grander venue: a throne room that would have made the best of bards fumble for words in describing its majestic beauty. It was redolent with opulence, between the marble pillars and walls studded with jewels, fluttering with tapestries. It was so large it looked to have been built by giants.

The throne in the center of the room was the same one from Galba's circle. He was sure of it. Only now it was alone. No statues flanked it, but it did rest on a marble dais. It also had an occupant. If he had to guess, the large man looked like the mustached statue he'd seen inside Galba's circle.

Olive skinned with long white hair, he kept his eyes closed, his mind focused on the collection of fist-sized worlds slowly orbiting his head. How Hadek knew the transparent globes of white light were worlds he wasn't sure; he just did. There was utter silence. And something else. Something that didn't feel right.

A twinge of dread fluttered up his spine. "Saredhel?" He tried keeping his voice to a whisper, but it resembled a shout growing weaker as each echo reverberated around the chamber.

"I'm here." Her voice sounded as if it was coming from everywhere.

"Where?" He searched the area, but saw no sign of her.

"Listen and watch."

Suddenly the door to the chamber burst open. When the man opened his eyes, the glowing worlds vanished. Both he and Hadek watched a pale, black-haired giantess hurry forward. She wore all black, made even darker in contrast to her porcelain-colored flesh. In her hand she held a sword, and she rushed at the seated man with a blood-thirsty cry.

He showed little concern, continuing to sit still until the dark-clad woman came within striking distance. Only then did he arise. But whatever action he attempted was too late. The giantess' sword had been sheathed in his chest. The man tumbled down the dais.

"Before Tralodren was formed, there were Vkar and Xora, his wife, both of whom were killed by Sidra, Gurthghol's daughter." Saredhel's voice narrated the scene of Vkar dying at Sidra's feet. "She'd been used by an entity who had existed before the cosmos to bring about this death, for it wanted to destroy the gods and Vkar's growing empire."

Everything around Hadek became distorted, like ripples on water. Once it stilled, a new scene was displayed. This one revealed Cadrith seated on the throne. This time, however, the throne was inside Galba's stone circle. In fact, it looked just like what he had left moments ago, save there were no others present but the lich upon the dais and throne. "Now that same entity has returned to finish what it began. Though it's decided to make use of Cadrith instead of Sidra, its desired result is still the same: the death of the pantheon and now Tralodren as well."

"So what am *I* supposed to do?" Hadek asked as Cadrith's eyes found him. Their haunting azure glow sent a shiver across his bones before everything was swallowed by darkness.

"You must help defeat him." Hadek's eyes widened upon seeing Gilban step out of the darkness. To say he was shocked to see the priest would have been a great understatement. It wasn't just the seer's sudden appearance that made the goblin go speechless, but *how* he appeared. He now had silvery-blue eyes where before blind orbs had rested. Other than this, he looked much as he had in life, though younger—probably no more than middle aged if the goblin had to hazard a guess. Finally finding his voice, Hadek opened his mouth to speak.

Gilban held up his hand, saying, "You're a key figure in this final battle, as are all who have survived Cadrith's attack." Gilban drew nearer. Even though he could now see, he still held his staff. The old stick followed the rhythm of his tread. "The destiny I spoke to you about before will be coming soon. You must be ready. When it comes, you won't have time to miss your opportunity."

"I don't understand," said Hadek. "I thought we were *all* facing Cadrith. Wasn't that the destiny you kept talking about? We were just fighting him and—"

"When I first gathered us all together, I was led by Saredhel in finding the candidates best suited to what I thought was a single purpose. I was wrong. Instead, what I discovered was that we'd all been chosen for a task grander than what brought us together at Taka Lu Lama. We all had been chosen as champions to stand against Cadrith's threat and would be united until that confrontation had been completed; thin threads of fate bind us all."

"So *I'm* one of these *champions?*" Hadek raised his eyebrows in mild disbelief.

"Yes."

"So *that's* my great destiny? To defeat Cadrith?" Hadek thought it didn't sound as great as he would have hoped. He didn't know exactly what he would have wanted instead—perhaps a fulfillment of the dreams he'd woven back in Taka Lu Lama.

"Yes and no." Gilban blurred the goblin's thoughts with his explanation. "We were all called to stand against Cadrith. How we do that is our individual destiny."

Hadek's brow wrinkled in troubled thought. "You're *dead* now, right?"

"I died, yes." It didn't seem to bother him to admit it.

"Then why are you here if you don't have to worry about it anymore? It sounds like we all failed. So why are you telling me this?"

Gilban smiled that familiar, enigmatic grin. It wasn't as intimidating with his new eyes, but still stirred up the same reaction in the goblin. "Because it is *my* destiny to do what I'm doing now. Each of us who has been called for this task has an integral part to play, and we must play. For if we lose, then so does Tralodren."

Hadek closed his eyes and brought his chin to his chest with a sigh. Keeping his head low, he asked, "Then I don't really have a choice in the matter, do I?"

"There is always a choice."

Hadek's smirk was facetious. "Where have I heard *that* before?"

An awkward silence followed, continuing until Hadek couldn't bear the crushing weight of it any longer. He knew where this was going. There wasn't any way to fight it even if he tried. He might as well get it over with and hope, once it was finally over, he still had a life he could return to.

"Fine." He sighed in defeat. "What do I have to do?"

"First we will have to get you in position so you'll be ready for your task when it comes to pass," said Gilban. "Then we just have to wait for it to arrive."

"Sounds like fun." His facetious expression fell flat.

•●•

Endarien's unconscious frame floated before Tralodren's sun, drifting in a silent orbit, alone and unaware. There was no one else to see the flare of searing flame that shot out from the yellow star. As the flare grew, it took on the form of a winged humanoid—a Galgalli. While the flame from whence it arose faded behind it, the avenging angel worked its wings, setting a rapid course straight for the hovering god.

When he arrived, the Galgalli took hold of Endarien's shoulders and gave them a shake. The god's sleepy eyes opened and then came into focus.

"A Galgalli?" Endarien's voice was still waking with him. "Haven't seen your kind for a while."

"Are you well?"

The question brought Endarien fully to his senses. He rapidly righted himself, taking stock of where he was.

"How long have I been here?" This certainly wasn't what he was expecting. From the look of things, he'd had an interesting journey. The last thing he could recall was Cadrith's final punch. But it wasn't just Cadrith's own power that had sent Endarien on his way. Nuhl was infused in it as well. Even with Vkar's essence flowing through his veins, Endarien had been unable to resist it.

"Long enough for the others to begin their plans for facing Cadrith," the Galgalli replied.

"And what's happened with him?" He craned his head over his shoulder, observing Tralodren behind him. It was some distance away but still visible to his keen eyes. Nothing seemed out of the ordinary, but he couldn't see everything in its finest detail from his present location.

"He's still on Tralodren, but will soon find his way to the pantheon."

"How?" Endarien spun around and faced the Galgalli. No divinity could get in or out. That barrier was secure and solid, and he should know.

"I wasn't told."

"I can't imagine Rheminas had you created on just my account."

The Galgalli said nothing, remaining stoic before the winged god. This wasn't doing any good. Time was already short, and he was wasting more of it with each heartbeat.

"Do you *know* what the other gods are planning? You can tell me that at least."

"They're preparing to make their stand on Thangaria."

"*Thangaria?*" Endarien raised his eyebrows in amazement. "Are they that desperate?"

"Determined," said the Galgalli. "They've set aside the old rules to make sure they'll succeed and now want you to join them."

"And they're *sure* Cadrith will head to Thangaria?"

"They believe Nuhl will make sure of it."

Endarien nodded. It made sense when he thought about it. Nuhl had come to Thangaria before to destroy it—what better place could there be to finish the job? He supposed there was more than a little irony in the location, which Rheminas and even Khuthon could appreciate. He couldn't really blame them. He'd just about done the same thing with Cadrith and the ruins of his temple.

"Then why come to me?" asked Endarien. "You should be headed to Thangaria or Tralodren."

"I'm headed there next but need a small portion of Vkar's essence so I can pass the Divine Barrier."

Endarien lowered his head and made a fist, noting how much of Vkar's essence had left him. He'd let it all fade away while he floated around like some corpse. What a waste. And for something that should have been so simple. He could almost hear Cadrith's mocking laughter. He deserved it. He'd been a fool.

"It's gone." He couldn't bring himself to face the Galgalli. "You left me out here too long."

"I don't need much, just enough to pass the barrier."

"You'll need more than a touch. If I couldn't take him with what—"

"We don't have much time. Whatever you can give will be enough."

Endarien found the divinity's face once more, pushing aside the rising guilt that felt like a crushing vise clamping down upon his shoulders and back.

"Fine. Whatever's left is yours." He held out his hand, palm facing the Galgalli. Endarien reached down into the core of his being, taking up what fragments remained of his grandfather's essence. He expelled it through his hand in a white bolt of crackling energy and into the Galgalli's chest.

The Galgalli absorbed it all, then bowed his head. "Thank you." He spread his wings and left for Tralodren at incredible speed.

Endarien stretched his own wings as he watched the Galgalli devour the distance between him and the planet. It was out of his hands now. He'd done his part and failed. He needed to prepare for the next stand, hoping this time he wouldn't make the same mistake. Focusing his thoughts on Avion, he summoned a vortex of cumulus clouds a short distance from him. Flying into the vortex, Endarien began forming his plans. There was much to do.

•●•

"Even so, we have come." The cold tone of Perlosa's words finished her greeting to the gathered gods. She wore no armor, only a fine mink-trimmed gown of shimmering ivory silk that blended with her smooth alabaster skin. Form fitting and augmented by blue and white diamonds, it told all who saw her she wasn't looking to fight.

"And with no warriors?" Khuthon growled. "Even your *mother* is here to fight—and with other Lords of Life, no less."

"As we have said"—Perlosa peered fully into her father's displeased face—"they would not come."

"Would not or *could* not?" Rheminas chided his sister.

"They would not set foot on Thangaria. They hold it too sacred and reminded us many times of the ancient oath we all took not to come here with weapons and warriors, and in our true form." Her ice-blue eyes crackled with a chilling anger carefully simmering beneath the surface. "An oath which we are all breaking, and they felt that to be a bad omen."

Olthon's brow wrinkled. "Still, the Lords of Water—"

"Have stated their displeasure with this plan as well," came Perlosa's frosty reply. "And we are not about to waste our followers in a vain battle that will serve only one purpose."

In a burst of rage, Khuthon struck Perlosa with the back of his hand. The goddess of ice and waves crumpled to the floor. It wasn't a strong strike, not as he could truly deliver, but the humiliation it brought was far more damaging.

"You go back to your realm and get those insubordinate *worms* you call *subjects* and bring them here." Khuthon gnawed the very words in his rage. "They *will* fight and they *will* defend this pantheon and Tralodren. I will not have my own daughter mock me to my face when even her own *mother* finds and brings warriors to this battle and looks to fight alongside us." Khuthon's eyes became slits. "Get out of my sight!"

Perlosa rose with a jerk, rubbing her jaw. Her icy glare never left her father. The doors opened again, and Endarien entered. He'd removed his helmet and was carrying it at his side. He held his long spear on the other side, where he also carried his shield.

"If you had lived up to your boasting, we would not be dealing with *any* of this," Perlosa snarled at him as they approached one another.

"What's done is done," said Endarien. "But if we're able to stand together, we'll be able to put this threat to rest."

"We thought all the wind got knocked out of you," Perlosa sniped as she continued her retreat. "It seems we were wrong."

"If words are your only weapons, then you're going to be the *first* to fall." Endarien's comment followed Perlosa, causing her to freeze in her steps, eyeing her cousin coldly.

Olthon consoled her son. "She's not really mad at you."

"But she does have a point," Endarien confessed to the others around the table. "If I had acted with more prudence, we wouldn't be here."

"Hah." Rheminas snorted. "You wanted your revenge, and you nearly got it. And now you'll get a second chance."

Endarien's mood lightened at the idea. "Thanks for sending the new Galgalli. Who knows how long I would have floated out there before coming around?"

"Galgalli?" Khuthon locked a curious eye on Rheminas. He wasn't the only one.

"And when did we vote on the right to allow the creation of a new Galgalli?" Ganatar crossed his arms, observing Rheminas more closely.

"Sorry." The rising tension wasn't lost on Endarien. "I wasn't looking to cause any trouble."

"You didn't," Rheminas assured him, ignoring the group's disapproval.

"Yes, you did that all by yourself." Perlosa delighted in her barb. She hadn't moved another inch since hearing mention of the new divinity.

"Shouldn't you be going somewhere?" A serious scowl burned away Rheminas' good humor.

"In a moment," she replied. "We would like to see how this plays out. Perhaps we will learn of other things you have been keeping from us."

"Now's not the time for accusations," he replied.

"Nor to keep things hidden," said Olthon.

"Is this true?" Khuthon looked his son full in the face. "Did you send a Galgalli to Tralodren?"

"Yes," said Rheminas.

"Why?"

"It's all part of the plan."

"Not *my* plan."

"Well, maybe not yet, but you'll see the potential soon enough."

"We agreed to a course of action." Ganatar's face grew more stern. "If you have something at work, you'd best tell us now. We can't possibly plan if we don't know all that's going on."

Rheminas relented. "All right. But after the others arrive. I only want to explain myself once. Which means you'll have time to go have a chat with your people," he told Perlosa over his shoulder.

Perlosa gave a small huff and was about to reply but caught sight of Khuthon's hard stare and decided better of it. Turning, she made her way from the room in a dignified rush.

"Do hurry back," Rheminas said airily. "I'm sure you won't want to miss a single detail."

Perlosa slammed the door behind her.

• ● •

Outside, in the rapidly crowding courtyard, another company of warriors appeared. Walking through a large steel-gray portal of light, a party of dwarves moved onto the dead chunk of a world. Amid the warriors were some priests who kept to the front of the others, near their god. Warrior and priest alike wore the same half plate armor. All carried matching axes and round shields bearing Drued's crest. Bearded and crowned with open-faced helmets, they followed their god into the courtyard and the war to come.

Drued, the dwarven god who led them, resembled his troops in all respects save height. Standing more than twelve feet tall, he made for an inspiring sight for those who followed behind. His long silver beard spilled out of his partially open-faced steel helmet. Each of the beard's twelve braids was capped in gold. His armor wasn't ostentatious but practical: hard forged steel plate mail shining under Thangaria's gray sky. A wolf-hide cape fluttered behind him as he marched for the large assembly already gathered around Vkar's hall. At his side swung his axe. On top of his back and cape rested his round steel shield.

"Make rest here," Drued said, turning to his priests. "I need to see how we plan to fight this battle." Raising his voice so the rest of the men would hear him, he continued, "You've served me honorably in life. I expect nothing less in the time to come."

"We would rather die than dishonor you or our tribes, my lord," said a nearby priest.

Drued considered the priest who had spoken with an emotionless face. "Today you're not just fighting for the honor of forefathers, clans, or families." Again the dwarven god looked out over the rest of the dwarven warriors as he raised his voice. "Today you stand to defend Tralodren itself. It's not only the clans that look to you but everyone who calls that wondrous world home. You volunteered to stand in this fight, so I know none of you are cowards. Keep up that courage, for the battle is sure to challenge us all. But if we stand firm to the end, we will have our reward, in either this reality or whatever comes after it.

"Stand firm," said Drued as he thrust his axe overhead. "Stay true."

"Hail Drued, Lord of the Dwarves!" rose a rumbling shout from every dwarf present.

Drued lowered his axe, singling out one of the warriors with his purple eyes. "Vinder," he said.

"Yes, lord," answered Vinder, locking his two ice-blue eyes upon him.

"Help the priests secure a decent spot for our camp. The rest of you, keep those axes sharp. I don't plan on taking any longer than I have to. And neither will our enemy." This said, Drued started walking toward the Hall of Vkar. He didn't get more than a few paces before he began glowing with a steel-gray aura and then faded from sight.

CHAPTER 18

C adrissa moved as if in a dream. She heard the soft whispers in her head growing clearer and then fading back into the whirlpool of others swirling around her. These distinct voices were telling her many things—*urging* her to do many things. For now she pushed past their demands while at the same time sifting through them in case they might hold any clues on what to do next. Once she learned that some of the whispers were sharing hints of the very thing she needed to know, she'd learned how to better examine them for items of interest. Combined with what she'd already learned, it was all coming together.

She ran down the strangely familiar hallway, rubbing the necklace as she went. She felt she'd traveled down it many times before. She was aware it was the work of the necklace that had taken hold of her once more—compelling her forward into this mad dash—but was far from fearful. Instead, she was happy, though rushing to try to get to her destination before some unknown deadline she felt in her head had expired.

Her ears managed to hear Alara and Rowan behind her over the constant whispers, but she was focused on the task at hand. Her thoughts were feverish and driven—compelled to one end: finding the information currently eluding her. Details were finally falling into place.

She gripped the scepter tighter as she ran. It felt good there, like it belonged there. She had no intention of letting it go anytime soon. Not when they were getting close to their destination. She could barely contain her excitement. She sensed the necklace was deeply pleased with this commitment . . . Eventually, she slowed and then stopped before a wooden door. She sensed there was something behind it that might be of use. She reached out and touched the rough, dry wood, soaking in the hope it offered.

"You found something?" Rowan came jogging up behind her. Alara was at his side. Since their encounter with the Troll, he'd opted to keep both sword and shield at the ready.

"I think so," she said, returning her hand to her side.

"If it's a Troll," said Rowan, "just let it have one of those blasts. I don't really want to fight another one."

"That makes two of us," Alara concurred.

He stepped forward and pushed on the door with the point of his sword. It opened silently. "Remember what I said," he warned as he took the lead.

Cadrissa followed closely while her fingers caressed the necklace. She was aware of the action and how it was probably a sign of how much pull it had over her, but she was confident she still had things under control. Even if her fingers might be demonstrating something different, she was still the master of her mind.

Behind the door was a world of opulence. The circular room was spacious, more so than any of the other rooms they'd seen so far. Around the walls were more sconces, which flared to life as soon as the trio entered the room. White bear hides, wolf skins, and rich tapestries hung on the walls amid crystal chandeliers, bronze braziers, and golden statues of young Nordic male and female warriors. White and silver carpets covered the floors. Indeed, amid such creations of bronze and gold, silver and brass, one could easily forget where they were.

"We must be in one of the towers," Cadrissa surmised. A great fire-place opposite the doorway was the first thing to catch her eye. It had to be as wide as she was tall and twice her own height. It was cold and dead like the rest of the keep.

"Is that good?" asked Alara.

"Very good," she said. In the center of the room was a massive round oak table. Cadrissa made her way up to it, tracing her fingers across the dark red wood like a lover's caress. "We're very close."

"I don't see any books or scrolls," said Alara.

Cadrissa cautiously continued her examination of the room. Yes, there was definitely something here. They were *very* close. She sorted through the whispers more carefully, combining them with what she'd already learned of Lann. Then it all fell into place. She knew what to do next—everything.

"There," she said, pointing with the scepter to what looked like an ordinary wall with a statue of a rather savage-looking Nordic male dressed for battle. A long-handled axe was clasped tightly in his grip.

"Cadrissa, are you—"

"We're *very* close." She cut Alara short as she hurried for the statue's base. "We're in one of Lann's private chambers, by the looks of it." She kept her eyes locked on the statue while her fingers moved even faster as they fumbled with the necklace. "You can see that it was his by the way it's decorated." She was vaguely aware of Alara and Rowan coming up behind her.

She was losing the fight for control, and it terrified her. It wouldn't do any good to tell Rowan and Alara. There wasn't anything they could do. And they probably knew already. She'd been slipping in keeping the necklace's pull hidden from them since arriving in Frigia. Best to just focus on what she could, while she could—and that meant getting to the statue.

She raised her left hand to the statue, touching the nose and face ever so slightly. Before anyone could do anything else, the statue began melting like snow in the sun. The fine, lifelike details faded into a blob of white goo. A few breaths later, the incredible sculpture was a puddle of snow-white ooze at the trio's feet. Cadrissa stepped over this mess and traced her fingers along the cold marble wall behind it.

"We're *very* close now." Her voice was faint.

The whispers in her head were louder than they'd ever been. They told her what to do next—*compelled* and *commanded* her. There was no choice; she had to do what they willed . . . The necklace had finally gained control. It was then she realized the truth of the object: it was very much alive.

"Sopek toth nola dorn." The spell revealed the outline of a door. "Yopek." She spoke with a solid, authoritative voice that wasn't entirely her own. The outline grew into a solid door crafted out of the same white marble as the wall.

"I thought all the counterspells were taken care of," Cadrissa heard Rowan whisper.

"So did I," Alara replied.

Cadrissa ignored them. What did they know anyway of magic or the power needed to do what she did? Power that she was so close to gaining . . . the knowledge of power . . . She motioned with her hands, and the door opened into darkness. She wasted no time in claiming entrance.

The room beyond was rather plain, with white pine paneling and the same illumination common throughout the rest of the keep. It was well furnished compared to the rest of the complex, but not as majestic as the room they'd just come from. Square oak tables with matching chairs were covered in a thin layer of dust. They held only a passing interest for her as she aimed straight for a tall desk resting on top of a wooden dais. She was drawn to it—pulled to it like a fish on the line. On top of it rested a fat tome. Her eyes opened wide when she saw the white scale hide in which the old tome had been covered. It was what she'd been searching for. All that knowledge at her fingers . . . all that power . . .

"Is *that* it?" she heard Rowan ask.

"Yes." She could barely get the word out of her mouth. It took so much concentration to hold her own against the necklace. But it was a lost battle. Hunching over from a sensation similar to what she'd experienced in Arid Land with Cadrith, she attempted to steady herself as the necklace's pendant blazed into a shimmering bronze nimbus. This aura of light transformed into a column, fully enveloping her. An eyeblink later it was spreading out and swallowing the dais where the desk rested.

She held her pose as if frozen. The light from the necklace continued its bright glow, but it didn't venture outside the area immediately surrounding the dais. Inside this cylinder of illumination she listened to a single strong voice pounding into her head, until it finally succeeded in mentally shoving her aside. She was unable to do anything now, not even think, as what she had come to believe was the necklace's presence, the fierce heat it occasionally emitted, flooded into her veins, heart, and brain before pooling in her eyes. It was unbearable—like molten lead coursing through her veins—and she screamed in agony.

Cadrissa was back in the study in Cadrith's tower—back to where she'd been left shortly after he'd raised it up and pulled her inside. And in many ways it was as if she truly had somehow been transported back in time to that exact moment. Everything was the same. The door was closed and locked—she knew without having to investigate. And the strange omnipresent illumination revealed all the books and scrolls resting in the bookcase to her right. It was just like she remembered it, even down to the musky smell and feeling of hopelessness.

And then she started to lose track of her own chronology. With each new heartbeat she forgot more of where she'd just been and focused more on where she now stood. She was the prisoner of Cadrith in his tower. There was no escape. She—

No! She gritted her teeth as she fought to hold on to the truth. She was free from here. Free from Cadrith.

"No!" Cadrissa expelled a blaze of fire from her outstretched hand at the scrolls and tomes. "I'm free from you! I escaped!"

"I let you." Cadrith's voice froze Cadrissa in her tracks.

"You said you were done with me," she said, searching the room as the fire continued consuming the shelves and the material stored on them. "You said I'd served my purpose."

"And you did. But now you have another."

Cadrissa dashed for the door, only to quickly retreat as it slowly swung open. "There's nothing more you could need from me. You're a god." Out of the opening slithered an inky blackness that drained all blood and courage from her body.

"No," she whispered.

The room around her faded into shadow and then total darkness, yet she could clearly see the amorphous night swirl into a collection of humanoid shapes. And while relieved it wasn't the twisting tentacle mass she'd encountered before, she was just as alarmed as these shadowy beings rushed her with grasping, clinging hands, seeking her out with reckless abandonment.

"Let me go!" She struggled desperately, but it wasn't enough. One hand grasped her ankle. Another found a tight grip on her thigh. Others followed suit, grabbing wherever they could. Each pulled and held her in the darkness rapidly enveloping her. All the while she could hear the chattering words of thousands of whispers scuttling about like fingernails on cobblestone.

Don't fight us. She heard a single voice emerge from the smaller whispers around her. *You only risk bringing greater harm to yourself.*

"What do you want?"

A vessel. The words came back to her like a spike of ice shoved into her spine. For a brief moment she thought of Cadrith, but this wasn't his work . . . and it involved more than one being. There had to be dozens of them, if not more, given how many hands were now assailing her—pinning her down.

"Who are you?" She fought away a new claw trying to cover her mouth.

"They're my new servants." Cadrissa felt the ice in her spine explode throughout the rest of her body as she watched Cadrith emerge out of the darkness. He was dressed in black with a black staff in hand, his smile still the same bone-chilling expression she'd come to loathe and fear.

"And you're going to be my new champion—the key to casting off the last shackles that remain," he said, drawing closer. The shadowy beings scurried from his advance like rats before the light of a torch.

"You didn't really think I'd let you live this long out of any sense of *mercy* or *obligation*, did you?" He came within inches of her.

"But you're a god." She didn't understand any of this.

"And you're a perfect pawn. You proved that in Arid Land."

"But you said—"

Cadrith grabbed her chin, cutting off any further comment. She tried her best not to squirm under his touch. She didn't want to give him any additional pleasure. Thankfully, the bone-numbing cold was gone.

"Yes, so much like her . . ." He held up her face, examining it as if he were trying to find something that wasn't clear on the surface. "But not so much as to frustrate my plans . . ." He released his hold. "The necklace was an added bonus. It helped tie everything into place now that all the curtains have been pulled back."

"What are you talking about?"

"Didn't you wonder why I didn't just kill you once we got to Galba? I didn't trust her, and if I failed with the throne the first time, I needed a way to try again."

Cadrissa tried to wrap her mind around what Cadrith was saying. "If you'd failed with the throne, you'd be dead. Galba said—"

"Yes, I would have been . . . in *that* body." He smiled his familiar haunting grin. "But if I had implanted a part of my spirit into *another* body . . ."

Her heart skipped a beat. "You were going to *possess* me?" Possession wasn't that common and was rarely discussed among wizards. It was more of a matter for priests, since none of what she'd read so far had given her the idea that such a thing was possible. Now it seemed that assumption was wrong.

"Actually, I *did* possess you, but thanks to that trinket"—he jabbed a finger at the necklace—"I was kept from doing much of anything until I finally could gain the upper hand.

"It turns out the necklace was meant to hold spirits and magical energy," he said, motioning to the shadowy beings gathered around them. "That's why *these* are here. Eventually, I was able to modify it to magnify my own essence so I could have increased control over my vessel, as I do now."

"But why me?" Cadrissa asked, feeling the familiar twinge of dread rising from her stomach and into her throat.

"Why not? You're the perfect specimen. I realize now how you were dangled in front of me so I'd snatch you up and use you back in the ruins, but now I have the chance to turn the tables."

"The black tentacles?" She was beginning to see a connection.

"Yes." A sour expression played over Cadrith's features. "A manifestation of Nuhl. It used us. You. Me. Your friends. *All* of us."

"Why?"

"That's really not much of your concern anymore."

"Let me go and we can stop it," she said, struggling for release. "We have the Scepter of Night and—"

"I know. I knew it back when that blind fool tried to use it against me in the circle, and I would have claimed it after my ascent if not for Galba. But then there was you—and now this necklace—both of which will fit very well into the last part of my plan."

"You can't use the scepter without the incantation." She desperately sought whatever bargaining chip she might have.

Cadrith laughed. "You think Lann Mirson was the only wizard king to know of the scepter? By the fourth age it was being studied probably more than any other enchanted object. Especially as the Divine Vindication neared. My master's former master had been working on a way to re-create it—even improve on it—before he died. And if my master hadn't taken a different approach in his studies after getting ahold of the Mirdic Tome, he probably would have forged a new one."

"Then let me go. If you're here, you also have to know where I am. Just come and take the scepter and let us live."

"It's not that simple. There's still a fine line I have to walk, and you and your friends have proven to be a loose thread in the tapestry that needs trimming. But if it's any consolation, I couldn't have successfully undertaken as much as I have if not for all we share."

"There's *nothing* we share."

"You're wrong. We share the same bloodline. Oh, it's diluted a great deal from what it once was, but it's still there. An incredibly thin red line connecting you to me and your extremely great-grandmother."

The blood fled from Cadrissa's face.

"Ah, you see it now, don't you?" Cadrith grinned. "Yes, your family tree runs right through me and the woman who, out of anyone, could have been my equal."

"The robes in the wardrobe." Further revelation dawned. "And then the—the clothes for the child . . ."

"Our child, who must have survived, if *you're* any proof."

"What happened to her?"

"She died like everyone else," Cadrith said dismissively, "afraid to lay hold of her true potential. Which was a good thing. She was too far into the path of knowledge, and eventually it would have been necessary to curb that." Cadrith studied her carefully again, and she felt her skin crawl. "Just *one* of the traits you two seem to share, although you have a weaker adherence than she had. But that doesn't mean you can't still be useful.

"Like my new allies." He motioned for one of the shadowy beings to come forward. Even then she couldn't make out much of the figure. It was roughly humanoid and perhaps seven or eight feet in height. "They tried to fight me at first, but once I showed them we had the same agenda, they came to my side quite readily."

"The trip from the Great Library." Cadrissa's eyes widened with yet another epiphany. "You were fighting the necklace."

"That and your other ally. It took some thinking to figure everything out. It *was* a rather clever ruse—giving you some extra time—but easy enough to reverse." So they *were* back in the present, but how much along in it were they? If Cadrith had any more of an advantage—

"The necklace was something different. It was created to hold the spirits of some fifty dranors seeking escape from the Abyss so they could continue their war against the gods. You just happened to stumble onto it when you were in those ruins where I used you to release me. But now, with this small army behind me, I'll be free to possess all the power in the cosmos."

And it will be a new day for the dranors, who will reclaim what the gods stole from us long ago. The coal-colored spirit beside Cadrith spoke into Cadrissa's mind.

A new hand covered her mouth before she could say any more.

"Serve me well, and I might let you reclaim your body," Cadrith informed her. "Fight me, and I'll shred your spirit into nothingness." Immediately, a fresh frenzy ensued among Cadrissa's captors as more hands clamped onto her body. Some of them covered her eyes, introducing her fully into darkness.

CHAPTER 19

Swift are his righteous wings, bringing justice to the oppressed;
His sword, a weapon of hot wrath.
Safe shall you be from his powerful gaze,
Lest iniquity be found within.
All who are evil have reason to fear, but the innocent he shall not harm.

—Ancient poem

B ack in Lann's private room, Alara and Rowan witnessed the burst of bronze light around Cadrissa fade before she unceremoniously tumbled to the floor. Alara ran to her side, Rowan right behind. Both remained cautious. Rowan had no idea what to expect next. While Alara rolled Cadrissa on her back, he squatted across from Alara. He tried to assess Cadrissa's condition but wasn't able to learn much more than that she appeared unconscious. Thankfully, she hadn't sustained any injuries in her fall.

She moaned and rolled her head from side to side, sweating and shivering. Rowan noticed the scepter was tightly clutched in one hand, and the necklace in the other. If he'd just come upon the scene now he'd have probably thought she was sick. But they both knew better.

Alara placed her hand on Cadrissa's moist head. "She's burning up, but her hands are ice cold."

"Don't get so close," he warned. "We don't know what's going on and—"

Cadrissa grunted.

"Cadrissa," Alara said, gently brushing a few slick sable strands from her face. "Can you hear me?"

Before anyone could react, Cadrissa's eyes flashed open. At the same time, her fist hit Alara in the stomach, flinging her across the room, where she crashed into the solid wall. The impact was so strong it cracked the pine paneling. Alara slid down its surface and slumped to the floor. Rowan leapt back with reflexes honed from his years of training while Cadrissa rose on shaky legs. The eyes that greeted him had changed from green to a brilliant azure and were laced with an incredible cruelty.

"Much better," Cadrissa said as she began admiring her body. Though it sounded like Cadrissa's voice, Rowan knew it was someone else speaking through her. The necklace, it seemed, had finally won. He dared a glance back at Alara. She was alive . . . for now. If he was going to do anything, he would need to do it soon.

"Cadrissa?" He cautiously took a step back, sword casually pointed at her with his shield raised. He didn't want to provoke a fight but wasn't about to lower his defenses either.

"*Gone.*" She closed the gap between them. Her voice was deepening. "Just like you'll be in a moment."

"Who are you?"

Cadrissa only smiled. It was a hideous thing—with too much teeth and dead eyes. "You can't be that thick headed, can you?"

Rowan's eyes became slits as everything connected. "Release her." Did this mean he was facing a god, or something else? Whichever it might be, he was the only one left to stand before it . . .

Cadrith's voice laughed through Cadrissa's mouth.

"Why torment her?" Rowan asked as he tried to add some more space between them. "You're a god now. Why bother with her? With us?"

"You're annoying pests whom I should have dealt with back in the circle." Cadrissa took another step forward, the unsettling grin still plastered on her face. "And that will have to be corrected. The cleaner the board, the easier and faster I win."

Cadrissa lunged for the knight. Rowan swung his blade, but found it ineffective—partly because he didn't really want to harm Cadrissa, and partly because the thing inside her was an apt combatant. The opening

Rowan's weak strike created allowed her to sock him in the face. The punch sent a spray of stars across his vision.

He staggered away from his attacker as she continued pressing him. Another blow to the face split his lip, followed by one that dug deep into his stomach. Cadrissa was moving too quickly for him to anticipate her movements. Rowan bent over from the latest strike. A gulping breath later and she had clamped a hand on either shoulder, sending a charge of magical energy running up and down his body. In that instant, he saw beyond Cadrissa's unnaturally blue eyes. The woman he'd once journeyed to save was nowhere in sight.

He shook violently, dropping both his shield and sword, before collapsing in a twitching heap at Cadrissa's feet. He couldn't move his body, but he could still think and see all that was going on about him. He could do nothing but watch as the possessed wizardess peered down at him with dark, hooded eyes. Everything that had once resembled Cadrissa—everything marking her as her own person—melted away as Cadrith's cruel visage glared out at the helpless knight. "And now," she said, stepping closer, "it's time for you to die."

Suddenly, there was a thunderous explosion. Rowan didn't see what happened next. Everything was a blur of motion and sound. As the dust began clearing, what he saw would remain with him for the rest of his life. A Galgalli towered above the possessed mage, debris and dying light drifting from the roof and ceiling where the massive angel had made his entrance. Miraculously, the rocks and timbers hadn't fallen on anyone, but did a good job of demolishing the rest of the room.

He'd heard stories and read in the Sacred Scrolls of angels who served Panthora. He'd also read that some had come to the aid of various priests in times of great need. But this was something different. A Galgalli was an agent of judgment, an avenging angel sent to do the will of the pantheon in dealing out divine retribution to those who warranted it. Everyone, no matter their religion or beliefs, knew this, which just made its dramatic appearance all the more unsettling.

Cadrissa was unfazed by the Galgalli, pressing on like a cat slinking toward its prey. "So they think you'll be able to stop me?" She lifted the scepter with a hearty air of defiance. "Come and judge me, if you dare."

The Galgalli remained still, peacock wings calmly folding behind him. "I've been given the authority to judge you for your trespasses against the pantheon and the inhabitants of Tralodren." The Galgalli's stern voice rattled the room even as the strange letters written on his mask glowed a searing white. "You've defied the god of death, slaughtered many in your pursuit of power, and sought to challenge the pantheon by siding with your current patron. For these crimes, you've been sentenced to death, your spirit and soul sent to the Abyss for eternal imprisonment."

"Let's see if you're as bold as your words." Cadrith's voice snarled out of Cadrissa's lips.

Rowan watched the Galgalli draw his sword and slash it a hair's breadth from Cadrissa's face. The white flame that wrapped the blade when drawn had burst to life and extinguished in one breath. It happened so fast it was over before he could fully register it, and Rowan wondered if anything had really happened at all.

A series of spasms shook Cadrissa's body, driving her to her knees and then the floor, where she continued flailing about like a fish out of water. As she did so, the necklace fell off. It was then Rowan understood: the gold chain had been severed by the Galgalli's sword. That had been his target all along, not Cadrissa herself.

"I will judge you face to face," said the Galgalli. "Not through the guise of this innocent woman."

As soon as Cadrissa fell, Rowan felt himself able to move again. Taking advantage of the situation, he retrieved his sword and shield with still slightly numb digits and ran to Alara. He could see she was conscious, though not fully alert. Some blood dripped out of the corner of her mouth and her face looked ashen.

"Rowan?" A weak voice fluttered from her lips.

He bent down beside her. "How badly are you hurt?" Though she tried, Alara was unable to fully hide the pain from her face.

"Do you think you can stand?" Over his shoulder, Rowan saw Cadrissa had stopped her shaking and was lying still . . . *too* still for his liking. A low groan from Alara returned his focus to her.

"I won't make it outside the tower." Her words were followed by a violent stream of moist, bloody coughs. He did the best he could to ease her suffering, but knew that she was bleeding internally. There was nothing he could do to stop it.

Across the room, Cadrissa began uttering some strange language and shaking. Before this macabre display, the angel kept a silent watch. His white eyes calmly observed everything with a powerful amount of concentration. Her body arched up from the floor, and she expelled a pale blue mist from her lips. Rowan and Alara both watched as the mist twisted and twirled into something vaguely humanoid. It reached out to them in seeming frustration before dissipating. Violent shudders followed, and then Cadrissa dropped flat on her back. Her mouth remained wide open.

"What did you do to her?" Rowan rose with sword and shield, making sure he was ready to defend Alara should this towering figure attack. He didn't know if he could, though. While he'd regained feeling in his body, he wasn't sure he could hope to even *scratch* the divinity.

As soon as the Galgalli's eyes washed over him, Rowan felt as if he had been laid open for all to see. He could hide nothing; it all just spilled out of him . . . and was seen by this . . . this agent of judgment.

"Have no fear, I mean you no harm." The words were softer now, but still resounded with the strong authority the Galgalli carried. "I've begun the judgment of Cadrith Elanis and those who would ally themselves with him."

Rowan shivered, suddenly realizing just how cold it was getting with the large hole in the roof and the broken wall. The temperature dropped at night in the mountains—especially in Frigia. Thankfully it was still light outside, not full daylight, but enough to help see them through the last part of their journey. Just what that last part would be, though, would be decided in the next few moments.

"We're not with Cadrith." Rowan held his blade and shield level, keeping one eye on Alara, continuing to monitor her degrading condition. She was still awake.

"I know," the Galgalli returned. "But you have something I need to finish my judgment."

"The scepter." Rowan spied the object lying beside Cadrissa. "What did you do to Cadrissa?"

"I freed her from Cadrith's possession."

"He was *inside* her?"

"A part of his spirit was, yes."

He'd heard tales of people becoming possessed by fiends and through other sinister means but didn't think such things happened anymore. He now stood corrected. And to think, Cadrith was there with them the whole time. He probably heard everything and knew all about what they were planning. The thought was far from encouraging.

"Where is he now?"

"Making ready to attack the pantheon, which is why I need the scepter, along with the spell to activate it."

"That's the *real* battle, isn't it?" Rowan tried again to read the Galgalli's face but still came up with nothing.

"The scepter." The angel's tone had grown harder.

"We're all that's left of nine people who were pulled across Tralodren to put an end to Cadrith," said Rowan, staring the Galgalli in the eyes. "As far as I see it, we still have a job to do." Brave words. Alara was near death, Cadrissa was probably dead, for all he knew, and he didn't feel so wonderful himself. But it was the right thing to do—to follow this through to the end . . . even if it meant his own death in the process.

"And I have my orders," the Galgalli replied.

"Which are to forsake us after we've come this far?"

"You are not being forsaken"—the Galgalli's face softened—"but saved, so that you can live out the rest of your days."

"We won't live much longer if you don't help us or take us to someone who will." Rowan was shaking as he fought for control over his seething emotions. "Or take us with you. There has to be someone who could help Alara." As if on cue, Alara released another string of bloody coughs, drawing Rowan's attention.

"If you're on our side, then can you heal Alara?" he asked as humbly as he could. "She won't make it much longer without some healers or divine aid."

"I'm sent to judge and bring retribution, not heal and comfort."

"Then we're just supposed to die here?" Rowan's face grew hard. He had to fight back the rage thickening his Nordic blood. He'd come too far, seen too much. He was being led by his goddess—that had to count for something, didn't it? "We're just some game pieces that aren't needed anymore, and now it's time to clear the board?"

"I have my duty," the Galgalli returned.

"And so do I!"

The Galgalli fell silent. Rowan held his breath in an attempt to hold back the rage threatening to spill out. He needed to use all he'd been taught about diplomacy. What he now fought for was the most important thing in his life . . . second to his faith in Panthora, but a *close* second.

He attempted what he hoped would be a strong barter. "If we give you the scepter and the way to activate it, then you must take us with you."

The Galgalli pondered Rowan's statement. Alara wheezed closer to Mortis. Cadrissa still didn't stir. The only noise in the chamber was the slow, stress-induced fragmenting of the wood paneling and the stone holding together what remained of the room.

"I don't think you understand where I'm going," the Galgalli explained. "It's about to become a battlefield."

"If there's going to be a battle, then there are going to be healers too," Rowan reasoned, noting Alara's worsening state. She was even paler, her head nodding sleepily over her chest. "We don't have much time," he informed the Galgalli. "I'm speaking for all of us, and this is what we want. Now, do we have a deal?"

"You don't know what you're asking." A small degree of empathy peeked out between the angel's words. "If I take you with me, you probably won't be able to return."

"I'm willing to take the risk," said Rowan. "*We're* willing to take the risk."

The avenging angel looked from Rowan to Alara, then at the motionless

Cadrissa. As he did it was almost as if he was looking through them and at something inside them instead. When he was satisfied, his eyes locked back on Rowan. Once again he pushed aside the feeling of utter defensiveness before the angel.

"Very well."

"Cadrissa will have to help you with the incantation," said Rowan. "We were about to get it ourselves before . . ." He trailed off while his mind reenacted the confrontation that had followed. They never did get it, he knew, but perhaps she could still find it. If not, all this would have been for nothing. It was a wild, foolish gamble, but it was all he had left to offer the angel if Alara was going to get the help she needed.

The Galgalli gave a flap of his wings, birthing a flash of light. After it had faded, Dugan stood in the Galgalli's place, dressed in the same garb minus the dark hood.

"*Dugan?*" Rowan was unable to say anything more. It couldn't be, but there he stood. Dugan gently stepped beside Cadrissa. He stooped low and placed a strong hand upon her delicate shoulder. A soft nudge roused a low moan. He continued to rub her shoulder until she lifted her head from the floor.

• ● •

Fluttering her eyes, Cadrissa managed to sit up with Dugan's gentle assistance. Upon doing so, she looked him full in the face, unsure of just what she was seeing.

"Dugan?" she hoarsely whispered. "I thought you were dead."

And then a thought came to her. "Am *I* dead?"

"No. Not yet."

"Then—"

He put a finger to Cadrissa's lips, surprising and delighting her at the same time.

"I need the incantation for the scepter," he said, then removed his finger. She wished he'd left it longer. "What is it?"

"You look better in this outfit than that black one with the face paint." A half-delirious, lopsided grin parted her lips. "Course, you'd look good in *anything* . . . especially that breechcloth."

"Cadrissa, I need you to focus." Dugan's green eyes blazed into hers.

Her eyelids fluttered again as a greater sense of understanding washed across her brain. "I don't hear the voices anymore."

"They're gone," said Dugan.

"Cadrith—"

Sudden realization of what had happened flooded her mind. Only she wasn't in his horrid room anymore, and the dark shapes holding her down were gone as well. She was back in Lann's tower.

"He's gone now too," said Dugan as he gripped her shoulders firmly but gently. "You're safe. I need you to tell me how to make the scepter work. I need the incantation." Cadrissa had become like a statue, absorbing all that he said with a blank expression. She was trying to process everything that was flying at her but couldn't get a handle on it.

"Cadrissa." Dugan's voice had an edge that pulled her out of her stupor rather sharply. Focus. She needed to focus. She was safe. She was in Lann's tower. She was free from the voices and Cadrith . . . and Dugan was standing before her . . .

"Do you know how to activate the scepter?" he asked. This wasn't really right. She'd seen his dead body. Seen his body burn up in flames, actually. He was definitely dead. So did that mean that she was dead too? She'd asked that before, but should she really trust him? After all, if he was dead already, then—

No. Focus. She needed to focus. A quick check told her she was still very much alive. A little sore, but still very much alive.

"The scepter, Cadrissa," Dugan repeated. "Do you know how to activate it?" It was as she took a closer look at Dugan that she could see what wasn't right. While it looked like him, it wasn't him. There was something slightly off—something she couldn't put her finger directly on, but it was there. And it was enough to mark him as the counterfeit he was.

"You're not Dugan."

"The scepter, Cadrissa." Dugan shook her slightly in an effort to emphasize his point.

"Please, Cadrissa." She noticed Rowan for the first time. "We need to know how to activate it." She also saw the room with fresh eyes. It looked like it had been through a war. That wasn't right either. It should have been clean and pristine, like she'd last seen it, not this wreck surrounding them. What took place with Cadrith hadn't taken longer than a few moments . . . right? But how did she overcome him when *she'd* already been overcome? And how did this Dugan look-alike fit into everything?

"Tell him what you know," Rowan insisted. "We don't have much time. He's here to help us."

Seeing she wasn't going to get her answers, she decided to trust Rowan. Nervously clearing her throat, she said, "We found a book that should contain it." She pointed out the desk and the tome still resting upon it. Amazingly both had remained undisturbed by whatever had laid waste to so much of the interior. "I was going to investigate it but got . . . distracted."

Dugan released her from his grip.

"So who are you really?" She watched him pick up the scepter beside her and then head for the desk.

"Right now, an ally." Dugan's voice was calm yet authoritative as he climbed the dais' last step, stopping before the desk. He peered at the book with an intense gaze. Cadrissa slowly nodded, letting the words sink in.

"What happened?" she asked Rowan. "This place—"

"There was a fight."

"With *him*?" Cadrissa pointed to Dugan.

"No."

"Where's Alar—"

Her tongue froze upon catching sight of the elf slouched against the broken paneling. She was far too pale. And there was blood and—

"What happened to—"

"He said he'd take us with him if we gave him the scepter and the way to activate it," said Rowan, glancing at Alara longingly. "It's her only hope."

She knew he was right. She could hear Alara's slow, labored breathing even from across the room.

"How long was I out?"

"Long enough. You find it yet?" Rowan asked Dugan, who, Cadrissa saw, was flipping through pages at a steady rate.

"I think so," he said, lingering on one page in particular.

Intrigued, Cadrissa took a few steps toward him, adding, "You can only use it once in your lifetime."

"Once is all I'll need." Dugan ripped the page from the book and stuffed it behind his belt.

"What—"

Cadrissa rushed forward but was stilled by Dugan's piercing eyes. He unsheathed his sword with one smooth motion. Cadrissa took a step back as the blade burst into white flame. With a steady hand he touched the tip of the weapon to the naked pages, setting them alight.

"What are you doing?" She was beside herself upon seeing the rest of the book catch fire.

"What I was told to." He descended the dais' steps.

"But—all that knowledge . . ." Her voice grew small.

There was a flash of white light where Dugan had been standing. When it was gone, a towering figure of a Galgalli had taken Dugan's place. The scepter had grown in size, matching its wielder's new proportions. A flutter of his wings stirred small pieces of rubble in the air.

Cadrissa was speechless. Like Rowan before her, she felt the pressure of his gaze upon her for a moment along with the terror of being laid so bare before another being. She sighed in relief when his intense gaze faded.

"You sure you want to come with me?" the Galgalli asked Rowan.

Rowan's face was set. "Yes."

"And you?" Dugan inquired of Cadrissa.

"W-where are you going?"

"Thangaria."

Cadrissa's mouth dropped open. "*Thangaria?*" This was incredible. To walk along the very halls of the gods—what was that compared to this tower and whatever else it might hold? This was a once-in-a-lifetime opportunity—no, once in *several* lifetimes. She had never heard of anyone other than the gods going to Thangaria. How could she *ever* turn such an offer away?

"I'm in." Cadrissa released a simple spell, knocking the tome from the desk and down the dais. The action extinguished the flames with a whooshing slap. She didn't want this place burning down before she'd had a chance to look it over. And now that she knew where it was, it would be easier to find it again once she'd finished her time in Thangaria. *If* she finished it, she supposed. When this was over, she would be free to spend as much time as she liked here. With just that one thought the past few days of her life—the terrible times and torments she'd endured—faded far into the background.

Dugan's white eyes went from the book to Cadrissa. Again she felt her discomfort under the gaze increase until at last he spoke. "Very well," he said with a sweep of his wings. "But your safety will be your own concern."

"Agreed." Rowan gently began picking up Alara.

As much as her thoughts were alight with the approaching wonders of Thangaria, she was still struggling to understand what had happened while she was possessed. But no matter how hard she tried, she couldn't put together the pieces. All she had were the memories of being trapped in her own mind and of Cadrith trying to take her over . . .

"Wh-what happened to her?" Cadrissa tried again to get an answer. Rowan's eyes didn't reveal more—didn't *want* to reveal more. But they didn't have to. She knew what had happened . . . what she must have done.

"Rowan . . ." Cadrissa didn't like the unease growing inside her.

"We have to hurry." He sounded like a captain addressing his guards. "She's getting worse."

Cadrissa bit her lip and tried to help him. Everything was a blur again, but a more normal sort of blur—nothing like the daze induced by Cadrith's grip. She was aware of Rowan slinging his shield over his shoulders and carrying Alara to Dugan—the angel. He took her in his larger hands while both she and Rowan climbed onto his feet.

No sooner had she taken hold of the thongs of his sandals than they were away, flying through the sky. Like when she was carried by the roc, she saw the clouds thicken and then disappear and felt the cold air wrap around her. But unlike with the roc, they didn't stop ascending. Instead they moved beyond the planet and then into the open cosmos between worlds.

She heard the mighty wings flapping, and then she figured out their destination. It was the sun.

Wait? The sun?

"Hold on." She heard the Galgalli's words clearly in the cosmic silence.

She was about to scream for him to reconsider, but he put on a burst of speed. It was unlike anything she'd experienced before. Even the roc's death spiral was like a leisurely descent in comparison. Worse still was how rapidly the sun was approaching. She could feel the heat—almost taste the fire. There was a strange sort of metallic tang to it she found oddly out of place.

And then they were mere feet from the colossal ball of flame. When a wild flare of fire burst straight at them, she closed her eyes and pressed as hard as she could into the Galgalli's leg. And then an incredible wave of heat encompassed her.

CHAPTER 20

THIS THRONE IS THE KEY TO OUR ULTIMATE FREEDOM.

—Vkar, first god of the cosmos

Once his eyes cleared from the brilliant flash, Gurthghol found himself no longer in Galba's circle. There was nothing around him but stony wilderness. He still was in the chair but was now nestled against a rugged outcropping. His location was a mystery. He ran through a mental inventory of the possible realms. Each of the gods' realms had its own unique look and nature. And from what he could see of the wide panorama around him, he wasn't on any of them. Nor did it look like any of the planets that made up the Tralodroen system. So where was he?

Of course, it was also possible none of this was real. All of this could be an illusion—another of Galba's tactics to keep him from taking the throne. Assuming what he'd done—the actual taking of the throne—had been real, then it was conceivable this would be her next move to try to stop him. Then again, maybe he never made it to the throne. *That* could have been the illusion instead.

Testing out the bands on his wrists and feet, he found them real enough. The sensation of being totally trapped in the throne was the worst part of all of this. He could deal with strange locales and unknown situations, but being stuck to the throne itself was his worst fear come to life. The throne had never done such a thing before; he didn't even know it could. Vkar had never built it for confinement. It wasn't meant to be a prison, even though that was ironically what it had become in the end—for both father and son.

No, this wasn't right. This couldn't be real. The scenery. The bands. All of it. It had to be Galba. She was still trying to hinder him with whatever was left at her disposal. He didn't really believe she'd just let him take the throne from her. If all she had left were tricks to turn him from his goal, then that showed him how desperate she truly was.

"I don't know what you think this will achieve," he accused the air, "but it won't stop me."

He struggled again against the bands. They wouldn't budge. Not even a fraction of an inch. If they were an illusion, they were a good one. Of course, they could be real. He had to consider that possibility too. Perhaps Galba had found a way to augment the throne since it had fallen into her keeping. Maybe it was another safeguard to keep the wrong people from claiming it. If so, then it shouldn't have been used against him. If anyone was the rightful heir to the seat, it was him. The firstborn of the gods, he was next in line for the empire—assuming the empire had remained after his father's passing, that was—and thus the legal and appropriate candidate to take the throne as his own. But the brief span of time in which he had sat in it showed him the utter folly of anyone who lusted after it.

And yet here he was again, taking it once more for the same reason he'd done so the last time: the preservation of their reality and way of life. As much as he would have liked to think otherwise, it seemed not much changes in the cosmic scale of things—or perhaps in their understanding of and interaction with it.

"Galba!" Gurthghol vented his rage.

How was she doing this? As long as he sat on the throne he was in command of it. That truth couldn't be denied. Which meant if he really was sitting in the throne right now, then he hadn't been picked up and deposited anywhere else. So was he really in command of the throne?

Closing his eyes, he focused his thoughts upon it. Focused on what he remembered and knew to be true about it after having sat upon it for all those years. Looking inside himself, he realized the connection between him and the throne was as it should be. No illusion could mimic that, as it was a part of his own spirit tapping into and grabbing hold of the very heart of the cosmos. So he was sitting on the throne and had connected with it once again. That meant the rest had to be an illusion.

Once more, Gurthghol tried to free his hands and feet, straining against the bands. Once more nothing came of it. He had to focus. Senseless flailing would accomplish nothing. Closing his eyes once more, he sought to tap into the throne, drawing on its great power to aid him. How could Galba be standing against the throne like this? It wasn't possible.

He should have been in Thangaria, making ready to stand against Cadrith. Taking a few calming breaths, he forced himself to still his mind and spirit. Once finished, he opened his eyes. Before him stood his father, the first god, Vkar.

"You couldn't keep away from it, could you?" Vkar asked. He wore a rich samite tunic over black pants with tall black boots, appearing just as he had in his prime. Long white hair flowed from his head, highlighting his wise, powerful face. His familiar long white mustache outlined his strong chin. Gurthghol was speechless. His voice, his manner, everything was a perfect match. Only it was all wrong. Vkar was dead. His father had been killed by Sidra—the older, *true* form of his father, not this younger version before him. The throne was real. He knew that in his core. The rest was the lie, and the sooner he unwound it the faster he could be off to Thangaria.

"I'm not going to play your games," Gurthghol growled.

"You think I'm an illusion, don't you?" Vkar asked, taking in Gurthghol and the throne with a curious eye. "I don't blame you. They'll try anything to get the upper hand and keep you from victory."

"My father's dead," he replied coldly. "I saw him die. You aren't Vkar."

The other stared into Gurthghol's eyes for a moment before nodding briefly. "Maybe not the Vkar you were expecting, but real enough for the time being, until what's left of me runs its course."

"His essence!" Gurthghol had completely forgot about having some of it left in his veins when he took the throne. Could *that* be what was causing all this?

"It makes for a unique combination when added to the throne," said Vkar. "It was never meant for two gods, just one."

"So you're *real*?"

"More like a shadow," Vkar continued, "for as long as this present sun is shining."

Cold, hard reality latched its firm hand on Gurthghol. "How can I even be seeing you? I thought what remained—"

"Wasn't me." Vkar gave a knowing nod. "You thought it was just an energy source of mine."

"So then, it's not?"

"It is and it isn't."

"What does *that* mean?"

"That for a very short while, I can talk with my firstborn son."

"If you're from his essence," said Gurthghol, "then why don't you look like he did when he died?"

"Our spirits never really age. You should know that by now."

"So then, all this time we kept you locked away in the tunnels of Thangaria—"

"It wasn't really me, Gurthghol," said Vkar. "It was just a part of me. And it will be gone soon enough."

The sense of finality to those words snapped Gurthghol back into his present situation. The longer he wasted what precious time remained, the less of his father's essence he'd be able to access.

"Am I still in the circle?" he asked.

"You haven't left," said Vkar.

"Then what's going on? How do I get free of these bands?" He struggled once more against the iron bindings.

Vkar seemed in no hurry to deal with that, instead asking, "Why did you take the throne again?"

"To save Tralodren."

"That planet you and your siblings created?" Vkar raised an eyebrow.

"How did you know about that? We didn't do that until after you'd died."

"You already know the answer."

"The essence." Gurthghol quickly put everything together. "It's in me, and so you know what I know."

"More or less."

"And Endarien too, I suppose."

"For the short time what's left of me remains." Vkar's face became serious. "You really shouldn't have taken the throne again."

"I didn't have any other choice," said Gurthghol.

"One world, son. It's hardly worth it."

"And the pantheon," Gurthghol added. "Nuhl wants to finish off what it started with you and Mother."

"And you're so sure of that?"

"It won't rest until we're all dead, you know that."

"There can be other things worse than death," said Vkar in a voice that was too flat for Gurthghol's liking.

"We lost you, Mother, and Thangaria," Gurthghol told his father, forgetting that if he really was already inside him, then he was privy to such knowledge already. It just felt good to talk to him after all these years, even if it wasn't really his Vkar. "The empire's in ruins. All we have is our own realms and each other. And if we lose that, we lose everything."

"I never would have figured you as one so dedicated to family," Vkar mused.

"As we get older we often see things differently."

"Yes." Vkar nodded. "We do, don't we? But taking the throne again . . . Haven't you learned anything from when you last had it?"

"I have," Gurthghol confessed. "I can finally see why you did what you did. Everything about Nuhl and Awntodgenee—it's all clear to me now." He allowed himself a small measure of delight upon seeing his father's pleasure in his statement.

"I always hoped you would in time. You were so close to me in so many ways—a worthy successor in many regards."

"You were a visionary, Father, and I'm going to build upon that vision. Today, I'm going to achieve what you couldn't."

"Then be prepared to stand alone," said Vkar. "Your brothers and sisters are still stuck looking at only a part of the larger whole and are content with the status quo. Only they don't know that the status quo—"

"Will destroy them in the end," Gurthghol finished. He'd come to this realization recently as he pondered the upcoming threat.

"Yes." Vkar shared another proud grin. "You are my son . . . and my pride."

"I only wish you'd lived long enough to see this day."

"Who's to say I haven't?"

Gurthghol said nothing, enjoying the moment. He almost allowed himself to imagine it could very well be real. That his mother and father lived, the empire never fell, Thangaria was still in existence . . . that his daughter . . . He snapped back to his senses.

"So how do I get back to the circle?"

"You *are* in the circle," said Vkar. "You never left, remember?"

"Then what's all this?"

"Remember what I told you about two gods in a chair meant for one? You're both in the circle and outside it at the same time."

"How? All I did was sit down."

"And I sat down with you at the same time."

"So now there's a contest of wills," Gurthghol concluded.

"The throne knows its maker and master, so it naturally defaulted to me and what my preference would have been."

"Which is?"

"The Expanse," answered Vkar. "I always had a place for it in my heart. Seems I still do."

"And the bands?" asked Gurthghol.

"Probably a manifestation of that conflict."

"*Probably?*" Gurthghol raised an eyebrow.

"I don't know everything, son. But I do know that if you focus on putting the last of my essence into the throne, that should clear things up. Once it's out of your system, it will recognize you completely."

"But won't that interfere with the throne even more?"

"No. It was created to withstand a great deal more than that."

"But what will happen to you?" asked Gurthghol.

"Does that really matter?"

Gurthghol mulled it over for a moment and decided that, given what was at stake, he supposed not. And he could always pull what remained back out of the throne later to investigate further.

"It would have been nice to have you stand beside me while I dealt the final blow," he confessed. "Even if it *was* just for a moment."

"And who's to say I won't be there?" Vkar's question filled Gurthghol with new strength. "If we truly are united in purpose, then *your* victory will be *our* victory. You have the potential to do it. You know that. Out of all your siblings, you're the best suited and most prepared to see it through."

"I won't let you down, Father."

"I know. Now go. Finish what I started."

Gurthghol closed his eyes and willed the last of what remained of his father, the first god to arise in the cosmos and challenge the Cosmic Entities, to flow into the throne. He forced it deep inside its incredible well of might, waiting for the last drop to leave his system. When he opened his eyes, he was back in the circle. There was no Galba, only the empty glade and ancient stones. The bands had also vanished. He was one step closer to *true* freedom. The last few were still ahead of him. No more tricks. No more hindrances. Only him and the last vestiges of the past that needed clearing away.

He closed his eyes. The ring of stones around him crumbled away with a small earthquake. This let what was behind the stones—hidden for centuries—come into view. Twelve thrones, similar in design to Vkar's but less ornately decorated, encircled the dais. Once he and his family had used them in the creation of Tralodren. Now they would serve another purpose.

None of the pantheon had any idea what he had done when he'd created their thrones. He had wanted them to have a taste of what Vkar's throne allowed. He thought it could put an end to the conflict that had raged between them for sole ownership of Vkar's throne. It also provided a way finally to be free of it. Each throne was an anchor that tied Vkar's throne to Tralodren.

Like a web, the twelve other thrones held the first in place, preventing it from going anywhere else.

The plan had worked wonderfully, allowing Gurthghol his long-desired freedom. And now here he was, back to imprison himself once more. But a sacrifice had to be made, and he was ready to make it. Just like his father before him had been ready to do the same to free the cosmos from its imprisonment. In that, he guessed he truly was his father's son.

The earth shook again, and the thrones uprooted themselves from their ancient locations. Each flew straight at Gurthghol, or more specifically at Vkar's throne. As they neared, they became transparent and merged into Vkar's throne in rapid succession. Gurthghol felt every throne lose itself in the majesty of the main throne. Like buckets filling a pond, the lesser thrones augmented Vkar's throne.

When the last of the twelve thrones had been absorbed, Gurthghol opened his eyes. There was now nothing but the glade and the pine trees encircling it. The crater created by his arrival still smoldered. The stone circle that had stood since the creation of Tralodren was now gone. Only the central throne and the dais remained. He willed himself and the throne to hover above the dais. Turning around in midair, he observed the two statues that flanked him. Vkar and Xora, the first gods. His parents.

"You *will* see our victory, Father." A wave of his hand melted the marble forms as though they were slabs of butter in a fire. The statues became a soupy white mass that seeped into the earth along with the shrinking dais. Satisfied, he took off for Thangaria faster than a shooting star, passing through the Grand Barrier as if it were nothing but mist.

CHAPTER 21

FREE WILL ALLOWS FOR CHOICE; INACTION INVOKES FATE.
ON THE ONE HAND THERE IS FREEDOM TO PLOT OUR DESTINY;
WITH THE OTHER DESTINY IS THRUST UPON US.

—**Callum, Elyelmic philosopher**
(1254 BV–1057 BV)

On the surface of Thangaria, in the middle of the crowded courtyard of Vkar's hall, a new arrival added to the growing throng. Those gathered from across the realms hushed as the Galgalli set foot upon the ancient rock. His majestic peacock-feather wings folded behind him as the others looked on. Rowan could feel their stares firmly affixed to his person but didn't give them more than a passing thought. His full attention was on Alara and what needed to be done next.

Both he and Cadrissa detached themselves from the avenging angel's sandals, where they'd hung on through a truly amazing ride. They'd flown straight at the sun and then, as far as he could tell, through it—coming out of what he thought looked like some sort of portal similar to, though much larger than, the one he'd seen in those jungle ruins back on Talatheal. He wasn't given much time to take it all in; their course took them straight to the largest of a group of floating rocks in what Rowan discovered was a near-endless ocean of them. And now that wild journey had come to just as sudden an end.

"This is amazing," Cadrissa said as they stepped away from the Galgalli. "No mortal has set foot on Thangaria—ever. And yet here we are."

The avenging angel stooped to lay Alara carefully beside Rowan. She didn't look any better but thankfully also didn't look much worse than when they'd left Lann's tower. They still had some time.

"Thank you for honoring your word," Rowan said while watching the Galgalli return to his full height.

"If you want to live, stay away from the battle," said the divinity before taking wing for what appeared to be a palace in the distance. Following his departure, Rowan took interest in the bizarre and wonderful figures gathered around him. All of them seemed as interested and unsure of these new arrivals as they were of them.

"I need your help," he beseeched them in Telboros, hoping some among them could understand him. "She's dying, and we need a priest or healer to bring her back to health." His eyes searched the varied faces that were still trying to make sense of these new arrivals.

No one came forth.

"Please," Rowan pleaded. "She doesn't have much longer."

A white-robed figure emerged from the gathered host. As tall as the Galgalli who had brought them, he seemed eternally youthful, though his eyes spoke of a wisdom gained from many a year of life. His clean, smooth skin and dark brown hair had the sheen of eternal health.

The brass circlet studded with cream-colored jasper stones complemented his wide segmented brass belt whose buckle was an ankh.

"That's a Lord of Life," said Cadrissa, dumbfounded. "An *actual* Lord of Life."

"You've come to an odd place to ask for healing, given what's about to take place." The lord's words were in Telboros and were as gentle as his soft blue eyes.

"Can you help her?" Rowan watched the lord draw near.

"I'm a Lord of Life, the very servant of Asora," he replied, taking a knee. "If her time has not yet come, as it must for all things, then I will do what I can to save her." This said, he focused his full attention on Alara.

Rowan saw Cadrissa draw nearer out of the corner of his eye. Her excited expression had turned into something more somber. "Rowan." He felt her hand upon his shoulder. "I wanted to—I wanted to say I'm sorry."

"For what?" he said, splitting his focus between Alara and Cadrissa.

"If I hadn't given in to the necklace—"

"You weren't yourself." Though he knew it was the truth, Rowan couldn't help but be troubled by Cadrissa's confession. "It wasn't you who attacked Alara."

"I know, but still—"

"Let it go," he said, becoming fully engrossed in the titan lord's actions. "I don't hold anything against you, and I know Alara doesn't either." He was pleased to hear himself say it. Even more pleased that he actually believed it. He really couldn't blame Cadrissa. Not if he was going to be honest. Who knows how long the necklace had a hold on her? Perhaps from the time in the ruins when she'd first picked it up. She clearly hadn't been herself, and so really couldn't be held accountable for what happened. And even if she was, doing so wouldn't help Alara or anyone else.

"I've done all that I can for her," the titan lord informed Rowan.

"That's it?" He'd been hoping for—expecting—something greater and more involved. This *was* a divinity, after all.

"There wasn't much more that could be done."

Rowan didn't see any discernible change in Alara's condition. "She doesn't look any better."

"Her wounds were deep," said the Lord of Life. "Asorlok's call is also strong upon her."

Fear settled and took deep root in Rowan's soul. "What do you mean?"

"It means that she's very close to Mortis," answered the titan lord. "It might be too late to save her from its grip." The Lord of Life's countenance further melted when he took in the pain his words inflicted upon Rowan. "Rest easy. There's still a chance she can live through this. Don't let hope die when there's still some fruit on the vine."

"Rowan?" He turned upon hearing his name.

"Vinder?" Rowan almost didn't recognize the dwarf moving his way. He looked younger than he remembered, and then there were his eyes: he had two of them. Even so, the features and manner belonged to the same Vinder he'd gotten to know during the time they spent trekking across Talatheal.

"I thought I recognized the voice," said the dwarf, stepping closer. "The lich got you too, huh?"

"We're not dead," said Cadrissa, clearly surprising him.

"Then how did you get here?"

"It's a long story."

And then Vinder caught sight of Alara. "What happened to her?"

Rowan was about to reply when Cadrissa beat him to it. "She was wounded while looking for a way to stop Cadrith."

"She doesn't look too good."

"I'm hoping the Lord of Life helped change that," Rowan explained.

Vinder noted the nearby titan lord with a nod. Apparently such things were more common sights in one's afterlife. Or maybe certain things just lost their previous importance after dying . . . "So you came to fight, then?"

"Not really," she replied.

"Then you picked a poor time for a visit."

"We were really coming here for Alara," Rowan heard Cadrissa explain as he watched Alara for subtle signs of improvement. "Rowan figured where there was a battle, there were bound to be some healers."

"So, *you're* dead, right?" Cadrissa asked. "I mean, you really *died*, right?"

"Yeah, I'm dead," said Vinder as plainly as one might comment on the weather.

"I just didn't know dead people looked so good. You even have both your eyes."

"They'll come in handy soon enough."

"So, *you're* here to fight?" she asked.

"I volunteered to come with Drued and some others. He wanted to bring warriors to stand before Cadrith. I figured I could do with a rematch. And it might brighten my prospects later."

"What do you mean?" Rowan couldn't miss the curiosity in Cadrissa's voice.

Vinder paused, hesitant about speaking what was just behind his lips. "I have some old debts to repay," he finally managed.

"So you weren't just padding your pockets." There was a kindness to Cadrissa's words that surprised Rowan—and actually pulled him back into their conversation.

"No. There were certain obligations I needed to attend to."

"And you're still attending to them now?" Despite her soft tone, Cadrissa's question weighed heavily upon all three. Rowan shared Cadrissa's mixture of amazement and pity for the dwarf. To learn that even in your afterlife things weren't fully at rest was unsettling to the young knight.

Again Vinder struggled to say something, though this time the battle was less intense. "I want to apologize." This got a fresh hold of Rowan and Cadrissa's attention. "I shouldn't have judged you as harshly as I did. I see that now. I didn't know anything about anything and should have just let things be."

"Well, I said some things too," Cadrissa confessed.

"Some of which were true," Vinder pointed out.

"Even so, I probably shouldn't have said anything. You were grouchy enough without me egging you on."

"You too, Rowan," Vinder continued. "You actually weren't half as bad as I first thought you were."

Rowan wasn't sure how to respond or if he should at all. Vinder and Cadrissa continued to stare at each other until a low moan from Alara broke the silence.

"Do you mind if I stay a moment?" he heard Vinder ask softly beside him. "I'd like to pay my respects while I can."

Rowan nodded softly.

•●•

"We've waited long enough." Khuthon spoke for the majority of the gods who'd taken their place around the table, waiting for the last of their number to arrive. So far the only holdout was Gurthghol. Ganatar had urged them to wait a little longer and give his absent brother a chance to show up, but the longer they waited, the more he doubted his brother would appear. Soon frayed nerves and escalating concerns took hold of the entire council. It was time to move things along.

"I agree," said Asorlok. He wore silver plate mail over a richly adorned outfit. The armor wasn't a whole suit. Instead pieces were layered over luxurious fabrics at strategic places: his chest, the front of his legs, his shoulders and forearms. A pair of long black leather gloves matching the leather hooded cloak completed his attire. "Gurthghol's obviously not going to appear, so why waste any more time?" He carried no weapon to war—not one that could be seen on his person.

"We will all stand against this threat," Saredhel calmly replied. She was also the only god—outside her husband—to not have changed her garb for the coming battle. Neither Dradin nor Saredhel wore any armor nor carried any weapon, outside of Dradin's staff. Even so, none doubted either of the gods' commitment to the coming fight. The two may have had curious ways, but they were loyal to their family, and had brought additional warriors to the battle.

"What's that supposed to mean?" Khuthon snapped. "Is he coming then?"

Saredhel remained silent, bald head bowed and white eyes on the collection of parchment and plans scattered across the table. Dradin remained silent beside her, body cloaked in dark green robes and hood. Only his well-trimmed white beard was discernible under the hood's shadow. His emerald eyes reflected the sparking light of his strange and wonderful staff.

"Well, at least we have made *our* presence known." Perlosa tilted her nose toward the ceiling. She'd returned to the council, bringing with her the required warriors, who were now with the others in the court-yard . . . meager though their number were.

She'd also donned a suit of silver armor. It had been molded to fit snugly on her upper body and shone over her torso to her shoulders. Her legs were bare, as were her snow-white arms. Her waist, though, was encircled with a silver skirt made of sharp, jabbing points of metal, which matched the style of the diamond icicles hanging over them for extra protection. In each of her fur-lined boots she'd placed a dagger, and she carried a long spear at her side.

"Please, sister," Rheminas mockingly scolded her. "Father's angry enough."

"We were merely stating—"

Khuthon cut her off. "You're fortunate to remain here as it is. That pathetic force you brought back with you won't—"

"At least we brought more than a *stick* to keep the—"

"Enough!" Ganatar's displeasure rang throughout the chamber. "We don't have time for this bickering. Rheminas has said he has something to add to our efforts, and now it's time to hear it."

"Thank you, uncle." Rheminas nodded at Ganatar. "After carefully pondering the matter before us, I've concluded the easiest way to resolve this threat is *not* to fight it."

"I can't believe it." Khuthon shook his head in disgust. "I've raised a coward from my loins."

"No coward," Rheminas continued, "but a wise warrior. I've created a new Galgalli to be our champion. With him taking up the fight, the risks are greatly reduced."

"I'm still waiting for you to explain why you went about creating one without consulting the rest of the pantheon," said Ganatar.

"As I said, there wasn't any time. We all had plenty to take our attention."

"And yet you found time to make a new divinity." Perlosa coldly eyed Rheminas. He didn't like the subtle smirk playing across her face. He'd seen it before whenever she thought she might have found a way to get her brother into trouble. Such ideas rarely worked, but just the sight of it was annoying.

"There's creating one and then there's debating that creation," he hurriedly explained. "We didn't have time for both. I simply did what was needed."

"But what good is a Galgalli against an agent of Nuhl?" voiced Olthon. "You've just created him to go to his death. And how would that leave us any better off?"

"That isn't much of a plan, Rheminas." Khuthon also wasn't impressed. If he didn't know better, Rheminas might have thought there was actual pity in his father's eyes.

"No, it wouldn't be—at least not by itself." Rheminas flashed his teeth. "But I've added a few other matters to make it more successful. After what happened with the battle in Galba's circle, I began to make some new plans. As I'm sure others have as well." He let his eyes slowly pass over Asorlok and Saredhel. The others wouldn't get it, but both of them would, which was just the point.

"Yes." Aero's eyes became shadowed in speculation. His short black hair contrasted with his soft brown eyes, which burned with a strong inner focus. "I don't recall us ever learning the full story behind those waiting to ambush Cadrith in the circle." The twelve-foot elven god wore pure shining silver-banded mail. It sloped over his shoulders and down his chest to where black, brass-studded leather strips made a skirt about his waist. His cape was a deep purple silk, matching the tunic under his armor. His helmet was open faced with cheek and nose guards and a purple-dyed strip of horsehair going across it.

"No, we haven't," Rheminas continued, "but it's safe to assume there were some backup plans in place. Seeing as we already had one . . . which failed . . . I figured it was safe to put forth another."

"Get to the point," urged Asorlok.

Rheminas remained unmoved. There was a certain timing to all of this, after all, and he wasn't about to stray from it. "I took one already destined for my service and simply promoted him into a Galgalli. And to further even the odds I sent him after the same weapon those in the circle were going to use against Cadrith."

"What weapon?" Drued's eyes narrowed.

"The Scepter of Night," Rheminas said while glancing Saredhel's way. "At least that's the name I understand it's known by. Saredhel will have to correct me if I'm wrong on that. Though why you left it in the hands of such a worthless servant is beyond me."

"You mean that old scepter that blind elf was carrying back in Galba's circle?" Drued apparently was putting things together.

"The very same."

"And how did you learn all this so quickly?" Olthon studied Rheminas with greater scrutiny than before. He let her. He didn't have anything to hide—not about this. "The battle at Galba's circle wasn't that long ago."

"I have my ways." Rheminas tried to turn his smirk into a harmless smile. If anyone wasn't fooled by his efforts, they made no indication otherwise. "Someone who knew more about the matter firsthand was able to fill in the missing information for me."

Drued snorted. "I still don't see what's so special about that scepter. It didn't look like much to me."

"Probably because it didn't have an opportunity to be used," said Dradin.

"Wait." Causilla grew concerned at Dradin's casual remark. "*You* know about this too?"

"The scepter was created by the wizard kings when they sought to take our power and place in the cosmos," Dradin explained. "It was intended to weaken any divinity or god it struck."

"And how come we're just hearing about it now?" Olthon's question was clearly shared by others of the pantheon. No matter. Things were nearing their end. And everything was moving in just the right rhythm.

"It was never used," said Dradin, "and was far out of the hands of anyone who might want to get hold of it. It wasn't a threat."

"And yet here it is." Perlosa often enjoyed stating the obvious. "And being used by some mortals you also wanted to keep a secret from us."

"Thankfully, it's in the hand of *our* champion now instead." Rheminas regained control of the conversation. "And with it, he should have a *tremendous* advantage against our enemy. He might even *slay* him outright."

"We doubt that," Perlosa scoffed. "But at the moment we are more concerned with all this secret plotting."

"Whose side are you on anyway?" Panthora growled. In her true form she resembled a twelve-foot Celetoric woman with black dreadlocks. She wore a simple sleeveless dress made of hide and cured leather stitched together. Other than this she wore hide boots tied with strips of leather and carried a short sword and a hide-covered wooden shield.

"We could ask you the same thing," Perlosa snapped back. "It *was* one of your knights with those others in Galba's circle, was it not?"

"Don't you ever get tired of looking for something to criticize?" There wasn't outright anger in Panthora's face or voice, but the glint in her eyes conveyed her thoughts for all to see. "It's a wonder you're even tolerated here at all."

Perlosa made a rigid face of hate before retreating from Panthora's glare.

"The scepter could change the outcome." Khuthon raked his goatee in thought. "But this Galgalli has just been created. This isn't a seasoned veteran like those who used to serve us. How confident are you in his abilities?"

"I would think him good enough to take on the task or at least help *tenderize* our opponent to give us a significant advantage. He did well enough when put to the test when just a human. With this new rank and the scepter, he should be a worthwhile opponent."

"Are we really going to do this?" Causilla searched for any sense of dissent from her mother and father. Both Ganatar and Olthon remained silent.

"It wouldn't be a bad idea to test Cadrith's limits—expose any weaknesses," said Khuthon, still mulling new plans through. "And if the Galgalli got in a good strike with that scepter, well, that would *really* change things."

"And if the Galgalli should fail?" Shiril let the question linger a moment before asking, "Won't that be the same as giving this scepter to Cadrith?"

"He doesn't know how to use it," said Rheminas. Let them keep poking at the edges of his planning. All he had to do was get a few onboard. The others would follow after that. And he was close to getting those few. "Even if he did get it, he wouldn't know how to turn it against us."

"You sure about that?" Panthora's question brought a momentary pause to the discourse.

"Are you really suggesting we're going to let this battle hinge on *one* warrior?" Aero's tone was a mixture of anger and confusion. Rheminas didn't expect the Race Gods to be the first to adopt his idea, so he wasn't surprised. "I thought we just did that with Endarien. Have I brought my best warriors here for *nothing*?"

"No, not nothing." Rheminas calmly continued explaining the plan. "They'd be a safety net should the Galgalli fail."

"But we *are* putting our hopes on this Galgalli," the god of the elves continued. "That's what you're saying, isn't it?"

"We tried sorting through what Saredhel had given us," Rheminas continued, "but it didn't work out. We either misunderstood or—"

"Or he was not strong enough to do what was expected of him," Perlosa interrupted.

"Foolishness, if you ask me." Drued's face was lined with pragmatism. "If one warrior couldn't defeat the first pawn, and Endarien with Vkar's essence couldn't do it, then why send this new avenging angel into the fight?"

Rheminas was about to open his mouth when the large chamber doors opened. Behind them was the very Galgalli of whom they spoke. Perfect timing. Just like he'd planned.

"Ah, welcome, Dugan." Rheminas cheerily motioned him inside. "I trust you were successful in retrieving the scepter." All eyes followed the newly minted divinity as he strode toward the table.

"I was."

"And the incantation to use it?"

"I have it as well."

"*This* is what is going to stand before Cadrith?" Perlosa sniped with obvious disapproval.

"If *you* wish to take his place, you're more than welcome to do so." Rheminas mockingly made an inviting gesture to his sister, which brought a round of low laughter and muttering from around the table. Perlosa rebuffed him with an icy huff.

"So it seems we're agreed on this option." Ganatar pulled everyone back together. "Since I've heard no real opposition, let's put it to a vote." His powder-blue eyes surveyed the faces of all gathered. "Who is in favor of letting this Galgalli fight as our champion in the coming battle?"

All present raised their hand.

"It's been decided." Ganatar lowered his own hand, the others following his example.

"We're still using the same plans that I've laid out," Khuthon hurriedly interjected, "but we'll wait until *after* the Galgalli's death before we put it all into action."

"*If* he dies," Olthon added. "If Rheminas is right, we can save a good many lives today with this Galgalli's success."

"But what about Saredhel's prophecy?" asked Panthora.

"What about it?" Endarien brushed such concerns away like bread crumbs off a table. "I already proved we didn't have the right interpretation."

"I thought it spoke of us being able to stop—"

There was a great rumble across the room.

"He's here." Asorlok's words brought a soft veil of dread upon the assembly.

"You know what to do." Rheminas' hard stare burned deep into Dugan's white eyes.

"I do." There was another rumble—this one louder than the previous one.

"Then fight well." Khuthon's words were a mixture of command and blessing.

The Galgalli ran out of the room as still another rumble shook the room and the sound of fighting started to draw near.

"Well." Khuthon slapped his hands together. "It's time to join the fray. Even if we're starting out behind the lines, this is still going to be a *very* impressive battle."

"What about watching it from here?" Asora pointed at the nearby Great Eye.

"No." The unusual amount of steel in Dradin's voice surprised many. "Some things need to be done in person."

"Indeed," Khuthon concurred joyfully. Perlosa rolled her eyes, but nobody seemed to notice or care.

CHAPTER 22

"Where are we?" Hadek took in what appeared to be a large system of labyrinthine tunnels. Both he and Gilban had emerged out of the darkness—or had they appeared there? He wasn't quite sure.

"You've been brought closer to your destiny." Gilban still had his new eyes, but now his body was transparent—ghostly in nature.

"So how come everyone seems to know so much about my destiny except me?" Hadek asked while looking around the seemingly endless underground corridors. Getting no reply, the goblin returned to the priest. Gilban stood still, head cocked as if waiting to hear something.

"What is it?"

"The battle is about to start."

"Battle?" Hadek dared another look around, fearful now of hordes of attackers rushing at him from all over the honeycombed rock in which he stood. "Here?"

"Not here." Gilban raised his insubstantial staff, pointing out the ceiling still several feet above them. "Up there."

Hadek raised his eyes to look. "Where are we?"

"Thangaria—well, *under* it, to be more precise."

"Thangaria?" Hadek tried the word out on his tongue. "Where's that?"

"The former home and now council seat of the pantheon."

"The *pantheon*?" Hadek's eyes went wide. "What kind of destiny do you think I *have*, anyway? I'm not a god and—"

"As I said, you've been brought *closer* to your destiny."

"Which lies *here*?" Hadek kicked a heel into the earth.

"Yes . . . well, above us, really."

"So I still have a choice, huh? I can still *refuse* it, right?"

"You always have a choice."

"Yeah, you keep saying that—you *all* do—but I'm beginning to think it isn't really true."

"Are you?" Gilban sounded slightly concerned. "What would life be without free will to choose our own course?"

Hadek didn't answer, letting his gaze sink to the dusty ground instead. He wanted an escape from those strange eyes and the unsettling feeling they caused. Seeking to calm himself, Hadek wandered a few yards away from the ghostly priest. The silence that followed became oppressive. Still, he held to his thoughts a while longer, for they were big thoughts—important thoughts—almost too great to have come from such a small creature.

"So you won't tell me what my destiny is?" he finally asked. "You're just going to bring me closer to it?"

"Did I tell you when you wanted to know about your death?"

"Then how do I know that I *want* this destiny?" He stared through Gilban's ether-like frame and into the sprawling tunnels beyond. They could have allowed a giant easy access without so much as scraping the top of his head.

"By having faith that you're able to endure the mantle waiting to be placed upon you." Gilban's words were soft, yet potent.

Hadek drew within himself yet again. This was a far cry from where he'd seen himself in the ruins of Taka Lu Lama. Once he had dreamed of being great, of finding his way out of the jungle and ruins and the tribe that oppressed him to seek his—

Suddenly time ground to a halt, the gravity of the revelation coming into place for the first time. The idea consumed him. Had he really been looking for this . . . for this destiny?

"Seems like we all have our fates linked in dealing with Cadrith, and there's nothing else. That doesn't sound like free will to me." Hadek didn't like Gilban's lack of a reply and decided to continue speaking. "So what happens if I refuse to do what you brought me here to do?" Again he found himself looking both at and through the former priest.

"Then you won't fulfill *this* destiny and will walk into another instead."

"So you aren't going to tell me what the other destiny would be either, huh?" Hadek's eyes wandered. He could feel Gilban's eyes looking through him as he did so, tugging Hadek's thoughts directly to the dark chasm of uncertainty, led by the strong faith that it was the right thing to do. Such thoughts were frightening, as Hadek would have preferred to know what awaited him in the chasm, not leap in blindly.

"If I told you, you'd be given an unfair advantage in making up your mind," said Gilban. "It could hardly be a fair choice. No one knows what their choices will hold in and of themselves. One may guess and perhaps rightly surmise some of the outcome, but there's much more to every choice we make. All choices come to form a life and then the destiny which is part of that life."

"But you said all of us have already been chosen to deal with Cadrith," Hadek reasoned. "We're champions who are supposed to stop him. So if I've already been chosen, then how can I have a choice in what I'm supposed to do? And why choose me anyway?" Hadek was still having a hard time wrapping his head around such a grandiose idea.

Gilban smiled.

"What now?" He was perturbed by Gilban's air of smugness, which still clung to him in the afterlife.

"You've asked a very wise question." Gilban's smile widened. "There are currently two great forces in the cosmos: Awntodgenee and Nuhl. They're old and have existed since before the beginning of creation. They also have a pact. This agreement grants them the right to destroy worlds, among other things, and the time has come for Tralodren to meet this fate.

"However, they've also decided to give each world a chance to save itself from destruction. It was a clause put in by Awntodgenee, which is never interested in destruction but rather in finding ways to preserve the cosmos. For this reason, Awntodgenee has called its champions to keep Tralodren from its looming end."

"So we're all *Awntodgenee's* champions?" Hadek's face wrinkled in thought.

"Yes."

He was amazed Gilban gave him such a simple answer.

"And we're supposed to *save* the world?" At this his brow grew even more furrowed. He was beginning to understand things better, but the ramifications that came with that understanding . . . "So Cadrith is *Nuhl's* champion?"

"Yes."

"So we have to stop Cadrith from winning so Nuhl doesn't win and destroy Tralodren? And you didn't know *any* of this until you were dead?"

"Not all of it, no. But once I crossed over, many things became clearer."

"And how does the gods getting destroyed come into all this?" As long as Gilban was being less cryptic in his replies, Hadek thought to press him for more answers. "I thought you said it was just Tralodren Nuhl wants to destroy."

"Another matter," Gilban said almost dismissively, "but tied to all this nonetheless."

"It has something to do with Sidra, right?" Hadek's eyes glimmered as more insight dawned. "That was what Saredhel said when I saw that woman kill that other man on the throne."

Gilban gave Hadek a pleased nod. "Sidra was Nuhl's first champion, and she was the first to try to kill the pantheon. The first world Nuhl came to destroy was Thangaria; killing the gods was just a side benefit. When Sidra had served her purpose, she was destroyed."

"But we're on Thangaria now."

"A small fragment of the world survives, housing the council, who are above us right now preparing for war."

"With Cadrith?" Hadek tried imagining such a thing going on above him but couldn't get beyond the rough rock.

"Yes. They know Cadrith will come to them and try to kill them off, as Sidra once attempted. Cadrith craves and is driven by the same thing. Any action taken against Tralodren would be blocked by the pantheon. They're the natural protectors of the planet. It's one of the few things they all agree upon. So you have to remove the pantheon if you want to do anything to Tralodren—either before or during your tampering—as you're going to meet up with them at some point along the way. That's why we are here—why *you* are here."

Hadek thought he felt a tremor in the rock around him. It was faint, but he could have sworn—

Another one shook the tunnels. This one was so strong that dust and tiny pebbles spilled down from above.

"What was that?" The goblin's eyes widened. There arose another rumble, this one much louder and more forceful than before, shaking the tunnel system from top to bottom as more fine debris rained down.

"The battle's started." Hadek's body grew cold at how fatalistic Gilban's voice sounded. "I have to attend to another matter, but I'll be back before you have to make your choice, though deciding now would be much easier than waiting to the last moment."

"Wait." He tried reaching out to Gilban as he began fading from sight. "You're just going to leave me here?"

"I'll return. Have no fear," he said before disappearing into nothingness.

"But—"

"Make your decision." The seer's disembodied voice hovered near Hadek's ear. "For when the time comes to act, you'd best be ready."

•●•

"She's not getting any better." Fear soured Rowan's stomach. He, along with Cadrissa, Vinder, the Lord of Life, and a fair number of onlookers in the courtyard, had been watching Alara's progress. Those who'd come from mortal stock seemed to be the chief watchmen among the gathered host. The rest made ready for battle, while those manning the walls kept their vigil.

"Can't you do anything else?" Rowan's vision blurred from the forming tears.

The Lord of Life was sympathetic. "I've done all I can. As I told you, she was very close to Asorlok's grasp. I may not have been able to pull her from it."

"This can't happen! This—"

Suddenly everything started to shake, accompanied by deep roars of thunder. The gathered warriors focused on the walls and the giants who manned them.

"The enemy is upon us!" came a shout from one of the watchers. "To arms!"

Vinder snapped to attention.

"To arms!" The shout of another watcher was followed by trumpet blasts and the din of rushing feet and clashing armor as the assembled troops made ready for war.

"If you don't want to fight, then you'd better find someplace safe," Vinder told Cadrissa. "She was a good woman." He slapped Rowan on the shoulder before dashing off into the increasingly frenetic flow of bodies around them.

"It's too late for her." The Lord of Life rose and began scanning for a place to take his stand. "Best to let the living deal with the matters of life. If you value your own, then you'd get far from this place." The titan lord left them and joined the wave of shouting bodies.

Rowan's chin fell onto his chest as tears began to flow. "This isn't right." Once more, he felt Cadrissa's hand upon his shoulder.

"Rowan . . ." Alara's weak words pulled him up from his melancholy.

"Alara?" His face brightened, if just for a moment. Her violet eyes moved his way, but there was hardly any force of life behind them. Her breathing had slowed and her skin had turned the palest he'd yet seen. Her eyelids were drooping as if trying to fight back sleep. This wasn't a natural sleep, though, but the rest of eternity. The blood around her mouth, which had dripped down her chin, neck, and over her breasts, told him that much. The slurping sound of her breathing filled in the rest.

"Hang on," he pleaded. "I'll get you out of here and take you to a healer who can—"

Alara's head moved slowly from side to side.

"Yes. There's still hope." Tears continued to flow down Rowan's cheeks. Alara attempted a deeper breath. It was a terrible sound, conjuring up an image of sodden bellows. And then she closed her eyes.

"Rowan." Cadrissa's words were softer than silk. She had managed to stop her own tears for the moment, but the crestfallen expression on her face remained.

"No!" He shrugged off her hand and words. "I'm not giving up. Not now. Not on her." He grabbed the shriveled panther paw around his neck and closed his eyes in prayer. If there was ever a time he needed Panthora, it was now. Even though Alara was an elf and his training had told him Panthora was the goddess of humanity only, he had to believe that she could do something. After all, didn't he have some great destiny or purpose? So he grounded his faith on hope and hope alone, since there was nothing in his religion to support what he was about to do.

"Panthora," Rowan pleaded through his tears, "if I've ever been found worthy in your sight, if you have ever shined your favor upon me and my adherence to your faith, then I ask you to save this woman from death.

"Hear my prayer and look to this woman—this brave woman—who has given all in this fight against even *your* enemy. Bring her back from the point of death. Bring her back to me." Rowan continued holding himself in reverence as he waited for his miracle to manifest. But as he waited, he only heard Alara slipping further away—her breath growing fainter, her spirit unshackling from her body.

"*Panthora?*" Rowan could only whisper. He heard Alara breathe her last, heard the rattle of her chest, the weak, expired breath leave her lungs, and the stillness of death drape itself over her as a shroud. In that final moment, he took Alara in his arms, crushing her with an embrace as his tears flowed over them both.

•●•

Cadrissa could do nothing but watch and try to stay out of the way of the commotion around them. Things had grown even more frenzied. There came another shaking and what sounded like an explosion very near them. The frenetic bodies around them didn't stop their rush to and fro. Their tall frames prevented the shorter mortals from seeing what was happening. It was only by some great miracle the trio hadn't been stomped to death. She didn't believe that such fortune would stay with them forever.

"Rowan, we should seek shelter inside . . ." Her words pulled the knight's face in her direction. Her heart was wrenched upon seeing his sorrow-laced eyes. He held the woman he'd loved as if he'd never let her go, but in the end he released the cooling flesh from his arms. There came another loud explosion followed by some acrid smoke drifting into the courtyard. There were screams now too, war chants, and the sounds of death claiming another soul. Rowan looked swiftly over this escalating melee, watching the throngs of armed warriors rush out of the gates at the threat coming to claim the pantheon.

"What do we do now?"

"You find yourselves some shelter and live."

"Gilban?" Cadrissa was as amazed as Rowan at the priest's sudden appearance not more than a few yards from them. Only this wasn't the only amazing thing: he wasn't alive anymore. That much was obvious, since Cadrissa could clearly see through his incorporeal form. The next surprise was his eyes: they weren't blind anymore. Just as with Vinder, what had been marred in life had been restored in the afterlife.

"This isn't your fight, not anymore," he said and made his way closer. Surprisingly, his staff clicked on the ground as if it was solid wood instead of ghostly vapor. "We've all done our part now."

"Why are *you* here?" Cadrissa ignored the chaos around them and the strangeness of his greeting. First Vinder and now this . . . If they were going to get any answers on anything, this was probably their next—and last—best chance.

"To help *you* finish *your* path," Gilban calmly replied.

"But you just said—"

Gilban raised a hand. "I said you have finished your part in *this* matter. You both have lives of your own to lead—should this battle be resolved in our favor—and you won't be able to live them out if you don't survive to take part in them.

"Come now, take shelter and live." Gilban directed them to the palace they'd seen upon first arriving. "You can't win this fight, for it isn't yours to wage."

"So we just run and *hide*?" Rowan's face darkened as rage replaced his sorrow.

"You are free to do as you wish," said Gilban. "For each man molds his own fate. I just came to help guide you to a slightly better end before I come into *my* eternal rest."

The bedlam continued all around them, but Cadrissa and Rowan still remained in its midst. Nearby, a handful of freshly slain gigantic warriors toppled to the ground. The slight tremor at their fall stoked fresh fears inside the mage. And yet Rowan seemed unconcerned, caring only for Alara's body.

As time passed, Cadrissa grew more tense as she took quick glimpses of the raging war. Self-preservation was winning out over curiosity. Finally, she could wait no longer. "I'm not going to stay and get slaughtered, Rowan." She lifted the skirt of her gown above her knees. "If you want to stay out here, that's your business. I'm sorry for your loss, but not much more harm can be done to Alara. *We*, though, are not so invulnerable." This said, she began running for the hall and what shelter and safety she could find there, darting through the armored titans and shorter warriors as she went.

•●•

Rowan watched Cadrissa flee. The ground trembled more frequently now, the screams coming more often and closer. It would soon be too late to get to safety. He had to make up his mind . . . and quickly.

"Go, or what your goddess has planned for you won't be able to be fulfilled," Gilban urgently pleaded.

"And what do you know about Panthora?"

"That she has a great plan for you."

He said nothing. There wasn't anything he could say; Gilban had spoken the truth. In everything leading up to this moment, Rowan had lost sight of that. He'd been so focused on everything else, he'd forgotten the joy he'd first felt upon hearing that Panthora had a plan for him and a great place to fill in the time to come. She'd shown him so much already. This wasn't where it was supposed to end. There was still a future before him—a good one, from what he recalled. He might not be able to understand all of what was going on, but he could take strength from that.

Rowan bent low and lifted Alara's body. No matter what his own future held, he wouldn't leave her corpse to be trampled. "So since you seem to know everything," he asked the ghostly Gilban, "what am I supposed to do that's so great, then? Can you tell me that much?"

"Only that not all battles are waged by sword and spear; through faith and patience come all victories."

The rising clamor told Rowan it really was time to leave. He made his way to the palace, dodging what bodies he could, running into those he couldn't. From above, he heard a flap of massive wings. Glancing heavenward, he saw the Galgalli—Dugan—flying overhead, shadowing Rowan as he went out to face the enemy.

"Seems *some* of us still have some battles to fight," he muttered.

Rowan had had enough of divine wars, secret agendas, and death. Let those called to fight the battle do the warring. He'd find a place to sit and think about what he'd heard and what he was supposed to do next. At the very least, his wounded heart could perhaps slow its bleeding . . . maybe even start to heal.

CHAPTER 23

Cadrith was able to escape the protective barrier around Tralodren with ease. He'd appeared before it with but a thought. Nuhl's augmentation would only accelerate the gains he'd already made, providing him with the bridge needed to span any divides of space or time he might encounter. Tapping into that power had allowed him to simply reach out and touch the barrier. The supposedly impenetrable structure became like fog.

Once on the other side, he hovered above the planet, seeing things in a truly new and wonderful way. This was his *true* destiny. Unshackled from Tralodren, he was free to embrace the entire cosmos. And all that stood in his way would soon be lying dead at his feet. With but a thought, he flew deep into the darkness of space at an incredible rate of speed. He wanted to get some distance from the planet before opening the portal to Thangaria. He didn't want to encounter any surprises nor take any unnecessary chances.

He got as far as the moon and then stopped. Closing his eyes, he imagined himself being anchored in the center of the cosmos. It was getting easier to command his new abilities and power. He felt the disturbance like a subtle shift in air pressure. A swirling portal of darkness, large enough to allow for his newly increased size, spun into existence a few yards away. Like the portal that had taken him to the Abyss in the first place, and then back to Tralodren once more, this one would get him to his next destination. Opening his eyes, he flew into the darkness, ignoring the slight pinch over all his flesh as he was transported to what remained of the supposed first planet ever created in the cosmos.

On the other side of the portal was the debris of Thangaria, a world long since lost to time. A remnant of it still clung to scraps of life and purpose, this being the section Gurthghol had saved when he took the throne from his father. It housed the same palace where that fateful battle had been fought millennia ago. He found it fitting that another like it would be waged there again. He hurried toward it, giving the small bits of rock and clouds of dust no mind. They were nothing, as the pantheon would soon be.

Soon enough he spied the walls around Vkar's hall and the forces assembled to defend it. They actually thought this assortment of divinities and formerly mortal followers would put up a solid threat against him. It was almost too easy.

Staff in hand, Cadrith set his sights on the gate. Within moments, the assembled horde fell upon him, and for about an eyeblink of time he was reminded of the Syvani's attack in Arid Land. But unlike then he could now unleash the full breadth of his divine power against them.

It didn't matter if his victims were titan lords or other divinities—even a god's followers now risen to divine warriors—all fed his dark ambition as he pushed his way closer to the hall and the gods inside. None even got close enough to strike him. If this wasn't power at its best, he didn't know what was.

A blast of black energy from his staff struck the gate. It fell before him in a crumbling heap, displaying the insides of the courtyard beyond. All who could tried their hand at assailing the dark god, but none were successful. Cadrith conquered all by his force of will or his staff, which he came to use as a crude club.

A volley of arrows descending upon him from behind the decimated wall were quickly consumed by a splash of black energy. The attack drew Cadrith's ire at a band of Elyelmic archers. Undaunted, they readied another volley.

Tapping into the power of his patron, Cadrith extended a hand toward the elves, releasing a wave of hungry darkness that disintegrated each one like fat in a fire. They didn't even have time to scream. Nothing remained. No bow. No armor nor arrow. He could sense Nuhl's pleasure with his progress. The entity wouldn't enter the fray itself, but was watching intently.

Cadrith pressed onward. A Lord of Life rose up against him just as he stepped inside the gate. A thrust of his staff impaled the titan lord before he could react. Aghast from the shock and searing pain, the divinity slid down the ebony shaft until Cadrith flung him free with a twist of his wrists. The lord was dead before he touched the ground.

Another Lord of Life, who had risen up right behind the fallen titan, joined his companion in death via a host of sinister black daggers that had suddenly appeared hovering in the space between him and Cadrith before darting for and into the divinity with violent accuracy. Two of many Cadrith slaughtered. Humans, a few giants, along with other divinities—he couldn't keep track. And he didn't really care to. After all, these things were far beneath him—flies to be swatted. Why concern himself with them as he cleared them from his path? It wasn't important who he squashed under his heel, ripped asunder with his own two hands, blasted with his strength of will, impaled and wounded with his staff . . . This was all just a preamble to the fight to come.

He'd become so entranced with his single-minded bloodletting that he didn't notice the shadow darkening the sky above and ground below until its creator landed in front of him. When he did, all combat ceased.

Before Cadrith stood a Galgalli, the executor of the pantheon's judgment. All feared and respected them . . . except Cadrith. Even so, he stilled his attack with the others. He needed to calculate how best to defeat this more challenging adversary. He could feel those solid white eyes looking deep into him, peeling all he was away to evaluate every little thing about him. But Cadrith was doing the same to the Galgalli.

There weren't many in the cosmos—only a handful at most, if he recalled his history correctly. And then he saw the writing on the Galgalli's hood. It was the same text he'd seen back in the tower in Frigia. There was a sense of satisfaction in that. He'd get revenge for having the other part of his plan thwarted. He also noticed the Galgalli held the Scepter of Night at his side. Perfect. It may as well have just been handed to him. Everything was falling right into place.

No one on the battlefield spoke a word. Everyone gave the Galgalli and Cadrith a wide berth, forming an arena-like opening in their midst. Their part in this battle was over. Whatever happened was on the Galgalli's shoulders now.

"We meet again." Cadrith's eyes narrowed as he tightened his grip on his bloody staff.

"Cadrith Elanis." The Galgalli's words were flat but strong. "I've been given the right to enact the full punishment afforded me by the pantheon: your total demise." The Galgalli drew his sword with his right hand. A white flame wrapped itself around the blade as soon as it was unsheathed.

Cadrith's mirthless smile widened. "They really *have* sent you to your death, haven't they?"

"Coo at limbea. Estorin gablin moor." The Galgalli began speaking what Cadrith realized was the scepter's incantation. The silver scepter started to glow white hot. Tiny letters, too small to be seen fully by the mortal eye, but not missed by Cadrith's, appeared all over the device in a shining purple radiance.

"You're wasting your time," he mocked.

"Uthran-koth. Uthran-koth. Japeth real!" As the words of the spell continued to pour from the Galgalli's mouth, the scepter's light increased in its intensity, exploding in a prismatic aura and covering the entire object before fading away. When finished, the scepter was plain again. Had he not seen the previous display, there wouldn't have been any sign that the scepter was anything special.

"Akeem. Akeem. Akeem. Yorn toth osiri latas!" The Galgalli charged forward with silent effort, his strong body forcing its way into Cadrith's personal space. For his part, Cadrith simply stood before the oncoming Galgalli. Calm and seemingly unconcerned, he waited for the divinity to draw closer . . . closer to his demise.

Cadrith blocked the first sword strike with his staff. Reacting just as quickly, the Galgalli swung the scepter up. Before he could complete the descending arc, however, Cadrith vanished, causing the Galgalli to stumble forward a step before he could regain his balance. Suddenly, the avenging angel was attacked from behind by a burst of black energy. The blast shot into him like a tidal wave, knocking him to the ground and sending singed feathers scattering.

The Galgalli leapt up and spun around, swinging his blade at his foe. Cadrith retreated a step from the strike that would have sliced his intestines wide open. The divinity tried again, this time thrusting his flaming sword forward in hopes of skewering Cadrith. This too failed. Cadrith simply sidestepped the action with the most condescending of smiles. He brought the end of his staff to bear upon the Galgalli. With a swift slice through the air he managed to cut into the forearm of his opponent, who failed to parry the attack with his sword.

"I'm not going to let you stand in my way," Cadrith said, slowly pacing around the Galgalli. The divinity stood watching, studying Cadrith's moves. Both were so engrossed in their tasks they'd failed to see the pantheon joining the silent crowd to watch the battle. They maintained a safe distance from the two combatants, keeping with the rest of the gathered warriors around the combatants.

Dugan kept up his study, looking for any weakness he might be able to exploit. This wasn't exactly like fighting in the arena, but similar in many ways. He had an opponent, and the fight was to the death. Only there was more at stake than just one life: what happened next would define the fate of millions.

"Your judgment is at hand." His white eyes shone under his mask as in the same instant he brought forth the scepter, swinging it with all his strength. Cadrith deflected the strike with his staff in an incredibly fast movement.

Before he could register what had happened, the scepter had been knocked free from his grip. Between the force he'd put behind it and the strength of Cadrith's swing, the scepter struck the ground with such an impact it sunk far into the rocky earth in one swift moment. He couldn't see how deep it might have wedged itself in the earth for the flurry of fists that followed.

He was able to block some, but not all, of the whirlwind strikes. Soon blood was dripping from his shoulders and even places on his wings. The strikes were too rapid for him—like a storm of hail pummeling him into a pulp—and he could do nothing against them. As soon as he defended himself against one, another would follow. He wouldn't be able to take much more. That would have been true, he supposed, if he was still just a human. But he wasn't a human anymore.

Dugan focused his mind, slowing the world. In this condition he was better able to observe his reflexes and gauge his reactions. In so doing, he was able to create an opening and avoid the crescendo of fists. In a heartbeat, the former gladiator started blocking the seemingly endless attack with growing ease. A moment more and he found himself countering the assault with well-placed punches of his own. Though not at the same pace of Cadrith's furious blows, they did the job of keeping the new god on his toes . . . until Cadrith grabbed hold of the blade of Dugan's flaming sword.

"I think I've kept your masters waiting long enough." His eyes dug into Dugan's white orbs.

"You overestimate yourself," said Dugan before daring a rapid glance to discern the state of the scepter. He couldn't see much of anything. Only a hole. That wasn't good. But if he could make an opening, perhaps he could—

"I don't think so." Cadrith gave a hefty tug, pulling the sword closer—and Dugan along with it. "Let's hope you die better than you fought."

Cadrith suddenly stopped, turning his head to look behind him, but keeping Dugan in his grip.

"Finally come out of your hole?" Cadrith mocked the pantheon gathered a safe distance from them. "You saved me the time of having to go inside and rustle you out."

Dugan tried pulling his sword free from Cadrith's grip but couldn't. Something held him back . . . and it wasn't just Cadrith. There was something else there. He could sense it. It was at that moment that he saw a glimmer of Cadrith's patron and was overcome with the grisly revelation of what it was he was truly facing. He'd known it before on an abstract level; it was part of his mission. He'd just been so focused on one thing after another he never really gave it a great deal of thought. That was, until it was staring him in the face.

Dugan beheld the swaying black mass of tentacles with their snapping white teeth. Instantly, he was reminded of his first encounter with it back on Colloni when Alara had been ushering him off the island. Once more he felt the shudder-inducing radiation of its being. Only now, he saw it with his new eyes, allowing a full comprehension of the might and nature of what it was he was opposing.

Another puppet ready to fall. There was a strong hatred dripping from the voice that came to his mind. A hatred not just for him and the others fighting it but also for life in general.

"Now"—Cadrith returned his full attention to Dugan—"let's end this."

Cadrith unleashed two attacks simultaneously. His fist rushed into Dugan's masked face with a loud cracking sound, birthing more blood from the Galgalli's jaw and mouth. While Dugan was staggering from the punch, Cadrith's eyes glowed an inky black. The same dark energy shot out of his sockets and into Dugan's chest.

He fell backward as if he'd been kicked by a mule, breastplate bubbling and melting on his bronze flesh like wax in an oven. And though he might have been knocked onto his back, Dugan's sword stayed in Cadrith's hand. He continued to hold on to its flaming surface without any sign of discomfort or injury. Dugan's flesh continued to sizzle and boil as the destructive energy ate away at the tissue beneath his skin. Now unarmed, he could do nothing but peer up at Cadrith with tired eyes. His breathing was labored, and he ached all over. The wound on his chest was more caustic than the worst acid as it burned through muscle . . . then bone . . . and then his heart . . . Unless he could find a way to reverse his injury or defeat Cadrith in one strike, he wasn't going to fulfill his duty. He clenched his teeth and tried with all his might to push back the pain and the darkness skirting his vision.

•●•

"I don't believe it," Khuthon cursed. "That was a Galgalli! A *Galgalli*! It should have at *least* slowed him down."

"So much for your plan." Perlosa shot Rheminas a mocking glance.

"He's too infused with Nuhl's presence," Dradin grimly assessed. "The time that we gained was the best we could hope for."

"What about the scepter?" Olthon didn't take her eyes off the battle for a moment, hopeful for some sort of sudden change in the situation.

"You saw what happened." Rheminas brought up his flaming sword and tightened his grip. "It's lost in stone or, who knows, in the catacombs."

"But we could still retrieve it." There was a sliver of hope in Olthon's voice and face. "If we—"

"We don't have the time," Khuthon growled. "We need to fall back on our original plan."

"So what do we—"

Panthora was cut short by Rheminas' scream as he took off for Cadrith at top speed.

"The time for talk is over," said Aerotripton before running after Rheminas. Khuthon followed, as did Drued, Endarien, Asorlok, and Ganatar in turn.

Dradin encouraged the rest of them. "If we all stand against him now, we stand a better chance of victory, but only if we *all* rise up to fight." Not fully convinced, those remaining hesitated, seeking Saredhel's counsel.

"I will join you," said the seer. It was good enough for the rest, who hurriedly charged into the fray.

• ● •

Cadrith heard Rheminas' shout from behind and was ecstatic. Whereas any other would have been petrified by the onslaught of so many gods rushing full force their way, Cadrith only grew more excited. He'd enjoy crushing them all, en masse or individually. As for how they wanted to meet their end, he'd leave it up to them.

Rheminas arrived first, fiery sword and dagger hungry for bloody retribution. Cadrith wasn't going to give it to him. He blocked the sword strike with the Galgalli's flaming sword and the dagger with his black staff. Rheminas snarled, gritting his teeth in his attempt to push through the blockade. Cadrith held him fast. Copper-colored fire flared in the corner of Rheminas' eyes and swiftly filled his sockets.

"Die!" the Flame Lord growled as the fire blazed from his eyes.

Instantly, Cadrith was covered in the coppery flame. But instead of being burned or writhing in agony, he remained unharmed. A simple mental command extinguished the flames at the same time Aero moved into the fray, swinging twice into Cadrith with his sword. But these attacks passed right through him, much to Aerotripton's amazement. Nuhl's added power was helping him anticipate their attacks and formulate rapid and fitting countermeasures. And Cadrith was enjoying every moment of it.

"Have you finished?" Before either could answer, Cadrith was upon them—sword flashing before Aero and a black blast of energy from his staff directed at Rheminas. The god of fire was sent flying backward. His place was quickly filled by Khuthon, who wasted no time in landing his meaty fist on Cadrith's chin. To Cadrith's surprise, he flew back a few yards, scraping his back upon the rocky earth as he skidded to a stop.

Khuthon was fast upon him, looking like he wanted to stamp him deep into Thangaria's crust. The temporary pain from the strike had already passed, but the anger from being put down was only rising. He leapt to his feet and brought his stolen blade down hard upon Khuthon. The sword struck the god of war's sword with a heavy clang. Moving faster than an eyeblink, Khuthon unleashed a series of swings and strikes Cadrith parried and blocked to the best of his ability.

He never had been much of a swordsman. Even with his new nature, it wasn't something he did well. Khuthon, however, was a master. Grim humor danced in Khuthon's eyes as he thrust and cut. He was enjoying this far too much for Cadrith's liking. But he was just one opponent. The rest had nearly surrounded him now. It was amazing to think it took a whole pantheon of gods to even come close to containing him. How powerful was he really? And how much more would he have to enjoy once they all lay dead at his feet?

Aero rushed him from his left whenever Khuthon allowed an opening for him to dart in. The Elyelmic god was bleeding from the last attack but still willing to suffer more in hopes of crushing Cadrith. But he wasn't about to allow him the chance. A swift punch to the head sent Aero spinning to the ground, unconscious. It was then the rest of the pantheon closed in around him.

Once again, Cadrith changed his location, moving to a new spot a few feet away from where the others had clumped together. Taking advantage of their temporary confusion, he lobbed the Galgalli's sword into Drued's back. The dwarven god groaned as he fell to his knees. Leveling his staff, Cadrith unleashed a burst of azure the pantheon's way. This was deflected by Dradin, who easily and harmlessly diverted the attack by means of a protective dome he'd erected with his staff over himself and the other gods.

"Stay behind me," instructed Dradin. "I'll see to the rest."

Cadrith laughed. "You really think you're stronger than Nuhl?"

"We'll find out." Dradin shot a green ray from his staff straight for Cadrith. He managed to hold it back with a raised palm, but only just barely.

Stop playing and take them out, Nuhl chided. *The longer you wait, the more likely you are to fail. You won't have my presence inside you forever.* Cadrith didn't like that assessment of his own prowess, but Nuhl was right. He needed to end this. He risked losing whatever edge he had the longer the battle lasted. And he wasn't about to let that happen. Thinking quick, he found a weak link and struck.

He made a fist. The ground beneath the gods crumbled. It was just as he thought. Dradin didn't think to cover the earth under their feet, just above and around them. As one, the pantheon tumbled into the growing hole underfoot.

He waited. He didn't need to move. Not yet. He knew they still drew breath, but as to their final end, he hadn't decided just yet. He was also making sure he'd taken care of all of them. He couldn't keep from counting their number again and again—putting names to faces. He'd been certain all of them had been buried in the debris at the bottom of the small crater, but something didn't feel right. And so he counted again. And again.

The sound of shifting debris didn't surprise him. The one who was the first to arise did, however. Asora, the goddess of life herself, had managed to claw her way up to her rather short-lived freedom. She was armed only with a rough club—not even armored—which made clear how much of a challenge she'd actually pose.

Kill her, Cadrith!

He didn't have to think about the order twice. Leveling his staff, he released a healthy dose of Nuhl's essence her way. Only it never reached her. In the time between her appearance and the attack, Khuthon had not only freed himself from the crater but also managed to jump into the path of the attack. The god of war took the full brunt of the assault, crumbling to his side.

"Khuthon!" Asora immediately sank to his aid.

"Cadrith!" Endarien bellowed as he flew straight into him. Cadrith was knocked to his back. Immediately Endarien began pummeling him with his bare fists. Pinned as he was from the collision, Cadrith had to work his hands free as his face was beaten into a pulp.

Finally, he got his right hand free. With it, he released a bolt of black energy into Endarien's side. The god gritted his teeth but remained fixed above Cadrith. The punches stopped. Cadrith used the opening to free himself from under Endarien. He willed himself healed of the recent abuse and stood between Endarien and the other gods rising from the pit.

Finish them! Kill them all!

As he readied to do just that, he finally understood why his original head count seemed off. He wasn't facing all the pantheon. There was still one missing. One he couldn't believe he'd so easily overlooked. Where was Gurthghol? Before any more could be said or done, there was an explosion of plum-colored light behind him.

Slowly, Cadrith made his way around to face the new arrival. "I was wondering when you might show up," he said as he studied Vkar's throne with renewed interest. "I didn't know you feared me so much that you'd steal the *throne* to fight me."

"I did what was necessary," said Gurthghol. "Sacrifices had to be made to keep you from getting out of your place."

"And where *is* my place?" Cadrith's sarcasm flowed richly from his lips. "If the rest of your family can't stand against me, then what hope do *you* have?" he continued, inching closer. This was almost too good to be true. He could retrieve the scepter later, and now he could claim the throne as his prize after defeating the pantheon. With both in hand he could make quick work of Nuhl and then set himself up as the greatest god in the entire cosmos. He couldn't have asked for a better table to be set in celebration of his victory. All he had to do was keep his wits about him long enough to assure that victory was his to claim.

Gurthghol only raised the index finger of his left hand. It was enough to hurtle Cadrith off of what remained of Thangaria and into the floating rocks and debris above it. He gnashed his teeth with each collision—some small and some not so small. He flew through them all, not stopping until he struck deep into the heart of a lifeless asteroid.

•●•

Gurthghol took in the carnage. He didn't have much time to do so. Cadrith would be stirring soon, thanks to Nuhl. Even with all his delays, from what he could see he'd arrived at just the right time. Surprisingly, the rest of the pantheon had been holding their own. It was clear, however, as they worked their way out of the hole they'd all been dumped into, they were already wearing down. Eventually, they would have fallen.

He watched Asora helping Khuthon to his feet. "Is he all right?"

"I'll live." Khuthon was winded but was making a rapid recovery.

"*Why?*" Asora, like the rest of the pantheon, displayed a mixture of confusion, amazement, and anger. "Why did you take up the throne again?"

"There was no other way." His reply was rather matter of fact. "It had to be done."

"We were willing to fight—were *already* fighting," Khuthon grumbled. "Things were well in hand."

"You would have failed." Gurthghol returned Khuthon's frustrated gaze.

"Is that right?" Khuthon gruffly replied.

"You *all* would have failed."

"So you had to break all the agreements we laid down at the beginning by bringing the throne back to us?" Olthon was less than pleased. "Now we not only have Nuhl against us, but you've also enraged—"

"Taking this throne was the last thing I wanted to do, but Saredhel's prophecy made it necessary."

"And how's that?" Rheminas' gaze was hot upon him.

Ganatar stepped into the conversation. "We don't have time for this."

"Agreed," said Gurthghol. "You see to yourselves and the wounded. I'll take care of Cadrith." Before anyone attempted any further rebuttal, he and the throne shot up into the thin atmosphere around what remained of the ancient planet.

CHAPTER 24

Hadek waited in the stillness of the labyrinthine tunnels. Waited and thought. What could he do? What *should* he do? That was a big question, and he felt he knew the answer—well, part of it anyway. He supposed he'd always known since just after his visitation in the small room in the temple on Rexatoius. The only challenge was getting the other part of the answer and following through on his decision. Following through was crucial.

He felt a few more tremors and watched a handful of dust and small pebbles fall from above. He feared being left alone in such a place and hoped Gilban would return soon. He paced the small section of tunnel he deemed safe enough for occupation—exploring further intimidated him more than the shaking and faint roars he could hear above did. He tried to imagine what it looked like when gods fought and couldn't even bring an image to mind. It was too fantastic for him to wrap his brain around.

"You have a great destiny." Hadek mimicked Gilban's voice almost perfectly. "Doesn't look too great to me." He switched to his own voice as he continued pacing. He found it helpful to pace and talk out loud as he thought. It helped bring some clarity to the whole matter, allowing him to reason it out as best he could.

"So I'm on Thangaria, gods are fighting above me, and I'm supposed to do something great . . ." He stopped and kicked a small stone down the facing corridor, sighing as he watched it skip away into the shadows. "Should have just stayed back at the temple on Rexatoius. At least there I was safe."

"But you were far from your destiny." Hadek turned to see the same dark-clothed woman who had visited him in the temple of Saredhel not more than a few feet from him. The exact same one who'd started him on this wild journey in the first place.

"*You.*"

"I'm here to help," said the woman, raising a warding hand to still Hadek's unease.

"Then get me out of here," Hadek cried as another tremor rumbled above. "You got me into this whole mess to begin with and now—"

"Is that what you really want?" The woman took a step closer, drawing back her inky hood as she did. Hadek watched her approach, transfixed by the transformation occurring as she neared. Her black robes lightened to a dingy gray and then a brilliant white as the hood fell away and vanished into nothingness, along with the former guise. What remained was quite familiar.

"*Galba?*" Hadek was taken aback by her supernatural brilliance and beauty. When he had control of himself again, he said, "I'd like some answers, please."

"About what?" Galba inquired softly.

"Everything. This whole quest, the war going on above us, the endless references to me having some great calling or purpose or destiny: *everything.*"

He waited for a response. Silence filled the chamber. Hadek soon grew restless and began to roll his right hand along in a gesture to indicate Galba should start talking. She didn't take the bait.

"Don't you have *anything* to say?"

Galba remained as calm as ever. "Why are you so troubled by being alone with your thoughts? Could it be you've already made up your mind, and now you're afraid to follow through on your decision?" It was Hadek's turn for taciturnity as Galba's words dug deep inside the core of his being.

"Gilban brought you here to make a choice," Galba continued, "or follow through on one you already made."

"That's what he said." Hadek was tight lipped.

"Has it been made then?" She took another step and leaned forward as if she were drawing closer to hear a faint whisper.

"Almost." Hadek's reply was smaller than his stature.

"Time isn't your ally, Hadek." Sadness tinged her voice.

"I know, I just . . ." He let out a sigh, then continued, "I don't know why anyone would pick me out for being a *champion*, like Gilban says I am. What can I do that's so great? What have I done to stop Cadrith? Nothing." Galba absorbed the goblin's dialogue with the most caring of green eyes. They made him feel like he was the only one in the whole universe worthy of their full attention.

"Awntodgenee must be pretty confused to have picked me with the others that were lumped together for this quest—or whatever it is. Dugan was tough. Rowan too. Gilban was . . . or is—or *whatever* he is now—he was good too. I'm just—"

"You're just *you*."

"Exactly." Discouragement slouched his shoulders.

"You're just you, and that's why I chose you."

"*You* chose me? Wait—*you're* Awntodgenee?"

"An aspect of it, yes." Galba's eyes twinkled.

Hadek shook his head. "I don't get any of this."

"I chose you because of who you are and what you represent. You have such wonderful qualities about you. Qualities that set you apart from all the others of your race. Haven't you often wondered why you were so different from your kin?" That was an understatement. Hadek had done almost nothing *but* that since as far back as he could remember.

"You've made good choices, hold to good beliefs, and have taken the step into a new world that few of your race—if any—will ever take. For these reasons you were chosen. You have the skill needed to be my champion. I've watched you since you were born, and have kept you safe until this time. You're the most important of the champions whom I've called for this task." Galba rested a hand upon his shoulder. Her words resonated with something deep inside him. He might not have known what was going on, might still have doubts swirling in his head, but inside—*deep* inside—it all made sense. It was all true. "In fact," she added, "all of the others were called merely to *help* you get to this point."

Hadek's head stepped to the forefront, debunking her claim. "Right."

"They all had a part to carry out, and they did it. Now it's time for you to do the most important task, which has been prepared for you."

"And what's that?" He still didn't know what he was being called to do . . . but he did have a hint, a *strong* hint, that was growing in strength with each passing heartbeat.

"My counterpart and opponent has raised its champion and so have I. It has used people, events, and situations to mold and create Cadrith. I've guided people, events, and situations to propel you to this point; the others helped you along your way. They found and helped free you from the ruins, took you all the way to the circle for the first confrontation with Cadrith, and now you're here for the last."

"Why, though? What's my purpose in all this?"

Before he could get an answer, there was a terrible commotion above. Rock and dust rained down and the tunnels shook from a tremendous explosion. He was blinded by debris and deafened by the thunderous crash. When his sight had returned, Galba was gone, and a silver scepter, the same one Gilban had retrieved from Gorallis, by the look of it—though much larger now—was sticking out of the ground a stone's throw from him.

It had crashed through the chamber's ceiling and was awash with an eldritch glimmer that was at once enticing and repellent. Nevertheless, he dared a step closer, looking up and around to make sure no more falling rubble would land on top of him.

As he neared the scepter, he heard Galba's voice in his head. *This is part of your purpose. Wield it as my champion and Tralodren stands a chance.* Hadek slowed to a stop before the enlarged scepter, ears still ringing and uncertain of what he was to do with it, how he was supposed to wield it . . . or if he even *wanted* to.

Of course, he knew he wanted to, and always had. He was just afraid to admit it—afraid to take the first step forward into grasping his dreams and making them a reality. Was it a dream of his to challenge Cadrith? No, but it was a dream of his to do something great—to *be* someone great. If he took the action presented him it could very well help him achieve that dream . . . *if* he should survive. But if he didn't, would that really be so bad either?

"It's time." Hadek jumped out of his thoughts at Gilban's shimmering manifestation beside him. "Decide quickly."

"Where did you go?" he inquired once he'd regained his composure.

"To places and matters that concern me, not you." Gilban's curtness amazed him. His time was nearly spent. It was time to decide. He just wanted to be sure—*had* to be sure.

"So Galba is an aspect of Awntodgenee?" Hadek studied Gilban's ghostly visage.

"Yes."

"And Awntodgenee can't lie?" His gaze meandered over to the shimmering silver scepter once again.

"It doesn't lie." Hadek could almost hear Gilban thinking: *Hurry up, Hadek, and make your move . . .*

"Then I've made my choice." He placed his hand on the scepter. Immediately it shrank back down to its normal size, fitting neatly into his grip.

"The scepter is already activated." There was some measure of pride in Gilban's voice that made Hadek less fearful of what was to come. But only *slightly* less so. "You just need to take it and strike true."

"And *that* will destroy Cadrith?" Hadek stared at the scepter. He was intrigued by its soft, steady hum and glamour.

"If you strike at the right time, yes," said Gilban as he pointed at one of the tunnels with his spectral hand. "Now go. Be quick and strike true." Sensing the last sand in the glass had finally begun its descent, Hadek ran down the corridor as fast as his legs would allow.

He'd thought the trek would have taken hours, given the tunnels' seemingly endless expanse, but he soon found the ground rising. Soon enough he was in a grand hallway decorated with all manner of finery found only in the corridors of the gods: riches beyond description.

Here he pushed himself as hard as he could to bring himself to the end of the breathtaking corridor, where a massive door happened to be slightly ajar. He was more than thankful. If it were closed, there was no way he'd be able to get it open. His small frame was greatly overshadowed by the door's solid, taller build. Squeezing through the opening, he made his way into the courtyard beyond, where the battle against Cadrith was coming to an end.

He couldn't see the fight, but he could hear it and smell it: electrical heat and blood mingling with the small fires and the odor of dying bodies. As he grew closer, Hadek could make out the form of a winged being lying prone and Cadrith gloating over him. He didn't have time to take in the whole scene; he could only focus on the most important matter. And there he was, the enemy to the pantheon and Tralodren, as Gilban had said.

Before he could get any closer, Hadek stopped. Cadrith was quickly surrounded by a handful of what he came to understand were other gods. Amazed at such a sight, he could do nothing but watch as they warred against the former lich, striking with blades, fists, and their divine power. Maybe he wouldn't need to attack Cadrith after all. Maybe all the gods would finish him off—as if gods could ever fail. And there were a lot of them too.

But just as he began entertaining the notion of getting a reprieve, his jaw went slack upon seeing them all drop into a large crater Cadrith created under their feet. He, like the rest of those gathered, could do nothing but continue watching in silence. Nothing seemed to move, not even time. He gripped the scepter even tighter, wondering if this was his time to strike. He was wide open if it was, because everyone else was giving him a very wide berth.

He snuck closer, though he doubted that any one of these giant-sized divinities and strong warriors would notice him pass among them. If not because of his height, then because their attention was focused elsewhere, but it was still better to err on the side of caution. He only had one chance with the scepter. It had to count. As he got closer, his stomach lodged in his throat. He could taste the rising bile. He willed himself onward, one foot after the other. He stopped in his tracks when he heard the sound of shifting rock and earth. It was coming from the crater. Someone was coming up.

Hadek watched Cadrith carefully, studying him between the tall pillars of people composing the crowded throng through which he waded. If he was to do something with the scepter, it would have to be soon. Even as he plotted his next course of action, a winged god—whom he assumed to be Endarien—collided with Cadrith. For a moment it looked like Endarien might finish off the former lich. But again, such thoughts were short lived.

Cadrith repelled him while looking like he'd never been attacked in the first place. Hadek was amazed. He grew even more so when yet another god arrived on the scene. This one, though, was seated in the same throne Hadek had seen at Galba's stone circle. Plum skinned and black haired, he had a long mustache and was dressed for war in dark armor. Thanks to the priests from his tribe, Hadek had learned a good deal about most of the gods—the Dark Gods most of all. And it was clear that Gurthghol had come to join the fight.

He didn't know if that was good or bad. He assumed it was good, since one more god in the fight was better than one less, but he was concerned about the presence of the throne. From how he understood things at Galba's circle, it was better for everyone if the throne had stayed where it was. He already knew it could make people into gods—Cadrith was proof of that. What it did to gods who sat in it, though, he wasn't so sure.

He didn't have to wait long to find out. Gurthghol flung Cadrith so far into the sky Hadek lost sight of him. This action not only surprised the gods and all the onlookers, but it left him wondering just what he was to do next. He wasn't about to try to go flying after Cadrith, scepter in hand. And no one said anything about the throne being here, nor

Gurthghol using it. Something wasn't right about this. And, worst of all, he didn't know how much time he had to sort it all out and do what needed to be done.

Resigning to a wait-and-see approach, he focused closely on Gurthghol and the rest of the pantheon. Hoping to hear what they were saying, he drew as close as he dared to the gods, who were speaking in tones he didn't take as being too friendly. Hadek felt safer remaining in the forest created by the taller divinities around him.

Gurthghol departed as quickly as he had arrived. Hadek assumed he was headed to find and probably finish off Cadrith. Again, he found himself wondering just what he was doing there in the first place. With Gurthghol's departure, a silence hovered over the place, allowing the groans of what looked like a large peacock-winged angel to catch the attention of all nearby.

Hadek watched as a pregnant goddess, who he thought might be Asora, made her way to the angel's side. Inching closer, Hadek noticed the divinity's flesh had been eaten away around his chest, muscles fading to bone over pulsating, moist organs underneath. Whatever had left such a wound must have been a pretty awful sight.

"Rest easy and be made whole," he heard Asora say as she placed her hands over the wounds. "You helped do a great service today."

Under the goddess' hands the other's ragged breathing eased, and his pallid complexion filled with a healthy color once again. New tissue grew over his bones, and his flesh wrapped up the wound completely. When he could breathe freely once more, he removed his mask and sat up to see what had happened around him.

"Is it over?" Hadek heard the divinity ask as he stood up with only minor effort—Asora aiding where she could.

"It seems that way, yes." Asora released a tired sigh.

"So all that fighting was for nothing?"

"I hope not," she said. "But not all the fighting is done." She shifted her gaze skyward.

Hadek mirrored the action, imagining what might be taking place in or even beyond that drab gray sky.

"Hadek?" The voice sounded familiar to the goblin. Turning, he discovered someone he wasn't expecting.

"Vinder?" he cautiously inquired as the dwarf drew near. He was dressed in armor and carrying an axe and shield that had obviously seen some action. The dwarf was sweating and looked tired.

"You have your eye again," he blurted out before he realized what he'd said. Thankfully, Vinder didn't take offense. Nor did he seem as bothered by Hadek's presence as he had been in times past. Instead, he actually seemed like he *wanted* to talk to him.

"You dead too?"

"No." He paused and waited for a heartbeat—just to be sure. "Not that I know of," he continued once he felt the comforting rhythm in his chest.

"First Rowan and Cadrissa and now you too."

"Rowan and Cadrissa are here?"

"Yeah," Vinder paused. "And Alara . . ."

I've guided people, events, and situations to propel you to this point; the others helped you along your way. Hadek rehearsed Galba's words, wondering if everyone had been brought here just to smooth his way forward. It was an intriguing thought, but not one he could afford entertaining at the moment.

"I saw Gilban too," Hadek continued. "Well, his ghost."

"So that would be everyone then—well, outside of Dugan, I guess. But he could still be here too somewhere, hidden among the warriors . . ." Vinder's gaze fell upon the scepter. "Is that the scepter from the circle?"

"Yes," he replied.

"What are *you* doing with it?"

"I thought I knew," Hadek began, "but now I'm not too sure." For once Vinder didn't fire back a sour retort. Instead, the dwarf merely nodded. It was almost sympathetic.

"I can understand that." He craned his head heavenward. "And so can everyone else here, I'd imagine. I guess we'll all just have to wait and see what happens next."

Hadek lifted the scepter, letting his eyes rest upon it. "I guess so."

CHAPTER 25

IF CONFLICT SHOULD ARISE, ONE MUST BE CAREFUL TO NOT BECOME
LIKE THE ONE THEY FIGHT. FOR IF VICTORY SHOULD BE ACHIEVED,
THEN THE FORMER VANQUISHED EVIL WILL BE REPLACED WITH A NEW ONE INSTEAD.

—The Book of Peace, one half of the Holy Dyad

Gurthghol was above the atmosphere with a thought. Already he was speedily tracking the path Cadrith left in the clouds of dust and debris. He'd wanted to get his attention, shake his confidence, as well as get him away from Thangaria. The place had suffered enough as it was. He wouldn't allow Nuhl the satisfaction of destroying any more of it.

He found the asteroid Cadrith had slammed into. It was still solid enough. But it didn't reveal where Cadrith was now, nor his present state. That could be easily corrected: a small gesture cracked the large chunk in half like an egg. There was nothing inside.

So where was he? He didn't have to wait long for an answer. As one, the floating debris took on a life of its own. Centering on Gurthghol, it rushed to meet him with a suffocating embrace. There was a large clapping shudder of force and then darkness. He wasn't wounded. The throne had protected him. What had tried to grind him into bits had instead been pulverized itself. Gurthghol calmly whisked the dust and debris away. When it had cleared, he saw Cadrith standing on a small rock a short distance from him. He didn't look too pleased. Gurthghol could understand his displeasure. If that was any indication of what Cadrith's best might be, he was in trouble.

"So what do we do now?" Cadrith sneered.

Gurthghol answered with a searing blast of plum-colored flame. Cadrith was able to block and redirect it with his staff. This was to be expected, of course. But he wouldn't be able to find what he was looking for if Cadrith was guarding things from him too closely. He needed to lull him into a false sense of security, let him get sloppy. He'd still have to play by the perceived rules if he wanted to keep both Nuhl and Awntodgenee distracted from his real goal. And to do that he'd have to have a few rounds with Cadrith while searching for the thread that bound the new god and his patron together. Then, when ready, all he had to do was pull that thread, and the rest would unravel. From there everything else would fall right into place.

"Finished?" Cadrith didn't wait for a reply. He gave a shout as he swung his staff Gurthghol's way. Accompanying it was a collection of black energy that was flung at him like mud from a stick. The sloppy darkness splashed across Gurthghol's body and throne, covering just about everything. He could feel the burning sensation seeping into his skin like acid, but with the slightest force of will the effect evaporated in a plum-hued mist.

Gurthghol raised his hands and let loose a surge of plum-colored light. Even as it neared the former lich, it thickened into something like syrup, running over and coating him. Just as rapidly as it attached to him, it hardened and encapsulated him in a crystalline cocoon. Gurthghol made another gesture, and the cocoon plummeted to Thangaria. He followed in the throne.

He directed the cocoon behind the wall and shattered gate Cadrith had forced his way through earlier. Gurthghol chose a spot between it and the hole where Cadrith had tried to bury the pantheon. The crystal cocoon smashed into the old cobblestone with all the charm of breaking bones. Cadrith's body was pressed into a small crater of its own from the collision. It wasn't enough to do any real harm to Thangaria, but hope-fully enough to tip him to the point of utter rage.

He landed the throne a few yards from Cadrith as he rose to his feet. The rest of the pantheon and divinities looked on uncertainly.

"I'm not your daughter." Cadrith's eyes twinkled with a black sheen before releasing a spray of deadly, inky energy. But what should have consumed Gurthghol in terrible agony did nothing but pass into him.

Gurthghol absorbed the attack into himself by channeling it through the throne. The consuming darkness was redirected to the heart of a lone black hole in a distant part of the cosmos. Being tapped into the throne again allowed him access to anything—anywhere in the cosmos. It was a powerful reminder of what was possible—truly possible—without any opposition blocking his way.

"And I'm not my father." Gurthghol stared Cadrith down. He thought he could see an inkling of a possible thread, but it was still too faint to clearly discern.

Cadrith howled as he raced forward, loosing a series of black bolts from his hands as he went. Though directed at Gurthghol's face, they were harmlessly sucked into his flesh, as with the previous attack. Undaunted, Cadrith resorted to a more primitive method, throwing a punch after closing the gap between them. His hand struck hard upon Gurthghol's unrelenting jaw. The sound of his hand cracking told all who heard it how badly Cadrith had failed.

Roaring, he slammed his staff into the earth, creating a large rift, which quickly swallowed the throne. Bystanders rushed out of the way to avoid becoming one of its victims. Cadrith managed not to fall in himself by hovering over the earthen tear. Though not long enough to reach the palace, the angry rent covered most of the courtyard, extending beyond the toppled gate.

"You may have the throne," Cadrith shouted into the darkness of the chasm beneath him, "but I have Nuhl. Who do you *really* think is greater?"

A blast of white flames shot up from the rift and enveloped Cadrith with a death grip.

He screamed and dropped to the ground. The flames didn't leave him but spread across his body and clothing, no matter how hard he tried to put them out. Finally, he was able to gain control of himself and, with a blast of azure light, extinguish the fire. With another thought he restored his charred body and garb.

Gurthghol used this time to his advantage, setting himself a few yards from Cadrith and carefully pondering what appeared to be that loose thread he'd been seeking.

"I'm through playing with you," Cadrith growled.

"Me too." Gurthghol extended his arms and turned his palms to Cadrith. He unleashed another vortex of living white flame. This time Cadrith was lost in the inferno, preventing Gurthghol from seeing anything from where he sat. But he was patient. He almost had what he needed. He was sure he'd identified the thread, but needed to make sure, so kept up the show for just a little longer. The flames would weaken Cadrith enough to get one last look before he made his final move.

Only that wasn't what happened. Instead, he felt Cadrith's staff against his throat.

"You. Will. Die," said Cadrith from behind the throne.

Clearly, Gurthghol had given him too much rope. It was time to rein in the slack.

Reaching up, he took hold of the staff on either side of his throat and found himself evenly matched. He was surprised but not alarmed. Cadrith was clearly learning how to tap into Nuhl's power. But he still had the throne and knew how to wield it.

"You're scared of me," Cadrith continued. There was a hint of satisfaction in his voice. "*All* of you are. I can feel it. You know this is inevitable. One day you knew your end would arrive, and today—"

"Is not . . . that day," Gurthghol countered.

Cadrith laughed as he jerked his staff harder, yanking Gurthghol's head back against the throne. Enraged, the god called upon the full power of the throne while pulling his neck and head forward. The staff snapped in half.

The action caught Cadrith off guard, slamming his head into the back of the throne. Gurthghol wasted no time, flipping Cadrith up and over both him and the throne. Cadrith slapped down face first into the hard cobblestone with such force he left an indentation at the point of impact.

It was then Gurthghol saw it: the thread. It was clearer to him now than ever before. Now he could finally end this, and he hurried to do just that. Cadrith was just a symptom. The real battle was yet to come.

•●•

Every part of Cadrith screamed for death's release. Every muscle. Every bone. He'd never felt such pain nor the hard hand of humiliation so heavy upon him. He needed to concentrate. Will himself whole. Will himself to tap into everything at his disposal. He was wasting time. Wasting Nuhl's precious essence. He could feel it now. He was weaker, less invigorated than before.

You don't have much time. Nuhl's voice in his head hammered the point home.

"I know," Cadrith muttered under his breath.

That last attack had almost killed him. The first blast of fire had nearly done him in, but the second would have been worse. The fire was right out of the deepest well of power he'd ever known. Pure divine might flared across every particle of his being to render it into dust. And that was what he would have become if he hadn't transported himself away at the last moment. The maneuver had bought him some time to set up his next attack. An attack he thought would finally put this all to an end. He should have been cleaner in the execution and just chopped off Gurthghol's head. Though in hindsight he realized it wouldn't have worked anyway. The throne would have kept him long enough to enact a counterattack. He needed to find another solution—and fast.

"You finished?" Gurthghol's mocking voice grated Cadrith's bones.

Gritting his teeth, he forced himself upright. It might have been a shaky effort, but he did it. And the action had its intended effect, at least on the gods whose faces he saw upon rising. No matter how powerful they thought they were, all had seen just how great an opponent they were facing. It was a small victory, but he would take them where he could.

He slowly turned around. As he'd expected, Gurthghol was only a few paces behind him. The pain was steadily decreasing. Bones were back in place, muscles and organs whole again. He could still win. And there was still the throne . . .

He'd been looking at this all wrong. He'd been trying to take on Gurthghol—go blow for blow against him. But that wasn't the answer. The answer wasn't in dealing with Gurthghol on the throne but in removing him from it. If he could unseat him, then he'd be just like the rest of the gods, whom Cadrith had been beating before Gurthghol arrived. And then there would be an empty throne he could take possession of.

Finish him, Cadrith. Do it now!

Cadrith squared his shoulders. "I'll still bring this pantheon to dust." He was looking past Gurthghol now, noting the various angles and the space around the base of the throne, figuring out all the proper dimensions needed to make everything flow just right. He'd only have one chance at this, and then everything putting him at an advantage would be gone.

"Is that Nuhl talking or you?"

"We're one and the same." It was close enough to the truth at the moment to keep Nuhl at bay. Cadrith didn't need anyone suspecting anything until he'd achieved his final victory.

He prepared another attack. Gurthghol would counter it, of course, which was just what he wanted. Cadrith shot another black bolt of energy from an outstretched hand. As Gurthghol once again absorbed the attack into his body, Cadrith willed himself right before the throne. In rapid fashion his left hand found purchase on Gurthghol's neck. It was then he unleashed the full brunt of his power—the entirety of Nuhl's essence—into Gurthghol.

A series of ropy black tentacles burst from Cadrith's fingers, wrapping around Gurthghol's neck and descending onto his chest and torso. As they spread, they swelled in size, sprouting small white-toothed mouths. Gurthghol was surprised. His focus, naturally, shifted to trying to tear away the tentacles spreading over him. This was just what Cadrith had been waiting for.

Jabbing his heel into the earth, he produced a small series of cracks and fissures under the throne. They had been created in such a way as to tip the throne and its occupant just enough to allow Cadrith some leverage. Using it, he lifted Gurthghol from the throne. He wasn't able to lift him fully into the air but managed to put a few inches between the god and his seat. Gurthghol's feet were still on the ground, allowing him some means to try to resist. And he did so at once, pushing down into his legs. But for the moment the two were evenly matched.

There arose a rumble deep beneath Cadrith's feet, but he managed to keep his footing. With the throne empty after being tied back into the cosmos, there was now the threat of the entire cosmos fracturing into the Void.

Yes. Keep him there. Nuhl's voice was again in Cadrith's head. *Let it all go to ruin.* For the moment, Cadrith was tempted to do just that—let it all end. But he quickly got ahold of himself. He wanted to defeat Gurthghol and take the throne, not destroy it or the cosmos.

After Gurthghol managed to pull a few of the tentacles free, he latched his right hand on Cadrith's throat. The rumbling increased as each of the gods tried to squeeze the life out of the other.

Cadrith reached out with his right hand for the throne, trying to lay hold of the back so he might be able to pull himself toward it. Gurthghol's solution was trying to reach out for the armrest near his left hand. But each pulled just enough to keep the other from reaching the throne. Cadrith was just a finger's width from his goal and so was Gurthghol.

The shaking increased as more of what remained of Thangaria quaked. Cadrith ignored it. He was so close . . . A rising shout caused him to dart an eye to his left. A lone dwarf was rushing him with a raised axe and shield.

"You again," he muttered upon recognizing the dwarf from Galba's circle. If this was Galba's last counterattack, it was pathetic.

In frustrated anger he swiped the air with his free hand. The dwarf flew headfirst into the pit Cadrith had created for the gods. This done, he locked his full attention on the throne. So engrossed was he that he never heard the small figure that came running up behind him, bellowing out a sort of battle cry. Not until it was too late.

•●•

Hadek, like the rest of those around him, was made breathless by what he was witnessing. He'd watched Gurthghol return with Cadrith and then the fight that followed. The fight that very much looked as if it was going to be over and Cadrith defeated when he did something Hadek was still trying to make sense of. Cadrith struck so fast he wasn't sure what happened other than to know that he'd somehow gotten past Gurthghol's defenses and had actually removed him from the throne.

Gurthghol fought against it, but it looked like the two were evenly matched. The longer they contested each other, the more the world around him trembled and shook. He didn't need to think it over long to know this wasn't good. If the shaking got worse, he had the horrible thought that everything would be ripped apart, and he and everyone else would be flung into the wilds of some terrible destruction.

"You were going to try and use that on Cadrith, weren't you?" Vinder was apparently finally putting the pieces together.

"Yes."

"You got a plan?"

"Not really." Hadek tilted his head. "Why are you so interested?"

"Because I think I've finally found a way to regain my honor." Vinder smiled. Hadek wasn't sure when had been the last time—if ever—he'd seen the dwarf smile. "If you're going to have a chance of hitting him, you're going to need something to distract him."

"Like what?" Before he could say more, the dwarf bolted for the warring gods, battle cry on his lips. Hadek watched in amazement.

Now, Hadek! He heard Galba's words in his mind. *Strike hard and true.*

A surge of energy ran through the goblin's body, sending his feet into a hard run right for Cadrith and the throne. Weaving through the legs of the few divinities between him and his goal, he was into the open area before he realized what was at stake. If what he'd been told was true, this was it. Everything was resting on his shoulders. If he missed . . .

He was vaguely aware of seeing Vinder soaring off into the pit and even less aware of the dwarven god, Drued, catching him by the ankle before he was lost to the dark void. He pushed away all distraction. Pushed away the pressure and fear. He focused only on Cadrith.

He finished his energized run with a boisterous yell and a flying leap. The height difference between him and the greatly enlarged Cadrith put him at a disadvantage. He wanted to be sure he struck something solid and didn't miss. He hoped the jump would give him enough height for the job.

Hadek swung with all his might. The scepter struck hard across Cadrith's lower back. Hadek landed firmly on his feet as Cadrith cried out in pain. Spinning around, he faced the full might of Cadrith's wrath-washed face. It was a terrible thing, the sight of which iced up his joints so he couldn't move. An eyeblink later, Cadrith unleashed a blast of azure flame from his right hand. Hadek could do nothing as he felt the flames completely consume him.

•●•

Cadrith knew something was wrong once he felt the pain explode across his lower back. He screamed in agony as it felt like his entire body was tearing apart, particle by particle. But the pain wasn't the only thing he felt. His strength and power were draining away like blood through an open artery. It was then he knew the full extent of what had just happened. He'd been struck by the Scepter of Night.

He had to take the throne. It was the only way to reverse the effect so he could triumph over the pantheon. But he also needed to make sure he wasn't going to be subject to another strike from the scepter. One more strike could very well kill him. None of this was lost on Gurthghol, who pushed back with renewed strength. He started crushing Cadrith's throat with a greater force than what Cadrith was able to resist.

Blinking away the tears, he searched for his attacker. He didn't have to look far. A quick turn of his head revealed the same bald goblin he thought he'd taken care of back at Galba's circle. The short green creature stared up at him with frightened eyes, but Cadrith was more concerned with the object in his hand.

Enraged that the goblin not only had possession of the Scepter of Night but somehow had been able to use it—and on him—he unleashed an azure burst of flame that enveloped the small mortal where he stood. An instant later, only the smoking scepter remained, rattling on the ground where it'd been dropped from the goblin's now-nonexistent hand.

Gurthghol took that moment to grab hold of Cadrith's right wrist. He gave it a fast snap. The bone cracked loudly. But the god of chaos didn't stop there. Keeping his hold on Cadrith's broken wrist, he used the leverage he still had in his legs to pull Cadrith's right arm further across his body and out of joint. The force of the tug twisted him around enough to shake his left hand from Gurthghol's throat and spin him around so that his feet fumbled and he fell.

The good thing was that Gurthghol was no longer choking him. But that was the only positive. He'd not only lost his hold on Gurthghol but was without Nuhl's essence. This might not have been a problem in and of itself, as he could use his own divine abilities to take on the rest of the fight, but he was far from his full strength . . . and Gurthghol had reclaimed the throne. Even as he tried to will himself whole, it was more of a struggle than it should have been. He was losing his power, his godhood. Forcing himself to his feet, he put on as bold a face as he could before Gurthghol. He'd managed to pull the last of the tentacles free and was staring down Cadrith with a burning hatred.

"Now you see the truth," said Gurthghol. "Without your patron behind you, you're nothing. And whatever you thought you achieved was a lie. All your divinity—all your *power*—is draining away."

A violent pain deep inside made Cadrith hunch over. He couldn't put his finger on what it was exactly, but it was far from good, of that he was sure. His wrist was healed and his arm was back in joint, but he felt cold, as if his body was a hearth where the fire had long since died out.

"I'm a god!" Cadrith shouted. "*That's* the truth."

"Really? That's not what I see." Gurthghol motioned at him. "Go on, see for yourself."

Cadrith cautiously brought up his right hand, looking over the wrist and the rest of it. It was whole and sound but something wasn't right. It was still pale but also cold. Moreover, the cold was very familiar. Something he'd long felt emanating out of his bones. Frantically, he put the same hand to his left chest. There was no heartbeat.

"No!" It was impossible but true: he was a lich again. Every trace of the power he'd recently wielded had been drained away. But that wasn't all. Even access to his well had been taken from him. He was now naked and defenseless before Gurthghol and the throne.

"I'm a god." The words were less forceful this time. He knew it was a lie, as did all who heard it. But he wasn't going to give anyone the pleasure of seeing him defeated—for as much as he was able.

"You were a pawn who got a taste of something greater." Gurthghol stoically sat and watched his misery worsen. There was no pleasure in the act, just simple observance. Both he and Cadrith knew there was nothing more he need do. He was finished. "You weren't even half as great a mage as you thought you were. You're just a plaything who's outlived his usefulness." Gurthghol's eyes glowed a brilliant white. "*That's* your truth. And it's time you embrace it."

Cadrith felt every fiber of his being shatter at once. He'd thought he'd known pain before, but this was an agony he'd never imagined. The worst part was knowing that he'd come so close and failed. He'd had the throne in hand—literally—and had failed. This truth made the torment ten times worse. The only consolation was none of it lasted long. In the blink of an eye, he and all he wore crumbled into a mound of dust at Gurthghol's feet.

CHAPTER 26

NOTHING CAN BE GREATER THAN THAT WHICH CREATED IT.

—The Theogona

"What have you done?" Olthon's face was awash with dread. It was an expression shared by the rest of the gods that were slowly making their way to Gurthghol and the throne.

"What was needed," Gurthghol calmly replied. "A sacrifice had to be made in order to stop this threat."

"A sacrifice to stop *Cadrith* from claiming godhood," Endarien pointed out. "We all made plans for that and voted on the matter." He jabbed an accusatory finger at Gurthghol, adding, "None of us would have voted for *this*."

"I know," he said. "But that wasn't the real meaning of the prophecy, and that's why what we decided to do didn't work. I saw the true meaning to Saredhel's words in time. It was right there in front of my face: I had to shackle myself to the throne again, sacrificing my freedom to save the pantheon as well as Tralodren. Everything else we tried failed, but this"—he struck the armrests with an open palm—"this was a success."

"A success?" Perlosa scoffed. "You *do* realize you almost *lost* the throne?"

"He wasn't even *close* to taking it." Gurthghol knew this wasn't really the truth, but for the moment it was better than the truth, which unnerved him more than he liked to admit.

"Have you finally gone mad?" The dread had only deepened across Olthon's face. "You almost brought about the destruction of the entire cosmos."

"And if it wasn't for that goblin, things could have very easily gone the other way," added Khuthon. While his tone wasn't the same as Olthon's, there was a fair deal of concern in his voice.

Gurthghol knew Khuthon was right—they all did—no matter how much he wanted to pretend otherwise. And it was because of Cadrith's near success that the need for action against Nuhl and Awntodgenee was vital. It was quite possible that the next time the threat returned, the throne alone wouldn't be strong enough to stop them.

"The same goblin that was in the circle, if I recall," Rheminas mused aloud. "Part of your doing?"

"No," said Gurthghol. "Yours?"

"Not mine," he replied, "but I have my suspicions."

"Well, however it happened, it worked out. What?" he asked at seeing so many concerned and even disappointed faces among his family.

"That dwarf looks familiar, though." Rheminas narrowed his eyes as he observed the dwarven warrior Drued had saved from the pit. "Weren't you at Galba's circle too?"

"Yes," said the dwarf.

"And now you fight Cadrith again? This your doing, Drued?"

Drued squared his shoulders. "Vinder volunteered to fight in Thangaria with the rest of our troops." There was a softening to his stance as he faced the smaller dwarf again. "But what he did just now was his own choice. And a very brave one."

"I don't know if I like all these coincidences." Rheminas eyed Vinder in a contemplative manner.

"Well, I like his bravery." Drued beamed. "He's honored me and all my kind today."

"Thank you, my lord." Vinder's voice trembled.

"Return with the others to New Druelandia and await your reward." He bid the dwarven warrior to leave his side. "I should be along soon enough." Vinder bowed and left his god in a run, tears of joy streaming down his cheeks.

"So it looks like everything is over, then." Aero had a note of optimism in his voice.

"Not quite," said Asora, glaring at Gurthghol. "You shouldn't have taken the throne."

"I told you already . . ." He sought out Saredhel for some assistance. "Tell them I was right."

Thirty eyes instantly locked onto the enigmatic goddess.

"This is what I told you: If one of us were willing to make a great sacrifice, we would gain an advantage over this new threat; confrontation with the dark patron's agent would take something dear from the confronter as payment for success. If you are looking for validation of your actions, I can only say that what was done by Endarien *and* Gurthghol was in accord with what I've spoken."

"So we were *both* right?" Endarien wrinkled his brow. "How can *that* be?"

Saredhel gave no further reply.

"So then, this was all for nothing?" Perlosa was clearly not amused.

"Not for nothing," Gurthghol insisted. "It's time we finally put an end to our enemy and its threats." He took a tight hold of each armrest and closed his eyes in concentration.

"What are you doing?" Endarien's rising concern echoed the thoughts of the other gathered deities.

"What needs to be done." Gurthghol was focused on nothing but the throne now. He had to tap deep down into its core and then tie himself to it.

"Make sure this is the course you wish to take," he heard Saredhel declare.

"I'm sure."

"What's he doing?"

Causilla never got a reply. There was a terrible rumble followed by an ear-piercing screech as the thin grayish atmosphere over the remnant of Thangaria was ripped in two, cleft down the center from horizon to horizon.

"Stop him!" Asora screamed. "He's tearing apart the cosmos!"

Before any one of them could respond, there was a massive change in pressure, popping ears and bringing on headaches. On its heels was a raging windstorm that rushed over the terrain. The strong gales picked up bits of fallen weaponry, the recently slain, and other debris that churned and funneled above the hall and the gods who stood outside it.

Ganatar raised his voice over the roar. "Gurthghol—"

"I know what I'm doing!" His rebuke held back any further questioning. As the wind settled a very unsettling calm fell. Divinities, formerly mortal soldiers, and other creatures alike were filled with great dread, for they could see the unease—even feel it—emanating from their pantheon.

The airborne bodies and debris fell to the ground or, in some cases, drifted off toward the scattered chunks of the former world, where they entered their own orbit. As the winds died down there appeared two beings before Gurthghol: one robed in light, the other in darkness. The one in light was similar to Galba in appearance, now the same size as the rest of the gods. The other had a humanoid frame and was equal in height to the figure of light, but the finer details of its appearance were hidden by a long hooded cloak covering it from head to toe.

"What have you done?" Dradin was fearfully reverent. Gurthghol recalled Vkar's words, reminding him of how his family were so afraid to upset the status quo. They'd rather be slaves than dare to be free. That was no life he wanted any part of.

"He made his choice," said Galba. "And it is a very poor one at that."

"We'll see about that." Gurthghol remained as confident as ever. This would work just like he envisioned. "I'm going to get rid of this threat to our existence once and for all. No longer will we have to cower before them and be part of their games. I'm going to free us and the cosmos from them forever."

"You'd be wise to reconsider," Galba cautioned.

"Don't patronize me," he snapped. "I know you both fear the throne and now that I have it again, you'll try anything to keep me from using it," he said, closing his eyes once again in concentration. "For you, Father," he said as he willed the two entities into the throne, the very object that had been created to tap into their essence in the first place. All were amazed as Gurthghol began pulling light from Galba and darkness from the cloaked figure, first in a thin trickle and then in a wide beam, sending it into the throne.

"Arrogant worm," growled Nuhl's adopted guise. "I'll gnaw your bones before you even come *close* to fulfilling your fantasy." The voice was at once male and female but also cruel and hungry. "You'll join your daughter in her failure soon enough."

"You used her for your own ends, twisted her with your games and schemes. She would have made me proud, but you robbed me of that, along with the lives of my parents." His brow wrinkled as he pushed himself to the brink of his abilities, willing the throne to do even more.

The flow of power increased to a river of energy being absorbed by the throne. He would win out in this matter in the end. He would achieve what his father couldn't, and be free of these meddling entities— beings who had turned his daughter against him and her true family. Beings who did nothing but keep them down—hold them back—from their greatest potential.

"I will destroy you."

He could almost feel Vkar standing beside him, urging him on. He supposed he was, in a way, given the essence still locked away in the throne. He imagined his father beaming with pride. He was actually going to do it. The thought invigorated him.

"Shall I now show *you* the truth?" Nuhl mocked. From out of the folds of the draping cloak a gelatinous black tentacle shot out and wrapped itself around the throne. The tentacle was covered in hundreds of tiny white-toothed maws, hungrily snapping. "Nothing can be greater than that which created it."

At first Gurthghol thought to shrug off the attack, but he found he couldn't. While he initially thought it was the same attack Cadrith had tried on him, he quickly realized something was wrong. This time there was something different about it. This wasn't a weakened form of Nuhl sent through a lesser agent like Cadrith. This was the full strength of the entity itself. The very embodiment of oblivion. Already Gurthghol felt weak. Nuhl was leeching the power and life out of him and the throne, reversing the very thing he was trying to do to them.

"No. I'm not going to let you win." He refocused on the guises of Awntodgenee and Nuhl. The beams of light and darkness being sucked into the throne had lessened. He could feel his hold over the throne slipping as more of his will and spirit weakened. Yet the more he tried pulling strength from the throne, the weaker he grew. He struggled against the forces trying to devour him and pushed on with his plan, willing the leeching of the two entities to continue. And it did . . . for a short time, before dwindling into a trickle.

"You've made your choice, Gurthghol," said Galba. "You've stolen your father's throne and now have tried to follow in his footsteps at the risk of ripping asunder the whole of the cosmos."

"I've done nothing but attempt to *save* the cosmos from *you*." Gurthghol leaned back in the throne, fighting with all his strength to stay focused. "Tralodren and the pantheon would have been safe . . . forever . . ." It was getting harder to remain conscious . . .

"You've made a poor choice," came Galba's authoritative words. "You almost placed the entire cosmos into Nuhl's hand after victory had been achieved."

"Lies!" Gurthghol spat. "You . . . can't hide the truth . . . my father was on the verge of discovering . . ." He was near the point of delirium as the thread of light and darkness slipping into the throne crumbled like spiderwebs in a strong wind. "He was going to liberate the cosmos from your tyranny and I was . . . I *am* going to bring his desire to pass."

Nuhl laughed in delight. "My champion may have failed, but I can claim at least *one* of your number before this is all done."

"Him only," Galba said, raising a warding hand. "My champion won the day. Yours has lost."

"Agreed."

"I still have the throne." Gurthghol was still weak, but had at least stopped getting weaker. It was hard for him to think clearly, harder to reason out what he could do, let alone should do. "You can't harm me."

"We shall see." The voice under Nuhl's hood was delighted.

Gurthghol roared in rage as the tentacle enlarged itself, enveloping the whole of the throne and hiding both it and its occupant from sight. Instead, only a coal-hued globe was visible. This globe was then drawn back to what was lurking under the guise's cloak like a fisherman reeling in his line.

The mouths on the smaller tentacles slithering out of the cloak twitched and chomped and drooled as the dark globe neared. The globe grew smaller and smaller until it fit quite easily under Nuhl's cloak. When the opening closed, the tentacle and what it had ensnared were no longer visible.

"Tralodren and your pantheon are safe from harm," Galba informed the rest of the gods and divinities.

"Enjoy the respite while you may," added Nuhl.

There was a bright flash of light and the two entities were gone. With their passing, the sky returned to normal, and all was as it had been before their appearance. Even the rift and the rest of the ruin wrought by Cadrith, save for the dead and the battered gate, were gone.

"What just happened?" Endarien found Saredhel, an action quickly duplicated by everyone else present.

"A sacrifice was made." Her words were flat.

"*Two* sacrifices were made," Panthora corrected. "That goblin—"

"Did his task well."

"What is going on here?" Perlosa's cold sneer was more twisted than usual. "It sounds like still more plotting behind our backs."

"Like I said," Rheminas spoke up. "There's much more going on than we first thought."

"Like with you and *your* plotting?" Perlosa wouldn't let the matter die. Not when she could poke her brother with it like a sharp stick.

"I doubt anyone is completely innocent here," Rheminas hotly returned. "Well, with the exception of Shiril, perhaps. But what *I* want to know is why Gurthghol took the throne. That was *the* throne, wasn't it? Not one of his tricks."

"It was Vkar's throne." Dradin settled any doubt.

"Oh, what have you done, brother?" Asora lamented.

"Saved Tralodren and us, by the look of it." Drued's pragmatism helped mellow the atmosphere.

"By trying to *kill* us all first?" Aero raised his voice.

"We would not be in this mess if Saredhel had just told us what we needed to know," Perlosa pressed. "*Everything* we needed to know about what was going on."

"I said what needed to be heard," Saredhel returned calmly.

"Of course," Asorlok said, curling his lip.

"We won't find any answers by bickering," said Olthon. "There's obviously much that needs to be explained, but right now we need to make sure the threat is truly at an end."

"It is," said Asorlok. "What Nuhl said was true. It won't be returning for some time."

"Hopefully a long time," said Drued.

"Then what do we do now?" Causilla asked while taking in the solemn divinities around them, noting the full extent of the conflict as if for the first time.

"We should at least honor Gurthghol," Shiril advised. "He gave his life—"

"No," Asorlok interrupted. "He's still alive."

"*What?*" Endarien was full of disbelief.

"He's not dead," Asorlok continued. "Not yet. He hasn't crossed over into Mortis."

"Then where is he?" Khuthon asked Saredhel.

"I don't know." The words were as unexpected as sunshine at night.

"We need to assemble a group to go find him," Rheminas urged the others.

"And where would they start?" asked Khuthon. "You heard Saredhel. We don't even know where he is."

"Nor how much longer he might remain alive." Asorlok took the line of reasoning further. "And if Nuhl wants to keep him prisoner, there's no telling where it might have him locked away."

"Maybe on Mortis," Causilla offered.

"No." Asorlok shook his head. "He isn't on Mortis. But Nuhl has the whole cosmos at its disposal. We could start looking now and never find Gurthghol."

"Then we need to prepare for the worst," said Khuthon. "The balance of power has shifted, and that needs to be addressed."

"I don't believe this," Olthon stated in disgust. "You can't wait until even a *day* has passed before you start lusting for his seat?"

"He's not here," Khuthon continued. "He's probably dead or at the very least imprisoned somewhere. So what can we do for him? Nothing. In the meantime, the council needs order, and we need to plan how best to rebuild and prepare for the future."

"If he's not dead, then he's still on the throne." Olthon let her gaze fall over all the others. "Which means he's still more powerful than any of us."

"He didn't look that strong after Nuhl got ahold of him," said Rheminas.

"But what if he finds a way to break free?" Olthon continued. "If he still has the throne—"

"That isn't our most pressing concern," Endarien interrupted. "Right now we need to focus on the present before we worry about the future."

"Yes, there are many matters before us," said Dradin, "but we're not going to make headway on them standing out here. If we're to have a discussion—a *thorough* discussion—on everything, then we should call another council."

"Agreed," said Ganatar. "But that doesn't mean things have changed or that they will," he cautioned. "We'll need to discuss this matter and redefine the rules of the previous council now that Galba is gone and we have broken our own rules by making Thangaria a battlefield and having Vkar's throne now somewhere in the cosmos."

"And don't forget those secret plots made by some among us," Rheminas chimed in. "Like I said, it's quite a distance for a lone goblin to travel all the way from Tralodren to Thangaria on his own. I think we're *all* due an explanation."

Endarien looked Rheminas full in the face. "Are you including yourself on that list?"

"We will have a full report and an in-depth discussion," Ganatar assured them. "On *everything*. We must be open with each other if we hope to make a full recovery of all that's been damaged and lost."

"Which means we'll be talking about the scepter too," said Dradin. "Such a weapon needs to be carefully considered—for all our good."

"Why do I see this being a rather long council?" Drued ran a hand through his beard.

"If we were able to agree on things rather quickly—"

"Then some of us might think something was wrong." Olthon was interrupted by a rather sardonic Asorlok.

"Then it's agreed?" Ganatar looked from god to god. "We assemble another council?" All gave their consent.

"Then that's it?" Panthora was confused and upset. "We're just going to leave Gurthghol to—"

"This has to come first." Ganatar was clear. "The order we've established among us and preserving it must be our chief concern."

"But he's part of your family." Panthora searched for some sympathy from the others.

"And he still is," Shiril replied softly. "But we can't do anything for him right now."

"He made a choice," Saredhel further explained, "and now has to live with the consequences."

"As do we all," stated Asora somberly before placing a hand on her stomach.

"You all right?" Khuthon asked from beside her.

"I guess all this has taken more out of me than I thought."

"Then let's get started," said Aero.

"Yes," Drued agreed. "I still have fallen warriors to honor and a realm to attend to."

THE WIZARD KING TRILOGY

"As do we all." Khuthon started marching to the hall.

"Bring the scepter." Ganatar motioned to two nearby Tularins. As they stepped forward, Endarien sought out one of his priests for a short conversation. The rest of the gods made their way to the hall as they conversed.

Rheminas took a few steps after them, then remembered something. Turning his head over his shoulder, he caught sight of the healed Galgalli. "You did well and have earned your rest," he told him. "Return to Helii and once this is all over, we'll have a proper chat about what's to come next."

•●•

Dugan gave a small nod as he watched the rest of the gods depart. He couldn't help but notice Asora's hand resting on her stomach as she walked. He thought he'd seen a small echo of concern ripple across her face, but it had faded as quickly as it arose. With the gods' departure, the other divinities slowly returned to the tasks at hand, such as seeing to the dead and clearing out the debris and rubble to try to restore whatever amount of glory they could. He watched them for a moment more before looking over at the two Tularins. One held the scepter firmly in hand, while both made ready to take it to the hall.

"You really think you can keep it safe?" he asked the one holding the scepter.

"We'll keep it well guarded," the other replied. "Which is nothing less than part of our calling in service to the gods, as I'm sure you are now fully aware of yours."

"It's clearer now than it's ever been," said Dugan. "But aren't you afraid one of the gods or another divinity will try to take it? Where could you hope to keep it safe from another god?"

"Let that be *our* concern," said the other Tularin. Both vanished in a flash of golden light, leaving Dugan alone with his thoughts, the rubble, and the masses of people trying to locate their own.

He didn't see any sign of Rowan, Cadrissa, or Alara. People were still sorting through debris and bodies, though, and they could have been swept away in the roaring wind. He wanted to think they took his advice and found some safe place to weather the battle—maybe even found a way to help Alara. But even if they had survived, his path was no longer connected with theirs. That last thread was cut while he was hanging from those two stone posts in Galba's circle.

Whether Alara, Rowan, and Cadrissa had made it through or perished along the way wasn't really his concern anymore. Nor was Vinder's future. The dwarf had clearly chosen his new path, just like they would in the end. Just like he had to. He was leaving the final pieces of his old life behind. The gladiator was gone. In his place was a Galgalli who needed to return to where he belonged.

He was still in service to another, but it wasn't the same as his previous life on Tralodren. There was some degree of freedom to his new existence. He was sure there would be rules and expectations as well. He'd get the full understanding once Rheminas returned. Which meant he had to get there first to greet him upon his return. It wouldn't do to start things off on the wrong foot. Not if he'd have to live with the consequences for the rest of his afterlife.

Raising his wings, he lifted off the dead chunk of a world and made his way to Helii.

CHAPTER 27

BLESSED BE THE HUMAN WHO SEEKS PANTHORA WITH A WHOLE HEART.
BLESSED BE THE HUMAN WHO KEEPS TO HER WAYS.
BLESSED BE THE HUMAN WHO HONORS HER,
FOR IN HIS DOING HE TOO SHALL BE HONORED.

—A Panian blessing

Cadrissa had decided to take shelter in what she quickly discovered were a set of stables rather than making a run for the palace. The stables were solid enough—built entirely of stone—and still stood after who knew how many millennia. Good enough signs for the time being. There was a faint odor of dust, but that was the worst of it. The only light streamed in through cracks in the wooden door and the gap where it had been left slightly ajar. She and Rowan had ducked inside the first stall that crossed their path.

It had obviously been built for much taller beings as well as an animal of some size, which made sense if these were the stables for mounts that would serve titan and god alike. The gate allowing entrance into the wooden box was left open, clearly showing the stone floor with a marble trough along the main stone wall. To Cadrissa's right was a stone block whose purpose was a total mystery.

Rowan had joined her shortly after her arrival, laying Alara's body parallel to the trough. He'd said nothing, only stared at the shield he'd placed beside her body. Cadrissa could do nothing but watch with some sorrow of her own. She had a hint of what Rowan was going through based upon what she had felt with Dugan's death, but didn't dare say she knew *exactly* what he felt. He and Alara had been able to express their feelings clearly and openly to each other.

A relationship had developed in her absence and blossomed far beyond the mere bud that had existed between her and Dugan. Or more accurately, just her own infatuation with him, since Dugan never had shown any signs of reciprocal interest. She didn't know how to comfort Rowan either. Near the point of numbness on all fronts, she knew she wouldn't be much help, let alone a sturdy shoulder upon which to rest. If anything, she might choke him with the dark clouds hanging about her head. Better to let him rest for the moment while the rest of the world sorted itself out around them.

Cadrissa had heard the crashing sounds of combat—the shaking explosions—and dreaded them. Fearful for her life, she breathed no sigh of relief when those same sounds ceased. Rather, the uncertainty of the situation called to mind a dawning dark reality. What had they gotten into and why? What was the meaning to all this madness? She thought she'd known before, but it all seemed to melt away in comparison with this . . . Then there was the guilt and fear she felt over what the necklace had done to her—what it had made her do as well as revealed to her about herself . . .

To say this was all rather surreal was a tremendous understatement. Here she was, in the very place where the gods met in council—and now even fought with small armies. No one had ever been to Thangaria before—at least no living person she knew of. She didn't even know of any myths or stories where anyone from Tralodren had made the journey there. If they tried, she now knew just how badly they'd fail. She'd seen the stars and planets closer than anyone ever could from the surface. She'd flown through the great expanse between worlds and even to the very center of the cosmos. For it was widely held in most circles that Thangaria was in the very middle of it, the first world created, with other things branching off from there.

She'd once held the Scepter of Night and had fought against the spirits of long-dead dranors. These were the things of legends and myths. Certainly they were the stuff good adventures were made of, and it was for adventure she'd left with Gilban and Alara in the first place. And now here she was, at the tail end of all those adventures: tired, sore, and deeply troubled by all she had seen and learned. What Cadrith had told her perhaps gave her the most concern.

It would partly explain how he was able to tap into her well so effectively back on Arid Land. Blood relation helped make such things, and other spells, less dangerous. But he also could have just been using something she didn't know about—some higher-level spell or training he'd mastered—that made the process safer. Or, of course, he could just have gotten lucky. But she couldn't bring herself to accept the idea of Cadrith doing anything by chance. So that left the other two options. She preferred the former over the latter. It was easier to accept. To think that in some way she was related to the lich . . .

Of course it wouldn't be a direct relation; it had been well over seven hundred years since the last wizard kings lived on Tralodren. But if true, then part of that potential from two very powerful wizards ran in her family. Not everyone started out with the exact same inclination for magic, but the potential was there to expand what you had with practice and training. And if she did indeed share some relation to Cadrith and his lover, then it was possible for her to reach for even greater things than she once thought . . . even greater power . . . and knowledge . . .

But why did he tell her? What purpose did it serve? He'd already taken her over and was content to let her fade from the world. A final gloat? A passing hint at what she could have had but now never would? Did he mean to show her what she had the potential to do but instead had wasted? Or did he know something else he didn't want to share? Something he only wanted to hint at instead?

Cadrissa shivered at the thought of some dark future he might have had planned for her. Willing her thoughts elsewhere, she put her mind on Rowan and their immediate future. That was the most important thing right now. That and the fact she was alive and on Thangaria. Better thoughts and brighter feelings than the darkness in which she waded.

• ● •

Rowan was lost in a sleepy gaze as his head hovered over his shield. The images of the two flame-spewing dragon heads held what concentration he had left. He'd removed the shield from his back and set it down not too far from where he'd laid Alara's body; his sword was next to the shield. Cadrissa had managed to find them shelter: a stone stable of some type where he'd set Alara's body beside an ancient, empty trough. Not the most fitting of places, but it was better than leaving her to be trampled in the chaos they'd just escaped.

It seemed like he'd been sitting and staring at the shield for hours. He hadn't heard any of the battle outside the stables. The whole world had been pushed away in favor of his internal landscape, which was darker than even Cadrith could have wished upon his foes. He had been half-aware of arriving at the stables and even less so of lowering Alara to her current resting place. After that everything had grown dim as his thoughts became increasingly myopic.

He tried to drive the thoughts away, but to no avail. He was now a man with a divided mind—divided opinions. He'd left for the southern lands on a mission with the most organized and strongest of beliefs in himself, his race, his goddess, and his order . . . And now all that was gone. He sat in the silence of the stable, uncertain and fractured. Nothing made sense anymore. Told by Panthora that the order he served was a lie, shown by Nalu and Alara that he'd been indoctrinated to hate the elven race, Rowan had a hard time latching on to anything anymore with any amount of strength. Was there nothing in which he could place his trust? Would there never be, outside of Panthora?

"Rowan?" His focus shifted dramatically upon catching sight of a transparent image of Alara standing beside her corpse.

"Alara?" Rowan hurried to her side, eager to reach out and touch her, only to find his hand pass right through her. He could see the concern in her eyes . . . but it wasn't so much from love as from pity.

"She's a ghost." Cadrissa joined him in his amazement. Apparently, Cadrissa had been beside him the whole time. Yet another thing he'd failed to notice.

"Is it really you?" Rowan took a step back, looking back and forth from Alara's body to her ghost. The spirit was much more lovely and breathtaking, but he wasn't sure if it was actually her. They were in the realm of the gods, after all. Here, anything was possible.

"It's me, Rowan." Alara's peaceful smile settled his fears.

"But how?" Cadrissa was still amazed.

"I don't have long. I'm being taken to Sheol and—"

"*Who's* taking you?"

"That's not important now."

"Oh yes, it is." He rebuffed the very notion.

"No." Alara remained calm but firm. "It isn't. Not for the living."

"This isn't right," he said, shaking his head in sorrow.

"Don't judge what you don't know." Alara was mild in her rebuke, but it stirred Rowan's Nordic blood just the same.

"How is this right?" His vision blurred as tears formed in the corners of his eyes.

"Rowan." Alara grew more serious, steeling herself. "I need you to listen. I was only allowed a small window of time. We won't have this chance again."

Rowan snapped his mouth shut upon hearing the finality of her words. If this was going to be the last thing he'd ever hear her say, he was going to give it his undivided attention.

"My time has come, but yours hasn't," she continued. "You have such a great purpose in your life. I can see that now—I can see *many* things now—and you will too once your spirit's been freed from your body. I also know that you can't get to where you need to be as long as I'm an obstacle in your path."

"*Obstacle?*" Rowan felt as if he'd just been punched in the gut. "What are you talking about? You've *never* been an obstacle to me. If anything, you've *helped* me—"

"You never really loved me, Rowan." Alara's words rocked him to the depths of his being. "Deep down, you know that. It's the truth, and it needs to be said."

He adamantly rebuked her, shaking his head. "No. That's not true."

"Deep down you know what you were really attracted to—and it wasn't me." He retreated a step from Alara's ghost, anger rising and mixing with his confusion.

"I don't know what sort of game you're playing, but Alara would never say—"

"Rowan? Look at me, Rowan. What you loved wasn't me, but the very thing you were longing for on your own—what I helped guide you to. That's what you were attracted to, not me."

Rowan could do nothing but stare through Alara's spirit. Was it true? Part of him wanted to entertain the thought, another warred against it.

"Why? You could have left me alone. Why come back and tell me this?"

Alara closed her eyes, took a hard swallow, and then said, "It's—I don't want to hurt you any more than I have. I don't want to be the thing that stands in the way of your future—for anything."

"And you thought *this* would *help*?" He bit back the furious retort ready to roll off his tongue. "I—the battle with Cadrissa . . . after all I did to get you here and then . . . And now you show up and tell me *this*?"

"I'm sorry." Alara's countenance fell with her voice.

"No." Rowan fought back the first hot tear starting to roll down his cheek. "I know the truth. I loved—*love*—you. And you loved me too."

"I wasn't in love with you, Rowan, just infatuated with the idea of your potential. We had respect for each other, if nothing else, but any love we thought we might have felt for one another was grossly exaggerated."

Rowan's jaw went slack.

"I'm sorry."

He tried to wrap his head around it. He knew this wasn't true—*couldn't* be true. So was this some sort of vision—a *lying* one—sent to deceive him, perhaps even a joke of Cadrith's meant to entertain him with some cruel sport?

"So it was all a lie?" Rowan's voice sounded so small, as if he was some distance from his body and listening to someone else speak. Tears were now running freely down his cheeks.

"We saw the best in each other and let it cloud our feelings and judgment," said Alara, clenching her lips tightly with a seeming force of will before continuing. "I'm sorry, Rowan."

Rowan said nothing more; he could say nothing more.

Cadrissa spoke up. "This is all my fault." Rowan noticed the fresh tears streaming down her face. "If I could have—"

"What's done is done," said Alara. "If anything, I should have acted sooner and taken that necklace from you."

Alara turned her head as if someone else was talking to her. She gave a nod to the unseen figure, then spoke again. "I have to go now. When this is all over, don't lose sight of your purpose. Not now. Not ever." Turning to leave, she began fading until she'd completely vanished from sight.

Rowan shuffled over to the stone block beside the row of spartan stalls and sunk onto it as he let the tears flow. He didn't know what was worse, seeing Alara again or listening to all that she just said. He let out the pain and the fear, the confusion and hurt—let it flow from his eyes and find full release in shaking sobs. He had lost all he thought he was, all he thought he had been. It was all a lie. All of it. From the faith in the knighthood he'd come to embrace, the woman he thought he had loved . . . maybe even his faith in Panthora . . .

Where could he go now? Where *would* he go? Why go anywhere at all when he could just die right here? If he did have a purpose, some great purpose like Panthora had declared and Alara just mentioned, he couldn't see it now. How could he dedicate himself to some higher calling when his life was built on nothing but half-truths and lies? Panthora hadn't even spoken to him or come to his aid when he had prayed for Alara's healing. A gentle hand on his shoulder pulled Rowan away from his thoughts to Cadrissa and her tear-streaked face.

"I'm sorry," she told him.

"So am I." He could barely voice the words. "But there's nothing that can be done about it now."

"I don't think she purposely came back to hurt you," Cadrissa offered softly. "She wasn't—isn't—that sort of person."

Rowan forced himself to swallow the hurt and confusion as he dried his eyes. It wouldn't do for a man, let alone a Knight of Valkoria, to be crying at a time like this. They were still in the midst of a battle, a war raging around them. But the profound silence from outside the stables suggested something else.

"I don't hear anything," he said. "Do you think the battle's over?"

"Maybe."

"So this is the end," said Rowan.

"It's the end of something," Cadrissa replied in halfhearted hope. "But it isn't *our* end."

"Not yet." He coated the room with some more Nordic pessimism.

"If the gods had fallen, I think we would have known about it," Cadrissa said, wiping the tears from her face and eyes.

Rowan considered that. "I suppose you're right." He stood to face the stable's entrance as he made an effort to push all he was feeling deep inside. This wasn't the time or place for it. They could still be in danger. "Do you think we should see what's happening?" He fixed his gaze on the door.

"I suppose we could." Cadrissa sighed and ran a hand through her dark tresses. "We can't stay in here forever."

•●•

Outside the stable was a great calm. Thangaria had returned to the dead chunk of rock it had been before, dotted with thin spires of fading fire and debris near the opening of the courtyard. Rowan and Cadrissa could see the warriors who hadn't fallen tending to those who had. Much of the shattered gate had been piled into two cairn-like mounds of stone, twisted metal, and other rubble.

"So did we *win*?" Rowan's words hovered in the air.

"Depends on who *we* is," said Cadrissa as she surveyed the scene. "If you mean the *pantheon*, I'd say yes, given the fact this place still exists and these warriors are dealing with their dead."

"Does that mean Cadrith's dead?"

Cadrissa paused. "I hope so. I can't see the gods wanting to let him keep drawing breath."

"I thought killing a god would be harder."

"Does any of this look *easy* to you?" She made a sweep of the surrounding area with her arm. "They had a small army gathered here, and who knows what else they might have made or brought to the fight."

Rowan paused, taking everything in, pondering. "So then it's done." There was a flatness to his words. "It's a pretty *hollow*-feeling victory."

"But Tralodren's been saved. That's a prize worth fighting for."

"But we didn't really *fight*." Rowan crossed his arms as he faced the palace he'd seen earlier. "*They* did all the fighting as we were led around like dogs to play in their games for some pointless sport. After all this, what do we have to show for it?"

"We have our lives."

"Not all of us."

"No. But *we*, at least, have ours."

"But nothing to live for anymore," Rowan gloomily continued.

"Rowan—"

"No." Rowan pushed Cadrissa's words aside. "You never had as much invested in this. It was just an adventure to you. You haven't lost *anything*, while the rest of us—"

"We've *all* lost something, Rowan." Cadrissa took hold of Rowan and roughly spun him around to face her. "We've *all* suffered, or have you forgotten my little *adventure* with Cadrith in Arid Land?" There was a fire burning in her gut now—a blaze of indignation she was hard pressed to find an origin for but ready to fan and embrace just the same.

"Now are you going to let the bad outweigh the good? Because the Rowan I got to know and the Rowan I saw before we came here wanted to believe in something greater than himself, something good in himself, in others, and in the cosmos.

"If you turn from that now—if you turn from who you are—then you've lost everything, and you have no hope, and you might as well just crawl back in that stable and lie down beside Alara." Rowan bristled, but Cadrissa wouldn't let him speak. She needed to say this, and she knew Rowan needed to hear it.

"Have we been used like pawns? Yes. Have we had to suffer to bring about this end? Yes. It hasn't been easy, but don't let it destroy who you are, Rowan. Not now. Not after what you've been through. You did what you set out to do: you stopped the information in Taka Lu Lama from falling into the hands of the Elyellium, and you rescued me from Cadrith.

"Now go back home, heal, and become the man you need to be. Don't throw away the good that Alara saw in you and that the rest of us respected about you. Just go home, heal, and grow . . ." Cadrissa returned to herself as the inner blaze fueling her speech cooled. She didn't understand the depths of her own words and was amazed at having said them, as well as the effect they had on the already troubled Nordican.

Rowan let out a deep, body-shuddering sigh before resting his gaze upon Cadrissa. "Where did *that* come from?"

"I don't know." She blushed. "But it's the truth."

Rowan said nothing, nodding slowly. He turned back to the courtyard, though Cadrissa doubted he actually saw any of it. "Yes. It is the truth, isn't it?" His voice was as distant as his thoughts.

She waited for him to say more but nothing else was forthcoming. And she wasn't about to try and say anything else after what she just unleashed upon him. Finally, he lowered his head with another sigh.

"I still have to accept my obligations." He faced her once more. She'd never seen him look so serious before. "No matter what's happened, I'm still a man of my word and have to honor what I said I'd do."

Cadrissa could only nod, unsure and unwilling to comment further.

"What about you, then?" he asked.

She absent-mindedly began to reach for the missing necklace and stopped herself when she realized what she was doing. Returning her hand to rest beside her, she said, "I suppose I'll go back to Elandor and retrieve the books I have stored there, and then decide what to do after that. Probably rest for a while too. It's been a long couple of days—or weeks or wherever we are in the year." She didn't know how time flowed on other planes and realms. She guessed she was about to find out, assuming they were able to find a way back to Tralodren.

Rowan nodded as a breeze picked up behind them and formed a whirlwind, revealing a new figure. A middle-aged Telborian man with the priestly robes of an Endari, a follower of Endarien, shuffled toward them. His long smoky-white mustache curled at the end of his chin and framed his smile in soft, regal splendor.

"Greetings." His voice was boisterous and welcoming.

"Hello." Cadrissa was hesitant. Rowan remained suspicious.

"I assume you're Cadrissa and Rowan?" Rowan kept his eyes on the strange quiver on the figure's back. It was filled with golden javelins. The long weapons poked through the quiver's bottom but were still held neatly in place. And neither of them could miss the silver war hammer dangling from his gray leather belt.

"We are," Cadrissa answered for the both of them.

"Good. I was running out of places to look." The priest's greenish-gray eyes sparkled in amusement.

"And why are you looking for *us*?" Rowan was still suspicious.

"Forgive me." The priest bowed. "I'm Bran, a high priest of Endarien. And Endarien told me to find you."

"Why?" Cadrissa inquired, not sure whether she should be curious or worried.

"To help you get back to Tralodren. In compensation for what took place when you arrived in Arid Land."

Rowan's eyebrows raised. "Brandon . . ." he muttered.

"What's he talking about?" she asked Rowan.

"It doesn't matter now," he replied.

"Well, I think if a god offers to compensate you for something, then that—"

"Trust me," Rowan continued, "it doesn't matter now." Cadrissa could see there was no use pushing and let the matter drop.

"Maybe not to you," said Bran, "but it meant enough to *him* to send me to you."

"We were told that if we got here we couldn't go back to Tralodren," Rowan explained.

"Not on your own, no," said Bran. "But thankfully you won't be making the journey on your own."

"So he's got us another ship, is that it?" Rowan's sarcasm was lost on Cadrissa.

"Better. Griffins."

"*Griffins?*" Cadrissa beamed. "I've never seen one before."

"Well, you'll get to see two of them up close," said Bran, obviously amused by her excited curiosity. She supposed to Bran such things were commonplace, but to her this day of wonders just kept getting more wondrous. And it felt good for once to not have to be fearful of being threatened, possessed, or stomped underfoot.

"But are you sure they can make it all the way back to Tralodren?" she asked when she recalled just how far away they really were. She knew griffins were strong, but strong enough to sail through the entire cosmos? And then there was the whole matter of how long they might be able to survive in the expanse between worlds. It was a brief trip when Dugan— the Galgalli—had brought them to Thangaria, but with griffins . . .

"Not to fear," said Bran. "We'll use a portal and get you safely back on your way. And the griffins are of native stock too, so they'll be eager to get back home."

Cadrissa watched Rowan's brow wrinkle as he asked, "But can animals survive outside their world?"

"You did," said Bran.

"Well, I'm not an animal," Rowan retorted, "and we had that angel to help us—at least I thought he did."

"You don't have to worry," said Cadrissa. "Griffins are amazing creatures. They can fly between planets."

"And more," Bran added. "They weren't a favored mount of the Thangarian Empire for nothing."

"And if they provide a portal," continued Cadrissa, "it will make things even easier." This seemed to settle Rowan's lingering concerns. "You plan on us leaving right away?"

"The sooner, the better, is how I understand it," said Bran. Cadrissa assumed that was a nicer way of saying the gods didn't want them hanging around. This wasn't where they belonged, after all. She and Rowan were still alive and needed to return to their proper place until death took them to the realms beyond.

"I'll need another moment," said Rowan in a voice that told Cadrissa all she needed to know. While she might have been tempted to accompany him for support, she knew he needed to do this on his own.

"Your mount will be here and waiting for you when you're ready," Bran cheerily replied.

"So then it *is* really over?" Cadrissa asked Bran as she watched Rowan walk back into the stable. "Our quest—or whatever it was we were called to do—is done now?"

"Yes. Nuhl and its champion have been defeated," said Bran.

"What happened to the scepter?" Cadrissa's heart skipped a beat when she mentioned the object. She was hoping she might get to take something back with her to make this whole ordeal worthwhile. She'd love to study it more closely, learn from it, and increase her insights so as to travel further along the path of knowledge. At least, that was what she told herself. She didn't want to acknowledge the subtle pull that object exerted toward exploring more aspects of power as well.

"That I don't know, and it's not really our place to know," said Bran. "I can say with some confidence, however, that it won't be found on Tralodren ever again."

"Probably for the best." As she spoke, Cadrissa felt the butterflies flutter out of her stomach. It would have been nice to get something more out of all that had transpired today. But her life was a suitable reward, she figured, given the circumstances. And she still had Lann's tower to explore after she'd rested up and sorted everything else out back in Elandor. There could be many things there of interest just waiting for her to claim them. Only given how things went with the necklace, she wasn't as eager to take up the venture as once she might have been.

"Indeed, as is you getting back to where *you* belong. So are you ready to leave?"

That was a good question. In truth, she didn't know. How could she decide to leave something so amazing as what she'd just seen? And this was only *part* of a massive cosmos. There was so much more out there, so many wonders—so much knowledge she could gain. She didn't think she'd ever see the night sky the same way again, nor Tralodren itself.

"I want to wait to say goodbye to Rowan, if that's okay." Bran's nod told her it was. "But do you think I could see the griffins while we wait?"

"Of course." He happily motioned for her to follow him. "You'll find they're not as frightening as some tales would have you believe . . ."

• ● •

While Cadrissa spoke with Bran, Rowan made his way back inside the stable, only to be startled by the low growl of a gray panther reclining on the stone block Rowan had rested on earlier. While he viewed the scene with some apprehension, the great cat was passive, greeting him with a tongue-stretching yawn.

You have done much. Again Panthora's voice spoke to Rowan's mind and heart. Oh, how he'd missed hearing it. *You've come so far and learned so much, and the trial is almost over.*

"*Almost* over?" Rowan dared a few steps closer to the panther, who calmly kept its place.

When you have returned home and made your stand as to who you are going to be and what you're going to believe, then you'll be able to enter into what I've made ready for you and take hold of what I have for you.

"But why did this all have to happen?" Rowan focused again on Alara's body. "Was what she said true?"

What does your heart tell you?

"A lot of things," he confessed, surrendering a sigh. "I just wanted to complete my first mission, and now—now I'm here." He motioned to the stables. "Why?"

You were called away from the world you knew to see the truth and given the opportunity to embrace one reality over another. There was no other way to do so.

"But why did Alara have to die? Why didn't you answer my prayer?"

The panther was now licking its paws. *I could do nothing more for her than could the Lord of Life who came to your aid. I heard your prayer, Rowan, but I can't take someone back from Asorlok's grip when their time has come.*

"So then what now?"

You move forward.

"I don't know if I can." The panther stopped its grooming to stare at him with its strangely intelligent yellow eyes. "I don't know what to believe about anything anymore, even you."

Let me be your strength. Panthora's words caressed his troubled thoughts. *Let me guide you. Have faith that I will direct you to where you need to be and move you into the places where you will come into yourself and your true potential. Don't take more than a few steps at a time and I will guide you, if you let me.*

Rowan allowed the words to sink from his head into his heart. When they'd done so, a great sense of calm—an eye in the center of the still-swirling storm of confusion about him—washed over him.

"But what about Alara's body? We should at least honor it."

The panther studied the dead elf with thoughtful eyes. *She's passed on to her own end, as you already know.*

"But what about her body?" He took another long look at Alara's remains. "It should at least be honored."

It will be returned to her family and homeland to get the proper burial, and her life will be honored as it should be. But that's not your journey.

"What's waiting for me if I follow your will all the way?" The panther rolled its eyes up to the young knight, keeping its head at rest over its crossed front paws.

More than you can possibly imagine. I have a plan for the human race that has yet to be realized, and the time to bring it about has finally come. And you are the one who will be able to carry it out.

You'll see much before you die. You'll witness many amazing things and see a land rebuilt and a world reforged, but only if you make the choice to stand firm in your faith in me.

Rowan dropped to his knee. "Forgive me, my queen. You're the only sure thing I have in my life. I'm not going to let you go, no matter what else might come my way."

There's nothing to forgive. Your heart has been pure from the beginning. Though your mind may be a bit troubled, throughout it all you have remained true to me.

"But I questioned you." Rowan kept his head low. "I doubted you."

But you didn't leave me. Even when challenged, your faith in me was still able to help you in spite of it all. And as you've stood by me, so I've stood by you, and will continue doing so in the days to come.

But what path will you be following?

Rowan remained on his knee in thought. Now was the time of hard choices, and he had to make them now or be under their heel for the rest of his days as they slowly crushed all the life out of him. Understanding his obligations and responsibilities, he knew, was part of being a man. And as he knelt in the stables, he saw two pictures of himself: one of how he was and one of how he could be. The choice, though, was where the strife would lie—the brewing maelstrom that he had to face.

"I can't go back to how I was after what I've seen and heard and now understand."

Then rise and return to Valkoria.

Rowan stood. "Will I still be able to speak to you as we are now?"

I'll be just as close to you as now, guiding and helping as you take on the purpose I have waiting.

Satisfied, Rowan retrieved his sword and shield. He was unable to resist one last lingering look at Alara. Though her body was bloody and empty of life, her sparkling beauty still remained. Closing his eyes, he did his best to fix the image in his mind, then turned his back and exited the stables.

EPILOGUE

1.

Alara closed her eyes with a breathless sigh. She wanted to let the stables and Rowan's sad, confused face linger a little longer. It wasn't the best way to remember him, but at least she knew he was alive and would remain so for some time to come . . . or so she hoped. When she was content it had soaked in deep enough, she parted her eyelids.

All around her was the waste of worlds lying strewn and crumbling amid an expansive field of dust. The sunless sky constantly flirted with twilight and dawn, not sure which to take fully by the hand. The silence, though, was the worst part. The suffocating stillness had nearly overwhelmed her when she'd first arrived in what she'd come to understand was Mortis. Then had come the shocking silence of her body. No heartbeat. No breath.

"Thank you," she told Tebow, who stood a short distance from her. "I just hope you don't get in trouble for letting me speak to him."

"It was brief enough to escape attention," he said. "And there are a few other matters going on right now to cause distraction." She almost hadn't recognized the younger-looking priest when she'd first met him shortly after arriving. It was certainly a far cry from the last time they'd seen each other in the flesh. As far as she knew, she looked the same as in life. Even her clothes were the same—though free of blood and any signs of battle—just as she last remembered seeing them when drawing breath. "Still, I trust you can keep the matter to yourself. I don't want word of this getting out to anyone."

"Of course," she said, not knowing whom she'd come across in this wasteland to tell anything to in the first place.

"So were you able to say your peace?" he asked.

"I said what I had to." She wasn't pleased with what she'd done, but upon entering Mortis so many things had become clear to her. She had hurt Rowan, but was confident he'd overcome the offense and sorrow. Her pain, though, was another matter. "I just hope he can forgive me."

"Come on." Tebow motioned for Alara to follow. "We've tarried as long as I dare."

"So how far away is Sheol?" Alara joined the priest as they started to walk in what seemed to her like a random direction. It was hard to orient oneself in a land with no sun, moon, or stars. When she'd first arrived in Mortis she had thought she was in some new part of Thangaria or maybe had slipped into a dream. Tebow showed up after she'd had some time to wander around. How long she couldn't say, as she was finding out time really had no meaning here—not as she understood it.

"We'll be there faster than you think."

Alara tried to find something to focus on other than what was before her but could find nothing. The whole place was like a tomb. That left just trying to make conversation until they arrived at what Tebow had said was the only inhabited city in the realm, where all went to discover their fate.

"Then what?"

"Then you'll be judged."

"Judged how?"

"Fairly."

"By you?"

"No. I'm not qualified to judge anything."

"Then who—"

"You'll find out soon enough if we keep to the path." Tebow quickened his step.

"So everyone—everything—comes through Mortis?" She reached back into the old rhymes and tales of her youth, trying to get a better sense of what lay ahead. She'd never really given them much thought—like others, she supposed—and now that she was in the midst of Mortis facing the rest of her afterlife, she wished she'd been more attentive.

"Every soul-possessing spirit, yes," answered Tebow.

Alara shook her head to clear it of what she was sure was a mirage. She was confident it hadn't been on the horizon the last time she looked. "What's that?" She pointed at the massive gray mountain.

"Sheol."

"But it wasn't there before—it just sprang up from nowhere. How—"

Alara stopped when she spied all the people now filling the terrain. Thousands of them appearing out of nowhere, all bedecked in robes of various colors. "Where did *they* come from?"

"The same place you and I did," said Tebow.

She was speechless as she stopped to try to take it all in. She couldn't. This was something too large for her—far beyond her grasp.

"Come." Tebow gave her hand a gentle tug.

Alara followed.

2.

The sun was bleeding away when Rowan reached the outskirts of the clearing that surrounded the knighthood's keep. The griffin had brought him to a location remote enough to hide his landing from the prying eyes of the watch or nearby towns or villages. His flight had been very short, made even shorter after arriving in a location he quickly came to understand was somewhere between the moon and Tralodren.

Bran hadn't been exaggerating when he said he'd help them on their journey. Of course, the major aid was the portal, which Bran had the griffins fly them to and then through, as it brought both him and Cadrissa across an unimaginable distance in a twinkling of an eye. It had all happened so fast he found himself already losing some of the details of what he'd seen of the portal—what he'd felt and thought as he passed through the massive glowing disk inside an ancient stone wall.

Before Rowan knew what was going on, he found himself overlooking the planet as he began to travel back to Valkoria. And while it was a breathtaking scene to see the planet and even the moon and sun in a way none on Tralodren had ever seen them before, his mind was too filled with what he was going to do next to fully take it all in. He didn't even try to understand how he was still breathing. Bran had said the griffins would help some with that and the priest would see to the rest, and Rowan was content to leave it at that. Why try to concern himself with something that was clearly working?

At this point, he was actually early for his report. He knew the *Frost Giant* couldn't have gotten here before him. For the ship was about a month's journey back, and it hadn't been that long since they departed. Had it? Everything had passed so quickly and run together; he was having trouble making an accurate account of things.

Not that it mattered whether they'd already arrived or were still on their way; he still had a report to give. A report whose finer details still eluded him. He wouldn't—couldn't—lie; he just had to stand up for the life he had chosen for himself. He'd decided that much on the journey after the brief and awkward goodbye between himself and Cadrissa.

He didn't know what to say to the mage. He didn't know her as well as the others, and it had shown when they parted. For her part, Cadrissa had managed well. Despite all she'd been through, she seemed healthy in body and mind, if not so much in spirit. Though as to what she must have been going through internally following her ordeals, Rowan was far from even waging a guess.

Cadrissa had wished him well and then asked what he would do with Alara's body. After he told her it was taken care of, she let the matter go. He supposed he'd never see Cadrissa again. They'd finally unwound the great ball of yarn that had bound them. He was just glad he'd been able to help see her safely through everything. He didn't want to think what could have occurred if she'd been left to her own devices. At the very least he'd been faithful to the cause he'd had when he'd set out from the ruins.

Coming home revealed to him just how little had changed in his homeland. The keep and the area around it were as he remembered they'd been all those months before he had set out on his first mission. But while the landscape might not have changed, Rowan had. And he was determined to follow that change and reach the destiny Panthora had set before him. He felt somehow *seasoned*, like something of his old self had passed away and been replaced with something different that was now at work defining his character. Because of this, he seemed out of place in the terrain. Not only because most of the equipment he'd left with had been lost, but because he somehow carried himself differently than before he'd left.

At least he thought and felt so. He'd seen more than most of his kinsmen, even his fellow knights, and he still hadn't reached twenty winters. Was this the measure of manhood: how much one has endured? If so, then he felt as if he'd grown up considerably. But what would he report about all this? What could he?

He didn't want to tell more than he had to, that much was certain. He already had hidden the necklace under his armor to prevent any questions. He wouldn't lie, but did he really have to tell Fronel all that had transpired? His short relationship with Alara? The battle with

Cadrith? That hadn't been part of his mission. A side trek perhaps, but not the objective. After all, how could he explain it to his superior? How would he understand what had happened to him? How would he react if Rowan said Panthora herself had told him the real story of the knighthood and he now believed she'd called him to some greater destiny?

But was it right to withhold all this from his superiors? Was partial truth regarding these matters the *best* truth? None of the knights knew their age-old origins, he was sure of it. If they did, many knights—and perhaps even priests—might start having some serious doubts. But should he allow those doubts to enter the order? And if he did, how could he prove the truth of what he said? He didn't have the book with him in which it was recorded, so it would come down to a new knight's words against those of the centuries-old order and his superiors. These were challenging matters to contend with—matters he wouldn't have been able to grapple with had he still been the boy he was when he'd left.

You're a man now, Rowan—he heard his father's voice in his mind— *and a man's world looks much different from a child's.* Rowan sighed from the heavy weight of his thoughts.

He spied the keep's thick walls standing like a giant in the distance. He studied the fat iron-clad oaken doors. They were latched with the finest steel and covered an opening large enough for two mounted men to comfortably enter side by side. Latched and bolted from the inside, the keep was impregnable. The gravel road leading up to it was kept clean and level so the knights could do their duties at a moment's notice.

He recalled how he'd been put in charge of keeping the roadway clear one summer soon after his admittance. Though it was a fond memory, it now seemed flat and hollow. In fact the whole knighthood seemed hollow to him. He found himself wondering if this was really for him now and what he was doing here. This was Panthora's will. That was what fueled him onward. She had something for him here, and he wasn't going to get it if he wasn't where he was supposed to be. It was the one thing to which he clung and anchored his faith. He wanted to—had to—pass through what followed if he really was to come into what awaited him on the other side. He had to believe it would be well worth it.

"Who goes there?" The watchman on top of the walls was a dedicate, and not much younger than Rowan, if he could judge the voice and frame from a distance. He couldn't place him, but that wasn't unusual. There were new recruits all the time eager to test their mettle for service in the order.

"Rowan Cortak, Knight of Valkoria. I'm reporting back to Journey Knight Fronel. I've just returned from my mission."

The younger Nordican didn't respond, instead turning around and motioning to men below to open the gate. In the next moment there was a loud clank, and then the doors opened.

"Welcome back, Sir Rowan. It's good to have you here safe and sound. Journey Knight Fronel has been alerted of your arrival."

"Thank you." Rowan entered the keep and the familiar life he'd left behind when the world seemed smaller and not so confusing. A world he now knew to be a shadow of the truth.

A short while later he was quietly walking through the warm halls of the keep, decorated with wool tapestries depicting famed battles and with stone busts of past grand champions, heroes of the order, and high fathers. Whereas he had nearly idolized these busts before, being fed on their tales in his training, he now found himself wondering which of them might have known the real history and purpose of the institution.

Panthers also made appearances in the corridors and elsewhere throughout the keep. Whether they were sleek onyx statuary, taxidermy specimens, or the stylized mosaics and paintings cluttering the walls, ceilings, and floors, the eyes of his tribe's totem—as well as Panthora's symbol—watched him as he neared Fronel's office.

He'd finally decided he wouldn't say anything more than what he was asked. That sounded fair and honest enough. It wasn't breaking the code, which he still honored, but getting very close to bending it. He'd have to be careful of the fine line he was setting himself up to walk lest he fall short of what was still expected of him, regardless of his new feelings.

Rowan remembered a time a few months ago when he had walked this same corridor after being inducted into the knighthood. Approaching from the opposite side of the altar room where he'd been knighted, he still felt a sense of completion as he neared the office, a sense that he'd come full circle with his life and was now ready to move forward.

He reached the door and stopped. Taking a deep breath, he asked Panthora for guidance, then rapped on the hard oak.

"Enter," came Fronel's voice from behind the door.

Rowan pushed it open. Inside, Fronel was just as Rowan remembered, though maybe a little older than when he'd first seen him. He seemed to carry a heavy weight on his shoulders. When Rowan had first come to his office, he'd taken it to be the air of authority. Now he sensed it was the responsibility of command, a duty Rowan could now understand in part and even sympathize with.

Fronel's office was unchanged since he last saw it. It still held the same wooden desk; the shield with the crest of the order, a profile of a roaring panther, behind him; and a shelf of ledger books, scrolls, and records of the knighthood's current and future missions and tasks. Pieces of parchment covered his desk as well as a few open books in which the journey knight had been writing. A simple oil lamp burned on the top left corner of the desk, casting some light over the desk and shelf, where it was aided by a candle on a circular bronze stand, dripping with wax, which illuminated the rest of the room.

Despite this, Rowan did notice some differences. A large map now decorated the western wall, revealing all of the Northlands. Each of the three landmasses—and even Troll Island—was rendered in such detail that to Rowan the map itself seemed a work of art. On the map, dotted here and there amidst the streams, rivers, towns, and terrain were small silver pins with heads resembling a roaring panther.

He studied them for a moment, then shifted his attention to the journey knight. "Journey Knight Fronel." Rowan bowed his head respectfully to the elder knight.

"Please sit, Sir Rowan," said Fronel as he motioned to a simple pine chair in front of his desk. "I see you noticed our new focus," he said, motioning to the map.

"New focus, sir?" Rowan joined Fronel's gaze, removing his shield from his back to sit in the chair. He made sure he kept the crest facing him and not Fronel. He wasn't sure if he wanted it to be the start of their conversation.

"We've decided to increase our presence more than ever before. The high father has put forth a challenge that we should have a keep on each of the Northlands, even Troll Island, in order to increase our and Panthora's influence in this part of the world and turn the savage religions of the tribes into the civilized and proper worship of the goddess."

"I see," Rowan stated flatly. He looked closer at the map, seeing that silver pins were inside the territory of his own tribe, along with several other tribes in other parts of the Northlands. He knew that each pin represented more than just one knight—in fact, it was probably a handful of knights, along with several priests. Enough to begin to teach the people the true faith and the authority behind it as well.

The thought of expansion, though, which once would have filled him with great delight, instead only made the hollowness of the institution seem that much more conspicuous. He wondered for a moment what his parents were experiencing with such an encounter. Then he wondered when and if he'd get to see them or his tribe again. Working the thought into the corners of his mind, he pulled himself back to the matter at hand.

"But that's getting ahead of ourselves." Fronel's words drew Rowan back to his desk. "You've returned from your mission alive and in one piece." He smiled. "Seems you've met with some favor." The journey knight turned a new page in one of the larger volumes, dipped his goose-feather quill, and began to write. "Something that will make for a good report, I'm sure."

The knot in Rowan's gut tightened as his mouth went dry and his tongue froze to the roof of his mouth. A light, cold sweat had started to cover his forehead and hands as his heart beat faster. "Favor through the help of some elves, actually?"

"*Elves?*" Fronel raised an eyebrow, along with his face.

"Yes, and it's a good thing I did come across them, otherwise I might not even be sitting here today."

"A most interesting report indeed, then." Fronel began working his quill over the parchment.

Rowan's throat tightened as he contemplated what to say next. "There were two of them, an older male and a younger female, and they led a group that was on the same quest as I was."

"Really?" Fronel's quill drank deep from the inkwell before flitting across the parchment. "Elves on the same mission as the Knights of Valkoria? So it seems our suspicions about them looking for the information were correct."

"So it would seem," Rowan said, staring at the quill between the journey knight's ink-stained fingers. A simple, silent prayer to Panthora was all he could do. The test had begun.

Moving his eyes back to Fronel's as they peered up at him, Rowan suddenly knew he was ready and just what to say. And with that revelation came a release from all the tension and fear that had been lurking inside him.

"I left the *Frost Giant* in Elandor, and no sooner had I departed the ship than I was robbed by a street urchin . . ." And so Rowan told his tale. It was the truth, but he didn't share anything about the revelations from Panthora, the battle with Cadrith at Galba, or even his trip to Thangaria. No, he stuck to the facts as they directly related to his mission. When he had finished, he left to pray in the altar room before heading to his room. When he did finally make his way into bed, he laid down his head with a clear conscience and, for the first time in many a night, fell into a restful slumber.

3.

It was nearing nightfall when a lone dwarven male dared peer inside Cael's lair. His white knuckles were clamped tightly around the handle of a strong mace kept in front of him. The cool air already had chilled much of the day's warmth, and the young man shivered. His shivers were intensified by his present location, which he didn't want to think too much about. Better just to get in, do what he had to do, and get out. Never mind that he was closer to the foul Troll's lair than he wanted to be. No, just look inside and see what he could see, then return back and report to the council.

The young dwarf was just old enough to put the first braid in his beard, having entered the first year of his adult life. His present task was a rite of passage in a way. Once he returned to the council he wouldn't have to worry about the Troll for a long while . . . for the rest of his life, hopefully. While many didn't think Vinder had survived his ordeal, there were a few who held out hope of him making it out with most of his body still intact. These were his family, of course, but many didn't know how well one dwarf could do against the onslaught of the deadly and dangerous Cael. This young dwarf, though, was about to find out.

Though his chest heaved and his heart rang louder than a forge's anvil, he made it around the opening of the cave and managed to peek inside, scoping out the lair without incident. His eyes quickly adjusted to the dim, rocky interior, and soon he could pick out the bones littering the floor. At first he didn't know what to think of them. They could have been from anything—including the remains of Cael's last meal. But the longer he gazed upon them, the clearer they became, until he could discern a familiar form.

Troll bones!

Astonished at the discovery, the dwarf dared a step further inside. Hunched over with legs spring loaded and ready to dash up and away at the first sign of trouble, he inched deeper into the lair. Having nothing leap out at him sparked some courage, which soon kindled a tiny flame that moved him still deeper into the cave. When he reached the bones, he looked around once more, scanning the lifeless rock in a panoramic sweep. If Cael should jump out now, he'd have little to defend himself with except his mace and fright. Not the best of weapons. He prayed for Drued to keep him safe a little while longer.

It wasn't until he got to the bones that he finally saw Vinder's corpse turned toward the skeleton—axe blade cleft into the vertebrae of the slain giant. The Troll's skull lay a short distance from its body, but the image was clear enough. However this battle may have been fought, Vinder clearly had managed to kill Cael, though he died in the process. Exactly how Vinder had done this was beyond him. He'd never known of a way to kill anything that left it devoid of its flesh and blood.

Be that as it may, Vinder, one lone dwarf, had stood up against Cael and had not only regained his own honor, but had also elevated his family and safeguarded his clan from further attacks the giant would have made. He would be remembered as a hero—a warrior of superhuman abilities. The bards would surely tell tales about him for generations. This was a feat few—if any—lone dwarves could ever hope to achieve. Vinder may not have been able to enjoy his reclaimed honor, but certainly his family's honor had been restored because of his deed.

Dropping to his knee, he maneuvered Vinder onto his back with a gentle push. Clearing the stray hairs from his cold face and beard, he smoothed them to make him more presentable to those who would later come to pay him homage. Hefting up Vinder's axe, he placed it over his chest and arranged his hands around it to hold it fast. With some more adjusting of Vinder's outfit and a few more gray strands of hair, the dwarf was finally satisfied. He stopped when he noticed the small icon of Drued attached to a necklace around Vinder's neck. It seemed somehow fitting that he should wear it, and so the young dwarf arranged the necklace neatly about Vinder's throat, the icon resting across the top of his hands as they gripped the hilt of the axe. Stepping back, he looked over the figure to get a better sense of the whole image it presented. It seemed to be missing something. After a moment he picked up Cael's skull and placed it beneath Vinder's feet.

"Rest well, honorable warrior," he said before leaving the cave. He'd make his way back to the clan and would soon be followed back here, he was sure, by a large portion of it, to see the spectacle of Vinder's redemption. Behind him the battle-scarred dwarf seemed to slumber in peace as the dark cloak of night descended over the Diamant Mountains.

4.

Cadrissa stood before what remained of Cadrith's tower. The once impressive structure was now a smoldering ruin. The sky was overcast but clearing, as if a heavy storm had just passed. Thinking back to the first storm she'd experienced in the tower and who had caused it, she shuddered. The smell of ozone was still heavy in the air and she found it hard to breathe, like a weight rested over her lungs. Turning in a full circle, she took stock of the scenery around her. She saw two craters and the evidence of a magical battle: scorched ground, the fallen tower, and faint vapors of magical energy still clinging to the air like a stubborn invisible fog. What it all meant, she wasn't quite sure.

Daring a few steps closer to the ruins, she picked up a piece of fallen masonry. When she did, she could hear voices faintly whispering something to her—telling her secrets she knew she wanted to hear . . . She paused and closed her eyes under the onslaught of words and images, trying to concentrate. But the whispers were too much, threatening to overwhelm her if she couldn't take control. With great effort, she opened her eyes and looked to the smoky ruins. Silence again reigned.

Letting the stone drop, she brought up her hand to push some hairs into place. In so doing, she noticed it had become completely skeletal. All the flesh had disappeared from both it and her other hand. And yet while no sinew or tissue held them together, both hands still functioned normally.

Frantically, she shoved back her sleeves, revealing both arms were now naked bone as well. Fear gripped her as she moved her hand up her arm to her shoulder, then her chest and back. Everything under her robe was bone! Not a shred of flesh remained!

Cold, familiar laughter spun her around, and she faced Cadrith as he'd first appeared in the ruins in Taka Lu Lama. The horrid, rotten form that had always unsettled her so much. "We share more than just our lineage." The lich clenched his bony hand into a fist. "Reach out and claim your *full* potential."

• ● •

Cadrissa shot up in bed. Sweat was running down her face, and her heart was pounding hard behind her rib cage. She immediately got up, heading for a plain wooden chair in the sparse room of the Elandorian inn. She'd recently rented it after returning to the city. Near the foot of her bed was the chest housing the books she'd placed in storage before she and the others had traveled to the Marshes of Gondad and beyond. As expected, they were still there and not the least bit disturbed. It was more than she could say of herself.

She took a seat cautiously, willing herself to calm. With the nightmare came the thought that maybe some part of the old lich still lingered in her. Perhaps what had once possessed her somehow snuck through all efforts to eradicate it and now was rearing its head for another confrontation. She told herself this wasn't the case. She was free of Cadrith, now and forever. No longer his prisoner and no longer part of some strange larger drama in which she had been made to play. She was free and had her life back. But even so, this truth was small comfort to her as she tried to calm herself by staring out her window.

Cadrissa watched the steady rain fall onto the cobblestone streets and walkways until she slowly regained control over her senses. She sighed and sunk lower in the chair. She was still weak and tired, and it felt good to sit down somewhere civilized. Somewhere safe. She'd tried for a quick nap, but evidently her conscience wouldn't let her rest.

The whole ride back had been a wonder, though. She'd never in all her life expected to see such amazing things on her flight back to Tralodren. The view of what remained of Thangaria was the first amazing sight. All those pieces of a dead world floating against such a wondrous star-speckled backdrop. And then there was the magnificent portal. To think it once had been used by the early titans and their kings and emperors, and it still worked—even after the world was destroyed. And then to get to travel through it herself? It was almost too much to take in.

And then there was where she'd exited the portal. Both she and Rowan had been transported from what Cadrissa quickly discovered was Tralodren's moon to the planet. Things moved fairly quickly after that. She didn't see much of Rowan and his griffin; both sped away to her right while she kept her course forward. She thought of shouting her final goodbyes but didn't think her voice would carry across the widening space between them.

As she'd made her descent, Cadrissa couldn't help but again recall her experience with the roc over Arid Land. This time, though, it was pure enjoyment—allowing her to safely take in all that she could for as long as she could. And what she saw . . . It was as if she was peering down at a living map, full of color and brightness. She could even see the lands past the Boiling Sea, putting to rest the theories of some that there was nothing beyond the constantly turbulent waters.

And to witness all this from the back of a griffin was truly a blessing she'd never have thought possible even in *many* lifetimes. It all happened too quickly to fully take in. She'd scarcely started to wonder how long the trip might take before she found herself back on Talatheal. The griffin landed in a wooded area outside Elandor. She made her way to the city on foot so as not to arouse suspicion. She had a strong desire to be an average person and quietly blend in for a while. She'd had enough confrontation and conflict to last her for quite some time.

Things had at last reached some form of closure. All the happenings since Gilban and Alara had recruited her were now past. All those adventures had now ended. She'd said goodbye to Rowan before she left, getting the impression he wasn't that much into farewells. Though he did his best to oblige, she could tell his mind was elsewhere, and his heart was in his homeland.

As for Alara, she had no idea as to her body's whereabouts. When she asked Rowan for an answer, he'd brushed her aside. Cadrissa knew Rowan didn't take Alara's body home with him and assumed he'd probably left it in the stable. It could have been in far worse places, she supposed. Knowing more now about how things worked, she wouldn't be surprised if Alara's body found its way to where it belonged, since it had been left in the very place of meeting chosen by the gods.

She was sure Rowan would be okay too. He was shaken from his journeys, obviously, but he'd survive. Cadrissa assumed the same of herself and had a feeling she'd feel even better after she took a bath. She needed some new clothes too. Not only was her current attire soiled from her travels, they continually reminded her of how she'd attained them. The further she could put herself from anything even remotely connected to Cadrith, the better.

She had planned to do this after her nap, but for now was content to recover from her dream and let her mind drift out of the paned window. She'd toyed with the idea of going back to the Haven Academy and continuing her training, but wasn't sure if that was what she wanted. Not only was there the problem of another year's tuition, but also the idea seemed somehow less exciting to her now. And, of course, there was the dream. The dream which unveiled the truth that she'd taken a step onto the path of power and had enjoyed it.

She didn't want to admit to herself that wearing the necklace had awakened something in her, a sleeping dragon waiting to be unleashed. It was so tempting—the rush of power—the unlimited well of magical might at her command. It was so wonderful to have that feeling at her fingertips.

Cadrissa stopped herself midthought. That wasn't her path. She was against it. She followed the path of knowledge, which abhorred the path of power. The two were opposites . . . weren't they? But wasn't knowledge in itself a form of power, and couldn't power be used to secure knowledge? Hadn't both of these points been validated in her recent adventures?

No.

She'd made a choice when she started her studies and chose the path of knowledge. It was who she was. It defined her and her magic. Even as she thought of these things, she was reminded of Cadrith's horrid face and her own fleshless appendages and body . . .

She didn't want to dwell on the other implications of the dream— that what Cadrith had said while attempting to possess her was true. Of course, after all that she'd experienced and seen, she wasn't one to put as much trust in luck as she once had. Could it be that Cadrith really saw her full potential? Was there something else about her life or maybe even her future she didn't know that tied them closer together still?

Perhaps it would be best to get those new clothes and bathe now, before the weather turned worse and while she still had some coin. Though her mind agreed this was best, her body was slow to act. Instead, she found herself staring out the window, dreaming of the days ahead . . . and the truth about knowledge and power.

5.

Upon opening his eyes, Cadrith saw the dimly lit chamber and felt the rough stone wall behind his naked back. His wrists were bound in iron manacles that were attached to thick chains leading to the wall behind him. Gone were his staff and clothes. Only a simple brown breechcloth kept him from total nakedness. But he was still breathing, which meant he was still alive.

The last thing he remembered was standing before Gurthghol. Then . . . then there was the pain. The terrible agony of having every part of himself ripped apart. He'd felt the divide between life and death again spread wide before him, but he didn't have another body ready to send his spirit into this time.

So he was dead. But that wasn't the worst of it. He could no longer feel his well of power within him. The magic that had once coursed through his veins was gone. As terrible as it might have been to realize he was dead, it was hundreds of times worse to know he was without the one thing that he'd thought made him what he was all his life. This was quickly followed by the understanding of where he was. No longer a deity, no longer a wizard, he was nothing but a man in the heart of the Abyss.

"Ah, you're awake." The familiar deep voice jostled Cadrith from his thoughts.

He lifted his head and saw Sargis' horrific face. The demon was no longer a shadow but had solid form again. His strong frame rippled with the rage contained behind his red skin. Cadrith dared a step forward but was restrained by his chains.

"Release me and I'll let you live," he bluffed. He had nothing left in his arsenal now *but* bluffs.

Sargis' laughter filled the rectangular room. It was just tall enough to allow the eleven-foot greater demon to comfortably stand and move about, even with his bull-like horns jutting a foot above his head. A smaller set of four-inch goat horns rose from his forehead.

The reality of Cadrith's situation sank deeper and deeper into the former wizard king. And as it did, he grew more panicked. This wasn't what should have happened. He had liberated himself from this place—had been set among the gods and had even shown his *superiority* over them. What faced him now was unacceptable—*unimaginable.*

"You're nothing here." Sargis' face revealed just how much he enjoyed this reversal of fortune. "You have none of your power, none of your tricks, and nowhere to go." Pushing a nearby iron lever forward, he added, "And this time you won't be able to escape. You're here for all eternity."

Cadrith said nothing, only stared into the fiend's bright yellow eyes with all the hate and boldness he could muster while cogs and gears moved about him. He knew what was happening but wouldn't give Sargis the pleasure of witnessing his fear. After a few more heartbeats, Cadrith rose up the wall. His chains were pulled by a series of pulleys that ran through a metal track built into the stones. The former lich was lifted a few feet off the ground, where he stopped with a sudden jolt that jarred his shoulders and back. He was now eye level with Sargis.

"As you can see, I've reclaimed my position and rule over my subjects," said Sargis as he spread his black bat-like wings in pride. "And you helped me all the way. I was driven by my hatred at being betrayed by you in those ruins. Can you imagine how my anger grew when I learned it was *you* who'd been keeping me from reclaiming my full form after your recent betrayal?" The demon's wings folded behind him as he drew closer, delighting in the chance to jeer his captive face to face. "I told myself it was only a matter of time before we'd meet again. When we did, I wanted to be ready."

"So here I am," Cadrith said, rattling his chains. He knew there was no way he could break them. Just like he knew the worst was yet to come. His fearful heart and once again living body made him quite sure of that. "But don't forget you weren't the only one I dealt with in this pit. I still have allies here. Allies that would stand with me in a heartbeat," he boasted. It was a lie, of course, but he felt better saying it. Hearing the lie offered a faint illusion of comfort. He knew that no demon—or devil, for that matter—could be truly trusted with anything. They were like wild dogs, only respecting the most ferocious and strongest among them. Show them a sign of weakness, and like all wild dogs, they'd tear you to shreds.

"I discovered that too after I returned," said Sargis as he neared Cadrith's face, a thick smile revealing his deadly teeth. He'd forgotten how tall the demon had been when they'd first met. He'd been so used to seeing him in his stunted shadowy form he didn't realize how, even at eye level, Sargis' hulking physique towered over him.

"However, any agreement they once had with you is now gone. They all saw how you reward your allies when I returned. You have no one left." Sargis' words were rich in the suffering they invoked. "It's just you and me now . . . and it will be that way until the end of time."

The greater demon unsheathed a sword from his belt. The blade was forged to look like a tongue of flame: wavy and tipped with a deadly point. The fiend's cruel face twisted with sadistic delight as he brought it close to Cadrith's chest. "One thing you'll learn here, Cadrith, is that you're immortal. Your old body may be gone, but the new one you have will live on for quite a long while." He sliced the blade down Cadrith's rib cage, stopping when he got to his thigh. Cadrith only gritted his teeth. He tried his best to contain the painful bodily convulsions, stifling his agony with his iron will as his flesh was filleted, breechcloth growing rich in spilled blood.

"Good for me," said Sargis as he thrust his large claw into the cut he'd just made, digging deeper into Cadrith's insides. Cadrith released a low, controlled growl and some more spastic jerking as sweat began flowing from his forehead, mingling with the river of tears from his eyes.

"But bad for you." The fiend moved his claw lower, digging around in Cadrith's innards some more before removing his hand. A clump of intestines exited with it. He let these topple to the floor, slapping against the wall as they fell. Cadrith let out a barely stifled cry of agony. He wouldn't give Sargis the satisfaction of a full scream if he could help it. No matter what had happened, no one would get the better of him. No one! He would still get out of this if he just bided his time and—

"The best thing is that you can be made to suffer some wonderful agonies that would have killed you before," Sargis continued while fishing out more intestines with his fingers, adding, "and then be made whole again to experience still more." Like a bloated string of sausages, the intestines continued spilling out in a wet, slurping mess. In the process, Cadrith's soiled breechcloth transformed into a gruesome apron.

"This just gives me some time to be more *creative* in my entertainment." One of Sargis' claws lit up with a silver flame that quickly leapt onto the intestines, worming its way inside the former mage. At this Cadrith let out a horrendous scream. He couldn't hold it back and hated himself for it.

"Ah, I think I've finally gotten through to you." Sargis dropped the intestines with a moist thud and then raised his sword.

"Welcome to the Abyss, Cadrith." The demon plunged the weapon into Cadrith's chest. He howled as he felt the cruel steel divide his heart even as it sliced through the front and back of his rib cage. He'd endured what he thought was terrible agony before, but this pain was beyond anything he'd yet suffered. It was almost unimaginable.

"I'm looking forward to enjoying your company for a *very* long time."

6.

Temperate breezes washed over Hadek's body as he rested beside a rock in an open, quiet glade. The blue skies overhead were thick with fat white clouds the same color as his silken robe. He was barefoot and relaxed, eyes closed to the wonderful beauty as he rested in the still, comforting nature of his surroundings.

The recent affairs that had led him here were now barely a gauzy mist in his mind. In time even that mist would be gone, and nothing but the pleasant thoughts and memories of this new place would dominate his thinking. For the moment, though, he could still recall that azure flame spinning toward him and the feeling as it seared over his entire body, until it suddenly stopped. It was then he found himself immersed in a world of light. He'd hovered in a great sea of it under a brilliant white sky—pure illumination all around.

He wasn't sure what had happened next. That much was already fading from his recollection, but he could still recall a reflection of what took place: a soft voice speaking something of encouragement into his ear and then . . . and then . . . What had happened? It was so faint now—so distant from his current state of existence—that he didn't even know for sure that it had happened at all. Only he knew that it must have.

All that made sense to him was he'd been told he had done well and then left the place of surrounding light for where he was now. Shortly after, he discovered he was dressed in a white robe, his feet were bare, and his heart and mind were no longer troubled. He was at total peace and in total comfort. Further, there was nothing here to disturb him, for all was at peace in this place called Paradise.

Hadek let out a dreamy sigh and wiggled his toes in the lush grass. Though many had come to call this place home for eternity over the centuries, it wasn't crowded. In fact, the place seemed an infinity unfolding in all directions, beauty flowing into still more beauty for farther than the eye could see or mind fathom.

Here he would be governed by no god, but by the Lords of Good, the rulers of Paradise. Administrating paradisal incarnates and angels carrying out their lords' decrees helping ensure that all who called this plane home would have an untroubled and peaceful stay. It wasn't what Hadek had expected for his afterlife, but he could get used to it.

Yeah, he could definitely get used to it.

7.

In a vast sea of endless, hungry darkness is a throne. It floats amid the empty, coal-colored landscape like a tombstone. In this throne sits a plum-skinned figure whose odd-colored eyes search out the ebony expanse in vain hope of release. Black iron chains bind him fast, keeping him lashed to his seat.

There is only the throne and its chained occupant. No sound. No light. No strength of will to free himself, just enough to sustain his meager form. The figure is forever alone, bound, and trapped in the emptiness and yet can't help but look for a way out, hoping for escape . . . for rescue. But no one will come. The sacrifice has been made.

And so he searches throughout the endless ocean of darkness but does so in vain, hoping against hope. So he has sat, sits now, and will sit in the endless years upon years to come. For he is a god, and time has no meaning, save when used, as now, as a scourge, striking him with further agony in his imprisonment.

This is the fate of Gurthghol, god of chaos and darkness, the first son of Vkar.

Chad Corrie has enjoyed creating things for as far back as he can remember, but it wasn't until he was twelve that he started writing. Since then he's written comics, graphic novels, prose fiction of varying lengths, and an assortment of other odds and ends. His work has been published in other languages and produced in print, digital, and audio formats. He also makes podcasts.

chadcorrie.com | @creatorchad

Scan the QR code below to sign up for Chad's email newsletter!